WHISPERS OF
THE VOIDBRINGER

M. ALLEN HALL

ISBN 979-8-9850231-0-7

Cover by federikary

For Logan, Madison, and Amelia,
who know to never split the party

Prologue

"Please, Amelia!" Madison begged her younger sister. "Please come play with us."

"Yes, Amelia," Logan joined in. "We really want you to play. And Dad said this is going to be a full campaign! Not just random battles. Three players are so much better than two."

Amelia glared at her brother. "You're just saying that because you need a cleric," she countered. "Why don't you just play both characters? You're always bossing me around when we play, anyway." She turned her focus back to the book she was reading.

"He won't boss you around!" Madison said quickly. "You get to choose everything for yourself. You can build your character and choose all the spells. Right, Logan?" Madison glared at Logan, hoping he wouldn't try to correct her.

"Right," Logan agreed, catching Madison's tone. "I promise not to boss you around. I'll just give helpful advice."

Amelia raised an eyebrow at him.

"And I'll only give advice when you ask for it," he conceded with a sigh.

"And you're going to share the loot and stuff. No more hoarding the magic items," Amelia added, laying out the terms of the agreement.

"Absolutely!" Madison said before Logan could respond. "Everything will be fair."

"Fine. I'll play the cleric," Amelia said as she put her book down. "Where are we starting?"

1

"Rose?" Halfred whispered. He waited.

"Rose," Halfred stated, a bit louder this time. He sighed and leaned on his golden staff. Another moment passed.

"Rose Fairfoot! It is time to wake up!" shouted Halfred, his cheeks turning red above his long, silver beard. Halfred Potts stood at the round door to Rose's bedroom, tapping his foot beneath his long, gray robe. He glanced at the symbol of the rising sun that sat atop his staff and muttered under his breath, "Selaia, give me strength."

At that moment, the door burst open, nearly knocking him over. He yelped in surprise and swung the staff around to keep his balance. Rushing through the doorway was a young halfling woman, her tangled, brown hair covering most of her face. Her robes were of the same gray color as Halfred's, but they lacked the gold trim and details that came with his position as the high priest of this temple to Selaia. Around her neck hung a golden amulet bearing the same symbol as the top of Halfred's staff. She clutched a small prayerbook to her chest, which she dropped as she reached out to help steady Halfred on his feet.

"I am so, so, so sorry, Halfred!" Rose exclaimed. "I was just, uh, finishing up my morning prayers." Her voice trailed away, and she looked down and tried to smooth some of the wrinkles out of the front of her robe. She made a half-hearted effort to sweep her messy hair behind her ears, but most of it ended up back where it had started. Only now did she notice that she had dropped her prayerbook, and she quickly bent down to retrieve it.

Halfred heaved an exasperated sigh. "Very well. In that case, I would advise completing your chores sometime before your midday prayers. Otherwise, you will barely have time to fit in your dinner before your evening prayers."

He turned and made his way down the tunnel away from Rose's room, his staff tapping lightly on the smooth stone floor as his slight form shuffled along. Once upon a time, he had been rather tall for a halfling, standing nearly four feet. But the weight of years of service had left him hunched, relying on the staff to navigate the tunnels of the temple.

"Thank you, Halfred!" Rose called after him. She made one last attempt to brush her hair out of her face and another to smooth out her robe, neither of which was successful. She placed her prayerbook back on the table next to the bed, took a single pink rose from the vase on the windowsill, and pinned it onto the front of her robe. She then set out to complete her daily tasks of cleaning and tending the garden on the hill into which the temple was built.

The sun was approaching the top of the sky as Rose finally began her chores within the temple's garden. She meandered from one bed to the next, pulling weeds from around plants that were just starting to bear fruit as spring turned to summer in the Mossy Hills. From the garden, Rose could see well into the Virdes Forest to the west, and she found herself quickly growing distracted by the gently swaying trees of its green expanse.

"Val, it's time to run!" Adelaide shouted up at the thin half-elf that was peering down from the tunnel opening. The human scrambled up and out of the hole, brushing red-hot embers from her bare arms. "That was definitely a trap. Someone knows we are here!"

Valduin let out a loud sigh as he tightened his grip on his crossbow. "I told you that I was better at checking for traps than you. Besides, you can't see in the dark. Next time, I go in first, and you stand guard."

"It was not dark in there! And this is not the time to be having this discussion," Adelaide hissed as she pulled herself to her feet. She took a moment to survey the surrounding forest. She could hear the sounds of many small feet running up the tunnel behind her. As she stooped and peered through the settling dust from the explosive trap that she had triggered, there was a sudden flurry of movement in the bushes on either side of the two treasure hunters. Bursting out of other tunnel openings that they had not noticed were dozens of small, brown, scaly creatures. The creatures ran on two legs and wore patchwork bits of leather and hide armor. They were snarling back and forth in a language neither Valduin nor Adelaide understood.

"Kobolds! I knew it!" Adelaide shouted as she took off running through the woods. "We're going to have to try to make it out of the forest. Maybe lose them at the river."

Valduin considered firing the crossbow, but with so many targets to choose from, he instead decided to focus on getting out of the woods as fast as possible. He ran after Adelaide as the kobolds began hurling rocks at them. Each time a kobold paused to sling a rock, Adelaide and Valduin's lead grew. They each took the occasional hit from the barrage of stones, but they pressed forward. The number of kobolds keeping pace with them gradually diminished as the subterranean creatures struggled through the thick undergrowth of the forest.

Moving at top speed, Adelaide did not know what other creatures might be taking notice of their retreat. She was sure, however, that the pack of kobolds would make short work of them if they slowed down. Neither Adelaide nor Valduin had any interest in being taken prisoner and forced to work in the kobolds' mines.

On they ran.

By midafternoon, Rose had completed her day's work tending to the garden. She was loading her tools into her cart when some movement at the edge of the forest caught her eye. Two tall figures had emerged from the tree line and were running across the intervening meadow. The tall ones were followed closely by what looked like a pack of small, brown creatures. At this distance, Rose could not make out any details of what either party looked like, but she could tell that they were heading toward the temple. As quickly as she could, she ran down the hill, pushing her cart of gardening tools ahead of her. She left the cart at the base of the hill and ducked into the cave that held the main entrance to the temple.

The cave extended about twenty feet into the hill. It ended at a circular door bearing the symbol of Selaia, the golden, rising sun. Rose hid as best as she could behind one of the large rocks within the cave. She considered fleeing deeper into the temple, but she was curious about the approaching figures. She stayed low and listened for the footsteps that she knew were coming.

Her heartbeat pounding in her ears, she whispered a prayer to Selaia as she tried to gain control of her breathing. Speaking in Halfling, she prayed, *"When the shadow of evil falls over my heart, Selaia will bring the light.*

"When the temptation of evil touches my mind, Selaia will give me strength.

"When the corruption of evil poisons my land, Selaia will purify.

"When the power of evil threatens my home, Selaia will be my shield.

"Selaia, guide my footsteps, and my path will ever lead to you.

"Selaia, watch over me, and my soul will forever be yours."

Adelaide glanced over her shoulder. She counted only six kobolds remaining in the group chasing them. She and Valduin had been running for several minutes now, and they were starting to tire.

"We need a plan," she panted. "If we can break line of sight with them, we might be able to hide and let them run past us. I don't think I can make it to the river at this rate."

Valduin glanced ahead at the upcoming terrain. "Let's head around that first hill," he suggested between ragged breaths. "Maybe there will be something on the far side to duck behind."

Adelaide grunted her agreement. She did not have the breath to say another word while they dashed toward the hill.

As Adelaide and Valduin cut across the edge of the hill, they saw the rocky outline of a cave entrance. Without hesitation, they threw themselves into the cave. They scrambled on hands and knees to hide behind some large rocks as they tried to catch their breath. Valduin drew his crossbow and shakily aimed toward the cave mouth; Adelaide wiped the sweat from her hands and unsheathed her two handaxes.

The pitter-patter of the kobolds' steps slowed to a stop. Adelaide guessed that the little lizards knew that they were hiding. In the moment of quiet as the kobolds searched, Adelaide took a chance to glance around the cave they had hidden in. She was surprised to see a round, iron-reinforced, wooden door about ten feet away from her. There was a golden emblem of a rising sun in the center of the door. She was even more surprised when she made eye contact with a brown-haired halfling kneeling just five feet behind Valduin's crouched form.

"Hello there!" the halfling broke the silence of the cave with what seemed to Adelaide to be an overly cheerful greeting. "I'm Rose."

"Shush!" Adelaide hissed as she brought a single finger up to her lips, but it was too late. Valduin was so startled by the unexpected voice behind him that he pulled the trigger on his crossbow, loosing the bolt out into the sunlight. The ensuing flurry of movement outside the cave could only mean that they were now cornered by the pack of kobolds.

"Come on out, intruders!" shouted a squeaky voice that held on to the *s* at the end of *intruders* for just a half second too long. The kobold was speaking Common now, but it then reverted to the guttural barks and snarls of what Valduin assumed was Draconic.

Adelaide looked at Valduin with wide eyes. Valduin had spun around and was looking at Rose in surprise and confusion. His eyes fell on the pink rose affixed to the halfling's robe. He cocked his head to the side and smirked as the flash of an idea crossed his face.

"I need this," he said as he reached out and snatched the flower. He proceeded to grab the bloom in his fist and tear the petals free from the stem.

"Hey! That's mine!" Rose protested, but it was too late to save her flower.

"There are a half dozen kobolds out there, and they are a little upset with us," Valduin hastily explained. "I have one trick up my sleeve, but if there is anything you could do to help us out, we could really use it." With that, Valduin nodded to Adelaide, stood up, and stepped toward the mouth of the cave.

"What are you doing?" Adelaide shrieked. She watched as Valduin began to chant in a language that she had never heard him speak before. His right hand traced a pattern in the air, leaving a faintly glowing green glyph hovering in front of him. When the symbol was complete, he threw the handful of rose petals through the glyph. The pink petals absorbed the pale green energy and hung in the air in front of him. Completing the incantation, Valduin pointed through the cluster of floating, glowing rose petals to a spot in the middle of the approaching gang of kobolds. Silently, five of the six kobolds dropped to the ground as the rose petals fell at Valduin's feet.

Adelaide's mouth fell open in shock.

Watching Valduin draw the glowing glyph in the air, Rose reflexively grabbed her amulet out from under her robe. *"When the power of evil threatens my home, Selaia will be my shield,"* she recited in Halfling. To her surprise, the rising sun in her hand began to glow with a faint golden shimmer. In a flash, the shimmer spread around her body. Emboldened by the sudden divine warmth that embraced her, Rose smiled. She stood up and strode past Valduin, out into the afternoon sunlight. She surveyed the fallen kobolds and then looked at the one kobold still standing.

"I suggest you run along back to your home. You are not welcome within this temple of the Watchful Mother," Rose proclaimed with a confidence that even she did not expect.

The kobold did not reply in Common or Draconic. Instead, it drew a dagger and charged toward Rose. Rose froze in place and cringed, bracing herself for the sting of the blade through her robe. But as the kobold stabbed the dagger up toward her chest, the golden energy sparkling around her condensed on the blade. The dagger stopped short; it did not even touch her robe. The kobold pulled the weapon back, shaking its head in confusion.

It snarled at Rose, and it turned its focus past the halfling, toward the cave. Adelaide had just stepped out, and she was preparing to throw one of her handaxes at their last standing foe. Before the human could attack, however, Rose raised her hand. When she spoke this time, it sounded as if another voice, deeper, louder, and larger than Rose's, spoke each word in synchrony with the halfling.

"I command you to flee," Rose stated. The golden shimmer surrounding her faded back into the amulet, leaving only the rising sun glowing. The kobold looked at Rose with fear on its face, its eyes fixed on the glowing amulet.

It turned its back on Rose and dashed away around the hill, heading in the direction of the forest.

"Did you just use *both* of your spell slots? On Sanctuary? And Command?" Logan asked incredulously.

"Yeah. Why?" Amelia replied, unfazed by Logan's attitude.

"You didn't even check if we needed healing!"

"You already used your only spell slot," Madison interjected, defending her sister. "And when they all wake up, what are we going to do?"

"Warlocks don't get a lot of spell slots!" Logan shot back, becoming defensive.

"You said you weren't going to boss me around!" Amelia shouted as she stood up from the table. "I get to use the spells I want to use. Or I'm leaving."

"Okay, okay, okay," Logan quickly tried to placate Amelia. He took a deep breath. "You're right. Everything is fine. Besides, we still have most of the minute that the Sleep spell lasts," Logan explained, reviewing the description in the rulebook. "I think we'll be able to get out of this."

"I hope so," Amelia said, slowly sitting down again. "I don't even have any gear yet to help in a fight."

2

"Quickly! They will probably wake up soon," Valduin said as he rushed out of the cave.

Adelaide moved forward, both handaxes still drawn. "It's going to get a little messy," she said to Rose as she positioned herself above the nearest kobold. "You might want to head inside."

"You can't!" Rose protested, trying to move between the motionless kobold and the advancing human.

"What are we going to do?" hissed Adelaide, trying not to raise her voice to the point of awakening any of the sleeping creatures. "They'll all wake up soon, and we can't beat them in a fair fight. They will overrun us, you included, and we will all get dragged back to their mines as prisoners."

Valduin was wringing his hands, unsure of how to get between the two women. He was looking over his shoulder to make sure the kobold that had fled had not returned when he noticed Rose's cart. He patted Adelaide on the shoulder frantically to get her attention. "Hey! If we can get them in the cart, we can tie them up together. Then we can use the cart to get them away from here."

Adelaide hesitated, still standing opposite Rose, still holding her handaxes.

"Yes, do that," Rose agreed with Valduin. "Take my cart. Take whatever you need. Just don't kill them."

Adelaide glanced at Valduin, and then looked back at Rose. After a moment's hesitation, her shoulders slumped. She shook her head and sheathed her weapons, moving past Rose to grab the first kobold. She let her pack slide off her back as she walked. "Get the rope out of my pack and put it in the cart," she barked at Rose.

Rose sneered at Adelaide's back, but she did not argue. This plan was better than butchering these creatures within sight of her temple. She grabbed the rope out of Adelaide's pack as the human lifted the first kobold into the cart. Adelaide sat the sleeping kobold against a small barrel that Rose had in the cart. Within moments, the rest of the snoring kobolds were likewise seated, forming a ring around the barrel.

Rose watched as the tall half-elf with short, dirty-blonde hair wrapped the rope around the whole lot. He secured the kobolds to the barrel and to each other with their arms tight to their sides. Meanwhile, the muscular human woman with the chocolate-brown braid reaching the middle of her back disarmed their foes, collecting five small daggers from the creatures' belts.

Just as Valduin was securing the knot with a final tie, the kobolds' eyes began to flutter open. It took only a second before the whole pack was snarling and spitting at their captors, pulling against their bindings.

"Well, look who decided to join the party," Adelaide taunted the kobolds. "So nice of you to wake up. Now, which of you little rats set that trap that almost blew me up?" Adelaide's voice rose as she moved toward the group, hands once again on her weapons. The kobolds seemed unaffected by her threatening demeanor, but they calmed down as they took stock of their predicament.

After taking a couple of steps forward, Adelaide felt Valduin's hand on her shoulder. "Maybe let me handle the talking?" Valduin suggested, his voice hushed. "You're not really the smoothest at this."

Adelaide paused in her advance. For a moment, she looked like she was about to fire off a retort at Valduin. Instead, she dropped her hands from her weapons and let her shoulders relax. "Yeah, yeah. Fine. You're just a big ball of charisma," she replied with only a hint of sarcasm. "See what you can get out of them."

Valduin sat down on a nearby rock, bringing himself to eye level with the small creatures sitting in the back of the halfling-sized cart. For a moment, he listened to the kobolds, who at this point were muttering amongst themselves in Draconic and glaring at Adelaide. While they talked, they had stopped struggling with the ropes.

"Hello there," Valduin said, trying to break the standoff. The kobolds' muttering died down, and a couple looked toward the half-elf, but none replied. "I was hoping that we could all have a little chat about recent events. It seems there may have been a bit of a misunderstanding."

"We *understand* exactly what you were doing, trespassers!" came the reply in Common from a kobold sitting on the far side of the barrel, facing away from Valduin. "Now, what did you do to Snork?"

As Valduin craned his neck to see which kobold had spoken up, Adelaide stepped up to the cart. She grabbed the ankle of the nearest kobold and spun the whole group around so that the one speaking was now facing

Valduin. One of the kobolds hissed at Adelaide as she returned to stand behind Valduin with her arms crossed.

"If Snork was the sixth of your group that chased us so angrily from the woods," Valduin continued, "then he has already fled back the way he came."

"Then he will bring word of the intruders back to the tribe. More will come, and you will all be digging in the mines tomorrow." The kobold bared its teeth in a strange, snarling smile.

"Do you speak for the group, then? What is your name?" Valduin asked, ignoring the threat and trying to keep the kobold talking.

"Snork was the boss of our team. Now he's gone. I am the boss. I am Crex."

"It is very nice to meet you, Crex. I would like an opportunity to explain the situation to you so that you can make sure you are making the best decisions for your tribe. You see, we allowed Snork to leave after he attempted to attack us. He found himself unable to even touch my small friend over there. Her magic is quite powerful. And the one behind me could probably break you in half. I'm sure she would at least try if I asked her to." This time it was Adelaide with the snarling smile on her face. "I find such spectacles rather nauseating and wholly counterproductive in such a circumstance. I would like, instead, to offer you a compromise."

The smile was gone from Crex's face, as was the tension in his neck and shoulders as he came to appreciate the helpless position they were in. The kobolds next to him each whispered a bit of Draconic, and then Crex replied, "We are listening."

"I would very much like a short truce. Mostly for the creatures that live beneath the hills here," Valduin said as he waved toward what he assumed was a settlement of halfling burrows within the surrounding hills. "We will return you all to the forest. We will leave you there, unharmed. And in return, you will not come back to this village. You will not leave the forest; we will not enter the forest. The next time we meet, if there is a next time, you may treat us in whatever way you see fit. But, today, we part ways with no intention of crossing paths again. How does this sound to you?"

Rose inspected Valduin as he gave this speech. She could tell that some amount of this offer was disingenuous. She wondered if the kobolds could see that as well. She doubted that they had the insight to recognize the half-elf's lies.

The kobolds began muttering in Draconic once again. After a few moments, Crex spoke up, "What about our weapons?"

Adelaide held up the fistful of small daggers that she had retrieved from the kobolds as they slept. "These? These are mine now. They'll make very nice toothpicks."

Crex hissed, but once again he seemed to accept his position in the negotiation. "Fine. Just let us go back to the woods. We never want to see you oafs again."

Valduin smiled. "A lovely arrangement! Adelaide, please help me with this cart." Adelaide took the handles of the cart and began wheeling it around the hill and back toward the forest.

Valduin turned to Rose. "Well, Rose, thank you so much for your help with this, uh, situation. I am not sure we would have made it out of there without you. By the way, I am Valduin Yesfiel, and that is Adelaide Bellamie. We are most certainly in your debt."

"You are very welcome. It is my duty to protect both the temple and all those who seek sanctuary. I don't think you knew that was what you were doing, but I am sure Selaia brought you here so that she could protect you."

"I do not know anything about Selaia," Valduin replied, "but I know that you were quite the protector today. Thank you, and I hope to see you again one day." With that, Valduin turned to follow Adelaide toward the forest. As he was walking away, he called back over his shoulder, "We will bring the cart back soon. This evening at the latest."

He disappeared from Rose's view around the hill.

Rose sat on the stone by the mouth of the cave until Valduin was out of sight. She then leapt up and sprinted into the temple to find Halfred and tell him everything that had happened.

"Logan, you are so lucky! If you hadn't rolled so high on that deception check, we would have a million kobolds coming for us!" Madison said.

"That's why you should always let me do the talking. I've got the highest Charisma score," Logan explained.

"You were about to chop them all up!" Amelia cried, pointing an accusatory finger at her sister. "That would have been so mean!"

"Well, I am chaotic neutral," Madison replied with a grin. "You guys chose goody-two-shoes characters. Not my fault."

"Being chaotic neutral doesn't mean you get to act like a monster," Amelia grumbled.

Madison gave a smug smile, and then she turned to Logan. "Alright, back to the plan. We are still going into the woods, right? Looking for treasure?"

"Obviously," Logan answered. "Maybe we can get some more information out of the kobolds as we walk. Maybe get a lead on some loot. We need gold!"

3

The walk back to the forest seemed longer than the run from it, but Adelaide did not mind. The halfling cart was small, and the cargo was light. She walked along, her pace steady, the cart rolling behind her. She did not bother to ask Valduin for help. She had seen him attempt tasks requiring strength before, and it was usually a rather humorous display. Besides, at the moment, he was doing what he did best.

"So, are there many tunnels and traps around this area of the forest?" Valduin asked, casually probing the kobolds as he walked behind the cart. "Was that the only entrance to your tunnels nearby?"

The kobolds glanced at each other. They looked nervous. They exchanged a few hushed words in Draconic, but none spoke up to answer Valduin's questions.

"You do not have to worry about us," offered Valduin, sensing their hesitation. "Remember our agreement? We will not be entering the forest. I am just curious, as I have never met kobolds before. I thought you all mostly lived in the mountains where you could dig your tunnels and mine for metals and gems. I would not think there would be much in the way of precious materials under a forest."

"We can find gems anywhere," came the reply from a kobold facing the left side of the cart who could just see Valduin out of the corner of his eye. "We always know where to look."

Valduin moved up to the side of the cart to get a better look at the one speaking. "Is that so? What is your name?"

"I am Brok," the kobold responded.

"Are you a team of miners then? Or do all kobolds work the mines?" Valduin continued to probe.

"Yes, we are miners. Snork's crew. Snork is the boss. We are the best crew in the tribes! We find all the diamonds he needs." The kobold spoke with hurried excitement. But his final comment drew a chorus of hisses from the rest of the kobolds. "What? We are the best. We can find the diamonds anywhere. Even under the forest. We know where to look," Brok continued, narrowing his eyes.

"So, are you only looking for diamonds? Or have you found other sorts of treasures under the forest?" Valduin tried to hide his excitement at the thought of looting a hoard of gems within the kobold tunnels.

"We find lots of things. But he just wants the diamonds. We get to keep the rest," Brok replied.

"You have to give Snork all of the diamonds? What does he want with them? That doesn't seem very fair," Valduin commented innocently.

Brok's smile faltered, and his voice fell to a whisper. "No, not Snork. Azereth." After speaking that name, the hisses and snarls from the rest of the kobolds returned. Crex, who was seated next to Brok, leaned over and bit Brok on the shoulder. Brok yelped in pain and tried to headbutt Crex. Crex was too fast, though, and he pulled away from Brok and started shouting at him in Draconic.

With that response, Valduin figured he was not going to get any more information from the kobolds, so he walked forward to keep pace with Adelaide. She looked over at him with a raised eyebrow. He responded with a shrug and a half-smile. They had been traveling together for a few months now, and that look was enough for both of them to acknowledge the opportunity that was in front of them.

"Halfred!" Rose shouted as she tore through the tunnels of the temple. "Haaalfreeed!"

She ran first to the central chapel, and when she found it empty, she headed toward Halfred's quarters. As she rounded the final corner to Halfred's study, she ran straight into the older halfling as he was coming out to investigate the shouting. Despite her attempts to hold on to him, and his attempts to brace against his staff, both Halfred and Rose ended up on the hard floor of the tunnel.

Halfred groaned as he pushed Rose away and rolled toward the wall. Using the wall and his staff, he struggled back to his feet. He straightened his robe and turned to face the younger halfling, his eyes burning with frustration. "How many times have we talked about shouting within the temple? Or running through the tunnels? What could possibly have happened to merit such an interruption to my work?"

Rose, back on her feet and panting with excitement, tried to recount the events of the last few minutes. "There was a fight! And one attacked me! And there was a human and an elf, and there were these lizards, and then the elf—or maybe he was a half-elf—did some magic, and the human wanted to kill all the reptiles, but I stopped her! And then they took my cart, but they said they would return it, and they tied up the reptiles, but one ran away."

Halfred's look of exasperated impatience was unmoved by her disjointed tale until Rose mentioned one particular detail.

"And then I asked Selaia to protect me, and my necklace started glowing, and when the one little reptile tried to attack me, the glow stopped him, and the half-elf had a crossbow, and he took my rose, and then—"

"Stop!" Halfred interjected, holding up a hand in Rose's face. "Say that part again."

Rose, still breathless with excitement, replied, "Well, the half-elf, I think his name was Valdoo-something, took the rose I had on my robe and tore the petals off it and used them to—"

"No," Halfred interrupted again, his face still stern. "Tell me about your necklace glowing. And slow down. In fact, come into my study, sit down, and tell me exactly what happened."

Rose took a deep breath. She once again tried to smooth the wrinkles from the front of her robe before she followed the shuffling Halfred back into his study. Halfred gestured for Rose to sit on the couch in front of the large bookshelf, and he took a seat in an armchair opposite her. He paused for a moment and studied the young woman in the low light of the single lamp on the table next to him.

"Now, Rose, please tell me, slowly, what happened in the moments leading up to you seeing your necklace glowing. Think carefully about the exact order of events and what you were doing during them." Halfred fixed Rose with a stern gaze. He sat with his elbows on the arms of the chair, his fingers steepled in front of his mouth.

"Okay. So, the half-elf—Valdoozie maybe?—grabbed my rose and tore off the petals. Then he used the petals to cast a spell on the angry reptiles. I think they called them kobolds. I couldn't see at first what was happening outside the cave. But when he started doing the magic, I got scared. I grabbed my amulet and said a prayer to Selaia. After I said that, I could feel the amulet getting warm in my hand. I looked down, and I saw this golden glow on the amulet that spread out to cover my entire body. I felt the warmth of Selaia, and I *knew* that She was there with me, protecting me. I had to uphold my oath to Her, so I walked out of the cave to protect the temple. I saw that all but one of the kobolds had fallen down. I told the last one to leave. It tried to stab me with a dagger, but the golden light grabbed the dagger and stopped it from hurting me! And then I commanded the kobold to leave, and my voice got really big and loud. It felt like Selaia was speaking through my mouth, and it worked! That last kobold ran away. Then we tied up the other five kobolds in my cart before they could wake up. Adelaide and Valdoogar are taking them back to the Virdes Forest now, but they said they would return my cart later today." Rose finished her story, paused, opened her mouth to start again, and then thought better of it. She sat quietly and waited for Halfred's reply.

At first, Halfred did nothing. He sat in the chair and stared at Rose. His expression did not change, though Rose could tell his mind was racing. Then, without a word, he reached out and snuffed the lamp on the table next to him. The windowless room plunged into complete darkness.

"Halfred! It's dark in here!" Rose exclaimed. She got to her feet, but she did not move for fear of tripping over something. "Please turn the light back on," she pleaded into the darkness.

A moment passed.

"Don't ask me for light," Halfred said to break the silence. "Ask Her."

Rose called out in exasperation, "Selaia, it's dark in here."

After another moment of silence, the room still dark, Halfred instructed, "Do what you did before. Hold your amulet and pray to Selaia for aid."

Remembering what she had done in the cave, Rose held her amulet in her hand and whispered to it, *"When the shadow of evil falls over my heart, Selaia will bring the light."* The amulet began to glow with the same pale golden light as before, but this time it grew brighter until it lit the entire room. Rose looked up from the amulet with wide eyes to meet the gaze of Halfred, who was grinning in a way that Rose had never seen.

"Selaia smiles upon you, child," Halfred said with a warmth that Rose was not expecting. "It seems she may actually have a plan for you." As Halfred talked, the emblem atop his staff began to glow, just as Rose's amulet was glowing, further lighting up the room. "You are now, truly, a cleric of Selaia. Come, we must get you ready for your journey!"

Halfred turned and left the study, an unusual spring in his step. Rose was so stunned by everything that had happened that she could hardly force her feet to move. After a moment, Halfred reappeared in the doorway, smiling, and beckoned for her to follow. Rose shuffled along behind Halfred, looking back and forth between his brightly glowing staff and the equally bright glow of her amulet.

Halfred headed deeper into the temple. They stopped at a door that Rose knew led to the armory, though she had never before had a reason to enter there. As far as she knew, the Mossy Hills halflings had not needed to use this armory since it was constructed a century before. Halfred pushed the door open and briefly surveyed the racks of armor that stood within the wide, dark chamber. He took another look at Rose, sizing her up, before moving toward the nearest rack.

Rose stepped into the room, slowly processing what lay before her. The room was larger than she expected. Dozens of racks of armor stood in rows down the middle of the room, like wooden soldiers waiting for orders, disappearing into the darkness deeper within the chamber. Along the wall on the left were numerous weapons hanging on wooden pegs, and down the wall on the right were tables neatly displaying all manner of tools and supplies. As she refocused on Halfred, he was waving her over to a rack of armor on the left side of the room.

"Come, come. Let us see if this one fits," he said as he pulled the top of a chainmail suit down from the rack. Rose approached meekly, and she nearly collapsed under the unexpected weight of the chainmail shirt as Halfred dropped it over her head. Once she had steadied herself and stood up straight, she saw Halfred handing her more pieces of the armor. With his help, she donned the suit of chainmail.

"Perfect!" Halfred exclaimed, clearly enjoying himself as he moved on to the wall of weapons. He glanced back and forth between Rose and the weapons before pulling down a small mace from the wall. He laid it on a table near the front of the room, and then he headed back to the wall of weapons. From here, he took a light crossbow with a small quiver of bolts, all of which he added to the table with the mace. Again, he headed deeper into the armory, his glowing staff lighting the way. This time he returned with a silver shield bearing the golden emblem of Selaia on it.

"If you ever lose that," Halfred explained, pointing at Rose's glowing necklace, "the emblem on the shield should suffice as a channel for Selaia's divine magic." He placed the shield alongside the weapons. He then began to work his way through the tables on the right side of the room. He stuffed object after object into a leather backpack until it seemed like it wouldn't hold even a copper piece more. The backpack as well ended up on the table with the rest of the gear.

At this point, Rose finally found her voice. "Halfred, what are you doing? Why would I lose my necklace? Where am I going? Why do I have to leave?" Rose found she was not quite able to keep the panic out of her voice as the questions came rushing out.

"Well, I'm sure I don't know!" responded Halfred, giddy with excitement. "That's the best part! That's why it's an adventure. Now, get all of your gear together and get outside. You said the other two were going to bring back the cart, right? You should wait for them. Otherwise, you'll need to track them down, which might be a little difficult at your level." Halfred was already moving toward the door as he mumbled the last few words.

Rose stood her ground. "Halfred, I am not going anywhere until you explain to me what is happening and what you are doing!" She stomped her foot, and she was startled by the loud rattle of armor that accompanied this small movement.

Halfred stopped walking. He slowly turned to face Rose. His smile faded a fraction, from unbridled excitement to gentle reassurance. "Rose, Selaia has chosen you to be a cleric of Her divine might. She has given you the ability to channel Her power and use it to help others. She did the same for me, long ago. You must now find your way out into the world to use Her gift to its fullest. I am sure that the meeting with those two adventurers today was not by chance. Go with them. Protect them. Help them make the world better and safer. There are many evils in this world, and you will be Selaia's weapon against them. You will always be welcome here; this will always be your home. One day, when you return, I will share stories of my adventuring days in exchange for the stories you are about to make. But now, it is time to go."

Adelaide stopped the cart about a hundred feet into the shade of the forest. She was sweating, and her back ached, but the lure of treasure kept her spirits high. With a heave, she lifted the handles of the cart and dumped the band of kobolds out on the ground. She chuckled at their shouts of protest at the rough landing.

"As we agreed, we have safely returned you to the forest," proclaimed Valduin when the kobolds had settled down, the barrel and the five reptiles sitting among the moss-covered roots of the forest floor. "We will now take our leave of this place, upholding our side of this agreement. I thank you in advance for respecting your promise not to return to the halfling village." Adelaide rolled her eyes at Valduin's grandiose speech to these evil creatures.

As Adelaide and Valduin started to walk away, rolling the cart behind them, Crex spoke up, "Wait! You can't leave us tied up like this."

Valduin stopped walking, and Adelaide did as well after a few more steps, clearly planning to ignore the kobolds' complaints. Valduin held a hand out to Adelaide and asked, "Could I please have just one of their daggers?"

Adelaide sneered at the kobolds, but after only a moment's hesitation, she pulled one of the small blades from her pack and held the handle out to Valduin. Valduin took the dagger lightly between his fingers, and then he spun and threw the dagger toward the kobolds. The ones that could see this movement yelped in fear at the sudden aggression. There was a collective sigh of relief when the dagger struck only the wood of the barrel, with one edge nearly touching the rope that wound around the group.

"That should be enough for you all to work with," Valduin called with a smile as he and Adelaide turned once more to walk out of the forest, heading toward the halfling temple to return Rose's cart.

"Should we go back for Rose? Or just wait here for the kobolds to lead us back to their tunnels?" Logan asked with a mischievous grin toward his younger sister.

"Hey!" Amelia shouted. "You have to come and get me! Why did you even ask me to play? Just to be mean? Besides, if you don't, you'll both die because you can't heal." She stuck her tongue out at him.

"Well, then, make sure you save your spells for healing," Logan retorted.

Madison spoke up, again, on her sister's behalf, "Of course, she will heal us. Right, Amelia? You know what spells to prepare?"

"Sure, I'll heal *you*," Amelia replied. "But I'm not sure *Valdoobie* is going to make it very far in this campaign. What class will your next character be, Logan? Will it have more spell slots?" Now it was Amelia with the mischievous grin as Logan raised his voice in protest.

4

Adelaide and Valduin rounded the base of the hill that held the halfling temple. As the cave that concealed the temple's entrance came into view, they saw Rose sitting on the same rock where they had left her only an hour before. Now, however, she was clad head-to-toe in shining chainmail with a mace hanging from her belt. The golden amulet that hung around her neck stood out against the silver of the chain shirt. Leaning against the rock was a leather pack with a shield strapped to it. She looked up at them and smiled as they approached.

"Hello again!" Rose called out.

"Hello," Valduin replied, curiosity clear in his voice. "Are you going somewhere?"

"I was hoping that I could go wherever you are going. You seem like you could use a protector. It's time for me to bring the light of Selaia out into the world!"

Valduin and Adelaide stopped in their tracks, staring at the cheerful halfling. Eventually, Valduin looked at Adelaide. "Sounds okay to me, I guess," he said with a shrug.

Adelaide, however, was a little more suspicious. She looked Rose up and down and said, "And what's in it for you? Do you expect us to pay you for your service?"

"Oh, no!" Rose replied, appearing sincerely offended by the question. "I think I'm just supposed to help you, you know, find creepy things and destroy them. Or something. Honestly, this is all new to me. But Halfred said that I should go with you and make some good stories to bring back and share with him."

"Who is Halfred? And what makes him so sure you are supposed to help us? You could make stories by yourself somewhere," Adelaide continued as she returned the cart to its spot next to the cave entrance.

"Halfred is the high priest of this temple. He is very old, and he has been a cleric of Selaia for a long time. He said that your arrival and the magic that I was able to use are signs that I should help you with your adventures. If you really don't want me to come, I understand. I'm not even sure I want to go yet. I just know Halfred suddenly thinks it's what I'm meant to do. Unless he's just trying to get rid of me, which actually wouldn't surprise me." Rose's voice was slowly trailing away, as she seemed to be having more of a conversation with herself than with the human.

Adelaide still did not seem completely convinced, but she returned Valduin's shrug. Rose's uncertainty was actually reassuring to Adelaide. To Rose, she said, "Alright, you can tag along with us for a bit. But if you end up slowing us down with those little legs of yours, you'll get left behind. Got it?"

Rose smiled at her. "That sounds just perfect. A test run, then. Are either of you hungry? We could grab some food from the garden before we set out. Also, where are we going?"

The party of three walked through the garden, and Rose pointed out what was ready for picking. They sat down for a short rest on top of the hill, with the massive forest within view, to discuss their plans. Valduin explained to Rose that he and Adelaide had ventured north from the city of Tarsam and that they had set off into the forest in search of treasure. There were many folk tales of magical places deep within the Virdes Forest, and travelers would bring stories of the fantastical creatures and haunting dangers of the forest. Recently, there had been rumors of travelers disappearing from the main road that traversed the forest.

"Do you think the kobolds are the reason why people are disappearing?" Rose asked.

"It could be," Valduin replied. "Or at least that could be part of the problem. I can't imagine that one tribe of kobolds could have spread through all of the forest or along the entire length of the road. The Virdes Crossway is a long road through the forest from Tarsam in the south to Barnsley in the north. It goes over the Valnear Viaduct, an ancient bridge that is the only permanent crossing of the Virdes River within the forest. The bridge is said to have been built by elves that once lived within the Virdes, but those elves have long since abandoned this region." Now it was Valduin's voice trailing off as he gazed wistfully out over the expanse of green that lay on the horizon to the west.

Noticing Valduin's look, Adelaide leaned over to Rose and whispered, "Valduin believes he is descended from those elves, from the city of Eydon. Eydon was lost to the forest long ago, but some people of elvish descent around here claim that city as their ancestral home. The bridge is pretty much the only remaining evidence that those elves ever existed."

After a minute or two of awkward silence, as Valduin stared over the forest, Rose's patience ran out. "So, where are we going?" she asked loudly.

"Back into the woods," Adelaide replied.

"Yes," Valduin agreed, dreamily, "back into the woods."

"I figured as much from the way you were talking to those kobolds," Rose said. "Are we looking for anything in particular?"

"Well, you know, gold, gems, magical items," Adelaide explained. "All the things the best adventurers have. Besides, we will need to buy supplies again soon, and we are running low on coin."

"Sounds good to me!" Rose said as she got to her feet and wrapped up what was left of the food she had collected from the garden. She tucked it in her pack and slung the bag onto her back. She then went over to Valduin and kicked him lightly in the leg. "Hey, Vardoon, on your feet. Rest time is over. We've got an adventure ahead of us!"

"It's *Valduin*," he grumbled as he gathered his gear.

"Come on, Val," Adelaide called over her shoulder. The women were heading down the hill toward the forest. "I'm sure the kobolds have broken out by now. We don't want the trail to go cold."

Together, the three adventurers returned to the Virdes Forest, retracing their steps to the spot where Adelaide and Valduin had left the tied-up kobolds. As Adelaide had predicted, all that was left were fragments of her rope and the small wooden barrel. She sorted through the rope for a second before admitting there was no piece left long enough to be worth keeping.

"Fifty feet of hempen rope, down the drain," she muttered to herself.

"Don't worry," Rose tried to cheer Adelaide up. "I'm sure we will be able to find more rope for you soon. And I have some in my pack if we need it."

"Thanks, Rose. Alright, let's see where those over-grown iguanas went," Adelaide said as she surveyed the forest floor for the kobolds' tracks. "They weren't being particularly careful to cover their tracks. Come on, follow me quietly. Let's find some gems."

Adelaide led the way, tracking the kobolds through the forest. Valduin followed her, keeping his hand on his crossbow and an eye out for any suspicious movement. Rose brought up the rear of the group, moving with as much stealth as she could muster, which was unfortunately not very much. With each step, her chainmail vibrated with the sound of a bag of coins being shaken. After just a few minutes, Valduin glanced back at her with an apologetic look on his face.

"That armor is going to give us a huge disadvantage in trying to sneak up on those kobolds," he said. "Is there anything you can do to be quieter?"

Rose looked down at the chainmail shirt, and she lightly ran her hand over the chain links as she considered this question. "I'm not sure," she eventually answered. "I've never worn armor before. Maybe I'll get better at it over time?"

"Shhh," Adelaide cut their conversation short. "There's something ahead. The kobolds went into this clearing."

As they entered the clearing, they saw the remains of a campsite. There was a ring of stones around a campfire that was still smoldering, a thin trail of white smoke rising toward the treetops. Around this ring of stones were a couple of logs that were being used as benches at the fireside. As Valduin investigated the remains of the camp, he picked up signs of a struggle and a rapid departure amid the scattered materials that had been left near the fire. A few bedrolls were still laid out on the ground, and there was a leather bag that had been dumped, presumably by someone looking for valuables. There were also splatters of blood on the green moss that carpeted the clearing. Valduin pointed out each of his findings to Adelaide and Rose.

"It looks like those dirty kobolds attacked whoever was staying here," Valduin concluded. "You can see lots of their small footprints still, and on the other side of the clearing, it looks like they were dragging something large. Maybe the bodies of the people that were here? From the size of the bedrolls, I would guess they were medium-sized, like a human."

Adelaide grew visibly angry as she said, "I *knew* we should have finished them off when they were sleeping! Evil little beasts weren't free for an hour before they attacked someone else. Let's keep moving forward. Their tracks will be easier to follow now that they are dragging something. And when we find them again, we won't make the same mistake as last time." She started moving toward the far side of the clearing. As she stepped over a fallen tree at the edge of the clearing, she froze. On the ground in front of her was the unmoving body of Crex.

"Well, I guess whoever got attacked put up some kind of fight," she remarked as Valduin and Rose caught up to see what Adelaide had found. Valduin patted down the body but found nothing worth taking.

Valduin and Rose fell back into line behind Adelaide as they continued to move through the forest. As the hours passed, the light filtering through the canopy grew fainter, and darkness eventually brought their progress to a stop.

Just as Adelaide stood up to tell Valduin that she was going to lose the trail in the darkness, he whispered, "I think I see another tunnel entrance up ahead. There is some light coming from the ground next to that large rock. Can you see it through the trees?"

Rose now joined the other two, squinting through the darkness to try to make out the light that Valduin was pointing toward. "Yes, I see it. Should we back off a bit from the entrance and rest for the night? I am pretty tired after all that walking in this armor. This will definitely take some getting used to."

"Yes, let's back away so we can be out of sight from that rock," Adelaide agreed. "Then we can make camp, but I don't think we should make a fire tonight. It isn't too cold, and we still have food from the garden. Getting caught sleeping by another pack of kobolds would not go well for us."

The party made its way back a few hundred feet from what they assumed was another entrance to the kobolds' tunnel system. They laid out their bedrolls and quietly ate what remained of their midday meal.

"I'll take the first watch," Adelaide offered. "Before it's pitch dark. Then Valduin can take watch since he can see in the dark. Rose, you can take the last watch, as dawn approaches."

"Sounds good to me," Rose replied sleepily as she started taking off her armor and dropping the pieces in a pile next to her bedroll.

Valduin cringed at the sound of the armor piling up. But before he could say anything, Rose had completed the task and was already half asleep. Valduin rolled over and muttered to himself, "Strange little halfling." Before long, sleep came to him, along with dreams of the magic that he had used and the intoxicating feeling of control the magic brought with it.

"Do you really have to take the armor off every time we sleep?" Madison asked.

"I think so," replied Amelia. "It's heavy armor, and I think it's uncomfortable to sleep in or something."

"And I guess you'll have to put it back on in the morning. It's going to be hard to move quickly if we have to wait for that," Madison grumbled.

"And it is so loud," Logan added. "Your stealth roll was awful. What do you think about changing it out for lighter armor?"

"How about we have a battle first? Then we can talk about my armor. You two are going to be so squishy in your leather armor. I'm gonna need to be alive if you want me to heal you," Amelia shot back. "We just need to find a magic item that improves stealth, or maybe you can get a spell to help me with being stealthy."

5

Come dawn, Valduin, Adelaide, and Rose packed up
their camp and crept toward the tunnel opening they
had found the night before. Rose did her best not to
move her arms too much, lest the clinking of her chain
shirt give away their approach.

All was quiet as the group reached the large rock and
peered into the hole. Perceiving neither movement nor
traps within the entrance, Adelaide led the way, followed by Rose and then Valduin. After squeezing
through the opening, they found themselves standing in
a long tunnel that sloped down into the ground ahead of
them. The tunnel was about six feet high at its tallest
point, giving Adelaide plenty of room to stand. Valduin,
however, was forced to stoop to avoid hitting his head on
the irregularities of the roughly hewn ceiling. Every
thirty feet or so, a torch was mounted into the side of the
tunnel, and beneath each torch lay small piles of fresh
and expended torches.

"This looks pretty much the same as the tunnel I was
in yesterday when that trap went off and we got
swarmed with kobolds," Adelaide remarked.

"Someone has been maintaining this tunnel," Rose
commented as she noticed the stacks of torches. "They

must use it regularly. Maybe they have been bringing in other hostages through here like the people they probably took from that campsite."

"We probably are not far from the Virdes Crossway, either," Valduin said. "That could be what this tunnel is for. I do wonder why it is so tall, though. The kobolds we saw would not need so much room."

Adelaide dropped to one knee, inspecting the floor of the tunnel for tracks. "Well, I'm sure that the group we were following came through here with whatever they were dragging. But there are lots of other footprints going both ways, and some are definitely bigger than kobolds'."

"That is strange," Valduin thought out loud. "I am pretty sure kobolds do not like to mix with other types of creatures, especially ones bigger than they are. They are pretty sensitive about being small, and they do not like working for or living around larger creatures."

"Be sure to remind them of that when we find them," Adelaide snarked. "Until then, how about you take a good look around that torch? Yesterday, I was walking past the first torch in that other tunnel when all of a sudden there was an explosion, and I nearly got set on fire."

Valduin inspected the torch and the tunnel around it as he edged forward. When he was level with the first torch, he saw the tripwire. It extended from the metal ring the torch was perched in, down behind the pile of dead torches, and then across the tunnel at ankle height to the opposite wall. There was tension on the wire, but Valduin could not tell if cutting the wire would disable the trap or trigger it.

"We should just step over this wire," Valduin suggested. "And we should definitely all keep an eye out for other traps as we go."

The party continued deeper into the tunnel, checking each torch that they passed for another tripwire, though it appeared that only the first one in the tunnel was trapped. After about three hundred feet, the tunnel turned sharply right and opened up into a small, round cavern. Within this cavern were piles of mining supplies, crates, and barrels. After pausing at the entrance to check for traps and to ensure there was no movement within the chamber, Adelaide led the way in. She moved hesitantly toward the three other tunnels that opened into this room, which stood in a group directly across the cavern from them. Again, she inspected the floor for signs of the group they were tracking.

Valduin's eyes went to the crates and barrels stacked around the room. He looked through them, checking the crates for ones that would open quietly, and rummaged through the barrels and piles of equipment. After a minute of searching, he emerged from behind a small stack of boxes with a wide grin and two leather pouches.

"What did you find?" Rose asked.

"It looks like about fifty gold pieces in this one, and there are some rubies in this one!" It was all Valduin could do to keep from shouting with joy. "Adelaide, it's our *first treasure!*"

Adelaide hugged him, lifting his slight frame up off the ground and bumping his head into the ceiling.

"Ow!" Valduin grunted, rubbing his head.

"Sorry! But, treasure!" Adelaide said gleefully as she stared at the rubies.

Rose took a look through the pile of gear as well, grabbed the little bit of food that had not spoiled, and walked back to Adelaide.

"I found something for you," Rose said with a smile as she held up a coil of rope.

Adelaide gave a little laugh as she accepted the rope. "That's perfect. I don't think you can call yourself an adventurer without some hempen rope." She hung the rope on her pack. The loot tucked away, she returned to inspecting the myriad footprints on the dirty stone floor.

"The tracks we are following definitely went this way," Adelaide said as she pointed down the tunnel on the right. "I can tell by the path of what they were dragging. But there are lots of other tracks going in and out of all of these tunnels. Some look like kobolds, but others look like different small creatures, and definitely some larger ones, too. We better keep moving before someone comes along."

Back in single file, Adelaide led the way down the tunnel, following the path of whatever the kobolds were dragging behind them deeper underground. After another couple hundred feet, the trail stopped at an alcove about five feet deep on the right side of the tunnel. Glancing into the alcove, Adelaide froze. Lying on the stone floor were a human man and woman, as well as a child. The three humans were gagged and bound with their hands behind their backs and their legs together with their knees bent. The child and the man looked like they were sleeping, but the adult woman was staring at Adelaide in silent terror.

As Adelaide stood there, Rose and Valduin came around the corner to see what she had found. For a moment, they all locked eyes with the woman on the floor.

Rose whispered, "We're here to help. We're not going to hurt you." She moved into the alcove and began inspecting the woman's bindings. Over her shoulder, she whispered, "I need something sharp." Valduin stepped forward, handed her a dagger, and then returned to the alcove opening to keep an eye down the tunnel.

After a few seconds, Rose freed the woman's hands. Letting the woman work on her other bindings, Rose moved on to the child. As Rose started working on the ropes tying the girl's hands, the girl woke up. Her eyes grew very wide at the sight of the new people, but she did not make a sound. Once the woman had freed her own legs, she crawled over to help with the child. From the stiff way that the woman moved, Rose guessed that they really had been tied up and dragged through the woods. Nearly all of the woman's visible skin was covered in scrapes and bruises.

"Moire, stay very quiet," the woman whispered to the child. Then, to Rose, she said, "Thank you so much. You are our saviors."

"Don't thank us yet. Let's get you out of here first," Rose replied, still focused on cutting through the thick ropes without accidentally hurting the child.

Once they had freed Moire, the woman hugged the girl, fighting back tears. Rose moved on to the man. As she began to work on his leg bindings with the dagger, the man startled awake. At first, he pulled away from Rose, but after seeing the woman and child freed, he instead tried to talk through the gag. Rose continued to work on cutting through the ropes on his legs, but the man kept wriggling away from her, trying harder and harder to talk, panic clearly rising within him.

"Stay still," Rose whispered. "I won't be able to get you loose if you keep wiggling." But the man kept trying to talk and move away from her, cowering against the wall of the alcove. Finally, Rose sighed and shifted her attention to the gag, quickly releasing it.

"You've got to leave me!" he said once he could speak. "Just go."

Rose paused in her attempt to free the man, looking from him to the woman and then to Valduin, trying to sort out what to do. Valduin stepped toward them. Rose said, "Just lie still; we still have time. I just need to reach your hands." With that, she grabbed the man's shoulder and rolled him away from the wall.

"No, don't!" the man shouted, but it was too late. As he rolled forward, Rose heard a snapping sound. She watched the now-broken wire that had been attached to the man's belt disappear through a hole in the wall. This was followed by a low rumbling and then the sound of breaking rock. Splintering cracks spread out across the ceiling of the alcove and the adjacent tunnel. Rose froze, but Valduin's reflexes were good enough to grab Rose by the collar and the man by the rope binding his legs.

He dragged them out into the main tunnel as the alcove collapsed, spilling rocks and dirt out into the tunnel, almost filling it. While no one appeared to have been injured in the rockslide, their exit was now blocked by the mound of stone and earth. They were also certain that their presence within the tunnels would not be a secret for much longer.

"Time to run," Adelaide said as she knelt down to help finish freeing the man. With Rose and Adelaide working together, he was soon standing and shaking the final loops of rope from his wrists. Adelaide stood up, pulled out her handaxes, and took off at a jog down the tunnel away from the cave-in. She knew that she would not be able to sprint while their new companions were still getting their legs back after being tied up for so long.

After another hundred feet of downward-sloping tunnel, the group reached an intersection with another passage. "Which way do we go?" Adelaide asked over her shoulder, trying to keep the panic out of her voice.

"Do any of them seem like they are going up?" Valduin asked from the back of the party. He had his crossbow drawn, and he kept glancing up the tunnel behind them.

Adelaide surveyed the three passageways, trying to decide which one might head to an exit. "I don't know! Maybe right or left. I think straight ahead keeps going down."

At this moment, Rose began to hear sounds coming from the tunnel to the right. "Don't go right. Someone's coming from there. Lots of someones, I think!" When Rose pointed it out, the rest of the group began to hear it too: rapid footsteps and the shouting of many angry voices.

"Left it is!" Adelaide led the way, followed by Rose, the human family, and Valduin. After a couple hundred feet, they reached another intersection.

"Go left again," Rose suggested. "Maybe we can get back to the first cavern we were in."

"Works for me," Adelaide replied.

As she rounded the corner, she nearly ran over two goblins standing in the tunnel. They looked as though they had been walking away from the intersection, and one of them was just turning around at the sound of Adelaide's approaching footsteps. Adelaide did not hesitate. She did not break stride. As she ran, she brought an axe down on the goblin. The goblin did not even have time to shout out before the axe made contact, slicing through its leather armor.

As the first goblin fell, the other goblin turned around with a surprised hiss. But as it drew its scimitar, Rose came around the corner. Seeing the goblin about to attack Adelaide, she grabbed her amulet and reached her other hand out toward the goblin.

"Selaia will purify!" she cried out in Halfling, despite being out of breath from running. The amulet grew warm in her hand as radiant, golden flames erupted over the goblin's body. It collapsed against the wall of the tunnel as the silent flames subsided, its weapon falling to the ground with a clatter.

Adelaide felt no heat from the flames, though she could have reached out and touched them. She gave this only a passing thought as she continued to lead the group down the corridor. As Rose had hoped, they soon found themselves back in the chamber stacked with crates and supplies. As the party rushed across the circular space to the exit tunnel, they could hear foot-steps and voices behind them, much closer than they had been earlier. Valduin glanced over his shoulder to see a mixed group of kobolds and goblins rushing into the room.

Adelaide continued toward the exit, with Rose, the woman, and the child close behind. The man took a second to pull one of the stacks of crates down across the entrance to this tunnel, hoping to slow their pursuers. While he did this, Valduin got ahead of him into the final tunnel. The party raced ahead, increasing their lead on the kobolds and goblins that were climbing and hopping over the debris left behind. As they approached the mouth of the tunnel, Adelaide remembered the tripwire at the last torch.

"There's a trap on the last torch!" she called out over her shoulder. "Jump where you see me jump!" With that, Adelaide leapt over the tripwire and closed the distance to the exit.

Rose made the leap, and the woman grabbed the child and also succeeded in avoiding the trap. As Valduin jumped, he heard the man behind him cry out in pain.

Valduin had time only to glance over his shoulder and watch the man stumble through the tripwire. As Valduin turned and covered his head in anticipation of the coming explosion, he covered the last few feet to the tunnel entrance and dove through. He felt the explosion before he heard it. He had gotten far enough away not to be injured, however, and he tumbled to the ground outside the tunnel.

The man was not so lucky. Valduin rolled and turned to see him facedown, with only half of his body hanging out of the tunnel. Valduin could also now see the arrow sticking out of the man's back, with its ratty, black fletching, and he knew why the man had stumbled.

"I need help!" Valduin shouted out to the rest of the group, who had gotten about twenty feet away from the tunnel's mouth. He grabbed the man by the arms and pulled him out of the hole. Before anyone could move, however, the pack of creatures pursuing them poured out of the cave mouth, and Valduin found himself surrounded. The kobolds dashed around to flank him while the goblins rushed forward with scimitars drawn. Within moments, Valduin had four kobolds and three goblins closing in on him.

"Val!" screamed Adelaide as she tightened her grip on her handaxes. While she took in the scene and calculated her next move, Valduin started to change. The space around him became drained of color, and he began to grow until he looked almost ten feet tall. His already pointed ears grew longer, and as he turned his head from side to side to face down his many assailants, Adelaide could see him sneering with far too many pointed teeth. He let out a maniacal laugh that made Adelaide feel as if her heart had stopped. One of the kobolds let out a scream, and the goblins' faces dropped from snarling anger to whimpering fear. All but one of the kobolds seemed to shrink even smaller than their usual size at the terrifying sight Valduin had become.

"What was that?" Madison and Amelia shouted in unison.

"That, my dears, is my Frightful Presence," Logan replied with a smile. "It's like one of the only warlock things I can do at level one. They must have really low Wisdom since most of them failed the saving throw."

"So, they are frightened now, right?" Madison asked.

"Yes, all but the one kobold, but only for one round," Logan replied. "After my next turn, it wears off."

"Okay. Amelia, you need to get to the man," Madison said as she surveyed the battle map. "And I need to get in there with my handaxes. I don't really have any special abilities yet. I'm just gonna need to start chopping."

6

Seeing their enemies cowering in fear, Adelaide made her move. With both handaxes drawn, she advanced to the only kobold that was still snarling at Valduin. With one swing of her right hand, she planted the handaxe in the back of the monster, and it dropped to the ground. With her other hand, she swung at the next kobold, but, as it was already starting to run away from Valduin, she couldn't quite connect with it.

The three goblins panicked, each fleeing in a different direction past the tunnel opening. After getting some distance from Valduin, they all turned and took shots at the half-elf with their shortbows. Their hands were shaking so badly, however, that only one arrow connected with Valduin, sinking into his thigh. He instinctively grabbed the arrow as the searing pain spread through his leg.

"Rose! A little help here!" he shouted out to the cleric as he pulled the arrow out.

"Coming!" Rose called back, running forward as fast as she could. She slid between Valduin and Adelaide as she dropped to one knee, holding her amulet in her hand. She reached out to touch the unconscious man with the other hand.

"*Selaia, spare this man*," she whispered in Halfling as she felt the amulet grow warm. Golden light sprung from her fingertips and into the man's back, and he inhaled sharply as the goblin arrow fell to the ground next to him. Rose stood up, holding her shield at the ready as she stared down the nearest kobold.

The kobold in front of her tried to attack her with its dagger, but with most of its attention still focused on Valduin, the blade dragged meekly across Rose's shield. The other two kobolds retreated as the goblins had. Each one hurled a stone from its sling as it ran, but their fright put them at such a disadvantage the stones could not find their targets.

Valduin, having returned to his usual appearance, glared at the goblin that had shot him with the arrow. As he pulled the arrow from his thigh, he cursed the goblin under his breath, muttering in Sylvan, "*To the depths.*" To his surprise, a spark of pale green energy appeared, circling around his right hand. He pointed at the goblin, and the mote of energy streaked through the air to it. On impact, it exploded against the evil creature's chest. The goblin collapsed to the ground, unmoving. Valduin, shocked by this new magic, let the arrow fall to the ground as he stared at the hand that had summoned the spark.

Adelaide turned to the kobold that had attacked Rose, and with an upward swing of an axe lifted it off its feet. It dropped onto its back, motionless. Before it had even hit the ground, Adelaide was striding forward toward one of the goblins, and she hurled her other axe through the air at it, striking it in the shoulder. There was a spray of green blood as the axe continued past the goblin and landed on the ground behind it.

Seeing Adelaide advancing on their position, the two remaining goblins loosed arrows toward her before retreating behind the boulder that was next to the tunnel opening. One arrow hit her in the shoulder, and the other pierced her hip. She doubled over, but she quickly pulled the arrows from her body. She stood up again, letting out a howl of pain and anger. "Don't let them get past you!" she shouted at Rose and Valduin. "We can't let them get reinforcements."

Rose started moving toward the rock, trying to follow the goblins, but she could not keep up with them. As they moved out of her line of sight, she turned her attention to the last two kobolds. Once again, she pointed at one of the creatures, and radiant, golden flames erupted all over its body. The flames made no burns nor smoke nor ash, but the kobold dropped to the ground, nonetheless.

The one remaining kobold snarled at Rose and rushed at her, dagger drawn. Despite the ferocity of its attack, which Rose was not able to block with her shield, the reptile's small blade was unable to pierce Rose's chainmail. She pushed the kobold back, unharmed.

"Keep going around that way!" Valduin shouted to Adelaide. "I'll get them from this side." He ran toward the large rock, waiting for the goblins to come into view. When he could not find them quickly, he turned back to the kobold that was harassing Rose. Looking at his hand, he repeated the Sylvan command that had summoned the orbiting spark of eldritch energy. He released the spark toward the kobold, but in his effort to avoid hitting Rose, the mote of green light flew over the head of his small target.

Adelaide, with only one handaxe remaining, briefly considered retrieving her other one. But she heeded

Valduin's call instead, and she maintained her pursuit of the goblins. She was hurting badly from the arrows that had hit her, but she knew they needed to finish this quickly and get away from the cave before more enemies arrived. She ran as fast as she could around the boulder, searching for the remaining goblins.

As Valduin grimaced in disappointment at the errant attack, the two goblins reappeared around the side of the rock in front of him. Each one had its short bow drawn as Valduin turned to face them in surprise. The first arrow hit him squarely in the chest. He fell backward to the ground as the second arrow flew through the space his neck had just left.

"Valdan!" screamed Rose. She sprinted toward him. As she turned away from the kobold, it took the opportunity to make another attack with its dagger, this time finding purchase in Rose's back. Rose grunted at the pain but kept moving over to Valduin's side. Amulet in hand, she reached down and touched Valduin's chest where the arrow had lodged itself, shouting her prayer to Selaia to heal him. The arrow came loose in Rose's hand, and Valduin gasped. When Valduin's eyes sprang open, they glowed briefly with the now-familiar golden light of Rose's divine magic.

The final kobold rushed up to Rose and tried to find the spot where its dagger had injured her just a moment before. However, Rose was able to turn in time to raise her shield and deflect the attack. Realizing that Rose's armor was too much for its small weapon, it turned its attention instead to Valduin. As the kobold tried to close the distance to where the half-elf lay on the ground, Valduin threw another spark of pale green energy at it. The impact spun the small reptile around as it fell to the ground. Valduin took a deep breath before slowly getting back on his feet.

"Wow, it doesn't even hurt," he said to Rose as he gingerly pushed on the spot where the arrow had hit him. "Thanks." He then refocused on the task at hand, looking up at the two goblins as they were readying their bows for another volley.

Before they could fire again, however, Adelaide came around the boulder behind them. With one swipe, she dispatched the goblin that she had already injured and moved to engage the other one. As she came within striking distance of the final goblin, it released its arrow, striking Rose in the leg. Rose dropped to one knee in pain. The goblin darted away from Adelaide, who was unable to get an attack off at the nimble creature. Their one remaining enemy was making its way back toward the tunnel entrance as Rose once again summoned Selaia's sacred flames. In a burst of golden light, the goblin fell out of a full run, tumbling head over heels until it disappeared through the tunnel entrance.

All three of the adventurers breathed a heavy sigh as the last enemy vanished.

However, instead of the moment of calm that they were hoping for, there came another noise from the hole. With a grunt, the limp body of the goblin came flying back out, and the head and shoulders of a new creature forced their way through the opening. It was vaguely goblinoid in the shape of the head and ears, but it was much hairier and much, much larger. It was so large that it was having difficulty getting itself through the hole. As it struggled, waving a large morningstar around in one hand, it looked over at Rose and Valduin and roared.

"We gotta run!" Valduin shouted. He headed toward the woman and child who were still standing, mouths agape, near a tree thirty feet from the newly-arrived bugbear. Valduin shot off a spark of eldritch energy as he ran, easily hitting the enemy where it was struggling to get through the small hole.

Rose ran after Valduin, and as she ran, she once again reached for her amulet. When she pointed at the bugbear, a beam of golden energy flew from her outstretched hand, searing the monster across the torso and causing it to glow with radiant energy.

With the divine target painted on the bugbear by Rose, Adelaide took aim with her handaxe. She heaved it at the monster from where she stood above the fallen goblins. When it struck, the blade sinking deep into the left side of the monster's chest, the golden glow subsided, as did the struggling of the bugbear. The gruesome weapon it carried fell to the ground limply. Now came the calm that they had been expecting.

Adelaide retrieved her first thrown handaxe, and then she removed the second one from where it had lodged itself in the bugbear. The woman and child ran to the man. He was breathing easily, but he was still unconscious. Rose took a deep breath and inspected the wound in her leg, dabbing it gingerly. Valduin approached the bugbear, not quite trusting that it was really finished. With his foot, he moved the large morningstar out of the monster's reach.

"Didn't the kobolds say that they got to keep the gems that they found?" Adelaide asked Valduin. "Check out whether they had anything on them."

"Great point," Valduin agreed. He dashed from kobold to kobold, patting down pockets and removing pouches from belts. "I don't think there's a whole lot here," he said at last. "I only got ten silver pieces off the whole group."

The man was just coming around as Rose and Adelaide both stiffened, their heads whipping around toward the body of the bugbear. They could hear faint voices and scratching sounds from within the tunnel below.

"Now it is definitely time to go," Rose declared as she helped the man to his feet. He looked around in a daze, trying to put together the sudden change of surroundings and the ache in his back. "You are going to be fine, but we really need to get moving," she said to him.

Together, the party ran from the bugbear-clogged tunnel. Not having any particular destination, Adelaide led them back toward the humans' campsite.

"That was awesome!" Madison exclaimed. "We seriously rocked that battle!"

"I told you that you were gonna be squishy," Amelia teased Logan as she poked him in the side with one finger. "You and the man would totally be dead if I wasn't there."

"Yeah, yeah, I know," Logan admitted. "This does give us an idea of what we need to focus on. We need healing potions and better armor for sure."

Madison opened up the rulebook to the equipment section. "Ugh, forty-five gold for studded leather armor. We need more money! Let's get these people to safety and then come back here. They said they were collecting diamonds. If we could just get a few of those, we would be in a much better place."

7

"I don't think they are following us," Adelaide said as the group reached the campsite. "Let's hide here and wait for a bit. If they're still coming, maybe they'll pass us."

Rose disappeared into a bush at the edge of the clearing while Valduin and Adelaide climbed trees. The humans covered themselves in the remains of their camp, the woman and child hiding under the collapsed tent and the man beneath a pile of bedding.

The group waited for thirty minutes that felt like hours. Rose lay in her hiding spot, replaying in her head the image of Valduin opening his eyes at her touch. He had come back from near-certain death because she had decided he should. She held her amulet in her hands, remembering the warmth of its magic. She thought she could understand what Halfred had been saying about her having purpose now. "*Selaia, guide my footsteps, and my path will ever lead to you,*" she prayed quietly as the wait dragged on.

Finally, Valduin came down from the tree he had hidden in.

"Looks like we are clear," he said, still not raising his voice above a whisper. The rest of the party crawled out of their hiding spots, except for Adelaide, who stayed in her tree to keep watch.

There was a sudden release of tension as the three humans hugged each other, the adults weeping and dropping to their knees to hold their child. Valduin looked around awkwardly, unsure of what to do, then proceeded to start breaking down the campsite in preparation for travel. Rose watched the family celebrating their freedom, a content smile on her face. The adults looked to be middle age, and the child now seemed older than she had at first glance. Rose guessed the girl was in her late teens as she stood two feet taller than the halfling.

After a minute or two, the humans stood up and addressed Rose and Valduin. "Thank you so much for your help. We didn't think that we were ever going to get out of that tunnel," the man began. "I am Brian Ware; this is my wife, Anna. And this is Moire," he said with a wide smile as he put his hand on the girl's shoulder.

"It is a pleasure to meet you! I am Rose Fairfoot." Rose gave a small, stiff curtsey which made her chainmail clink around her. "That one is, uh, Valdooeen, and the one in the tree is Adelaide." Adelaide gave a small wave from where she was sitting, but she kept her attention on the surrounding forest.

"Yes, I am *Valduin* Yesfiel, and that is Adelaide Bellamie. Why were you here? The Virdes Forest is a dangerous place," Valduin asked as he returned to stand by Rose.

Brian replied, "We live in Tarsam, but Anna's family is from Barnsley, north of the forest. We had received word that their farm had been attacked by creatures from the forest, and we were hoping to travel there as quickly as possible. We usually take the coastal road around, but we didn't think we could spare the extra days of the journey. So, we tried to make it on the Crossway. We stayed off the road to avoid bandits that might attack us there. Clearly, we were not prepared for what awaited us in the forest."

Listening to their story, Valduin felt a pang of guilt. If they had taken those kobolds somewhere else, or if they had just killed them like Adelaide had wanted to, this family would not have been attacked. He wondered whether Adelaide felt the same, but he knew that he couldn't talk to her about it here.

"We also ventured out from Tarsam. We could bring you back there if you like," Valduin offered. "We are not equipped to guide you all the way to Barnsley at the moment. You should probably take the coastal road next time, or hire some security."

Brian and Anna looked at each other for a moment. Finally, Anna replied, "We would very much appreciate the escort back to Tarsam. We will find a way to Barnsley." She reached out and squeezed Brian's hand. They were both clearly disappointed.

"Adelaide, let's move," Valduin called to the ranger. Adelaide deftly descended the tree, barely using her hands as she leapt from branch to branch.

"We should head west until we hit the road," Adelaide said as she started leading the group out of the clearing. "Then we can follow it south to Tarsam. We aren't very deep in the forest; we may even make it back to the city tonight if we push it." Grabbing what was left of their supplies, the Ware family fell in line behind Adelaide with Rose, and Valduin brought up the back of the group. The six of them walked in silence, still wary of attack by kobolds, or worse. Brian and Anna held hands while Moire fell a few paces behind to match step with Rose.

"Thank you for saving us. You were amazing in that fight," she said softly.

"I'm just happy we were able to get you all out of there," Rose replied. "I've never really been in a battle like that. We encountered some kobolds yesterday, but we were able to scare them off. We didn't have to kill any of them. I've never killed anything before." Rose's words slowed as she realized the importance of that statement.

"I didn't like that part, but it still feels like it was necessary. I'm proud I was able to save Valduran and your father." Rose smiled weakly, the realization that she had dealt the killing blow to a few of those creatures still weighing on her.

"Don't feel bad about killing them," Moire reassured the halfling. "They were evil; they would have enslaved all of us if they could have. The kobolds caught us off guard yesterday. We had just set up camp in the late afternoon. We had made a fire and were cooking. I was collecting firewood when they arrived. By the time I got back, my parents were already tied up. I snuck up on one of them, and I think I killed it. But once the rest saw me there wasn't much I could do," Moire recounted their capture to Rose, eyes staring hollowly forward as she talked.

"I'm sure you did everything that you could," Rose tried to reassure her. "It's amazing that you were able to do what you did! You must be so strong."

"I don't really think I am. I think I mostly just caught it by surprise. I can move pretty quietly," Moire replied. "But I didn't have the right equipment for fighting."

Rose realized that she still had the dagger that Valduin had given her to free the Ware family back in the tunnel. She pulled it out and handed it to Moire. "Take this," she said. "Next time you will be more prepared. I hope there isn't a next time, though."

Moire accepted the dagger, holding it lightly in her open hand before wrapping her fingers around the grip with resolve. "Yes, I will be ready," she said, with more energy than Rose had seen from her to this point. Moire sheathed the blade carefully with a strap of leather from her pack and hung it on her belt.

By midafternoon, the party had reached the Virdes Crossway. The road was twenty feet wide most of the time, and although trees arched together above it in places, nothing grew on the hard-packed earth of the road itself. The travelers headed south, back toward the city of Tarsam, within the hills to the south of the Virdes Forest. As the road left the forest, it was soon flanked by farmlands. The hours passed, and the sun sank low over the peaks of the Sandgate Mountains just visible to the west. The group began to see more life along the road as they approached the city. There were markets, shops, taverns, and houses built close to the road.

Finally, as darkness truly fell over the land, they came over the final hill and saw the walled city of Tarsam laid out before them. The much larger Seawalk Road could be seen leaving through the East Gate of the city, heading toward the coast. The city was roughly square, more than a mile on each side, and it was enclosed by four high, stone walls, with a gate in the middle of the north, east, and west walls. Rising from the center of the square city was a massive tower that looked like a single shard of broken glass.

"Whoa," Rose muttered, in awe at the size of the city in front of her. "You live here? What is that in the middle of the city?" She looked up at Moire.

Moire smiled at Rose as she said, "Yes, this is Tarsam. It isn't nearly as big as the cities on the coast, but it is nice. That is the Crystal Tower, where the Crystal Fist presides. The Crystal Fist has controlled the city for as long as anyone can remember."

"It looks pretty big to me," Rose replied, her voice hushed. "The Crystal Fist? That's a little intimidating. What's so special around here that someone would build such a big city?"

"Tarsam controls the trade going between the coast and the mountains. All of those farms we passed on the way here bring their goods to Tarsam's markets to sell, and everything coming out of Westray or the dwarven cities in the mountains must come through here to get to the coastal cities of Alomere and Verasea."

"Got it. Adelaide, you said that you and Valdugnan came from here, too?" Rose asked her compatriots.

Adelaide laughed at Rose's wide-eyed expression. "Well, we were here recently, and we left from here to explore the Virdes. But neither of us grew up here. I'm actually from Westray," Adelaide explained. Valduin nodded along, but Rose could tell that he was not listening. His eyes were focused on the city before them.

Before Rose could ask any more questions, the group of six reached the North Gate. Rose could see a few soldiers with crossbows atop the wall on either side of the arch. There was also a handful of soldiers standing in front of the gate, which was slightly ajar, leaving a space wide enough for a single person to walk through. One of these soldiers stepped forward as the travelers approached, his shield still on his back, and his sword in its sheath.

"Announce yourselves," he called. Rose could see a clenched white fist emblazoned on the chest of the man's leather armor.

"We are the family Ware. I am Brian. We live in the Mosaic District and always beneath the Crystal Tower. The Crystal Fist carries the light," Brian stated in a well-rehearsed way.

The soldier gave the rest of the group a cursory inspection. He raised one eyebrow in open surprise at the presence of a halfling among them, but he otherwise seemed satisfied with what he saw. He turned toward the gate, gave a wave to the other soldiers who had been watching the interaction with half-hearted attention, and returned to his post.

"Follow. Quickly," Brian whispered to Valduin, Adelaide, and Rose. The group moved in single file through the gap in the large doors and into the city of Tarsam.

The streets were paved with wide, flat stones within the city, and there were streetlights burning along the major streets. The city streets made a grid, and Brian led the group a few blocks south, deeper into the city, before turning west.

"Our home is in the southwest part of the city," he explained. "We will pass through the West Market to get home. It is better than going straight through the center of the city. There will be many guards close to the Crystal Tower at this time of night."

They made their way through wide squares lined with tall buildings. The squares were connected by streets that passed through the buildings like tunnels. Then they entered an enormous outdoor market, though the traffic seemed thin in the deepening night. South of the market they passed street after street of homes, mostly connected to each other by common walls and each one painted a different color.

Finally, exhausted, the group stopped in front of a bright orange home flanked by a dark green one and a vibrant purple one. Brian opened the wooden door with a key, and the group filed inside.

"Welcome to our home," Anna said, sighing with relief. "You are free to stay the night if you like. You can actually stay as long as you need. We are very much indebted to you for rescuing us."

"That would be wonderful," Rose replied. Then she remembered Valduin and Adelaide. "Or should we go to your home?" she asked.

Valduin and Adelaide exchanged a nervous glance. Adelaide replied, "Well, we don't really have a home here. We were just passing through the last time we were in this city."

Though Rose was curious, she did not want to pry in front of the Wares, so she shrugged and turned back to Anna. "Thank you very much for your hospitality. Where should we put our things?"

Within minutes, the adventurers had set up their bedrolls on the floor of the main room of the house. In the comfort and darkness of the small home, they fell dozed off quickly, each one reliving the excitement of the day before giving in to much-needed sleep.

"Level two! Level two! Level two!" Madison and Amelia chanted as Logan reached for the rulebook.

"Do you get anything cool?" asked Amelia. "I get another spell slot and my Channel Divinity things."

"I get spells!" Madison exclaimed. "Hmm, but only two. That's okay though. Hunter's Mark and Cure

Wounds it is. That way I can get you up if needed. How about you, Logan? Anything interesting?"

"Actually, I get a bunch of things. Another spell slot, a new spell, and some abilities. I need to read through these invocations. There are a lot of choices here," Logan mumbled as he scanned the rulebook.

"Wow, two whole spell slots," Amelia teased. "Warlock is such a useful class."

Logan paused his reading to glare at her.

"Well, you make your big decisions," Madison said, "while we go shopping. We've got gold to spend!"

"Ugh! Real-life shopping isn't enough? We have to go shopping in the game, too?" Amelia whined as she buried her face in her hands. "I'm going to go read. Come get me when something exciting happens."

"No, Amelia, you can't!" Madison begged. "Please stay. Maybe we can find something for you." But Amelia was already out the door.

"It's okay," Logan said, marking down his new abilities on his character sheet. "I'll go get her in a few minutes."

8

Valduin realized that he was awake before he opened his eyes. He lay still, wondering what may have caused him to awaken. Eyes closed, he tried to listen for any change in the room. At first, he heard nothing.

Then, he continued to hear nothing. No footsteps in the room, no voices from upstairs, no creaking floorboards, no shouting from outside the house. As he listened, straining to get any hint of what was happening around him before he opened his eyes, he noticed that he couldn't hear Adelaide or Rose breathing. As panic began to set in, he realized that he couldn't hear his own breathing, either.

Valduin sat up with a start, looking first to see that Adelaide and Rose were still on the floor near him. Seeing them sleeping as he expected, he jumped to his feet and spun around, surveying the room. He suddenly found himself face-to-face with a strangely familiar, elven-appearing man. The man was tall, probably closer to seven feet than six. He was thin, with a sharp jawline, a strong cleft chin, and pointed ears that were much longer than those of the usual elf. He had long, straight, silvery-gray hair that reached the middle of his back. As Valduin stared into his face in shock, the creature before him smiled a wide smile that showed too many teeth, grabbed Valduin by the wrist, and appeared to start speaking. Valduin had just enough time to realize that he still could not hear anything when there was a rapid, sinking feeling in the pit of his stomach. He felt as though he was being pulled forward, though he did not feel off balance. He tried to resist the pull, but he could not stop it.

A moment later, he was standing on a hillside. The sun was low, though Valduin could not tell if it was setting or rising, and a warm breeze blew through the air. All around Valduin was knee-high grass dotted with strange, colorful flowers. While Valduin could name the colors he was seeing, everything seemed more vibrant than he was used to. He looked at the creature who had brought him here. He had let go of Valduin's wrist, and he was standing with his hands clasped behind his back. The creature's unnervingly wide smile remained.

"You have done well, Valduin Yesfiel," came the soft voice of the creature, speaking in Sylvan. The voice seemed small coming from so tall a person, and Valduin was reminded of the last time he had heard that voice.

"It's you! How did you do that? Where are we? Who are you?" Valduin's mind spun as he struggled to comprehend his current situation while simultaneously reliving the events of his last meeting with this being.

The creature's smile settled from unbridled excitement to warm reassurance, with fewer teeth showing. "This is my domain, within what you were taught to call the Inner Plane of Light. I am Taranath. I have been watching you, Valduin. You have done very well."

"Taranath," Valduin repeated the name slowly, cautiously testing it as someone might test the temperature of a hot cup of tea. "Yes, I've used the magic you gave me. And just today I was able to use a new kind of magic. How did that happen? I feel like there is still so much to learn. How did you bring me here? Can you teach me that?" Valduin asked, his excitement for arcane knowledge overwhelming any sense of caution.

Taranath chuckled. "You are not quite ready for that skill. But your power is growing. You will discover new abilities in time. For now, I have a gift for you." With a wave of his hand, a large, black sphere appeared in the air in front of Valduin. "Look inside and tell me what you see."

Valduin hesitated for a moment, but then he slowly leaned his head and shoulders into the sphere. He felt nothing different within the sphere, but he could see nothing within it either. "I can usually see in the dark, but I see nothing here," Valduin replied, trying to keep the panic out of his voice. He felt a hand on his shoulder.

"Yes, your elven eyes can pierce natural darkness but not this magical darkness," came the soft voice of Taranath. "But tell me, what do you see now?" In a flash, Valduin's vision returned. But unlike his usual darkvision, he could see everything clearly, including the vivid colors of this magical realm. He leaned away from the sphere of magical darkness. He could sense where the edges of the sphere were, but his vision was no longer obscured as he looked through the sphere. He turned back to Taranath in amazement.

"Will I always be able to see like that?" Valduin asked.

"You will now. As your powers grow, you will be able to do a great many things," Taranath replied. "And your powers will need to grow. There are many evils across the planes, and I feel a strange one festering deep within the Virdes. I once could walk through the forest and visit Eydon whenever I liked. Recently, though, I have been unable to enter the forest, and even my vision into that place is obscured. It is quite unusual, and I cannot say exactly what is causing it yet. I must ask you to go there."

"You mean there is something powerful enough to block you from entering the forest, and you think *I* can do something about it?" Valduin asked, incredulous.

Taranath replied, "My powers are linked to the innate magic of this realm. I am not nearly as strong when I physically travel to your Material Plane. And yes, I do think that you can do something about it. I would recommend first seeking out the tomb of Galien. He was from Eydon, and he is a former, uh, associate of mine. In his tomb, you may find some items that will help you on this quest. You will find the entrance to his tomb just upstream of the Valnear Viaduct. It will not be easy to acquire these items. If it was, they would have been stolen years ago, but I am confident that you will be successful."

Taranath reached out to pat Valduin on the shoulder again. Just as Valduin was preparing another round of questions about Eydon, he felt Taranath's hand give him a push. Valduin's stomach dropped as he once again fell through the planes, arriving back in the Wares' home in Tarsam within a moment. Though there was no momentum to his arrival, his knees buckled, and he crumpled back onto his bedroll as his head spun with everything that he had just seen. After an hour or two of lying in stunned silence, he drifted back to sleep, thinking about how he would convince Adelaide and Rose to return to the Virdes.

Adelaide rolled over. Her body ached from yesterday's action. Between the battle and the several hours of travel afterward, she could use a day to rest. The sun was streaming in through the front windows of the room they had slept in. She squinted a bit as she looked toward the light, trying to make out the shapes of her companions. She could see that Rose had leaned her shield up against a chair and appeared to be praying in front of it. Valduin was just a lump on his bedroll, snoring softly. Usually, Valduin was the first to wake up, but Adelaide wasn't going to give him a hard time. He had almost died yesterday.

Rose was not quite as forgiving. When she finished her prayers, she started putting her armor back on. This was not a quiet activity, and before she was finished Valduin groaned and sat up.

"Good morning, Valdear!" Rose greeted him as her head popped through the top of her chain shirt.

"Ugh. Morning," he replied. He pushed himself onto his knees and began to pack up his bedroll.

"What's the plan, then?" Rose asked. "Where is the next adventure?"

Adelaide answered first, "I think we need to do a little shopping, and then head west. Toward the mountains, maybe? Or we could try to find someone in Tarsam that needs some work done."

"Let's go back to the forest," Valduin suggested. "We know those kobolds are mining gems. We know a fair bit about their tunnels and traps now too. I think we could get some good stuff off them. Also, I wouldn't mind disrupting their kidnapping operations."

"Are you serious?" Adelaide asked, her mouth hanging open in shock. "Do you remember the size of that thing that was coming out of the tunnel yesterday? Or were you still *dying* at that point?"

Valduin rolled his eyes. "Yes, I remember. It was a bugbear. We finished it off with one round of attacks. And I don't know about you, but I'm feeling stronger today than I was yesterday."

"You know, I am too," Rose agreed, holding up her arms and flexing her muscles underneath her armor. "But we should still buy you some better armor before we head off."

"So, you're okay with going back into the forest?" Adelaide glared at Rose.

"I guess so. We do know that those evil creatures are kidnapping and robbing people in the forest. I think I'm supposed to find evil and destroy it. I didn't get much in the way of instructions from Halfred. But I don't think Selaia would let me use Her power if the purpose wasn't righteous," Rose replied.

"You see, Adelaide? We have a goddess telling us that we are doing the right thing in stealing from, and probably killing more of, the kobolds. How can we pass up such a divine calling?" Valduin asked with feigned piety.

Adelaide narrowed her eyes at the two of them. "Fine. But if it doesn't work out this time, I get to pick where we head next."

"Works for me," Valduin assented to Adelaide's terms.

"So, you all are on your way out?" Brian's voice came from the stairs at the back of the large room.

Valduin turned to him and said, "Yes, I think we will be on our way. Thank you for helping us get back into the city. It would have been hard for us to do on our own at night. And thank you for your hospitality."

"It was the absolute least we could do," Brian replied. "You saved our lives. We will always be in your debt. You will have a place to sleep here if you ever return to Tarsam."

Valduin, Adelaide, and Rose packed their bags, said their goodbyes, and made their way out of the Wares' home. As they stood on the street, trying to decide which way to go, they heard a voice behind them.

"Need directions?"

Adelaide spun around, surprised by how close the voice sounded. Behind her stood Moire, dressed in loose, brown pants and brown leather boots. Her dark hair was pulled up in a bun, and she had a satchel slung across her body. Rose noticed the dagger hanging at Moire's side.

"Pretty sneaky," Adelaide commented. "And yes, actually. We need to find somewhere to buy some armor."

"Sure!" Moire replied. "You'll be able to find that in the West Market. It's the one we passed through on our way home last night. That's where I'm headed, too. I need to pick some things up before we leave for Barnsley again."

Moire led the adventurers back through the crowded residential streets until they emerged into the large square of the West Market. The center of the market was filled with a labyrinth of stalls, carts, huts, and tents. Vendors shouted to passersby, musicians performed as they walked through the market, and shoppers perused the wide variety of items for sale. At first, Moire led the group around the outside of the market, until she slowed at one of the storefronts that lined the square, clearly a more permanent fixture of the shopping scene in Tarsam. Without saying anything to her guests, she approached the front of the shop, which had a large display window on either side of the entrance.

In the first window stood a headless and armless mannequin wearing a long dress of green and blue that rippled as if standing in a light breeze, though it was behind glass where there couldn't possibly be any wind. Moire moved past this to the other window, where there was a suit of ornate leather armor on a similar mannequin and a pedestal displaying a pearl-handled dagger. The entire party stood staring in silent fascination at the beautiful items.

"What is *this* place?" Adelaide asked in excitement.

"This is The Lamia's Lair. It's a magic shop. They always have the coolest things for sale," Moire explained. "That dagger has been here for a long time. I can't imagine what it costs, but I'm just dying to know what it does."

"Can't you just go in and ask?" Rose asked.

"I mean, maybe," Moire replied. "But I could never afford to buy anything magical. And they say the enchanter that runs the shop is a mean old gnome. I've never seen him, but he would see right through me if I started asking about that dagger."

"Is this the place we are going to buy armor?" Valduin asked hesitantly. "Because there is no way we have enough money for that armor in the window."

"No, I just always have to stop and look in here when I come to the market. We'll find armor for you in the maze," Moire replied as she pulled her gaze from the dagger and walked toward the mass of stalls in the center of the market. The rest of the group fell in line behind her. They twisted in and out of the stalls, trying to avoid getting drawn into conversation with any vendors. After a few minutes, they found themselves standing in front of a large wooden structure, not on wheels, from which hung all sorts of simple armaments and armors. A pair of dwarves sat amongst the tables below the mass of hanging gear.

"This is where you want to shop," Moire said as she pointed toward the dwarves. One of the dwarves stood up and approached when he caught sight of Moire pointing.

"Welcome, welcome! I'm Harfall. That's my brother Harfell. What is it you all are looking for? Need something a little heavier to swing around?" the dwarf asked, gesturing to Adelaide's handaxes.

Adelaide rested her hands on her weapons. "These do just fine for me, thank you very much," she replied with only a hint of attitude.

"Very well!" Harfall chuckled. "So, what do you need? See anything that you like?" He waved a hand at the variety of gear hanging above him.

Valduin stepped forward. "I have been wearing this armor for quite a while, and I was wondering if you had anything that would hold up a little better to attacks but still give me decent mobility." Valduin laid out his leather armor on the table, which he had taken off at the Wares' home and not put back on.

Harfall inspected the armor. He put one finger through the hole the arrow had left in the center of the chest the day before. "Yes, I think we could help you. How much are you looking to spend? I have some basic studded leather that would be a bit better than this, or we may have some more interesting pieces if you have the coin," his voice trailed away, tempting Valduin.

"It depends on how interesting the pieces are," Valduin replied, not intimidated by the experienced salesman.

"Well, I may have an enchanted breastplate to give a bit of magical protection on top of the physical protection," Harfall offered with a smile.

"And how much would such protection cost?" Valduin asked, mimicking Harfall's smug tone.

"Oh, I would let this one go for maybe fifteen hundred gold pieces," Harfall said.

Valduin quickly shifted gears, becoming impatient with the gnome's game. "Not a chance. I'll take the studded leather. Forty gold pieces."

"The market price is fifty..." Harfall countered.

"I'll give you twenty gold pieces, the leather armor on the table, and this," Valduin replied as he pulled a small ruby from a pouch on his belt and placed it on the table.

Harfall leaned close to the edge of the table to get a good look at the gem. He called Harfell over to look at it as well. After a few hushed words in Dwarvish, Harfell grabbed a pole with a hook on the end of it and took down a set of studded leather armor from the rafters of their shop. He brought it forward and placed it on the next table over from Valduin's offer.

Harfall looked up at Valduin, his eyes gleaming, and said, "Very well. The armor is yours. Stay alive. Come back anytime. Bring some more beauties like that and maybe you could get something even stronger."

As Moire led the party back out of the maze of vendors, Valduin matched strides with Adelaide.

"What were they saying?" he asked.

"They liked the ruby. Dwarves love jewels. They thought they were getting a great deal," Adelaide replied.

"You speak Dwarvish?" Rose cut in on the hushed conversation.

"I am originally from Westray, in the Sandgate Mountains. There were lots of dwarves there from the nearby dwarven cities," Adelaide explained.

"Well, that's helpful!" Rose seemed sincerely impressed. "I'd love to see your home someday. Before meeting you, I had barely even left the Mossy Hills."

"That's why I suggested heading to the mountains next," Adelaide said as she gave Valduin a sidelong glance. "I haven't seen my family in a while. It would be nice to check in at some point." She grew distant at the thought of returning home. The group fell into silence as they followed Moire out of the maze.

At the edge of the market, Moire pointed them toward the North Gate. "We'll probably be gone for a couple of months to Barnsley. Please come back and visit when you finish your business in the forest!" Moire said as she waved goodbye. "Thanks again for saving my life!"

"Well, we found the magic shop! Too bad we don't have nearly enough money for magic items or even potions," Madison said. "We have got to focus on getting some good stuff on this trip to the forest."

"I want to know what that dress does! Why do you think it was rippling like it was in the wind?" Amelia asked.

"And I want that breastplate that the dwarves had. That would be the perfect kind of armor for me to use," Madison added.

"See, Amelia? You have to go shopping sometimes to get cool stuff. We aren't going to find everything locked up in chests at the end of dungeons. We can come back for these things once we get some more money," Logan said. "And maybe we can ask the dwarves to trade a job for the breastplate. We'll check back there after we go to the tomb."

"What do you think we are going to find in the tomb? Please let it have at least one magic weapon!" Madison remarked as she looked over her updated character sheet. "These handaxes are going to get old real fast as the enemies get bigger."

9

Arriving at the North Gate around midday, Valduin, Adelaide, and Rose found it wide open. There was still a presence of Crystal Fist guards, but people were passing through the gate freely. There were families walking together, individuals wearing uniforms bearing the symbol of the Crystal Fist, and merchants and farmers with carts of goods to sell in the markets of Tarsam. The adventurers hurried through and once again found themselves on the Virdes Crossway.

They headed north, stopping to buy food from a farmer who was leading a mule-drawn cart toward the city. As the sun descended toward the Sandgate Mountains in the west, the buildings thinned back out to occasional farmsteads as the group approached the Virdes Forest.

"So, Adelaide," Rose broke the comfortable silence in which they had been traveling, "you're from Westray. Why did you leave? And what happened when you two were last in Tarsam? You both seemed pretty anxious around the guards. How did you two even meet? Fill me in!"

"Okay, well, yes, I am from Westray. My parents are still there; they run a shop. My mother is a seamstress and a leatherworker. My father is a blacksmith. I didn't really want to learn any of those trades, and my parents couldn't afford to send me to school, so I grew up working in the shop and exploring the woods and mountains around the city," Adelaide replied.

"And why did you leave?" Rose followed up. "How did you end up here?"

"I had seen plenty of adventurers come through Westray. Sometimes they came to my parents' shop. They always looked so cool, and they had so much gold and nice clothes, and everyone wanted to hear their stories. I didn't want to work in the shop forever, so when I got a chance, I decided to try the adventuring life. I hope to someday get enough money so my parents can close the shop and retire."

"Aw, that's sweet!" Rose smiled at Adelaide, and then she turned to Valduin. "So, where did you come in?"

"I was her ticket out of there, I guess," Valduin explained. "I had been on the road for a while when I found myself in Westray. I found Adelaide's shop while I was looking for some warmer clothes for traveling in the mountains. We chatted a bit about adventuring since I was just getting started. The next thing I knew, she was packing a bag, and we were on the road together."

"That all makes sense, but what happened in Tarsam?" Rose asked.

Valduin winced at the question and made eye contact with Adelaide before answering. "The Crystal Fist isn't very fond of vagrants in the city. We were looking for work, but we didn't have enough money for lodging. After a couple of nights on the street, we got thrown out of the city. That's when we decided to head for the forest. With the stories we had heard about monsters and criminals, we figured we could scrounge up enough coin to return to Tarsam and get some real adventuring work."

"Criminals?" Rose looked at Valduin with wide eyes. "I hope we don't find any of those. Monsters are enough to worry about without having to be suspicious of people too."

Adelaide laughed at Rose's naivety. "Be suspicious of everyone and everything. That's one of the first pieces of advice I heard from an adventurer coming through my parents' shop."

The party fell back into silence as they continued their journey northward. By the time they reached the place where the road entered the trees, there were no travelers in sight in either direction.

"What do we think?" Adelaide piped up. "Rest here? Or push into the forest?"

"I think we should push forward," Valduin said. "We can make it a few more hours before we need to sleep. That way we will have access to the deeper forest tomorrow. Sleeping near the road should be safe, relatively speaking."

"Sounds good to me!" Rose agreed.

"I'm fine with sleeping in the forest tonight, but why do we need to go deeper into the forest? Aren't we just looking for another entrance to the kobolds' tunnels?" Adelaide asked.

Without hesitation, Valduin replied, "I think we need to get deeper into the forest. They would probably be moving whatever gems they were finding back toward the mountains. I think we need to head to the river and follow that upstream and look for a way into their tunnels there." He kept walking forward, not making eye contact with Adelaide. He knew she was good at spotting lies, and he was doing the best he could not to expose this one that he had prepared for this inevitable question.

Adelaide shrugged, seemingly satisfied with his explanation. The trio pressed on, moving at a leisurely pace into the forest. Adelaide had the time now to inspect the road as it cut through the trees. She knew that the road had been here a long time, probably hundreds of years. It did not look paved, however. Even though the ground seemed to be nothing more than packed dirt, nothing from the forest on either side encroached on the road. No vine, no bush, and no grass violated the borders of the path. Above, the trees would lean in far overhead, in some places creating a living tunnel. But even the trees close to the road did not send their lower branches out over it. Adelaide examined the trees as they walked. At some points it looked like branches may have started growing toward the road, but they bent away before they could cross over the road's edge.

"Hey Val, what's up with this road?" Adelaide broke a few minutes of quiet as the group strolled along the Virdes Crossway in the fading daylight.

"What do you mean?" Valduin asked.

"Well, how is it here? How has it not been overgrown by the forest? Does someone take care of it? I've never heard of cleaning crews or anyone working out here or anything," Adelaide replied.

Valduin looked around as if he was seeing the forest for the first time. "I never really thought about it," he said, half to himself and half to Adelaide. "I guess it's probably some kind of enchantment. The elves of Eydon built the bridge. They probably built the road as well."

Rose also looked around as well, and then she said something that neither Adelaide nor Valduin understood. Her amulet began to glow, and the usually dark brown irises of Rose's eyes turned to almost an amber color. Rose gasped and opened her eyes wide, looking up and down the road.

"Yes, it is definitely magic!" Rose exclaimed. "The entire road is shimmering with magic." Rose looked up. "And so is the space above the road. The magic fills the air fifty or sixty feet up."

Adelaide looked down at her feet but was unable to perceive any difference in the road from a moment ago. "You can see the magic?" she asked Rose.

"Yes, I asked Selaia to help me see if there was magic in the road, and She did," Rose replied with a shrug.

Adelaide smiled. "Remember that spell. That will be very useful for finding enchanted items. Maybe you'll be able to lead us to some next time we find one of those kobold hordes. Anyway, we should probably find a place to camp for the night soon. It's getting pretty dark for my human eyes."

At the mention of darkness, Rose made her amulet shine brighter, shedding light on the road around them. They continued walking for another few minutes before Valduin stopped, peering through the trees.

"I think there's a campsite over there," he pointed into the forest on the eastern side of the road.

"I don't see anything," Rose said, holding her amulet out to try to light up the woods.

"Let me check it out," Valduin said. He crept forward toward the trees. "Stay here and listen for trouble."

Rose and Adelaide waited at the edge of the road as Valduin disappeared into the darkness. Adelaide tugged at the loops of leather that held her handaxes to her belt. Rose tapped her foot.

They did not have to wait long, however, as Valduin called out to them only a minute later. "It's a campsite for sure, and it's empty. We can sleep here tonight."

With the light from Rose's amulet, the women made their way through the trees and undergrowth toward the sound of Valduin's voice. They found him starting a fire within a ring of stones. Adelaide surveyed the area. There was the fire ring with a pair of logs flanking it as benches. There was even a small pile of sticks that looked like someone had pulled together for feeding a campfire. There were many footprints from many different creatures. Adelaide could see bootprints from some medium-sized humanoids, small paw prints from four-legged woodland creatures, and even some bigger footprints of some sort of large, barefoot, bipedal creatures.

"It looks like this campsite gets a lot of traffic," she remarked. "It's probably frequented by people traveling on the Crossway. I hope no one else was planning on using it tonight."

The group ate the remains of the food that they had bought from the farmer earlier and then prepared to sleep. Rose went through the process of doffing her armor, which was getting faster each time she did it. She curled up in her bedroll and went to sleep, tired from a long day of walking.

"You should sleep while it's dark," Valduin said to Adelaide. "I'll take watch and wake you up when the sky starts to lighten."

"No argument here," Adelaide replied as she spread out her bedroll.

Valduin spent the next few hours thinking about everything that Taranath had told him. He was desperate to find out what was in the tomb, but he was just as desperate not to have to explain to Adelaide what had happened the previous night.

His watch passed uneventfully, and Valduin shook Adelaide awake. He opened up his own bedroll, laid it next to the still-warm remains of their fire, and fell deeply asleep. Adelaide looked around the campsite for a moment before picking a tree with a few low branches about thirty feet away from her sleeping compatriots. She climbed up the tree to get a vantage on the campsite and the surrounding woods. As she settled in for her watch, her mind wandered back to her parents, and the promises she had made before leaving home.

A couple of hours into the watch, as the sky was just starting to lighten, the sound of a twig snapping below her jerked Adelaide out of her reverie. Leaning around the trunk of the tree, she could see shapes moving through the woods, from the direction of the road. As they grew closer, she made out the silhouettes of five humanoids creeping through the dark forest, all with weapons drawn.

"I told you someone would take the bait," a raspy voice whispered from the front of the group. "Travelers always love a stocked fire pit." Another one of the shapes shushed him, and they continued forward toward Adelaide's position.

Adelaide smiled to herself as she drew two of the kobold daggers from her belt. She waited in silence as the humanoid in the front of the gang passed under her tree. Her heart was pounding in her ears as one by one they moved past her. The last one in the line trailed about fifteen feet behind the rest of the group, keeping an eye on the forest behind them. As this one reached her tree, Adelaide whipped the two daggers straight down into its shoulders. As both daggers sunk to the hilt, the figure dropped softly to the ground.

Adelaide jumped down from the tree, drew her last two daggers, and began stalking the next one in the line. This one was now twenty feet from her, approaching the place where the other three had stopped just outside of the campsite. Adelaide darted forward toward another tree. She threw her daggers at the next figure and ducked behind the wide trunk for cover. She saw the first dagger hit the man in the back, but the second one sailed over his head as he doubled over in pain.

The man screamed as he spun around and fired a crossbow bolt wildly into the darkness behind him.

Hearing the sound of the crossbow firing, Adelaide steeled herself, drew her handaxes, and came barreling out from behind the tree. As she ran, she shouted, "Val! Rose! Under attack!" Approaching the injured humanoid, she threw her first handaxe toward the figure closest to the campsite, hitting him in the thigh. She then slashed the injured man in front of her with her only remaining weapon, dropping him to the ground with a grunt.

At the sound of Adelaide's shouting, Valduin's eyes sprung open. Despite the darkness, he could easily see the attackers who were turning to face Adelaide. He leapt to his feet, throwing his blanket on the remains of their fire as he did. *"To the depths!"* he shouted in Sylvan to send a spark of pale green energy into the attacker closest to him, who was leaning forward to pull a small axe from his leg. The force of the blast first stood him upright, eyes wide in shock, and then he fell like a tree flat onto his back.

Rose jumped out of her bedroll, instantly regretting her lack of armor, and grabbed her amulet to light up the surroundings so she could see their attackers.

The remaining two humanoids, each with a crossbow drawn, took in their situation. Three of their comrades were on the ground, either dead or dying. They were being picked off from behind while being attacked with magic from the front. The sudden bright light shining from the small one burned their eyes, which had been accustomed to the darkness. They made eye contact with each other, and then both of them dropped their weapons.

"Stop! Stop!" the taller one cried. "Please stop. We're sorry!" They both dropped to their knees with their hands in the air.

Adelaide strode forward, removed her axe from the body on the ground, and then looked at Rose and said, "Do you mind tending to these guys? I think they are all still technically alive."

"Of course!" Rose replied as she hurried over. Her hands gave off their familiar golden glow as she touched each of the three humanoids on the ground. Each time she did, their bleeding stopped and their breathing became more comfortable, though they remained unconscious for the moment.

Valduin addressed the two remaining bandits, "Now, what are we going to do with all of you? What was your plan? Rob us? Kill us in our sleep? Is this campsite a lure that you use to get travelers to let down their guard?"

The taller of the two stammered out, "W-w-we weren't gonna hurt you. W-we just need coin. G-G-Garat found you." The man, who Valduin could now identify as human, pointed toward the man on the ground between them, who looked to be a half-orc.

Rose returned to the group. "They are all alive," she reported. "Not sure how long they will sleep for, though. Adelaide did a number on those two."

"Thank you very much, my dear," Adelaide accepted the compliment with a clumsy curtsey that made Rose giggle.

Valduin smiled as he looked at their situation. "I think we will use the old rope trick again, ladies. Adelaide, if you don't mind, could I borrow your rope?"

Adelaide realized what Valduin was suggesting, and then she grumbled a bit. "Fine, fine. Use my rope. But the next time we really need a rope you'll be sorry you keep wasting it." She walked off toward her gear.

Valduin turned to the bandits standing in front of him. "Please take your sleeping friends and sit them at the base of that tree," he said, indicating a nearby tree that was about eight feet around. "Then kindly seat yourselves next to them."

As the unconscious bandits were collected around the tree, Valduin started searching through their pockets, pouches, and packs. Other than Garat the half-orc, they were all human. Valduin set to counting through the loot while Adelaide finished tying the rope around the bandits at chest level, securing them to the tree. She walked over to where Valduin and Rose were finishing up looking through the bandits' things.

"What did you find?" she asked. "Anything good?"

Valduin looked up at her with a wide smile. "We pulled almost one hundred gold pieces off the five of them, another hundred silver, and this fancy ring," he said as he held up a small, silver ring with a single green stone in it.

"Oooh that's pretty," Rose said as Valduin held up the ring. "Can I have that?"

Valduin looked at Adelaide first, but she didn't seem interested in the ring, so he handed it over to Rose. Rose slipped it on and held her hand up to admire it.

With the adrenaline from the battle wearing off, both Valduin and Adelaide could feel their exhaustion creeping up again.

"You think we can go back to sleep?" Valduin asked.

"I think it would be fine," replied Adelaide, as she finished collecting and cleaning her daggers. "They aren't going anywhere. Rose, are you okay to take watch now?"

"Yes, I feel fine," Rose replied. "You two go to sleep. I will keep an eye on the thugs. I'll wake you up if they try anything." She started putting her armor back on, just in case.

Rose looked at the men tied to the tree. "My friends are going to sleep. I would very much appreciate it if you all stayed quiet and took some time to think about the decisions that landed you here. Thank you."

Surprised by her politeness, the tall man, who had been doing all of the talking, replied, "Uh, yes, Miss Rose. We'll be quiet."

Rose smiled. Satisfied, she sat against another tree where she could see Valduin and Adelaide while keeping an eye on their prisoners. She recited her prayers as the light of the morning sun shone through the treetops to the east.

"Now that's what I'm talking about!" Logan exclaimed. "Madison, you tore them up!"

"It worked because I had lots of weapons to throw. And because they had so few hit points. I feel like I've

86

said this a bunch already, but I definitely need to get something bigger to swing for when we battle something stronger," Madison replied.

"What do you think that ring does?" Amelia asked. "Do you think it's magic?"

"Maybe," Logan shrugged. "You can use detect magic to get an idea, right? Maybe we will be able to get the gnome at the magic shop in Tarsam to identify it for us."

"Even if it isn't magic, we could probably sell it for a decent amount of gold," Madison said.

"We aren't selling it!" Amelia protested. "It's the first pretty thing we've found in this whole game. And you said we were going to share the loot this time. I'm *keeping* it!"

10

By late morning, Valduin, Adelaide, and Rose had finished their rest, eaten their breakfast, and packed up their camp. The five bandits remained tied to the tree; the near-death experiences of three of them discouraged any attempt to break free. As the party of three began to walk away, the half-orc Garat spoke up.

"Do you think you could let us go now?" he asked. "We won't bother you all again. We do appreciate you not killing us."

Valduin and Adelaide looked at each other, though neither one made a reply or a move toward the tree. Sensing their reluctance, Rose stepped forward and said, "Of course. We won't leave you stuck like this. Just give me a second." She walked over to where the bandits' weapons lay piled on the ground and picked up a scimitar. Walking back to the bandits, she laid the scimitar across Garat's legs, below the knees.

"I think that should be enough for some clever folks like yourselves," she said as she turned to leave.

"Th-thank you!" Garat called out as he began to carefully lift his legs to get the scimitar to fall toward his hands.

Back on the road, Valduin led Adelaide and Rose northward again, continuing on toward the Valnear Viaduct. The party was mostly quiet, and Adelaide and Rose each kept an eye on the woods on either side of the road, alert for new dangers. The road rose and fell over small hills as it carved its magical path toward the Virdes River.

After a few hours of walking, the group was approaching the top of one of these hills when Adelaide spoke up. "Does the forest here look different to you two? It seems denser than what we've seen so far."

Rose stopped to look around with Adelaide as Valduin continued forward. "I think you're right," she agreed. "I don't remember the trees being this close together earlier."

"What in the world is this?" Valduin interrupted the women's discussion as he gazed off the top of the hill.

Adelaide and Rose stepped up next to Valduin. In front of them, obliterating the road, was an enormous crater. It appeared to be roughly circular, with a diameter of nearly one hundred feet. The walls of the crater were close to vertical where they met the surface, and they dropped at least sixty or eighty feet straight down before sloping into a bowl. Near the bottom of the bowl was a large opening into a cave or tunnel. While they could hear no creatures in the forest around them, the crater seemed to emit a low hum, and it smelled of charred wood.

"I am absolutely positive that this should not be here," Valduin continued, surveying the pit. "What could even make a hole this big?"

Adelaide thought for a moment before replying, "I have no idea. Maybe some kind of burrowing creature? Any thoughts, Rose?"

Rose, however, was not looking in the hole. She had moved off to the right side of the road and was peering between the tightly packed trees. "What? Oh, I don't know. I think I hear something over here, though. It sounded like whispering."

As Rose was inching toward the tree line to investigate the gentle whispers, she noticed another sound. At first, she thought it was just a few gusts of wind, but as the sound grew louder, it became regular and more frequent. It began to sound more and more like wings beating. A single pair of enormous wings.

"You guys hear *that,* right?" Rose asked as she looked up toward the sky, searching for the source of the sound. She walked back to the middle of the road to get a clear view through the gap in the trees above. What she saw there made her heart sink as she froze in place, mouth agape.

"Yes, I hear it…" Valduin began to reply. His words trailed off as he also looked up to the sky and found himself unable to move.

Descending through the gap in the trees above the road was a gargantuan, red-scaled dragon. Its leathery wings were halfway folded as it drifted to the ground; they would have hit the trees on both sides of the road at full extension. It landed in the middle of the road to the south of the three adventurers, trapping them against the crater. It lowered its head to inspect the small humanoids, and they could feel the heat radiating off the dragon's body. Thin trails of white smoke rose from its nostrils, and the smell of char that they had detected in the crater was now overwhelming. The dragon let out a small chuckle as it pulled its lips back in a sinister smile to reveal a mouth full of long, sharp teeth.

The dragon began to speak, but neither Rose nor Adelaide nor Valduin could understand it. However, after the interactions with the kobolds, they all recognized the language as Draconic. Rose and Adelaide did nothing, still frozen in place by the sight of this terrible beast. Valduin, however, steeled his nerves, took one step toward the dragon, and said, "W-w-we don't speak Draconic. D-don't you speak Common? W-we are very sorry for intruding on your home." From the smell, Valduin had concluded that the crater behind him was this dragon's lair.

The dragon furrowed its brow in apparent frustration at Valduin's response. It repeated whatever it had said in Draconic. The trails of smoke from its nostrils grew thicker and darker as the smile dwindled into a snarl.

"What are you doing?" Adelaide hissed at him. "Stop talking to the dragon and figure out how we can get out of here!"

Valduin's mind raced. He stepped back next to Adelaide, and in a forced whisper said, "I'm sure dragons this big speak Common. Otherwise, how do they get so many humanoids to serve them?" As he spoke, he dropped his pack to the ground and began rummaging around in it. Finally, he found a small pouch of salt among his food supplies. Taking a pinch of salt in one hand, he scraped some of the soot from his bedroll where it had fallen in the fire during the scuffle the night before. He rubbed the two components together between his palms while muttering to himself in Sylvan. He then put both palms on his forehead and rubbed them over the top of his head as if he was sweeping his hair back from his face.

The dragon's eyes narrowed as it watched Valduin cast the spell, but it seemed to understand what Valduin was doing. When the spell was complete, it repeated its statement in Draconic, which Valduin could now understand.

"What brings you thieves into my lair?"

Valduin interpreted for Rose and Adelaide, who were relaxing a bit as the minutes passed without any aggression from the dragon. "The dragon thinks we are thieves sneaking into its lair," he said.

"Well, tell it that we aren't!" Adelaide exclaimed in a harsh whisper.

"I can't!" Valduin hissed back. "This magic lets me *comprehend* languages. I can't speak Draconic with it."

"Well, that's not exactly the most helpful spell, now, is it?" Adelaide's eyes shot daggers at Valduin. "What do we do? We can't talk to it, we can't go north because of the hole in the ground, and we can't go south because of the massive *dragon* in the road."

The dragon's rumbling voice stopped their conversation again, but this time its words were less harsh. Valduin understood it to be the same question as before but in a different language this time.

"Wait, that's Sylvan!" he exclaimed. He shouted up to the dragon in Sylvan, *"We aren't thieves! We are traveling north to Barnsley. We don't want any trouble!"*

"Unfortunately for you, small one, trouble you have found," the dragon spoke louder now, still in Sylvan, and it sat back, spread its wings, and let out an ear-splitting roar.

Adelaide froze once again, but Valduin was distracted as his mind raced. Dragons were not supposed to speak Sylvan; they were supposed to speak Common. And red dragons make their lairs in mountains, not forests. He looked back at the dragon, inspecting it as closely as he could at this distance.

Then he saw it. When the wings spread, their tips passed through the tree branches. It was an illusion. As soon as this thought passed through his mind, the entire dragon seemed to dim. Valduin could see straight through it and down the road behind it.

He turned to Adelaide and Rose and said, "The dragon isn't real. I think it's an illusion." He started to walk toward the dragon. After walking five feet ahead of the other two, he pulled his crossbow forward from the side of his pack and fired a bolt at the dragon. It was an easy shot to take at such a large creature.

The bolt passed straight through it.

The dragon looked down at where the bolt had gone through its body, and then it grabbed at its chest dramatically as it staggered backward on its hind legs. It fell forward flat on the ground with a tremendous crash, though the sound seemed hollow to Valduin. Its snout lay a few feet from the party. It looked directly at Valduin, gave an exaggerated smile, chuckled again, and disappeared.

The tension broke for Rose and Adelaide as they realized that the threat had passed. Valduin, however, remained alert. "Whoever created that is probably still close, and probably has something to do with the hole in the ground," he said. "We'll need to find them to get through here."

Rose lowered her voice and nodded her head toward the forest on the east side of the road. "I heard whispers coming through the trees over here right before the dragon showed up. They were probably casting the spell then," she said.

All three of them came together in the middle of the road, and then they crept toward the tree line where Rose had been. They heard another chuckle, the same sound as the large dragon had made but at least three octaves higher in pitch, and then there was a sudden flurry of movement between the trees. As they all looked toward the movement, a blinding flash of colored lights erupted from the forest.

"I can't see anything!" Rose shrieked.

"Me either!" Valduin shouted. "Adelaide, are you okay?"

Adelaide blinked a few times to clear her eyes and found that she could see. "I can see," she said, "but I don't know what I'm looking at." Between the trees, Adelaide saw four tiny humanoids with matching butterfly wings. Their skin was pale green, and they all had long red hair. To Adelaide's eyes, the four creatures were identical, and as they flew, they swarmed around each other, making it hard to focus on any one of them. Adelaide squinted through the stinging in her eyes and the blur of the creatures' movement, and she magically marked one of them as her prey. She drew a dagger and threw it at the cluster of tiny creatures. It looked like she was going to hit one of them, but the creature dove out of the way at the last moment.

As Adelaide reached for another weapon from the side of her pack, the small creatures began whispering again while drawing a dark green, glowing glyph in the air. All at once, the four tiny beings pointed at Adelaide, and her vision erupted in a shower of colorful sparks. Her arms dropped to her sides as her face went lax. She stood in the middle of the road, mesmerized by the light show that only she could see.

The creatures chuckled again as they flew back through the trees. Just as they were about to disappear into the foliage, Rose's vision cleared, and she reached out her hand toward the cluster of winged creatures. As her radiant flames began to erupt within the four tiny beings' space, they dodged quickly out of the way, unscathed by Rose's attack.

Another moment later, Valduin's vision cleared as well. Following Rose's lead, his hand went out toward the retreating creatures, and he fired a spark of eldritch energy toward them. The spark appeared to make contact with one of the tiny, winged beings, which disappeared with the impact of the spell. The remaining creatures continued past the tree line, their path unchanged, and their demeanor unaffected by the loss of one of their number.

After unleashing their spells, and with their attention focused on the spot where their assailants had disappeared, Rose and Valduin heard rapid footsteps behind them. Glancing in the direction of the sound, they watched as Adelaide sprinted away from them, directly toward the crater. They continued to watch in horror as she ran at full speed over the edge of the hole. But to their surprise and confusion, she did not fall. She kept running as if the road continued unimpeded by the massive hole in the ground. She stopped about ten feet past the edge, and she stood there, suspended in the air, looking around slowly with awe on her face.

Forgetting about the small creatures for the moment, Rose pulled the coil of rope off her pack and handed one end to Valduin "Hold on tight. I'm gonna jump!" she said. She took the other end of the rope in her hand and broke into a sprint toward Adelaide. Reaching the edge of the pit, she leapt into the air.

She had expected to just barely reach Adelaide where the human floated above the crater, but as she took her last step before the jump, she felt a strange warmth burst from the ring on her finger. When she left the ground, she felt lighter than air, despite the armor and gear she carried, and soared over Adelaide's head. Twenty feet beyond the human, as Rose was expecting to enter free fall into the center of the crater, she landed hard on what felt like normal ground. Not prepared for the landing, she tumbled forward and ended up prone, staring down into the hole, as the warmth from the ring subsided.

Valduin, having watched Rose's incredible jump and impressive crash landing, held tight to the rope as he approached the edge of the crater. He inspected the hole, testing the edge with his foot. When he felt the road continuing at its normal elevation, he realized this was just another illusion. Again, as soon as this thought crossed his mind, he found himself able to see through it, as he had seen through the red dragon a minute earlier.

Adelaide was just coming to her senses as Valduin turned back toward the forest, searching for signs of the small creatures. Rose pulled herself to her feet, taking in the sight of the crater around her. She took a moment to look for signs of magic. Her spell revealed the expected aura of the road as well as the magic of the illusory crater. She also noticed a glow coming from her new ring, which she had by now deduced gave her the ability to jump terrific distances.

"Where are they?" Adelaide bellowed as she realized she had tried to kill herself running off the edge of a cliff while under the influence of the flying creatures' spell. "Where'd they go?"

"They went into the trees on the east side of the road," Rose replied. "They were pretty fast."

Valduin racked his brain, trying to remember where he had seen creatures like this before. After a moment, it hit him. "They are sylphs!" he declared. "They are like fairies or sprites. Tiny fey creatures."

"I didn't ask *what* they are," Adelaide snapped at him as she marched toward the trees, handaxes drawn. "I asked *where* they are!"

"I think they're gone," offered Rose, speaking softly in an attempt to placate Adelaide. "Maybe we should just keep going," she suggested.

"Also, honestly, they didn't hurt us." Valduin also tried to calm Adelaide down. "I think they were just having fun."

"*Fun?* Is it fun to make people try to kill themselves? Is it fun to scare people half to death with a massive red dragon?" Adelaide shouted in anger. As she stood at the edge of the trees and seethed, she realized that she could still feel the presence of the sylph she had marked. Her magic was still active. She went silent, her head clearing as she focused on the sense of her quarry, and she crept into the forest.

The hunt was on.

"Isn't it cheating that you know what all the monsters are?" Amelia asked Logan.

"He can't help it," Madison explained as she rolled her eyes. "He's memorized the whole book of monsters."

"First of all, it isn't cheating," Logan explained defensively. "It's called *metagaming*. And second of all, it's in my backstory. I went to a fancy elven school in a fancy elven city and now I know a whole lot of stuff about monsters and the planes and all sorts of things. That's how I explain why I speak five languages. I still had to roll an Intelligence check to remember details about the sylph."

Amelia looked back at Madison, clearly unimpressed, and said, "Please make sure to have Adelaide remind Rose never to ask Valduin backstory questions." The girls laughed together as Logan glared at them.

11

The party crept from one tree to the next as Adelaide led the way, tracking the movements of the sylphs through the forest. She did not think that the creatures had gone far, and she wanted to be sure that she got the first move in the next encounter. They descended the hill that the road had been climbing, and at the low point before the next hill, they came upon a small stream. At the edge of the water, Adelaide froze, holding up her hand to tell Valduin and Rose to stop moving.

Without moving her head, she whispered, "I see one. It's about fifty feet to the left on this side of the stream. Valduin, you're gonna have to loop around behind it while Rose and I cross the stream. Hopefully, it'll keep its attention on us."

"Do we really have to sneak up on it?" Rose asked. "It probably wouldn't bother us again if we just kept moving."

"And it's probably almost out of magic," Valduin tried to assist Rose in dissuading Adelaide. "Those were some impressive spells it was casting earlier."

"I don't care!" Adelaide hissed. "It needs to know that it can't just scare people like that." She took the first steps carefully across the stream. "Rose, let's go. We will circle back in a minute to corner it."

Rose gave Valduin a helpless look as she followed Adelaide through the stream. Valduin waited for a moment before backtracking until he could approach the spot that Adelaide had pointed out. A minute later, he had snuck into position above the stream. He could see the shapes of Rose and Adelaide on the far hill, well above the stream's bank.

Shaking his head at the situation, he ran down the final slope to the bank of the stream and spun around, searching for the sylph. He looked downstream, and, seeing nothing, he turned to look upstream. As his head whipped around, he found himself face to face with a smirking fairy hovering in the air. Another spray of rainbow lights shot from the sylph's hand, but Valduin was able to resist its blinding effects this time. The tiny creature's smile faltered for a moment, but it managed another chuckle as it disappeared into thin air.

Valduin could hear it as it flew away, but despite swinging his hands wildly he was unable to grab the tiny, invisible creature. He could now hear Rose and Adelaide rushing down the opposite bank, and his mind raced as he tried to decide how to find the sylph.

Finally, he settled on diplomacy. He called out in Sylvan, *"Please stay! I just want to talk to you! We need your help!"*

Rose and Adelaide had crossed the stream, and Adelaide was scanning the bank with wild eyes, one handaxe raised, ready to be thrown.

Valduin motioned for Adelaide to lower her weapon. *"We will not hurt you,"* he tried again, still in Sylvan. *"We only want to talk."*

"*She doesn't look like she wants to talk,*" came the Sylvan reply from the trees above.

All three adventurers looked to the tree branches above them, searching for the source of the voice.

"*She is just a little upset about what you did before. That red dragon was terrifying,*" Valduin explained.

"*Why, thank you. I have been working on that one for a very long time. I still don't get the facial movements quite right. It's hard to study red dragons, you know. They are so sensitive,*" the sylph replied, its voice shifting about the canopy above them.

"What is it saying?" Adelaide asked, eyes scouring the treetops for any sign of movement.

"We are just chatting," Valduin said. "It might help if you put your axes away. If the sylph has lived in the forest for a while, it might be able to help us find the tomb." The moment the last word came out, Valduin grimaced, knowing he had given away his intentions for this expedition.

"Tomb? What tomb?" Adelaide asked him, startled by this new information. "I thought we were looking for the kobolds' horde."

"Okay, there might be a little more to this particular outing. Can we please talk about it later? I promise I will tell you everything," Valduin pleaded with Adelaide as he turned his attention back to the treetops.

"You better tell me everything," she growled, waving an axe at him menacingly before sheathing her weapons.

"*Do you think you could come down now?*" Valduin called back up to the dragon. "*I would love to talk to you about something.*"

Before the reply could come, Valduin felt a weight land on his pack. The sylph whispered in his ear, *"Tell her to sit down on the rock there. Then we can talk."*

Both Rose and Adelaide jumped at the new proximity of the voice, but they still could not see the sylph.

"I think it would be best if we all took a seat," Valduin suggested to his companions. "Just to keep things polite."

The three adventurers each sat down, with Rose and Adelaide on one rock and Valduin facing them from a fallen tree about ten feet away. As Rose and Adelaide looked at Valduin, there appeared the light green, feminine face of the sylph peeking over his shoulder.

"Thank you," she said to Valduin.

"You are welcome," Valduin replied. *"I am Valduin, and my companions here are Rose and Adelaide. What is your name?"*

"I am Venez," the fairy said. *"I am sorry for scaring you. It was just a bit of fun. And once you found me, I was just trying to get out of there without getting hurt."*

"She apologizes for scaring us," Valduin interpreted for Rose and Adelaide. "And she says she was just defending herself."

"Please tell her that it isn't nice to scare strangers like that," Rose said calmly. "Also, where are her friends? Will we meet them?"

Valduin passed on Rose's comment to Venez, who smiled and gave a high, tittering giggle. She spoke to Valduin again in Sylvan, who relayed the comment to Rose, "She says that it is what she does best. And scaring strangers away has always been easier than fighting them. Sylphs aren't the strongest fighters. They are just tricky enough to avoid confrontations. Ones as old as Venez are very good at avoiding fights. And it was just her the whole time. The other ones were another illusion."

"How old is she?" Rose asked. "Has she lived here long?"

"Well, she did not say that part, but I assume she is quite old because of how powerful she is," Valduin explained. "Making those illusions we saw required some strong magic. Stronger than anything I can do. I have only seen sylphs do very small, simple illusions. Some of the elves in Alomere kept them. Not as pets, they are too smart for that, but as companions. Now, let us see if she will help us."

"Have you lived in the forest long? We are looking for a place, an old place. It holds the tomb of an ancient elf named Galien. Do you know it?" he asked.

Venez flew around to the front of Valduin so she could get a good look at the half-elf. She inspected him for a moment, staring into his eyes in a way that made him feel as if she was looking right into his soul. After an awkward pause, she replied, *"Yes, I know the place that you seek. Just up the river from the bridge. I used to live close to there, but recently there have been all sorts of evil creatures moving through the forest. I've had to stay on the move to avoid getting caught by them."*

"We have met some of these creatures," Valduin said. *"Kobolds and goblins and bugbears. We killed a few of them just a couple of days ago."*

Valduin was surprised when Venez shook her head and said, *"Those whiny kobolds and dirty goblinoids I can handle. There have been other creatures, not of this plane; fiendish monsters within the forest."* At this, Valduin's eyes grew wide. He thought back to what Taranath had told him about an evil growing within the Virdes.

"Whoa, what did she say?" Rose asked, sensing the change in Valduin's demeanor. "You look like you've seen a ghost."

"She knows where the tomb is. But she said that there have been monsters roaming the forest recently. Evil creatures from other planes. Fiends, she said," Valduin explained.

Rose's mouth fell open in silent shock.

"Yes, about that tomb," Adelaide cut in, unaffected by this news. She pointed an accusatory finger at Valduin. "When were you planning on telling us that this was more than just a trip to rob some kobolds? Where did you find out about a tomb, anyway?"

"Well, I found out about it while we were in Tarsam," Valduin said, his words coming slowly as he tried to sort out how to explain his meeting with Taranath.

"When? We were together the entire time," Adelaide countered.

"Actually, that is not entirely true." Valduin's voice trailed off.

He hesitated.

Adelaide's patience waned. She raised her voice and said, "You had better start talking, mister, or you'll be finding someone else to raid a tomb with you. Maybe your new fairy friend will help you."

"Maybe we can walk and talk," Valduin said to Adelaide as he turned back to Venez. "*Could you take us to the tomb today? Before dark maybe?*"

"*Yes, it will be only a couple of hours from here for you on foot. Go back to the road and head north. I'll let you know when to leave the road,*" Venez replied. She smiled at Adelaide and Rose, and with a wink, she turned invisible again. Valduin felt her leap off his lap and heard her flutter away.

"We go back to the road and continue north," Valduin reported. "She will tell us when we need to head off the road. We should reach the tomb by nightfall, so we can sleep before heading in there."

The party returned to the road, walking through the illusion of the crater as they headed farther north. As they walked, Valduin told Rose and Adelaide how Taranath had visited him while they were sleeping in Tarsam. He told them that he had been taken to the Inner Plane of Light and given new abilities. He also recounted Taranath's concerns regarding the evil growing within the Virdes Forest and his instructions to find the tomb of Galien before heading toward the ruins of Eydon.

"So, you went to another *plane of existence*? While we were sleeping?" Rose asked in shock.

"And this Taranath person, are you sure he's good? Are you sure you aren't being used?" Adelaide added.

Valduin thought for a moment. "Well, I guess I do not know for sure," he answered. "But I know that he has helped me in the past. He saved my life once, and he gave me the ability to use magic. I think I owe him the benefit of the doubt. I do not have to trust him completely, but I think he is good. I think he wants to help me, and us, do good."

"We'll see," Adelaide muttered. She was still suspicious, but she realized that a creature capable of taking Valduin to another plane was not the kind of creature she would want to start a fight with. Not yet, at least. Also, she was a little wary of the fact that this was the second time today that they had been talking about creatures from other planes. There was something about that idea that did not sit well with Adelaide. Creatures were not supposed to just move between the planes, especially when it meant monsters coming to her home plane.

Just as Valduin was beginning to worry that Venez was not going to come back, the group heard the light flutter of wings. Valduin felt the weight of the sylph landing on his pack, and Venez revealed herself once more.

"Go west through these trees," she whispered to Valduin.

The party turned off the road and headed into the woods. The once gentle hills of the forest were becoming more pronounced, and the trees were thinner here. The adventurers descended the steep slope from the road to the bottom of a hill. With Venez's directions, they wound their way along a stream until they stood before a dark stone archway set into the hillside. It would have been completely concealed to a viewer looking down from the top of the hill. However, Venez had brought them along the stream below it, and the recessed entrance was easy to spot.

As Valduin stared in awe at the stone archway, an ancient elven construction, Rose and Adelaide surveyed the rest of their surroundings. They both noticed the many footprints in the soft earth around the archway, and Adelaide was able to identify the creatures that made them after tracking similar footprints only a few days before.

"Kobolds!" she hissed. "And something bigger. Maybe another bugbear. If they looted this place already, I am going to be so furious." She glared at the ground for a moment. "With how soft the ground is here, these must be fresh. They are probably still in there."

The anger in her voice shook Valduin out of his dreamy stare at the elven handiwork. "We should rest," he said. "It is getting dark, and I doubt a few hours will make a difference. Let's set up camp across the stream and up the next hill where we can see this entrance. If we see them coming out, we can ambush them. Taranath implied that there are defenses within the tomb to protect it from looters. They might not be coming back out."

The group made their way across the stream and found a spot with a good line of sight to the stone archway. As they made camp, Venez said to Valduin, *Good luck. I hope to see you again. It isn't often I meet a child of the Fey in this forest. I would like very much to talk more with you.*"

Before Valduin could respond, the sylph had vanished once again, its light wingbeats fading into the dark forest.

"Why did she call you 'child of the Fey'?" Amelia asked. "Is that some other piece of your overly-complicated backstory?"

"I actually don't know," Logan replied. "Maybe just because I am a half-elf? Are all elves related to the Fey somehow? I'm not sure."

"More importantly, why aren't we just going in there? We didn't use many spells in the encounter with Venez, and we didn't even get hurt. Let's just do it!" Madison exclaimed.

"It's the end of the day. We have each used at least one spell. We don't want to rush in there and fight a bunch of kobolds and bugbears and also have to deal with the tomb. It's probably going to be a dungeon crawl. We need all of the power we can muster for this," Logan said, counting off each point on his fingers as he lectured his sisters.

"Ugh, fine," Amelia rolled her eyes as she stood up from the table. "Just remember that you're not the boss. Sometimes you're gonna have to do what we want to do."

"Where are you going?" Logan asked in a panic. "You can't leave again. We are about to enter our first dungeon!"

"Relax, elf-boy, I'm just getting some snacks. I'll be back," Amelia replied as she walked out of the room.

12

The night passed uneventfully as Adelaide, Valduin, and Rose each took a turn watching the archway for signs of movement. There was none to be seen. In the morning the group ate breakfast quietly before heading back to the tomb entrance.

"Any new footprints?" Valduin asked Adelaide. "Did we miss someone leaving the cave?"

Adelaide took a moment to look around, remembering the arrangement of the muddy tracks from the night before.

"I don't think so," she finally concluded. "I think these are all the same footprints from yesterday, and all of these tracks seem to be headed *into* the cave, not away from it."

"I'm not sure if that makes me feel better or worse," Rose said as she inspected the archway. "Hey Valdunie, what do you think of this writing?"

Valduin opened his mouth to tell Rose for the hundredth time how to pronounce his name, but his attention was drawn to the writing that Rose had found. There was Elvish script carved into the underside of the stone archway. It took Valduin a few seconds to identify all of the letters, as this was some very old text, but he soon was able to read the phrase.

"It says 'Here lies the Demons' Judge, Galien, Keeper of the Astral Peace,'" he reported.

"That's a cool name," Rose said as she studied the carvings. "Which of these words are *Demons' Judge*?"

Valduin pointed to three words as he read them, "'Judge of Demons.' I think Demons' Judge sounds better. Who knows what they would have called him in Common. I wonder what it means when it says 'Keeper of the Astral Peace.'"

Rose thought for a moment. "I'm not sure, but it sounds familiar. I think I may have read about that back at the temple. But I don't remember exactly."

During this conversation, Adelaide crept forward into the cave. She turned back to the other two and said, "Val, we need you out front. It's going to get really dark in here, and I don't want to be walking in the front with a torch." Adelaide laid out a torch and her tinderbox. Before she started trying to light it, however, Rose reached out and touched the top of the torch. It began to glow with warm, yellow light.

"Oh, right," Adelaide said, looking up at Rose. "I forgot that you could do that. That's perfect. Thanks." Adelaide lifted the coldly glowing torch, shouldered her pack, and followed Valduin into the darkness. Rose stayed close enough to touch Adelaide, not wanting to be left behind in the dark.

Valduin headed into the lightless tunnel. After about fifteen feet of level ground, the tunnel began to slope downward. Adelaide and Rose watched as Valduin disappeared ahead. They followed at a distance, trying to keep him at the edge of the torch's light.

For the first section of the tunnel, the walls were a continuation of the masonry that made up the archway at the entrance, but as they traveled deeper, the construction transitioned to smooth stone. They were moving deep into and below the hill. The tunnel continued downward and began curving to the left until it appeared to dead-end in the darkness. As Valduin approached, he saw that there was a flight of steps descending even deeper at the end of the tunnel.

He stopped at the top of the steps, listening for any sound of movement below. He inspected the top steps and walls of the tunnel for signs of traps or alarms. Nothing seemed threatening, and after a few moments, Adelaide and Rose caught up to him.

"What do you think?" Adelaide asked. She held out the torch and peered down the stairs.

"I do not see anything yet, but there must be traps around here somewhere. Taranath specifically said the tomb was protected," Valduin replied.

"Nothing to do but keep going and be careful," Rose said. "We can stay closer to you if you like. I don't hear anything down there, so I don't think we've caught up to the group that left the tracks outside yet."

"If any of them are left," Valduin muttered. He started down, taking a moment to inspect each stair before putting weight on it. The steps seemed to go on forever, and Valduin grew nervous in the silent darkness. After a full five minutes of agonizing descent, he saw the bottom. Just as he was about to whisper back over his shoulder that he could see the end of the stairs, he felt the world move sideways. Without thinking, he leapt forward. He cleared the set of four stairs that was swinging out from beneath his feet and landed with a painful slide on the last few steps.

Valduin groaned with the impact. He turned onto his stomach to look up toward Adelaide and Rose, and he wheezed out a warning, "Stop!"

The women had stopped when Valduin had jumped forward into the darkness beyond the reach of their torchlight. They now approached the upper limit of the trapped stairs and looked down at the trap. The door consisted of four stone stairs that swung down to reveal a pit. The pit was at least twenty feet deep, and Rose and Adelaide could make out rusty spikes rising from the floor. They saw bones laying between and around the spikes. There was also a bugbear impaled in the middle of the pit.

"Ewww," Rose groaned as she covered her mouth and looked away from the hole.

Adelaide did not seem disturbed by the sight. In fact, she sounded cheerful when she said, "Well, that takes care of one of them. Do you think we could get down there to look for loot? Those old bones could be from adventurers. There's no telling what they might have been carrying!"

As these words came out, however, the stone steps swung back into place. The seam where the stones met was all but invisible in the low light.

"Maybe we should focus on clearing out the tunnels and making sure nothing is going to come out and find us dangling over those spikes," Rose cautioned. "I don't like the idea that there are more of those bugbears wandering around here."

Adelaide sighed. "You're probably right. But if it's safe on the way out, we should totally go down there." She eyed the stairs as she considered the best way past the trapdoor. "How are we going to get over this?" she muttered.

"We can try to jump," Rose said. As the last word crossed her lips, she once again felt the warmth flowing from the magic ring. She looked up at Adelaide with a sly grin and said, "Watch this." Rose crouched down and leapt clear over the trap, descending several steps past it before touching down lightly a stair above where Valduin had landed. She looked back up the stairs at Adelaide and said, "Aren't you coming?"

Adelaide stood with her mouth hanging open. Not one to be bested, she retreated up a couple of steps, then ran down toward the trap. As she tried to jump, her heel slipped off the edge of the last step above the trapdoor, and she slid onto the trapped stairs.

Seeing her slip, Valduin took one step toward her and reached out, grabbing her flailing arms a moment before the steps dropped out from under her. Adelaide found herself hanging from Valduin, her feet dangling over the metal spikes at the bottom of the pit. The spikes seemed much bigger now that they were backlit by the glowing torch that she had dropped. Rose stepped up and grabbed Valduin by the belt. Together, they hauled Adelaide to safety on the lower stairs as the trapdoor swung closed once again.

"Nice one," Rose teased. "I'm sure no one heard that. Let's go see what's next!" She skipped down the final few steps and into the next room, lighting up her amulet to guide her.

Rose surveyed the chamber. It was a square roughly forty feet on each side. Across the room from where Rose stood was a large, stone door. This door was about ten feet high and ten feet wide, and it stood flush with the wall. The room was empty as far as Rose could tell, without furniture or objects or structures of any kind.

Valduin and Adelaide joined Rose at the doorway. They paused to take in the sight of the ancient chamber.

It was Adelaide who noticed the floor.

"What are all these symbols then?" she asked as she poked Valduin's shoulder with one hand and pointed at the floor with the other. "Are those Elvish?"

Valduin looked to where Adelaide was pointing. He saw that the floor was no longer hewn stone but rather covered in tiles. Each tile was a square with sides about a foot long, and every tile had a symbol on it. The symbols looked like they were once black painted on white tiles, however, both the tiles and the paint had faded toward shades of brown over the centuries.

Valduin inspected the symbols at his feet. He replied, "Yes, I think they are Elvish. Most of them are letters, but others I don't recognize. Maybe they are so old we don't use them in Elvish anymore? Or maybe they are something else? It is hard to say."

"Well, there aren't any bodies in here," Rose remarked before stepping into the room. She checked the corners behind her now that she could see them. Finding nothing, she proceeded across the tiled floor to the door, looking for any obvious switch or mechanism to open it.

Valduin and Adelaide remained at the entrance for a moment, looking at the letters on the floor. Even though he had watched Rose walk across the tiles without incident, Valduin crouched down and touched one of the letters. Nothing appeared to change.

He stood up again and entered the room. The Elvish symbols held his focus as he looked around. It was not a single set of unique symbols; there were duplicates of some of the symbols around the room. As he walked around, hoping that some sort of pattern would jump out at him, he came across a series of letters he recognized. Near the far right wall of the chamber, four tiles in a row contained the symbols that spelled *Galien* in Elvish.

Valduin knelt down and inspected the tiles. They did not look different from the others around them in any way. He tried touching them gently, pushing on them, stepping on them. He traced the symbols with his finger. He spoke the name in Common and then again accented in Elvish. Nothing seemed to have any effect. As he considered his options, Adelaide called out to him, "Are you coming, Val?" He looked up in time to see Rose disappearing through the door, which had not moved since their arrival. He walked over to join Adelaide, and as he got closer to the door, he saw what Rose had found. The bottom left corner of the stone door had been broken off to leave a hole big enough for them to fit through.

"I don't see any chips of stone, any tool marks, or any stone dust," Adelaide said to Valduin as he approached. "And the edges of the broken stone seem to have been rubbed down, probably by lots of creatures crawling through here. I think this was broken a long time ago, and people have been using it to get into the tomb ever since."

"I'm guessing there was some sort of puzzle with all these letters," Valduin replied. "I found the name of the guy who is buried in here written on the floor over there. I couldn't figure out how to activate it, though. This room would probably have stopped most people trying to get into the tomb, especially if they didn't know Elvish."

Adelaide was already halfway into the hole as Valduin spoke. A moment later, she had disappeared, and Valduin could see Rose's light filling the space on the other side of the large door. He crouched down and crawled through, disappointed in himself for not being able to figure out the puzzle.

Standing up on the other side of the door, he found himself in another hallway. Similar to the one at the top of the stairs, this hallway had smooth stone walls that gently arched overhead to a peak nine feet high. The passage extended about fifteen feet before another archway marked the entrance to the next chamber. Valduin took the lead and moved forward, listening for—but not hearing—any movement from the next area.

As he gathered his nerve to look around the corner into the next room, Rose's voice broke the silence of the tomb.

"Is this Elvish, too? It looks like it. And it's under the archway again like it was at the entrance. Doesn't that seem weird to you? I feel like you usually write on the front of an archway so people can see it as they approach. By the time you can see this writing, you are already halfway into the room."

Though frustrated by how loud Rose was being, the ancient Elvish writing above him drew his focus. He read each of the three words aloud in Elvish, and then he translated them to Common for the benefit of his companions.

"Mind Your Manners."

Rose furrowed her brow. "That's a strange thing to write in a tomb, isn't it?"

"I do not know. Maybe they just want you to respect the dead? Maybe this is a warning not to disturb the tomb? It is impossible to know for sure," Valduin replied, frustration creeping into his voice. "Now, please try to be quiet until we are sure this room is empty."

Valduin walked through the archway and was surprised, after the emptiness of the preceding room, to find this room a complete mess. The chamber was thirty feet wide, and there were two long tables, one on either side. This left a ten-foot-wide path down the middle of the room that ended at a single small table standing on a platform that was raised about a foot above the rest of the floor. The platform made up the entire far end of the room and looked like a low stage. Two large tapestries hung on the far wall, one on either side of the small table.

There were ornately carved chairs scattered about the room, and the tables and floor were covered in plates and silverware as if the tables had been set for a feast.

Then there were the bodies.

From where he stood within the entrance, Valduin counted a dozen dead goblins, bugbears, and kobolds. Some were lying across the tables or over the fallen chairs, but most of them were in a pile next to the archway where Valduin stood.

"Whoa!" Rose exclaimed as she looked around Valduin and saw the pile.

"Shush!" Valduin slapped his hand over Rose's mouth. He whispered, "Whatever happened here, we do not want it to happen to us. I will look ahead for the way through. Can you take a look at these bodies and figure out what killed them?" He released his hand from Rose's face.

"Sure," she whispered. "Got it." She carefully pulled the bodies of the kobolds away from the archway. She lined them up along the wall and inspected them for injuries.

Adelaide helped Rose lay out the bodies, and as she did, she started searching them for valuables. Valduin crept deeper into the room, scanning the tables until he reached the stage at the far end of the chamber. The chair at this table was bigger than the others, nearly a throne. Valduin looked at the old tapestries hanging on the wall, but he found them to be mostly blackened. Whatever they had once depicted, they had been thoroughly defaced at some point in their long history.

"Valduin!" Adelaide hissed into the darkness. "Where are you? Get back here!"

He returned to where Adelaide and Rose were finishing up their search of the bodies. "Sorry. I didn't realize you couldn't see me. What did you find?" he asked.

"Well, they haven't been dead very long," Rose started. "And they were killed in a few different ways. Some have large, blackened areas of their bodies that look like burns. Most of them, though, look like they were killed with their own weapons, or maybe killed by other members of their party."

"Yikes, okay," Valduin replied. He looked at Adelaide. "Any loot?"

"A bit. Maybe thirty gold pieces in total. Most of what they were carrying was just these," Adelaide said as she held up a handful of the fancy silverware that was scattered throughout the chamber. "More interestingly," she continued, "is that there were two skeletons underneath that bugbear. They both were also carrying some of the fancy silverware."

As Valduin narrowed his eyes at the skeletons lying in the row next to the other bodies, Adelaide and Rose spun toward the far end of the room.

"We need to hide!" Rose whispered as she dove through the archway into the dark hallway, extinguishing the light on her amulet as she went.

Adelaide tried to run after her, but she found herself unable to pass through the archway. She started to panic as she tried, again and again, to get through, but each time she was stopped by an invisible force. She soon gave up and dove into the line of bodies, pulling a bugbear's arm over her.

Valduin looked at his friends in confusion. Before he could ask what they were doing, however, he heard it too, the sound that had triggered their fear. Hysterical, cackling laughter echoed toward them from the other end of the room. It was muffled at first, but as Valduin moved into the hallway to hide with Rose, it clarified, as if the source had opened a door, filling the room with mad noise. Valduin did not dare peek out into the room for fear of being seen. He crouched next to Rose and waited, hoping Adelaide would be safe where she lay beneath the dead bugbear.

"*A natural one!*" Now it was Amelia's laughter that filled the room. "Big strong Adelaide couldn't even jump over the trap."

"You only made it because you have that magic ring," Madison snapped. "Besides, that was like an hour ago. Can we please focus on whatever killed all of these bad guys and is probably now coming for us?"

"Yes," Logan said with a smirk. "Let's not talk about how you almost fell to your death in a trap that we already knew about."

"I would not have died!" Madison shouted. "What I would have done is looted those skeletons and kept it all for myself. I bet there is some good stuff down there. Centuries of adventurers trying to raid this tomb, and it's all ours for the taking."

"Well, if you keep rolling natural ones, I think we'll be added to the pile here," Amelia teased Madison. "Why couldn't you leave the room? What do you think was stopping you?"

"I don't know, but I don't like any of this," Madison replied. "I'm sure this bugbear that I'm lying under right now stinks too. Not my first choice of hiding spots."

13

Adelaide lay face down with as much of her body under the cover of the bugbear as she could manage. She focused on keeping her breathing under control and not thinking about the bugbear's stench. The laughter had stopped only to be replaced by sounds even more sinister. Voices echoed from the darkness deeper in the room. She could hear no footsteps, but the voices were moving closer. They seemed to be arguing with one another, though Adelaide did not understand their words. There may have been three or four voices, each speaking at a different pitch but all in the same wheezing, hissing language.

As she lay and listened, the voices stopped. Adelaide guessed that the source of the voices was still thirty or forty feet away. There came a sickening crunch and a clatter that Adelaide thought might be a chair falling over. Silence followed, and Adelaide remained motionless, straining to hear any indication that it was safe to come out from hiding.

Minutes passed, feeling like hours, Valduin peeked into the long room. Seeing no threat, he whispered to Rose that she could put her light back on, and the two of them went to Adelaide's side.

"Why didn't you come out into the hallway?" Rose asked as she helped Adelaide out from under the bugbear. "It would have been much easier to hide there."

"I tried to," Adelaide responded, standing up and brushing herself off. "But I couldn't leave. It felt like there was an invisible wall in the archway."

"Is it still there?" asked Valduin.

Adelaide walked to the archway and put out her hand. It stopped just before breaking the plane of the arch. She knocked on it, leaned on it, and felt for an edge. The invisible wall filled the passage completely.

Valduin walked over and stepped into the hallway. No barrier stopped him. He inspected the archway again. Seeing the inscription he had already read, he looked again at the line of dead kobolds and bugbears. After a moment, he repeated the inscription. "Mind your manners. Adelaide, do you still have any of the fancy silverware?"

"Uh, actually, yes," Adelaide admitted as she pulled a handful of forks and knives from her pocket. "I thought we might be able to sell them."

"And you found those on every one of these bodies, right?" Valduin continued.

"Yes, they all had at least a couple of pieces," Rose answered, catching on to what Valduin was thinking. She picked up a single fork from the floor and walked back to the archway. She held her hand up in front of her as she did, and when she reached the stones with the Elvish words carved into them, she felt the barrier. She pushed on it, but she could not pass through. She dropped the fork to the ground, and almost fell over as the force that was holding her released her to stumble into the hallway.

"That explains why they all died here," Valduin concluded. "They were probably trying to run away from whatever we just heard out there, but they got stuck at the archway. They could not figure out how to get past the barrier in time to escape."

"Okay then, that's half of the puzzle solved. The next half is how we open the next door," Adelaide said as she took the silverware from her pocket and dumped the pieces on the end of one of the long tables.

"Unfortunately, it is a little more than that," Valduin replied. "I have not even found the next door. The other end of this chamber seems like a dead end."

"Well, those voices were able to come through the far wall somehow. Let's spread out and look around again," Adelaide suggested as she led the way deeper into the room.

Rose and Valduin followed, and Rose held up her amulet so that Adelaide would also have enough light to look around. At the far end of the room, Rose and Adelaide saw the blackened tapestries for the first time, and they stepped up on the raised platform to look for the next doorway. The group inspected every inch of the wall that they could, including Valduin using a fork from the table to pull the tapestries away from the wall and peek behind them.

Rose soon grew bored of the search, and as Adelaide and Valduin continued to study the stonework, she looked at the small table. The silverware and plates here were even fancier than those in the rest of the chamber, but they were spread over the table and on the floor around it.

Without thinking about it, Rose reached down and straightened the silverware on the table. As she moved the plate to the center of the setting, there came a distant rumbling sound.

"What was that?" Adelaide asked. She put her ear against the stone wall between the tapestries. "It sounded like something moving in the wall."

Valduin looked around to see if anything had happened in the room that might have caused the sudden noise. He saw Rose standing next to the small table and asked, "Did you find something? A button or switch?"

Rose looked down at the table. "I don't know. I was just sort of moving the stuff around on the table."

Valduin walked over and saw the plate and silverware neatly arranged in front of the fancy chair. He recited the inscription once again, "Mind your manners." He picked up a goblet from the floor next to the table. He placed it in its proper position above the knife, to the right of the plate. The rumbling within the wall behind them repeated, louder this time.

"The wall is moving!" Adelaide could barely contain her excitement as she felt a section of the wall slide to the side to leave a small, dark gap.

Valduin and Rose positioned the rest of the silverware, glasses, and small plates around the place setting. As each piece landed in its proper location, the door behind them slid farther into the wall until the doorway had fully opened. Adelaide stood at the doorway with her handaxes drawn, straining her eyes for any sign of movement in the darkness behind it. Rose and Valduin turned to join her, and the three moved ahead into the next hallway.

"Do I need to ask why you two knew how to set that table?" Adelaide asked as the party crept forward.

"I went to fancy elf school, remember?" Valduin replied without any hint of sarcasm.

"I worked in a temple. Halfred was particular about a few things when we had guests," Rose said with a shrug.

Again, they found themselves moving through fifteen feet of tunnel before entering another room. Valduin took the lead and peered into the next chamber. This one was smaller, about thirty feet square, and there were two square pillars, roughly ten feet apart on either side of the room. On the far wall, visible between the pillars, was a stone door.

"Is there another hint?" Rose asked Valduin as she approached the entrance, holding up her glowing amulet and looking at the stone archway for more carvings.

Valduin looked up at her suggestion, and he read aloud the Elvish writing that he saw there. "Come in Pairs," he said. "Or something like that. It might be 'They Come in Pairs,' or 'You Come in Pairs.' It's hard to tell what conjugation it is without any context."

Rose looked at Adelaide, who rolled her eyes. "Okay, book boy," Adelaide teased. "Let's see what's going on in this room."

The party spread out to inspect the room. The walls were made of the same stone as the previous chambers. There did not appear to be anything in the room except for the two columns. As they approached the columns, Rose spoke up. "Look at this pillar. Is that a button?"

Valduin and Adelaide walked over to stand by Rose. On the pillar on the left side of the room, facing the left wall, there was a symbol, about five feet off the ground, faintly glowing pale blue. As Valduin stooped to inspect the symbol, Adelaide walked over to the pillar on the right side of the room. Despite the darkness this far from Rose's amulet, she had no difficulty finding another glowing symbol on the far side of the pillar.

"Is it Elvish?" Rose asked, looking up at Valduin.

"I don't think so," he replied, a troubled look on his face. "This looks like a magic rune. Hold on a second." He pulled out the salt and scraped another bit of soot from his bedroll as he cast his spell to comprehend other languages. When he had finished, he inspected the symbol. Still unable to glean its meaning, Valduin held his hand up and rested his fingers lightly on the edge of the glyph, hoping its significance would become clear.

Before he could let the magic decode the symbol, the silence of the room was shattered by Adelaide's scream.

"Watch out!"

Valduin spun to the halfling standing beside him and recoiled in terror. Floating behind her was a seven-foot-tall, humanoid shadow. Before he could even raise his hand, the shadow dove toward Rose's back and seemed to bite her on the shoulder. She let out a scream as the blackness poured into her body. The shadow released its grip on her and rose back to its full height.

Adelaide took two steps toward the dark form behind Rose before instinctively ducking as a similar shadow dove toward her from behind the pillar she had been inspecting. She was able to avoid being hit, and she turned to face the shadow creature.

Rose, coughing and holding her shoulder, looked toward Adelaide. Seeing the second shadow looming over her companion, Rose raised a finger to point at the dark form. Radiant flames burst from the chest of the shadow, which gave a screech as it collapsed to the ground and dissipated in a cloud of black mist. Rose turned to face the shadow that had attacked her, bracing herself for another attack.

The shadow dove at Rose again, but this time Rose was able to raise her shield and fend it off. The shadow swelled with apparent frustration, dwarfing Rose as it stretched toward the ceiling of the chamber.

Adelaide watched the fading, shadowy remnants of the closer enemy seep into the stone floor. Satisfied that it was not getting back up, she turned and threw both of her handaxes into the looming form next to Rose. The first one drew a faint shivering reaction from the shadow, but the second one passed straight through and clattered against the far wall. Adelaide snarled and strafed around the shadow to collect her weapons.

Valduin raised his hand over Rose's head and released a spark of green energy. His eldritch magic exploded into a blast as it impacted the shadowy figure, dispersing its form with another screech.

Rose turned on her heel, her amulet in her hand, scanning the room for other threats. Seeing none, she relaxed, clutched her shoulder, and leaned against the wall.

"Rose, are you okay?" Adelaide asked as she picked up her handaxes. Valduin stepped forward and helped the halfling back to her feet.

"I just feel, uh, a little weak," Rose said as she started coughing again. "This armor feels too heavy all of a sudden."

"Well, you can't take it off yet," Valduin said. "I think you are going to need it again before we get out of here."

"So, Val," Adelaide asked, pointing an axe at the half-elf for emphasis, "what did you do?"

"I did not do anything!" Valduin cried, holding his hands up in surrender. "I was just trying to read this glyph over here, but I had to touch it to get my spell to work on it."

"Uh-huh, uh-huh, and how is 'I had to touch it' the same as 'I did not do anything'?" Adelaide's questioning grew more aggressive.

Valduin glared at her, but he said nothing.

"So, what does the glyph mean?" she asked, letting the tension fade.

"I still do not know," Valduin admitted. "It must just be a magical rune; a button like Rose suggested. The spell only works on actual language, not on symbols just used for magic. But I think we can agree touching it was the wrong move. Did you find anything over there?"

"Okay, for the record, don't ever use that spell again. That's twice it hasn't helped. Let's get back to the issue at hand. Yes, there's another glowing mark over there. Same glow but different symbol," Adelaide answered. She turned her attention to Rose, who was still rubbing her shoulder. "You gonna make it?"

"Just feel weak. And tired. It feels like that thing sucked the strength out of me," Rose replied. "Should we try touching the other one then? This one didn't help. But let's not get caught off guard again if those things come back. Keep your eyes open."

Valduin and Adelaide walked around to the other side of the room. Rose put her back against the first pillar and slumped down to sit against it, facing the center of the room.

"Here we go," Valduin muttered. He placed his hand on the glowing symbol. They heard nothing that made them think they had opened a door. Instead, they froze as they watched two more of the shadows come around from either side of the pillar Rose was seated against.

Rose saw the looks on their faces. She glanced up to see the two shadows closing in on her. She grabbed her amulet and whispered, *"When the shadow of evil falls over my heart, Selaia will bring the light."* The amulet, which was still glowing with Rose's light spell, started to pulse brighter with golden light. The two undead creatures froze where they were standing above Rose. The pulsing grew in strength until waves of golden light pushed the shadows away from Rose. The two dark shapes turned and fled through the archway by which the group had entered the chamber.

Valduin watched in amazement as the shadows ran away from Rose, terrified by her divine power. Once the room was clear, he said, "Uh, wow. Okay, that one did not work. The other one did not work. There has to be something else here. Adelaide, check that side of the room again. Quickly. Before they come back."

Adelaide and Valduin spread out, feeling their way around the walls of the chamber, looking for any sign of another way to open the door. They had not gotten far before Rose's panicked voice rang out, "They're coming back!"

Valduin and Adelaide looked up at the same time to watch the shadows pass under the archway before moving in toward Rose. Looking again at the arch, Valduin remembered the writing there. "'Come in pairs.' Maybe those creatures come in pairs, but maybe we have to come in pairs as well," he said. Then, with the excitement of an epiphany, he shouted, "Adelaide, on three, touch the symbol on your side!"

She gave a quick nod of understanding and held her hand over the rune glowing on the pillar.

"One, two, three!" Valduin called, and they both slapped their hands against the glyphs. Without delay, a familiar rumbling sounded from the back of the room as a section of the stone wall slid away to reveal another dark corridor. A the same time, the two shadows vanished from beside Rose without making a sound. Valduin helped Rose to her feet as Adelaide approached the doorway.

They were all quickly overwhelmed by the smell of rotting flesh coming from the next area.

"Oh, gross!" Rose said, holding her nose in disgust.

"Shush," Adelaide hissed. "This is probably where those things that we heard talking are. Don't blow our surprise."

The three adventurers crept down the hallway to the next room. As they reached the next archway, they stopped short as a screeching voice erupted within the next chamber. The sounds were gibberish to Adelaide and Rose, but Valduin understood the words. *"Thieves! Thieves have come again! Wake up, fools!"*

"Uh, what is that?" Amelia asked, her eyes wide.

"It's gotta be whatever was talking back in the dining room chamber," Madison said. "Did we say there were three or four voices back there? This must be the voice of one of them."

"What language do none of us speak?" Logan wondered aloud. "There can't be many we didn't cover with these characters, but if I only understood because of the Comprehend Languages spell, this must be a new one."

"I'm not sure we're ready for a fight against three or four enemies," Madison said. "You think you'll be able to talk to them, Logan? Or maybe distract them while we grab whatever it is we are here to get?"

Logan winced. "I can only *comprehend*. I can't speak other languages," he reminded Madison. "That requires the Tongues spell and that's a higher level."

"Well, whatever it is, I hope it's the boss battle," Amelia replied as Madison rolled her eyes at Logan.

"After getting hit with that strength drain my speed is only fifteen feet, and I'm at half of my hit points! We need to wrap this dungeon up and rest."

14

The room fell back into silence after the screaming stopped. Valduin took a deep breath to steady his nerves. He immediately regretted it when he tasted the rotting flesh in the air. He peeked around the corner of the archway to survey the room. Ducking back into the hallway with Adelaide and Rose, he relayed his findings.

"Okay, this is definitely the burial chamber," he began. "The room does not look too much different from the other ones, but there is a platform with what is probably a sarcophagus on it against the far left wall, about sixty feet away. There is some sort of podium in front of that as well. We will be entering from the corner of the room; the wall to the right is really close."

"Anything moving in there?" Adelaide asked. She adjusted her grip on her weapons. "Any sign of the thing we just heard?"

"I did not see any movement, but there are lots of bodies. Mostly along the walls and piled up in the corners," Valduin explained. He then noticed that Rose was leaning against the wall with her eyes closed. "Are you sure you are okay, Rose?" he asked. "We could go back and rest now that we know how to get through all the other chambers."

Rose shook her head, pushed herself off the wall, and stood up straight once again. She replied, "I think we need to finish this now. We heard the voices all the way back in the dining room. I think whatever this is can probably get us in any of the rooms. Let's just keep going."

As the three adventurers crept into the final chamber of the tomb, they spread out across the chamber. Valduin moved forward toward the sarcophagus, heading for the podium. Adelaide turned left out of the archway and stayed close to the wall, as close as she could get without wading through the skeletons. Rose followed a few feet behind Valduin, keeping her glowing amulet aloft so that she and Adelaide could see in the otherwise pitch-black room.

As Valduin reached the podium, he saw that there was a thick leather book resting on it. Despite centuries of lying here, the leather was still glossy black, clear of cracks or stains. There was no writing or designs on the cover, but the spine was reinforced with a brass plate, and there was a brass clasp holding the book closed. As Valduin reached for the book, he was interrupted by one of the voices that they had heard in the dining hall. It spoke in the same breathy tongue that they had not understood earlier, but Valduin's magic interpreted the words now. *"Why did you come here, thief?"*

"Taranath sent us," Valduin called out into the darkness, in Common. He repeated the sentence in Sylvan, Elvish, Undercommon, and finally Abyssal. After the final statement, there was a cackle from behind him, and a screeching reply in Abyssal from a different voice echoed through the chamber.

"Taranath! Slimy Taranath. Taranath has no power here! That worm dragged Gnash from the Deep In-Be-

tween long ago. He bound Gnash to Galien. But Gnash was patient. Galien's time ran out. Gnash claims Galien now!"

Before Valduin could find the source of the reply, he felt a burning pain in his back. He spun to the left, trying to get out of the way of whatever was hitting him, and he was able to reduce the force of the impact. He saw a sphere of flame that had deflected off the back of his armor impact the front of the podium; the wood blackened under the scorching heat. The leather book, however, appeared untouched by the flames as smoke rose around it. Tracing the attack back to its source, Valduin saw a monstrosity, unlike anything he had seen before. The thing floated above the archway by which they had entered this chamber. As Valduin's brain tried to make sense of what he was looking at, a pink sphere of energy jumped out toward Adelaide as she turned to face the monster. The sphere popped when it hit Adelaide in the face. Her eyes went wide for a moment, but then she shook her head and readied herself to attack.

Valduin studied Gnash briefly. He could best describe the thing as a large ball of writhing, black tentacles. Between the constantly moving tentacles, Valduin could see eyes that appeared to be moving as well. An eye would peer out from between two tentacles for a moment before blinking and reopening somewhere else on the monster. With everything in swirling motion, it was difficult to tell if this was one creature or multiple. Exactly how many of each body part it had was a mystery.

Adelaide seemed unfazed by the horror show in front of her. Before anything else, she muttered a few words under her breath and pointed one of her weapons at the monster to mark it as her prey. She heaved both of her handaxes up at the creature. It was still a good distance away, and the first attack flew high and bounced off the ceiling. The second one made contact, but it did not seem to do much damage. The weapon landed with a clatter on the floor below the floating mass of tentacles. Adelaide too off running toward where her weapons had landed.

Rose, still sluggish after the encounter with the shadows, turned and faced the monster. "What is *that*?" she screamed. Her eyes were wide with terror as she raised one shaking hand to point up at Gnash. "*Selaia, watch over me, and my soul will forever be yours,*" she prayed with desperation in her voice, and a bolt of golden energy leapt from her outstretched finger. The spell hit the monster squarely, drawing squeals of pain from multiple voices and leaving behind a glowing target.

Valduin could hear it say to itself in the strange language, "*Not only thieves, Gnash. They are murderers!*" As it talked, six small eyes all became visible at once as two of the tentacles unfurled from the mass and pointed toward its two attackers. A sphere of sickly green flew from the tentacle that pointed at Adelaide, and another red sphere of roiling flame headed toward Rose. Adelaide's eyes grew wide with panic for a moment, but again she shook off the effect.

Rose, however, was unable to get out of the way of the attack. The red sphere burst into flames across her torso. She screamed and fell to the ground, her face strangely lit by the golden light of her amulet and the reddish glow of her heated chainmail. The mass of tentacles giggled and shivered at the sight of Rose's fall. With a strange, halting motion, it began to move toward her unconscious form with what appeared to be a combination of hovering and teleporting.

"Rose!" Valduin shouted. He raised his hand toward the glowing target on the monster while stepping forward to shield the halfling's fallen body. The green spark of energy leapt from his hand, but it did not find its mark. Instead, a tentacle whipped out and appeared to catch the spark in another of its bubbles. Capturing the spark's momentum, the bubble whipped around the monster's body, orbiting it like a moon around a planet. Another tentacle uncurled from the ball, pointing straight down toward Adelaide.

The bubble popped, and Valduin's spell streaked toward the human, hitting her in the back of the head. She stumbled as she ran to retrieve her weapons. She looked like she might fall, but she kept her balance and grabbed both of her handaxes as she stumbled forward. Rearmed, she glared up at the creature hovering ten feet over her head.

Closer this time, both weapons found their mark. The first throw cleaved one of the outstretched tentacles from the rest. As the creature screeched and opened several eyes to look down at Adelaide, the second weapon sunk deep into the mass, the blade disappearing into a spot that had held an eye a moment before. The writhing of the tentacles accelerated as a gush of black liquid fell through the mass, splattering on the floor next to Adelaide.

"Adelaide, she needs you!" Valduin shouted as he summoned another spark of eldritch energy into his hand. This time the spell found its target, and the force of the impact tore Gnash apart. More of the black liquid burst out from the body of the monster, and the mass of tentacles plummeted to the floor with a sickening, wet slap.

Adelaide stepped around the mess that was left of Gnash to reach Rose. As she placed her hands on Rose's cheeks, a dark green glow spread from her fingertips and into Rose's body. Rose took a quick breath in, and her eyes opened. She was greeted by the rather rough-looking face of Adelaide, who had blood dripping from her nose, the corner of her mouth, and her ears.

"What happened to you?" Rose asked as she sat up.

"I'm not sure. I was running to get my axes and I got hit in the back of the head. Hard. The whole world went black for a second. I think I almost went down with that one blow," Adelaide replied.

"That was definitely a close one," Valduin agreed. He did not volunteer any explanation for what hit Adelaide. "How do you feel?" he asked Rose.

"Still weak," Rose replied. "But better with that thing dead." She held up her amulet and looked toward the creature, but she was surprised by what she saw. "What happened to it?" she asked as she looked back at Valduin.

Valduin came over to her side to see what she meant. On the ground, where moments ago had been a pile of black tentacles, there was now only a rapidly fading pool of black sludge.

"This is what happens when you kill creatures from other planes. Their bodies disappear and their spirits go back to the plane that they came from. Depending on what the creature is, sometimes they can come back to life on their original plane," Valduin explained.

"There we go again with the other planes of existence," Adelaide groaned. "I would really like it if we could just stick to this one. There are plenty of danger-ous things to deal with here without worrying about all of the other planes, too."

"I don't think that is up to us," Valduin replied. "This thing knew Taranath. Venez mentioned fiends. We will be seeing a few more creatures from other planes before we are done with this forest."

He turned toward the podium again. He inspected the book where it lay. When he did not see any sign of a trap, the lifted the book off its stand and turned it over in his hands. It did not seem as old as he knew it must be. His mind raced at what ancient knowledge or magic might be hidden away here. His fingers trembled as he opened the brass clasp. Inside, however, the book was empty. Blank pages. He flipped through the book, looking for any sign of its relevance or importance. He found none.

Rose limped past Valduin and sat down on the edge of the platform that held the sarcophagus. Her breathing was labored, and she was still rubbing her shoulder. "Did you find what you were looking for?" she asked. "Is that book why we came here?"

Valduin felt himself blush with embarrassment as he flipped through the blank pages again. "I do not know. Maybe. Maybe not." He slipped the book into his pack and started to look around the room again.

"Do you think we need to open the sarcophagus?" Rose asked. She glanced at the box over her shoulder.

Before Valduin could answer, Adelaide spoke up. "Can we take *that*?" There was excitement in her voice. Valduin and Rose followed her pointing finger to the back wall of the chamber above the sarcophagus. Hanging on the wall was a weapon. It was an axe, with a long, wooden handle that looked as if it was made from a gnarled tree branch. The bright metal of the axehead, like the fresh leather of the book, belied the centuries it had hung in the damp darkness of the tomb.

"Absolutely," Valduin said. He and Adelaide walked around the sarcophagus, and she boosted him up the wall so that he could take the weapon down. Looking closer, the handle was not secured to the axehead so much as it looked like the gnarled wood had grown around and through the metal blade. The head itself was adorned with etchings that looked like tree roots that spread from the point of attachment to the handle and ended in tips just at the sharp edge of the blade.

"It's beautiful!" Adelaide said, her voice hushed in awe at the sight of the weapon. "Can I keep it? Please?"

"Well, I cannot use it," Valduin replied. "Yes, I think you should. I am pretty sure that it is magic, too. We can figure that out later. We should loot the rest of this place and get out of here so we can rest."

"Yes! Loot!" Adelaide agreed.

"Take this so you can see," Rose said as she moved her light spell to her small mace and handed it to Adelaide. "I'm just gonna take a little rest here," she said from where she was sitting. She placed her pack next to her and laid her head on it. In no time at all, she was sleeping.

As Rose rested, Adelaide and Valduin tore through the piles of skeletons and corpses that lined the walls of the chamber. They dug through the remains of dozens of adventurers unlucky enough to have tried to explore this tomb over the centuries. Most of the gear was beyond salvage, having been destroyed when the wearer was killed or when Gnash had dined upon the remains afterward. They methodically collected leather pouches, packs, and anything else that looked like it was still useful, and they placed them on top of the sarcophagus to sort through.

Valduin was counting coins while Adelaide searched through the bags for items and gear, dumping money in the pile near Valduin as he counted. After an hour, they had retrieved everything from the horde that seemed valuable.

"How much was there?" Adelaide asked.

"Just about five hundred silver and four hundred gold," Valduin replied with a big smile. "What did you find?"

Adelaide's mouth hung open at the amount of coin they had recovered. After a moment, she held up the items that seemed worth taking from the remains. "A couple of fancy daggers," she said. She held up a matching set of gold-handled weapons. They each had a handful of gems set into the hilt, one with sapphires and the other with emeralds. "And this pack with what I think are potions." This time she held up a leather holster that could be hung on a belt. The holster had leather loops that closed with metal clasps that could hold four small vials. Two of the loops were empty; two contained glass vials with glass stoppers carefully secured by the clasps. Each vial was filled with a golden liquid that shimmered as Adelaide swirled it in the light.

"You think those are healing potions?" Valduin asked.

"Maybe. I can't be sure. I've never seen one before, but I know they aren't that rare. And it's the kind of thing I would expect an adventurer to carry. You should take these. Both Rose and I can cast healing spells, but you can't. If we go down, you'll need these to bring us back in a battle."

Valduin took the holster and secured it to his belt. He divided the gold and silver coins into three of the intact leather pouches they had found. Adelaide tucked the fancy daggers away in her pack and went about fiddling with an attachment for her new axe. She wanted to be sure she could bring it out at a moment's notice.

The looting complete, Adelaide sat down next to Rose. She did not want to wake the sleeping halfling, so she rested her head against the sarcophagus and closed her eyes. She reviewed the events of the battle in her mind. She spent a good amount of time thinking about how Gnash had turned to sludge on the floor of the tomb. The idea of killing something only for it to come back to life on another plane of existence bothered her. She preferred when the things that she killed stayed dead.

"You couldn't hit the monster even though Amelia gave you advantage, and then you rolled a *natural twenty* on me? If you had rolled higher on your damage, this campaign would have been *over*," Madison yelled at Logan.

"What did you want me to do?" Logan yelled back. "I don't have any other kinds of attack spells! I didn't know that thing could catch my spells. You told me to stop studying the monsters in the book."

"Well, I, for one, am glad Logan didn't kill you," Amelia consoled Madison. "Also, how am I the one that got knocked out? All this armor didn't do a thing for me against that ball of fire."

"Yeah, that's the downside of having a high armor class but low dexterity," Logan lectured. "Any enemy that is using magic that requires saving throws will go right through you."

"Well, we got the loot, and I got a sweet new axe," Madison said. "Do we know where to go next? Back to Tarsam?"

"Let's get out of the tomb first," Logan said. "But then I do think we have to go back to the city. I get the feeling that I need to talk to Taranath again, and he said he can't enter the forest. I'm guessing we will be headed toward the ruins of Eydon once we are geared up. But first, we need to find someone who can identify that axe and the potions for us."

15

A little while later, the light on Rose's mace faded away, plunging the chamber into darkness. "I guess that's our cue," Adelaide said. She shook Rose's shoulder. "Rose. Come on. We gotta move."

Rose opened her eyes and sat up. She lit up her amulet again. She stretched her arm above her head to test her shoulder.

"Feeling any better?" Adelaide asked as she situated her gear to start the trek out of the tomb.

"Actually, I feel a lot better," Rose replied. "Not nearly as tired or weak as earlier. I can't remember, Valdurin, did you say we should or shouldn't open the sarcophagus? There might be something cool that was buried with Galien."

Valduin had forgotten that Rose had asked that earlier. He gazed at the sarcophagus and considered the question. "I think we should *not* open it," he answered after a pause. "I feel like we got what we were sent here for, and I do not like the idea of disturbing the body. Besides, we were already attacked by undead things in the 'Pairs' room. Who knows what might pop up if we start messing with that."

"Works for me," Rose replied with a shrug. "I just wanted to put it out there before we left." With that, Rose finished collecting her gear, and the three adventurers headed for the exit. As Rose fell in line behind Adelaide, she noticed the axe hanging from her pack. "Whoa, that's pretty!" Rose said as she admired the gleaming head of the axe up close.

"I know!" Adelaide said with a smile. "I can't wait to try it out. Valduin thinks it's enchanted. I guess we'll need to find someone who knows magic to help us understand what it does."

"Did we get any other loot? Anything for me?" Rose asked.

"Indeed, we did," Valduin said as he held out one of the three leather pouches. "Over a hundred gold pieces and nearly two hundred silver pieces for you."

Rose took the pouch, glanced in it briefly, then tucked it into her pack with a smile. "That's just lovely."

The party entered the room where the shadows had attacked them. There was no sign of the undead creatures, but Adelaide did notice something that they had not seen before. There was a hole high on the wall, above and to the side of the archway they had entered this room through the first time. The hole was roughly circular, and almost four feet across.

"Check that out," Adelaide pointed to the hole. "I bet that's how Gnash moved between the rooms."

Valduin looked up at the hole, then thought about the dining room on the other side of the wall. "That must come out behind one of those tapestries," he concluded. "We heard Gnash coming to get one of the kobold bodies, and he was talking to himself the whole time."

"And the way he flew around," Adelaide added, "explains why I didn't hear footsteps as he moved through the dining room."

Feeling satisfied that they had figured out the secrets of the tomb, they moved through to the dining room and continued toward the exit. Adelaide stopped at the head table for a moment to rearrange the table setting. As she moved the pieces around on the table, the door behind her slowly slid closed. When she was finished, she had remade the place setting on the opposite side of the table. She moved the large chair around so that it faced the back wall of the room. She smiled to herself at her handiwork, and then she jogged to catch up with Valduin and Rose.

The group went down the final short hallway and crawled through the hole in the first door of the tomb to return to the room full of lettered tiles. As Rose and Adelaide pulled Valduin through the hole, they heard footsteps. Spinning toward the entryway, they saw a singular goblin standing at the bottom of the long staircase that led to the tomb entrance. The goblin stared at the three adventurers for a second, and then it turned and disappeared up the stairs. Valduin scrambled to his feet and ran to the archway. He raised his hand to throw an eldritch blast at the fleeing goblin, but the glowing, green spark soared over the goblin's head. Before he could cast another, the goblin was out of range and out of sight up the staircase.

"Well, we are out of time," Valduin said. "We need to get out of here before his friends show up."

Knowing the location of the trapped stairs, they each were able to safely jump past the trap this time. Adelaide paused for just a moment after clearing the trap, considering how she could get down there to look for loot. Before she could make any move, however, she felt Rose tugging on her elbow.

"We can't mess around right now. We've got to get out of here," Rose said.

Adelaide sighed and nodded. She turned to follow Valduin. Valduin crawled up the last few steps so he could peek down the tunnel to see if anyone was waiting for them. He found the final passageway to be empty. They crept toward the entrance of the tomb, where evening light had started to filter in. Rose dismissed the light on her amulet, worried that it would give their position away. As they approached the last archway, they could hear footsteps and shouting from outside.

Valduin took a deep breath and stepped forward to the tunnel opening. Outside the tomb, he could see dozens of creatures. There were kobolds and goblins. There were at least a dozen bugbears. And there looked to be a pink-skinned hobgoblin in heavy armor shouting orders at the rest of them. Valduin sprinted back into the tunnel as a volley of arrows descended toward him from a group of goblins off to one side.

"We are in serious trouble," he panted as he rejoined Adelaide and Rose within the cover of the tunnel. "There are a lot of baddies out there. All kinds of goblinoids, and more kobolds as well. I am not sure how we can get out of this."

"Should we go back down into the tomb?" Adelaide asked as she brought out her new axe. "Maybe we could wait them out. Or maybe we could pick them off as they crawl through that broken door. Or maybe we could even summon some of those ghost things and hope they attack them and not us?"

Valduin grimaced. "That might work for a while, but I worry that these guys will just keep coming. They seem pretty organized. There was a hobgoblin that looked like he was in charge. And there are a lot of them out there."

"Do you think you could talk us out of this?" Rose asked. "Maybe we can give the hobgoblin some of the gold we found, and he'll let us go."

"They were shooting arrows at me before I said anything," Valduin recounted. "I do not think they want to talk."

As the three grew quiet, considering their few options, they heard a familiar flutter of wings, and Valduin felt a weight drop onto his pack. The pale green face of Venez appeared over his shoulder, and the sylph began whispering to him.

Valduin smiled as he listened, and then he said to his companions, "Get ready to run. This is going to be interesting."

"What's the plan?" Adelaide asked. She still did not trust the tiny fey creature.

"You will see," Valduin said with a smirk. "All I will say is that it worked on us. And it is the best option we have right now." He said a few things in Sylvan to Venez and turned toward the cave entrance. Venez turned invisible again, and they could hear her wingbeats carrying her toward the mouth of the cave.

"When we hear the screaming, we run," Valduin explained. "We will head to the right and up the hill. Once we are out of sight, we go south. The end goal is to get out of the woods, but we will not be able to do that in one run."

"What do you mean by 'screaming'?" Rose asked. She had not finished the question before a chorus of screams erupted outside of the cave.

"You will see," Valduin said with a smile. "Run!" He took off toward the tomb entrance. Rose and Adelaide did their best to keep up.

As they emerged into the soft light of dusk, the screams were intensifying. Valduin cut to the right out of the archway and headed up the hill above the tomb entrance, but Rose and Adelaide were curious. What they saw in the sky above the stream made their hearts skip a beat, but it only took a moment for them to understand what was happening. It was all Adelaide could do not to let out a cruel laugh.

Hovering eighty feet in the air, just above the treetops, was a familiar ancient red dragon. It was roaring and blowing fire up into the air in a magnificent display of power, and the kobolds and goblinoids were buying every bit of the illusion. As Adelaide turned to follow Valduin, she felt a weight land on her back. She glanced over her shoulder, but she could not see anything. When she heard Venez's petite chuckle, she smiled.

"I don't know if you can understand me," Adelaide whispered as she started to run, "but nice work. And thanks."

Up the hill, the party ran. At first, Rose struggled to keep up. Soon, however, she realized that by using her ring of jumping to avoid particularly tight spots of underbrush, she was able to match the speed of her larger and faster companions. They were quite a sight, a human and a half-elf sprinting through the woods, being outpaced by a bounding halfling. After almost an hour of moving at top speed through the forest, they allowed themselves to pause and catch their breath in the closing darkness of night. With no sign of being followed, they walked on until they found a small recess in a hillside in which to make their camp.

Venez appeared once again, whispered in Valduin's ear, and then flew up into the air above the party. She looked down at the group for a second. Her eyes glowed as she made a few hand motions, sparkling flecks of golden light cascading from her waving hands. Then, she turned invisible again.

"Is she gone?" Rose asked Valduin, with a touch of sadness in her voice.

"Not completely," Valduin replied. "She said she would make us hard to find tonight, which I am guessing is that spell that made the crater in the road when we first met her. She also said she would keep watch so we could rest."

"That's so nice!" Rose said. "I wish I knew how to thank her."

"Maybe I will ask her in the morning, okay?" Valduin gave a yawn as he dropped his pack on the ground and started laying out his charred bedroll. "Remind me to buy a new one of these next time we are in town," he said to Adelaide. "This one is half-cooked."

Adelaide rolled her eyes as she set up her own bedroll. Rose barely got hers unrolled before she was asleep, only halfway out of her chainmail. Valduin pulled out the leather book as he lay down, inspecting it for any signs that it was the thing Taranath wanted him to retrieve. Finding nothing but blank pages again, he let himself drift off to sleep.

"This is why you make friends with the NPCs," Logan said to Madison. "Without Venez, we would have been in serious trouble back there. Either dead or captured."

"I still think we could have lured them into the tomb and killed them all one by one," Madison replied with a shrug.

"That's pretty gruesome," Amelia said with a grimace. "Anyway, what do you think we missed in the tomb? There was probably something cool in the sarcophagus, and in the pit trap on the stairs. Maybe in Gnash's secret tunnels, too."

"We don't talk about that!" Logan exclaimed. "We just say we got everything, and we move on."

"You're not in charge!" Amelia erupted. "If I want to think about the sarcophagus, I'll do what I want!"

"Whoa, take it easy," Logan said as he held up his hands. "Listen. There was probably a trap on the sarcophagus, and both of you were nearly dead after the battle. There's no reason to second guess those decisions, or else we'll never make any progress."

"Yeah, yeah," Madison said dismissively. "You're just mad you got an empty book, and I got a sweet magic weapon. Can you learn the Identify spell soon? It's gonna get real old if we have to haul every cool item all the way back to Tarsam to find out what they do."

16

Rose opened her eyes. She lay on the forest floor, unmoving as she soaked up the warm sunlight of late morning. She could see Adelaide lying a few feet from her. Over the sleeping human, Rose saw Valduin sitting with his back against a tree. Venez was perched on his knee. As Rose sat up, Venez turned to look at her. The fairy smiled, bowed her head slightly, and disappeared. Valduin said something in Sylvan, and then he stood up and walked back over to Rose.

"So, she's gone?" Rose asked Valduin.

"Yes. She is still looking for a good place to make her new home within the forest. I do not think that we can count on her to come to our rescue again," he answered.

"She was pretty magnificent back there," Rose said with a smile. "The look on those goblins' faces when her red dragon flew in! I won't be forgetting that any time soon. I wish there was some way to thank her."

"Well, she said that anything we can do to drive the evil out of the deep forest is helping her. She was forced out of her home because of these creatures roaming the forest freely. We have a bit more work ahead of us."

Adelaide sat up, yawning.

"Good morning, sleepy head!" Rose said with a cheerful smile.

"Morning," Adelaide groaned in reply.

"So," Valduin said as he sat down next to the other two, "what do we do now?"

"I thought you were the man with the plan," Rose responded. "You said we need to find the ruins of Eydon and destroy the evil there. That will fix the forest, right?"

"I think that's a long-term plan," Adelaide said. "Today, we should head back to Tarsam. We need to find someone to tell us what this axe does and what those vials are," she pointed to the leather holster on Valduin's belt. "We need to head back to that magic shop. The Lamia's Lair."

"Yes, Tarsam," Valduin agreed. "We could also try to sell those fancy daggers. Maybe we could get you some better armor." He gestured toward Adelaide.

"Yes! Do you think we could try to get that magic armor from those dwarves? That would be amazing!" Adelaide grinned broadly.

"Depends on how much we can get for the daggers. I would not get too excited yet. I am also hoping that Taranath visits again once we are out of the forest," Valduin admitted. "I think this book that was in Galien's tomb is important, but I cannot figure out how. He will also be able to give us some information on finding Eydon. Since its ruins have not been found for at least a few centuries, I would like all the help we can get to locate it."

"A few *centuries*?" Rose's eyes grew wide. "Woof. Yeah, he needs to help us find it."

"Well, let's get going then!" Adelaide got to her feet, excited at the prospect of going shopping and getting some new gear. She shouldered her pack and took a moment to observe the forest around them, looking to the sky to orient herself. After a few seconds, she decided on a southeasterly course. "We'll head that way. South toward Tarsam and east toward the Crossway. After that run yesterday, I'm not exactly sure how far from the road we are, but we'll find it eventually."

The trio moved through the forest with Adelaide in the lead. The ranger did her best to guide the group through the woods toward the road. After about an hour of walking, Adelaide slowed to a stop. She peered ahead through the trees. She could hear the gentle rustling of leaves above, and what sounded like flowing water just a little way ahead of them.

"Did you see something?" Valduin whispered as he stepped up next to Adelaide.

"I'm not sure," Adelaide replied, her voice hushed and tense.

Rose stopped behind her friends and scanned their surroundings for any sign of danger. As she took in the forest, she noticed a large centipede crawling down the trunk of one of the nearby trees. The centipede looked to be almost two feet long, and its jet-black, segmented body snaked back and forth as it came down from the canopy. Rose took a few steps toward the base of the tree, staring up at the centipede as she did. She had never seen a bug so large.

Without warning, the centipede leapt from the side of the tree, dropping onto Rose's shoulder. Rose felt a sharp pain in her neck as the creature bit her. She yelped and shook it off and onto the ground. For a moment she felt her head spin and a wave of nausea that made her eyes water, but she was able to blink it away and refocus on the oversized bug.

After watching in confusion as the centipede attacked Rose, both Adelaide and Valduin were surprised by sudden, sharp pains in the back of their legs. Spinning around, they saw three more of the large centipedes on the ground behind them. They had each been bitten by one.

As Rose looked down at the strange bug that had just attacked her, she drew her mace and brought it down on top of the centipede. While she felt like she hit it hard, the sound of the impact was unsatisfying. Instead of a crunch, there was only a light thud.

Adelaide reached both of her hands to where she had strapped the handle of her new axe. With a large over-head swing, she brought the axe off her pack and down onto one of the centipedes, splitting it in half. The axe gave off a satisfying vibration in Adelaide's hands as it carved through the centipede's glossy black exoskeleton. She pulled the gleaming head of the axe out of the bug. Somehow, the weapon was still immaculate despite the ichor that it had sprayed across the forest floor. As she admired the gleaming blade, there was a shimmer of purple light. Tendrils of energy extended from the roots etched into the axehead, through the edge of the blade, and down into the unmoving body in front of her. The light was drawn up through those seemingly decorative roots to the handle of the axe, where the light faded.

Adelaide stood agape, staring at the axe while this display of magic played out. When Adelaide looked back from the axe to the spot where she had killed the cen-tipede, instead of the large bug cut in two, there was a tiny humanoid cut in two. It was about a foot-and-a-half tall, green-skinned, with long, black horns on its head as well as smaller horns across its shoulders. It had a hunched back and sharp, hooked claws. It would have been a rather frightening sight if it wasn't already split in half.

"What is that?!" Adelaide screamed as she took in the remains of the creature in front of her.

"Do not know!" Valduin replied as he ran back the way they had come, trying to get some distance between himself and the centipedes. One of them tried to bite him as he ran past, but he was able to avoid it. "And do not care!" he finished. He released a spark of green, eldritch energy at the centipede that had just tried to bite him. The blast seemed to crush the centipede into the ground, where its form shimmered for a moment and then transformed into another of the tiny humanoids. As he watched, this one's unmoving body melted. Within moments, it was nothing more than a puddle of green and black sludge.

The one centipede left near Adelaide skittered up to her and bit her on the ankle. She screamed as she kicked it away from her. The one that had attacked Rose made a similar attack, sinking its fangs into Rose's lower leg. This time, her head spun as the centipede's venom took hold in her body, and she was unable to shake off the effect. She staggered backward a couple of steps, vomited, and collapsed to the ground, unconscious.

Adelaide glared at the centipede that had bitten her a second time, raised her axe, and brought it down behind the centipede's head. With a quick crunch, the axe cleaved through the creature, and again there was a flash of purple energy absorbed by the axe. The centipede transformed into another little green creature, but this time, instead of the legs being separated from the body, it was the head that had been removed.

Valduin, seeing Rose collapse, ran toward her, letting fly an eldritch blast at the creature that had knocked her out. It took the hit but continued moving toward Valduin. As Valduin and Adelaide faced down the one remaining centipede, there appeared in front of each of them another of the green, humanoid creatures. Both of the monsters came screaming out of thin air, spitting and snarling. The sudden appearance of more of these strange creatures annoyed Adelaide, but Valduin was overwhelmed with fright.

The half-elf screamed and stumbled backward, away from the newly arrived monsters. With its target distracted, the one remaining centipede crawled up his back and sank its sharp pincers deep into the side of his neck. He pushed the creature off his back as he staggered. His vision grew dark as he approached unconsciousness, but he was able to stay on his feet.

Adelaide did not even notice Valduin's troubles. She was busy bringing the axe back up in another wild, two-handed attack on the creature that had just appeared in front of her. The axe cut into the creature's shoulder, and it sunk over halfway down the length of its torso. Adelaide had to put her foot on the body of the creature to wedge the axe out, the ethereal purple tendrils again extending from the gaping hole in the monster's body before being pulled into the axe. With rage in her eyes, she turned to face her next opponent.

Valduin, breathing hard, eyes wide with fright, raised his hand once again toward the final centipede. This time the force of the green bolt of energy crushed half of the centipede flat against the ground. As with the last one he had dispatched, this centipede turned back into its humanoid form before melting into sludge.

Watching the last of its compatriots fall, the final green creature disappeared. Valduin could hear it running away, but despite swiping at it wildly, he was unable to connect with the creature. Adelaide, seeing no more immediate threats, stood up straight and relaxed her grip on the axe. With a sigh and a shake of her head, she walked over to Rose's unconscious body. Her hands glowed with her dark green magic as she healed the halfling, who awoke with a start.

Rose sat up with a start and looked for her attacker. "Where is it? Where did it go?" she asked in a panic.

"It's dead. We took care of them," Adelaide answered, her voice flat. "Get up, we need to move."

"Are you okay?" Rose asked Valduin as he staggered toward them and dropped to his knees next to her. "You don't look so good."

"I could maybe use a little pick-me-up," Valduin said. Rose's hands took on their golden glow as she touched Valduin's neck where the centipede had bitten him. The ragged hole closed without a scab or a scar, and Valduin took a deep breath as the divine healing spread through his body.

"Thanks, Rose," he said with a smile. He helped the halfling to her feet and brushed some of the dead leaves out of her wild hair.

"What are these things?" Adelaide asked. She stood over the bodies of the creatures she had slain. Rose and Valduin joined her.

"Also, why did the ones I killed turn to sludge, but the ones you killed did not?" Valduin added as he poked at one of them with his foot.

"I think I know what they are," Rose said. "They are quasits. Tiny, evil fiends. Demons. And, just like you were saying when we killed Gnash, these should have turned to sludge as they returned to the lower planes once these bodies were killed. I don't know why they didn't."

"Wait. Wait. How do you know all of that?" Valduin asked.

Rose laughed a little. "I did a lot of reading back at the temple. Halfred didn't trust me to do anything important, and tending the garden wasn't exactly a full-time job. There were all sorts of books about demons and devils in the library. Those were my favorites. I liked looking at the creepy pictures. I didn't really pay much attention to the ones about the planes or nature or anything."

Valduin raised an eyebrow at the mention of a library. "That sounds so nice. Maybe one day we could visit the temple and I could look in the library? I have not had much time to read since leaving Alomere."

Adelaide was bored at the mere mention of visiting a library. "Let's just keep going. I don't want that one that got away to come back with any friends."

"One got away?" Rose asked. Her body tensed, and she scanned the surrounding forest for movement.

"Yes," Valduin replied. "When there was only one left, it turned invisible and ran. I could hear it running but could not hit it."

"Yikes. Yes, let's get moving," Rose agreed.

"But don't we need to figure out why some of them melted and some didn't?" Adelaide asked. "It was only the ones I killed."

"I'm going to go out on a limb and say it's that axe," Valduin replied. "Think about it. Galien was called the Demon's Judge. When you killed these demons, they did not melt. I do not know why or how or what it means.

We still need to get someone who knows about magic to inspect the axe."

Adelaide considered this for a moment. "Maybe you're right. But just in case, let's take one. Maybe we can sell it."

"Take one? They are small, but they must still weigh forty pounds. I don't want to be carrying that all the way to Tarsam," Valduin said.

"Okay, fine. Just this then," Adelaide replied as she picked up the severed quasit head. She tied it by the horns to her pack.

"That is super gross," Rose said. "I love it!"

Valduin rolled his eyes. "Can we please leave now?"

Without responding, Adelaide turned and walked away, keeping a careful watch for any movement that might reveal an invisible demon. Beyond the next few trees was the stream that Adelaide heard before the battle. As the group made their way down the bank, Rose nearly fell into a large hole.

"Whoa!" she shouted as she caught herself against a tree branch to keep from stumbling into the gap in the bank of the stream. Peering into the dark, five-foot diameter hole, she could make out some indistinct piles on the ground. "Hey guys, look in here. I think it might have been their den or lair or something."

Valduin and Adelaide joined Rose as she lit up her amulet to inspect the contents of the small cave. She could see five or six piles of clothing and gear on the floor of the cave, which was not very deep. All around the piles were the tiny footprints of the quasits. The smell of decay was present, but not overpowering.

Valduin crept forward into the cave, inspecting the sides of the hole for any sign of traps. Finding none, he started poking at the first pile. He found a set of gear in the size and style of the kobolds they had fought. There was no sign of the former occupant of the gear, whom Valduin assumed the quasits had devoured.

"It looks like the remains of creatures the demons had eaten," he relayed to Adelaide and Rose. "Most of them were probably kobolds."

"Any loot? Those kobolds kept saying they were collecting gems. It would be nice to get a few for our trouble," Adelaide said.

Valduin rifled through the piles and emerged from the den smiling. "Not as much as we got from Gnash, but it is something!" He held out two leather pouches to Adelaide, who snatched them and turned to a nearby log to count them out.

"Oooh, nice," she said as she inspected the contents of the pouches. "Only about sixty gold in that one, but this one has gems. It looks like sapphires and emeralds. I'm not sure how much they will be worth, but I know Harfall and Harfell will want them."

"Let's get moving, then," Rose said, still on guard for the return of the last quasit. "We really don't want to fight anymore right now."

"You got it," Adelaide replied, smiling as she tucked the loot away. She headed across the stream. Valduin and Rose fell in line behind her, and the party continued on to the southeast, looking for the Virdes Crossway and heading for the safety of Tarsam.

"So much loot!" Madison exclaimed. "We are totally getting me some new armor now."

"How come you get all the cool stuff?" Amelia asked. "You got the magic weapon, and now you are going to buy new armor. When do I get something?"

"Well, you got the magic ring, and you started with a super high AC from that chainmail," Madison replied. "I need to bump mine up."

"A whole lot of good it's done me," Amelia grumbled. "I've gotten knocked unconscious in both battles."

"It's okay, Amelia," Logan reassured his sister. "You're going to start getting much more powerful spells soon. Clerics are super strong. You might need to stay out of melee a bit at these low levels."

Amelia glared at the other two. "Fine. I'll be the boring healer. But if Rose dies, my next character is gonna be a barbarian. Then I'll get to hit stuff."

17

As the hours passed, the tension diffused for the travelers. Eventually, they found the road and headed south. As they walked on the now-familiar packed earth of the Virdes Crossway, Valduin broke the silence.

"How are you feeling, Rose? That's twice in two days you have almost died."

"Wow, ouch," Rose replied. She chuckled. "My body feels okay. It's my pride that's bleeding out now."

"Sorry," Valduin said, sounding sincere. "It is just that of the three of us, you are the newest to adventuring. Are you feeling like you made the wrong choice yet? I know I felt like I had when we were running away from those kobolds the other day."

After a moment's reflection, Rose answered, "Honestly, not really. Sure, I took some hits, but we all made it through. I'd say I've been having fun! It's nice to be out of the temple and not have Halfred being disappointed in me all the time."

"Why would he be disappointed? Weren't you just the gardener?" Adelaide chimed in.

"Well, not really. I've lived at the temple for a few years now. My parents brought me there as a teenager. I hadn't really shown much interest in any craft or profession, so they figured Selaia would be able to figure something out for me. I'm not sure what they told Halfred to convince him to take me on, but he usually acts like he got the short end of the stick when it comes to me." Rose hung her head as she talked. She perked up as she finished, "But with the way he got so excited when I was able to use Selaia's magic, I think he will be much happier with me when I get back and tell him all the cool stuff we've done!"

"I'm sure he will be very proud of you," Valduin said.

"What about your parents?" Adelaide asked. "Are they dead?"

"Dead? No!" Rose cried. "They live less than a mile from the temple. We still talk and everything, and I see them once in a while. But I have my obligations now, and they are merchants so they travel around a lot."

"Did you tell them that you were leaving?" Valduin asked.

Rose looked stunned. "Actually, no, I didn't. I probably should have." She thought for a moment. "I'm sure Halfred will tell them. That's better anyway since they would not have been happy about me risking my life to help some strangers. Tall strangers at that." She gave Adelaide and Valduin a suspicious, side-eye glare before laughing.

Valduin laughed with her, but Adelaide only gave a half smile before turning her attention back to the road in front of her.

By the evening, they had emerged from the forest and were greeted by the rolling hills and patchwork farmland north of Tarsam. After another couple of hours, exhaustion was starting to set in. They were passing through some of the larger settlements on the road north of the city when they decided to stop for the night.

"Are we camping, or do you think we can get a room tonight?" Rose asked. "I never thought I would miss the little bed I had at the temple, but sleeping on the ground every night wears on you."

"Yes, a room would be nice," Adelaide agreed. "I wouldn't mind a bath either."

At the next cluster of buildings, the group entered a two-story, stone building with brightly lit windows. Above the door was a sign with an image of a metallic dragon and the name of the inn, The Tin Dragon. The door swung open to reveal a lively tavern. Along the right-hand wall was a bar being tended by a human man and a silver-scaled dragonborn.

The party approached the bar, where the dragonborn greeted them. "Hello there, strangers! I'm Naressi. Welcome to The Tin Dragon. Are you looking for a table or a room? Or a table and then a room? Or a room and then a table?" She gave a wide smile, clearly amused with her own presentation.

Valduin looked at Rose and Adelaide before speaking up for the group, "Nice to meet you, Naressi. I think a room first so we can unload our gear, and then a table. We have been in the woods a few days and could use some real food."

"In the woods! My, some real adventurers here!" Naressi's eyes grew wide, though Valduin was not sure if she was being sincere or not. "How many rooms do you need? And for how long?" She pulled out a large ledger, opened it to somewhere in the middle, and reviewed the last few entries.

Valduin glanced at Rose and Adelaide again, uncertain of the necessary accommodations. Adelaide glanced at Rose, and then she replied, "Two rooms should be fine. Rose and I can bunk up." Rose smiled at Adelaide's suggestion.

"Alright, then," Naressi said as she produced two keys from below the counter, each on its own ring with a charm hanging from it that looked like the metallic dragon from the sign. "Rooms five and six. There are washrooms at either end of the hall. Feel free to freshen up, then come on back down for dinner. The kitchen will be open for at least another couple of hours. Big crowd tonight with the caravan coming."

"The caravan is coming?" Adelaide asked, her voice rising with excitement.

"Yes, it just started arriving today! First word of it only came in a couple days ago, which is unusual. In recent years we have been getting more notice than that. It is late this year, too. We've had lots of people coming in recently and waiting for it. From what I hear, most of the taverns within the walls are full, which is good for my inn," Naressi replied. "Were you waiting for it?"

"Well, we were coming back to the city for other reasons, but if we can stay for the party, I'm sure we will," Adelaide said. "I've never seen this end of it."

"Well, I hope you enjoy it. That will be one gold per night for the two rooms. How long will you be staying?"

"We can say two nights for now," Valduin replied as he placed two gold pieces on the counter and picked up the keys. "And we will be back down for dinner." He led Adelaide and Rose across the tavern to the stairs and headed up. When they arrived at their doors, he gave Adelaide one of the keys.

"I am just going to drop my stuff and go get a table," Valduin said. "You can wash up if you want."

"We'll meet you down there," Rose said. She followed Adelaide into their room and fell face-first onto one of the beds. Adelaide dropped her own pack against the foot of the other bed. Valduin put his gear on one of the two beds in his room. He locked the door behind him as he headed downstairs.

While the dining area was busy and loud, Valduin had no trouble finding a small table off to the side opposite the bar. He sat quietly, contemplating everything that they had seen. The human bartender eventually came around to take Valduin's order, and he asked for three plates.

Not long after the waiter walked off, Adelaide dropped into the chair next to Valduin, startling him out of his thoughts.

"Okay, before she gets down here," Adelaide began in a hurried, hushed voice, "what are we going to do about the halfling?"

"What do you mean?" Valduin asked, caught off guard by the aggressive tone of Adelaide's voice.

"We have been in three battles with her, right? And *twice* she got knocked out and almost died. Twice I had to heal her. *She's* supposed to be the healer. If she keeps ending up on the floor, she's more of a detriment than anything else."

"True, but in that first battle it was me that almost died," Valduin countered. "And without her, I would not have made it. *And* she was able to stabilize all of those bandits in the woods. Without her, they would probably have died, too."

Adelaide's stern look softened a fraction. Before she could say anything else, Valduin continued, "Also, how are you going to see in the dark without her magic?"

"Are we talking about magic?" Rose asked as she approached the table. She hopped up onto the chair across from Adelaide. She had taken off her armor, but it did not look like she had tried to do anything about the dirt, twigs, and leaves in her hair. She looked around for a moment before she said, "What kind of establishment is this, anyway? No chairs for halflings?"

Valduin gave a chuckle at Rose's feigned indignation, and Adelaide managed a weak smile. Rose continued, "So, what's the caravan? Sounds exciting! There's going to be a party?"

Adelaide shelved her misgivings about Rose for the moment, and she explained, "Yes, it's a party. At least that's what I've heard. Up in the Sandgate Mountains to the west, during the winter most of the roads are blocked with snow. So, once spring comes and the roads are cleared, a caravan of traders assembles in Westray. You know, merchants and craftspeople that have been producing goods during the winter finally have a chance to get those goods to markets outside of the mountains. It's a vast assortment of peoples that come, but mostly you see dwarves from Khal Durum or some of the smaller dwarven towns in the mountains.

"The dwarves meet up with the people of Westray and form a caravan. The caravan heads east along the Sandgate Road to Tarsam and then east to Alomere and Verasea on the coast. Usually, it arrives by late spring, so it is late this year. I've only ever seen the caravan as it left, but it was always a party in Westray in the days leading up to the departure. From what I've heard, there is quite the reception here in Tarsam, as dignitaries from Westray and Khal Durum also come to meet with the Crystal Fist. I would expect the marketplaces to be absolutely crazy for the next couple of days. It's a great time for us to do some shopping."

"So, we should make sure we know what we need to get," Valduin said. "Adelaide, you need better armor. We need to get that axe identified. And we need someone to tell us what these potions do. Anything else? Rose, do you need anything?"

Rose thought for a second. "No, I don't think so. I'd like to take a walk through the market to see what's out there, but I don't think there's anything, in particular, I need."

Adelaide chimed in, "We also need to know what we are doing next. You have been saying that we need to go to Eydon, but you also said that no one has been there for a very long time. How are we going to find it?"

Valduin considered the question for a moment. He was gifted a little extra time to think as the waiter arrived with three steaming-hot dinner plates, and both Rose and Adelaide dug in. He joined them, and he was surprised when he realized just how hungry he had been. It had been a while since he and Adelaide had eaten a hearty meal. The party ate in silence for a couple of minutes before Adelaide spoke up again. "So, how do we find it?"

"I think I need to talk to Taranath again. I feel like this book is important, but I can't figure out why. And I need to tell him about the whozits we fought. He'll be interested in that."

"Quasits," Rose corrected him around a full mouth of food.

"Yes, the quasits," Valduin conceded.

"Okay, good plan," Adelaide replied with a patronizing tone. "How do you get in touch with a super powerful being that can jump between planes of existence whenever he feels like it? Do you have a spell for that?"

Valduin considered this. He had not yet thought about how he would find Taranath to get this information. "I don't know. I guess I was assuming he would come to me now that we are out of the woods and had completed the task he gave us. He told me he couldn't enter the forest right now. He seems to have a connection to me, so if we just go about our business, he should find us. That's what he did last time."

"Well, I guess that's fine," Adelaide replied, though her body language did not indicate that she was reassured at all by this plan. "We'll go shopping tomorrow and hope he pops up at some point to tell us how to find the ancient, abandoned, elven city deep in the evil heart of the mysterious forest. Just a regular day at the market."

After this uneasy conclusion, the group paid for their meals and headed to bed. Adelaide and Rose retired to their room, and Valduin did the same. Despite his anxiety about their path forward, Valduin had no trouble falling asleep as the exhaustion of the days of travel overtook him.

When Valduin awoke, the room was still dark, though this did not impede his vision of the wall he was facing. He lay as still as he could, listening for what might have roused him. There was still some dull commotion coming from the floor below, but it did not seem much changed from when he went to bed.

He noticed another sound, softer, but much closer. The scratching sound of a quill writing on parchment. The sound was almost certainly coming from within his small room.

Taking a shaky breath in, he prepared himself to confront the intruder. But before he could move, a familiar voice greeted him, "Welcome back, Valduin. It's nice to see that you can be counted on to complete tasks promptly. I appreciate reliable associates."

Valduin rolled over and sat up to face Taranath, who was focused on writing in a book. It took Valduin another second to realize that it was the book they had recovered from Galien's tomb. "I was wondering what that book was for," Valduin said. "I could not tell if that was what we were supposed to recover, or if it was the axe."

"The book is what I wanted you to have," Taranath replied. "But if you brought out Fiend's Lament as well from Galien's tomb, then you should be well equipped for the next leg of your journey."

"Is that the axe's name? Fiend's Lament?"

"Yes," Taranath said with a smile. "A particularly effective weapon against demons and devils. I enchanted it many years ago for a quest that Galien undertook."

"What does it do? Adelaide used it against the quasits we fought."

"What do you mean? You encountered quasits in the forest?" Taranath asked, his face growing stern.

"Well, that's what Rose said they were. Little green things with arms and legs and lots of horns. And they could change into centipedes. We killed a bunch of them, but one got away," Valduin recounted.

"Yes, that sounds like a quasit. This is most unsettling. Having fiends—even lesser demons such as these—roaming freely through the forest is a very bad sign. Whatever evil has found its way to the ruins of Eydon is growing, and this confirms its fiendish nature. You said Adelaide used Fiend's Lament on them? What did you see happen?"

"Well," Valduin tried to remember exactly what it had looked like when Adelaide had killed the quasits. "Each time she hit one with the axe, it died immediately. And then there would be this purple glow that the axe seemed to soak up. And their bodies would just lay there. When I killed one of them, the body turned to sludge."

"Then you have already witnessed the power of Fiend's Lament. The axe was created for the specific purpose of killing fiends, so it will hurt a fiend more than an ordinary weapon would. And when it deals the killing blow to a fiend, the fiend's essence is locked into that physical body so that it cannot return to its native plane. As the body dies, the essence is absorbed into the axe, killing the demon or devil outright." Taranath smiled gleefully as he described the enchantment on the axe, again showing an unnerving number of teeth.

Taranath closed the book that he had been writing in. "At one time this was Galien's as well. When he passed, the knowledge within it went with him. It is now ready for you to fill with your own magic. I put a couple of spells in there for you to get started." He held out the book to Valduin, who took it with respectful restraint, even though he could barely contain his excitement at increasing his magical abilities.

Valduin sat on the side of the bed, the book held tightly in his hands. "Where do we go now? How do we find Eydon?" he asked.

"Follow the river west. Where the river meets the mountains, there is a waterfall. Behind the waterfall is the entrance to Eydon. At the time of my last visit, there were a few stray creatures that had made their homes within or around the city. You will want to be careful and stay quiet. I cannot know what awaits you now.

Good luck on your journey, and I hope that the next time I see you this evil will be behind us." Taranath stood up and wrapped his cloak around himself. "And one other thing. I know that Adelaide is having second thoughts about bringing Rose along. I would recommend keeping the cleric around. While I find piety exceedingly boring, they usually end up being worth the trouble of protecting them."

With that, Taranath vanished from the room. Valduin could almost make himself believe he could smell the sweet grass of the Inner Plane of Light on the air as Taranath disappeared. Valduin opened the spellbook to see what new knowledge lay inside.

"What are you doing?" Logan asked as he watched Madison jump up from the table and dance around the room.

"It's my level-up dance!" she proclaimed.

He watched her for a second, and then he shrugged. "Well, okay," he said. He did a happy little wiggle in his chair.

"And we are just going to ignore the fact that you wanted to leave me behind?" Amelia said with a pout. "Rule number eight: protect the healer. I'm going to need help out there!"

"*I* don't want to leave you behind," Madison explained as she returned to her seat. "*Adelaide* might, though. She thinks people need to be able to fend for themselves. She doesn't like the idea of being dependent on others or having others depend on her."

Amelia glared at her sister. "Sounds like an opportunity for some character growth."

"We're only level three," Madison countered. "It's way too early for character growth."

"Fine then!" Amelia shouted. "First you beg me to play. Now you are trying to ditch me. I'm *out of here!*" She pushed back from the table and headed for the door.

Logan decided it was time to step in. "Okay, okay, that's enough. Amelia, you are doing great. We *both* want you to stay and play." This time it was Logan glaring at Madison. "Let's look at what we all get for level three. And now we know what the axe does. That will save us time on the shopping day."

"We are still going to check out the magic shop, though, right?" Amelia asked as she returned to her seat. "I want to find out what that dress does!"

18

Rose awoke to Adelaide shaking her shoulder. "Wake up if you want to go shopping," Adelaide was saying. "You'll sleep through the whole party at this rate."

Rose rolled away from Adelaide and pulled the sheets over her head. "Get me something pretty," she mumbled.

"Are you serious?"

"Do you always wake up at lunchtime?" Valduin added.

Rose did not move, but she responded, "No, Valdoonar. Sometimes I sleep through that too."

Adelaide sounded confused when she asked, "Why are you talking to Val? He isn't here."

Rose rolled over to look around the room, confused as to what she had just heard.

"Are you sure?" Valduin's voice spoke into Adelaide's mind this time. Adelaide tensed and looked around.

"You had better not be invisible in here," she said as she stepped toward her gear.

Someone knocked on the door. Neither Rose nor Adelaide moved. After a moment, Adelaide could hear Valduin again.

"Will you let me in? I know you are awake. I could hear you trying to get Rose up."

Valduin stood in the hallway with the black spellbook open, repeatedly casting his new message spell through the door at his companions. With a jerk, the door swung open, and standing in front of him was a stern-looking human woman with a battleaxe in her hand. Rose was visible in the room beyond Adelaide, still in bed, but at least with her eyes open.

"What in the world is wrong with you?" Valduin asked, feigning confusion as he stepped into the room.

"What was that? You've never done that before," Adelaide said, glaring at Valduin with narrowed eyes.

"Just a new spell I learned," he replied coolly.

"And how did you learn it?" Adelaide continued, still not trusting the half-elf.

"When Taranath visited last night."

Rose sat up at this statement. "He visited again? What did he say? What do we have to do?"

Valduin proceeded to fill in his companions with the information that he had gotten from Taranath during their midnight meeting, including how Fiend's Lament worked and how they would find Eydon. Adelaide took a long, hard look at the axe as Valduin described its powers.

"Well," Adelaide said when Valduin was finished, "this all makes sense then. And it's nice to know where we are headed. I must say I am not reassured by the fact that we may have to fight both more demons and whatever stray creatures Taranath may have seen at the ruins. He said to stay quiet? We already know we aren't the best at that," she concluded as she looked toward Rose.

Before Rose could open her mouth to argue with Adelaide's insinuation, Valduin reached into a pouch on his belt. He stepped forward while speaking in Sylvan, "*To *seek, but not to find.*" As his free hand glowed with pale green light, he tapped Rose on the forehead.

She disappeared.

The room went silent. The sheets on Rose's bed moved down, and the bed creaked as a weight was removed from it.

"Whoa," Adelaide said. Valduin and Adelaide could hear Rose's soft footsteps, but otherwise, they could not tell where she had gone. The halfling reappeared as she leapt from Adelaide's bed onto Valduin's back, nearly toppling him over. She dropped down to the floor and looked at her arms to see if she was visible again.

"Well, that's pretty cool!" Rose exclaimed. "That will definitely help me be sneaky."

"Let's hope," Adelaide muttered. She shouldered her pack and hung Fiend's Lament where she could reach it. "Now, are you ready to go shopping?"

"Okay, fine," Rose replied with a groan. "Let's get it over with."

The party collected their valuables, locked their rooms, and headed downstairs. Before they even got to the bottom of the stairs, the smell of cooking bacon was overwhelming. There were half a dozen groups of two or three people sitting at tables and eating hearty breakfasts. Naressi was behind the counter, yawning and working her way through a pile of dirty dishes. She bid them good morning with a small wave as they came down the stairs.

"Heading into the city, then? Would you all be needing some breakfast first?" she asked.

"Absolutely!" Rose spoke up. "Can I make a special request? Do you think you could put some cooked eggs and bacon inside of a bread roll cut in half? So that we can walk and eat?"

Naressi narrowed her eyes at the halfling, then replied, "Yes, I suppose so. Is that a traditional halfling breakfast dish or something?"

"Uh, not really," Rose replied. "It's just something I like to make when I'm at home. It lets you eat breakfast and still get on with your day."

"Very well," Naressi shrugged. She stood up and headed into the kitchen. "I'll be just a minute." Before long, she returned with three long rolls stuffed with eggs and bacon, per Rose's order.

"Those actually look pretty good," Naressi said as she handed over the sandwiches. "Maybe I'll try selling them. See what the other customers think. That'll be one silver apiece, I guess." Valduin dropped the coins on the counter, and the three adventurers walked out into the bright sunlight of an early summer day.

They walked, and ate, and discussed plans for reentering the forest and finding the lost city.

"You seem chipper this morning," Adelaide said to Valduin. "Excited to be going to Eydon?"

"Are you kidding?" he replied. "Of course! The city of my ancestors, lost for almost a thousand years. And we know how to find it! Just think of what we might find. What we might learn!"

"Just think of what we might have to fight," Adelaide retorted. "Just think of why no one has ever found it before. Probably because the ones that did never came back. I'm not one hundred percent sure we are ready for this."

"Well, we are going to buy some more gear," Valduin said, his excitement waning in the face of Adelaide's concerns. "What do you think, Rose? Are you a little interested in finding a lost city?"

Rose, not wanting to crush Valduin's mood, answered, "Absolutely! It will be so much fun being on an adventure with my two best friends." She smiled before taking another large bite of her breakfast sandwich. She did not notice the look that Valduin gave Adelaide, nor the pain on Adelaide's face as she digested being Rose's best friend.

After a half an hour of walking, the party approached the North Gate of Tarsam. The first time they entered the city together had been at night. The gate had been heavily-guarded and open just enough to let through one person at a time. When they left the city during the day, the gate was wide open under the watch of a handful of Crystal Fist guards. Today was a different story. The gate was wide open again, but there were a dozen guards standing along the wall above the gate, and another couple dozen on the ground. Passing into the city was a continuous stream of travelers; Adelaide guessed that she could see at least two hundred people filing through the gate as they crested the final hill on the Virdes Crossway.

"So, what do you both think?" Adelaide asked. "Head over to the West Market again, right? Do we want to start at the magic shop, or do we want to go into the maze first to find the dwarves?"

"Well, we know we want to go to the armorers again," Valduin said. "And since we know how the axe works now, the magic shop is more out of curiosity than necessity. So, we should start in the maze to make sure we can get you what you need. Then, if we have any money left over, we can maybe spend it at the magic shop."

"Sounds fine to me," Rose agreed. "I'd like to look around the market a bit, too. See if there is anything else interesting from the caravan that Adelaide told us about."

A short time later, they found themselves walking with the mass of people through the gate and into the city. They followed the crowd, which seemed to know where it was going, until they reached the center of the city and found themselves looking up at the soaring Crystal Tower. Near the base were several smaller towers—all constructed of clear, crystal plates—glittering in the sunlight like massive, faceted diamonds. The central tower soared high over the rest, and Rose could see balconies hundreds of feet up the sides of the tower, where tiny figures watched over the city.

"Do you feel like people are watching us?" Adelaide whispered to Rose, breaking her reverie. Rose blinked a few times to clear the sunlight from her eyes, and then she glanced at the people around them. The river of people was parting at the Crystal Tower. Half of the crowd was heading east, and the other half west. Rose guessed that they were headed to the two major marketplaces of the city.

There were, however, a fair number of eyes that lingered on the three travelers as they stood in the middle of the wide avenue, admiring the Crystal Tower. Those eyes included a couple of Crystal Fist guards off to the side of the street.

Rose took a moment to see where most of the people were looking, and then she said to Adelaide, "Turn around real quick." Adelaide turned her back to Rose, and Rose figured out why they were drawing attention. Hanging on Adelaide's pack, next to the gleaming battleaxe, was the quasit head that she had collected the day before.

"Do you have anywhere else you can put that thing?" Rose asked, struggling to contain her laughter.

"Uh," Adelaide took stock of her gear, "not really. Let's just keep moving." With that, the trio did their best to blend into the stream of people headed toward the west market, and they tried not to think about the guards who were following them a hundred feet back in the crowd.

They were soon approaching the market, which seemed to have grown since they last visited it. Instead of just the maze of carts and stalls in the center of the large city square, there were now vendors lining the streets for blocks leading to the square. People were shopping throughout the streets, and Rose, Adelaide, and Valduin had to push through the crowd at some points in order to stay together. Eventually, they reached the square itself, which was overflowing with shoppers and merchants.

"This is crazy," Valduin said as he pulled Adelaide and Rose to the side of the stream of people entering the market. "Are we really going in there?"

"Of course we are!" his companions said in unison.

"Are we still being followed?" Valduin followed up. He resisted the urge to look over his shoulder. He did not want to give away that he knew they were being followed.

Adelaide answered, "I'm pretty sure we are. They were keeping their distance, but those two guards are definitely still there."

"Maybe we should go to the magic shop first," Valduin suggested as he surveyed the market and tried to remember where the Lamia's Lair was. "I think it is just over there, and if we can get inside quickly, maybe we can lose those guards."

"Sounds fine to me," Rose replied. "And The Lamia's Lair is definitely just at the end of this row of shops," she added, indicating the side of the square they had entered through.

"Okay, we should move quickly, then," Valduin said as he reached into his pocket. A moment later, he turned Rose invisible again. They darted down the side of the market and ducked into the recessed doorway of The Lamia's Lair. Valduin tried the handle, and, finding it locked, knocked twice on the door. He tried not to make his knock sound too panicked. They waited, but there was neither sound nor movement from inside the shop.

Adelaide turned to look back down the street, where she could see the two guards surveying the crowd. They seemed to have lost sight of the adventurers for the moment, but they were heading toward them nonetheless.

Just as Valduin raised his hand to knock again, the door creaked open a few inches before being stopped by a chain. It was dark within the shop, but Valduin could see an elderly gnome peering through the opening. Before Valduin could say anything, the gnome said, "Where did you get that?" Valduin followed the path of the gnarled finger pointing to the quasit head on Adelaide's back.

"If you let us in, we will tell you," Valduin replied, forcing the desperation out of his voice.

The gnome peered up at Valduin through a crystal monocle that hovered in front of his left eye. It felt like the wizened gnome was inspecting Valduin's soul. Without another word, the door shut. A moment later, Valduin could hear the chain being released, and the door opened again. Valduin and Adelaide rushed in; they could feel Rose's invisible, armored form moving between them into the shop.

Adelaide shut the door behind her, and then she peered through the display window out at the street. Just a few seconds later, the two guards came into view, and Adelaide withdrew into the darkness of the shop. The group stood in tense silence as the guards continued past the storefront.

The three adventurers let out a collective sigh of relief, and then they turned to inspect the inside of the shop. The ceiling was low, and there were bundles and sacks hanging within range of Valduin's head as he took a few careful steps into the dark room. The three walls of the small shop were lined with shelves, and the shelves contained all manner of objects. There were glass jars filled with strange liquids. There were wooden boxes with metal locks. There were bundles of dried herbs and flowers. One entire set of shelves contained nothing but leather-bound books, and another shelf held dozens of rolled-up scrolls in what were apparently purpose-built cubbies.

In front of the shelves, separating the customers from the inventory, was a low countertop that wrapped around the room. At the back of the room, there was a section of the counter on a hinge, and behind this was a closed door. At first, Valduin thought that the counter was comically low, but he soon realized that it was at an appropriate height for gnomes. The old gnome had passed through the gap in the counter and lowered the hinged section down to separate himself from the party when Valduin finally found his voice.

"Thank you for letting us in, sir," he said.

Behind the counter now, the gnome walked around until he had reached the closest point to his guests. He pulled out a stool from under the counter and sat down. The monocle continued to hover in front of the gnome's left eye as he inspected Valduin again. It was only now that Valduin noticed the monocle was being held by a spectral, floating hand, and the gnome's own hands were folded carefully in front of him on the counter.

After a moment's silence, the gnome's attention moved to Adelaide, who was still taking in the sights of the room. She was looking at the objects hanging from the ceiling, making sure not to bump into any of them. The gnome then looked back toward the display window. Valduin followed his gaze to where a bare mannequin stood, no longer wearing the blue and green dress that Rose had been fawning over.

"It is not polite to slink about!" the gnome croaked out. He waved a hand toward the window, and in a flash, Valduin could see Rose standing there looking at the mannequin. Rose looked down at herself, realized she was no longer invisible, and turned to face the gnome, looking sheepish.

"There, much better. We must have everything in the open. Aboveboard. Yes. Quite." The gnome's gaze returned to Adelaide, who was leaning over the opposite counter and trying to read the names of the books on the back shelves. "I am very curious about that head. Where did you get it? How has it been preserved?" Valduin watched as the spectral hand placed the monocle on the countertop and floated over to Adelaide. The hand jerked the head from Adelaide's pack and brought it back toward the gnome. Adelaide spun around at the sudden tug on her back.

"Hey, that's mine!" she said as she chased the floating head across the room.

"Yours? You still have yours attached to your neck. This was never yours. But whose was it? Who took this trophy? Do you know? Did you steal it from someone? We can't have that. No, that wouldn't do," the gnome shook his head at his own suggestion. Adelaide's indignant run across the room was cut short by the gnome's harsh words, but Rose giggled at his strange demeanor.

Valduin spoke up, saying, "We took that trophy, sir. From the fiend itself. Do you know what this creature is?"

"Yes, I know a quasit when I see one. Dirty little demons. Always scurrying about. And stop calling me sir!"

"I'm sorry, sir. I mean, Mr. Lamia? Is that your name?" Valduin floundered under the gnome's intensity.

"Mr. Lamia? You are here purporting to have killed a quasit and preserved its head, and you think I am a *lamia*? Maybe try doing a little research before jumping into battle with fiends. Next, you'll be asking me to tell you if those vials you carry contain potions of healing! Ha! Yes? No? Now, I am Seer Brixim," he said. He bowed his head slightly as he introduced himself. Rose's giggling only intensified.

Valduin's voice quivered as he responded, "It is very nice to meet you, Seer Brixim. I am Valduin, and this is Adelaide and Rose. We took that head from a quasit in the Virdes Forest yesterday."

"Yesterday!" Brixim exclaimed as he inspected the head from several angles. To do this, his spectral hand had released the head in front of him, where it now hung in the air and rotated slowly. The floating hand returned to its position holding the monocle up to Brixim's eye as he considered the head.

After a few long moments, Brixim looked back at Adelaide. "This is quite odd. How did you manage to preserve it?"

"That happens to be a trade secret," Adelaide bluffed, turning her body slightly to make sure Fiend's Lament was out of the view of the gnome. "Information like that will cost you."

"Cost! Cost *me*?" Brixim bristled at Adelaide's suggestion. "Why, you little..." he muttered as he waved his hand toward Adelaide. She felt a tightness across her body, as if she had been grabbed by a massive, invisible fist. Against her will, she slid halfway across the room toward the gnome, and then she began to rotate while hovering a few inches off the ground.

"Hey! What are you doing!" she cried out as she struggled to free herself, but to no avail.

Brixim inspected Adelaide in much the same way as he had inspected the head, which was no longer floating but rather resting on the countertop. After a few moments, he had the information he needed. "That is a very interesting weapon. Preserving the body of a fiend. I've not seen an item that could do that before. And I've seen a lot of magic."

Adelaide felt her body released from the magical hold. She straightened her clothes and pack as she glared at the gnome.

"Okay, okay, okay." Brixim held up his hands in surrender, though even his empty hands did not make Adelaide feel safe. "I am Seer Brixim, and this is my shop, The Lamia's Lair. I am usually open by *appointment only*," he paused to let this sink in as he made intense eye contact with each of the three adventurers, "but you have brought a unique item here today, so I will *forgive your intrusion*." He paused again for effect.

185

"Was there a price that you had in mind for this object?" he indicated the head on the counter.

Adelaide and Valduin looked at each other. This had not been part of the plan, and they had no idea what this kind of thing would be worth. Valduin spoke up first, saying, "As you said, it is a unique item. Fiendish bodies do not last long in death on this plane, and by the magic of the weapon my friend wields, this head has been preserved. I am sure we could find many interested researchers within this great city, but we have heard great things about you and your shop. We wanted to give you the first chance to bid on it."

Brixim looked again at the head, and then he glared at Valduin through the monocle. Still looking at Valduin, things began to fly through the room, seemingly of their own accord. In no time at all, there were three items lined up on the countertop next to the head. "First of all, I find your tone *patronizing*! Do not lecture me on the mechanics of extraplanar dissolution! But, despite your own *naivety*, your position in this negotiation stands. My offers," Brixim said, indicating the items. "You may pick *one*. First, three hundred gold. Simple, functional, timeless. Second, as there are three of you, three potions of water breathing. Each will last for one hour, so be sure to plan your aquatic adventures appropriately. Finally, a Ring of Swimming. This will let one of you swim quite quickly, I suspect at least twice as fast as you currently can."

Valduin, Adelaide, and Rose surveyed and inspected the items, paying particular notice to the magic ring. After a moment, Valduin replied, "These are all very nice items, and certainly useful. I wonder, however, if you might have any items on hand that would aid me with my magics. Like you, I am a spell caster, and any help I could get to make sure my spells attain their desired effects would be most helpful on our adventures."

"First of all, little elf boy," Brixim retorted, pointing his gnarled finger up at Valduin, "you are most certainly *not* a spell caster *like me*. Secondly, of course I have such an item, but this would cost you more than just one severed quasit head." As he talked, a long, thin wooden box floated off a shelf at the back of the room, next to the door that led deeper into the building, and landed at the end of the row of Brixim's offers. The wood was the color of dried blood, and the box had brass hinges and a brass latch. The latch flipped up, and the box opened to show Valduin a wand of beautifully worked ebony with caps of lustrous brass that gleamed in the low light of the shop. Drawn to the beauty of this tool of magic, Valduin reached for the wand, and the box snapped closed. Startled, Valduin looked toward Brixim, who now had a sly smile on his face.

"Not only will this wand aid in the effectiveness of your spells, but also with just a moment's concentration, it can help you regain a bit of spent magical energy. Now, what else do *you* have to offer?" Brixim asked.

Valduin turned to Adelaide. "How much gold do we have?"

Adelaide, not exactly enamored of the magic wand, replied, "Maybe six hundred all together, but why don't we just take the gold or the potions? I will need some gold to buy the armor we had planned on," she hissed.

"How about the fancy daggers? Just one of them?" Valduin begged.

Adelaide considered this for a moment, and then she sighed. "Fine," she muttered as she reached into her pack and pulled out the gold-handled dagger with the emeralds set in it. "I don't like green and gold together, anyway."

Valduin set the dagger on the counter next to the quasit head. Brixim lifted it, again without touching it, and let it rotate as he inspected it through his monocle. Finally, he said, "This is well made. It will hold an enchantment. You have a deal." The first three offers zipped through the air back to their respective shelves. The dagger and the quasit head floated toward the back door of the room and disappeared behind the counter. In a moment, the only object left was the dark red box, which now stayed open as Valduin reached in and withdrew the black wand.

"It was a pleasure doing business with you all. Now that your pursuers seem to have moved along, please leave so that I can get back to my *important* work. Do come back, though. I am always interested in acquiring rare or interesting magic items. But next time, *make an appointment!*" Brixim concluded as he walked toward the back of the shop.

The front door opened of its own volition.

Valduin, Rose and Adelaide shuffled out onto the sidewalk before Valduin thought to ask, "How do we make an appointment?" The only response was the slamming of the door behind him and the sound of the chain being reapplied to it.

"He was rude," Madison said.

"I liked him!" Amelia shouted. "He was kind of silly, and he is probably like a level twenty wizard. But the dress was gone! And I didn't even get a chance to ask him what it did," her excitement quickly gave way to pouting.

"We were also supposed to find out what the dagger in the other window does, but we didn't do that either," Logan said. "In other news, this Wand of Recovery is amazing!" He read and reread the item card for the magic wand.

"Okay, you got a wand," Amelia rolled her eyes. "We have been shopping for like an hour already! Can we fast forward a little bit please?"

"No! I *badly* need better armor," Madison answered.

"You guys get all the cool gear," Amelia grumbled. "If we have to go shopping, I want to get something for myself too. It shouldn't cost very much."

"Of course," Madison replied. "And I promise we won't spend hours haggling with the dwarves."

19

Back on the street, Adelaide scanned the area for the guards that had been following them.

"Looks like we're clear of those guards," she said. She took another moment to survey the mass of shoppers that were swarming through the maze in the middle of the square. "Do you think we will even be able to find the dwarves in there? I think I remember where Moire led us, but with all these extra people here today, they might be hard to find."

"Only one way to find out!" Rose cried. She led the way into the maze of stalls and carts in the center of the marketplace. It took the group nearly an hour, as opposed to the ten minutes it had taken Moire, but they eventually found Harfall and Harfell's armory deep within the maze. While the shop had appeared full the last time they had visited, with items hanging from the rafters of the stall, this time, it was positively overflowing. One of the dwarves was standing on the top of the stall, stacking wooden boxes. There were sets of leather and metal armor hanging from nearly every rafter on the inside, and the tables below were covered with smaller bits of gear and weapons.

As they approached, the dwarf brother within the stall greeted Valduin, "I recognize that armor. Welcome back, friends! Did you bring any more fine gems? Looking to upgrade your gear again?"

Adelaide stepped forward and said with a smile, "Hello, Harfall. Actually, yes, and yes. I am in need of some new armor. I was wondering about that enchanted breastplate you had mentioned."

"Ah, yes, *the* breastplate," Harfall grinned as he rubbed his hands together. "A fine piece of armor that is. I believe I told you last time that the price is fifteen hundred gold pieces. I'll need to see the coin before I bring it out. No commitment to buy, but we keep the good stuff under lock and key, and I want to make sure it will be worth my effort to show it to you," the dwarf explained. "I'm sure you understand."

Adelaide made a show of looking through her pack. Finally, she brought out the pouch where she had kept all of the gemstones they had collected during their journey. She poured the pouch out on the table between them.

Harfall looked up through the open rafters to his brother and called out to him in Dwarvish. Harfell descended via a ladder leaning against the back of the shop to join them. Soon, the dwarves were inspecting the gems and muttering to each other in their own language. After a minute, they turned to Adelaide, and Harfall said, "Sorry, dear. This isn't nearly enough. You could get a standard breastplate for this, and even that would be a generosity for returning customers."

Adelaide looked a little disappointed, but she had known that the pile of gems was probably not worth more than three hundred gold. "That sounds perfect," she said. "Do you maybe have one that's not super shiny? I need to be able to hide. And a shield as well if you have one that matches."

Harfall glanced at Harfell, who thought for a moment. "Yes, I think we can do that," Harfell said. He climbed back up to the roof where he had been sorting crates. After a few moments of waiting, Harfell lowered a wooden box with a large crest painted on the side. Harfall grabbed the box and brought it over to the table. The lid had already been pried off, and out of the straw-packed crate he lifted a breastplate and shield of beautifully blackened steel, both bearing the same crest as the box they came in: an eagle with its wings spread in front of a mountain. He laid them on the table.

Adelaide could barely contain her excitement.

"Now this set," Harfall explained, "is from Khal Durum. Do you know this place?"

"Yes, I have been to Khal Durum," Adelaide replied in Dwarvish. *"And I know that crest to be that of the Line of Marin, ruling family of Westray. How do you have this?"* Harfall's eyes grew wide, and then he gave a hearty laugh.

"I knew there was something that I liked about you!" he exclaimed, also in Dwarvish. Then, reverting to Common, he continued, "This armor comes from a shop called The Gray Anvil. The shop has been in business for a couple hundred years and is quite well known. These pieces were made as part of a commissioned order for the rulers of Westray, for their elite guards. From what I've been told, the commission was canceled abruptly after they had begun production. This set is one of only a handful that were completed. Are you from Westray then?"

"Yes, I was born and raised there," Adelaide said, her eyes not leaving the armor. She took a breath to pull herself together before she asked, "With the gems, how much for the set?"

Harfall turned to Harfell, but before he said anything he glanced back at Adelaide and chuckled. He then started talking to his brother in a different language, one that Adelaide did not understand. After a brief exchange, they turned back to Adelaide. "Throw in two hundred gold and you can have the set."

Adelaide's face grew stern. "You already said the gems would cover a breastplate, and a shield does not cost two hundred gold. I'll give you fifty gold."

Harfall looked incredulous. "I was being kind when I offered the armor for those gems. And this is a special set, meeting your specific request in color and style. But you are return customers, and I trust you will continue to come to us first for all of your armor needs," he paused, waiting for Adelaide's agreement. "So, I will let you *steal* this set from me for these gems and one hundred gold pieces."

Adelaide sighed. While this offer did not sound much better than the first one, she needed this armor with the symbol of her home. "Deal," she said, trying not to sound too excited. She counted out the additional gold and picked up the armor. Without even walking away from the dwarves' stall, she pulled off her old leather armor and hung it on her pack. She strapped the shield to her pack as well, and donned the breastplate, letting her fingertips trace the outline of the eagle embossed on the chest.

"Thank you for your patronage, and stay safe out there," Harfall said in Dwarvish as Adelaide shouldered her pack again. The adventurers said goodbye and took off weaving through the maze in search of an exit.

"Did you catch what they said at the end there?" Adelaide whispered to Valduin as they walked away.

"I recognized it as Undercommon," Valduin replied, "but they were whispering, so I could not really hear what they were saying."

"Ah well," Adelaide shrugged. "I think the deal was reasonable. This armor is amazing! I can't wait to walk through Westray in this gear. It will definitely turn some heads!"

After a couple of turns, Rose spotted a row of small carts lined up with several halflings sitting in front of them, calling out to passersby to inspect their wares. As this was the first time Rose had seen halflings since leaving home, and as she had never met halflings from anywhere outside the Mossy Hills, she darted through the crowd toward them. Adelaide and Valduin were left trying to force their way through the steady current of shoppers, as they had much more trouble navigating the traffic than the nimble cleric.

Rose reached the carts and greeted the merchants in Halfling, *"Hello! Greetings from the Mossy Hills. Where are you all from? Did you come here with the caravan?"*

One of the merchants walked over to Rose. She was an older, but not elderly, halfling, maybe just past one hundred years of age. She was wearing clothes made for cold weather that Rose was not familiar with, and her gray hair was pulled back into a single long braid. She was wearing a leather headband with beads and feathers in it. *"Greetings, daughter. Yes, we travel with the caravan from the mountains. Biastal, our village, is at the base of the Sandgate Mountains, close to the main road. We join the caravan as it leaves Westray each year to sell our crafts here and in Alomere."*

"Is the caravan always so crazy?" Rose asked. "It seems like a lot of fun! There are lots more people here than the last time we were in the city."

"Actually, the mood was different this year," the merchant replied with a stern look. "More somber. We do not go to Westray, but it sounds like things are strange there, and it looks like it too. The state coach of Westray no longer bears the symbol of the Line of Marin. And it is guarded by giants. Evil, two-headed monsters that never sleep so as to keep a constant watch on the coach."

"Whoa, that sounds terrible! Did the giants come into Tarsam?"

"I'm not sure. We stayed far from that part of the caravan. A bunch of halflings wouldn't want to find themselves underfoot of a giant! Anyway, to business. Do you see something you like? I'm sure we have something here for you," the merchant opened her arms toward the tables and carts around her.

Rose took a moment to look over the crafts for sale. The tables were covered with leather and bone jewelry, beaded pouches and satchels, and halfling-sized accessories like gloves and belts. After a moment, Rose picked out a small brooch bearing the rising sun that was the symbol of Selaia and two braided leather headbands similar to the one the merchant was wearing. The headbands each had a cluster of bone beads threaded onto them, and one had three long feathers attached.

"What kind of feathers are these?" Rose asked the merchant as she picked up the headbands.

"Those are from the wing of a mountain eagle," the woman replied. "The bones on the headbands also come from the eagles, but the brooch comes from the antler of an elk."

Rose smiled as she looked at the items. *"These are perfect. How much for them?"*

The merchant considered Rose for a second, her eyes moving from the shining chain mail to the mace on her belt to the golden amulet of Selaia around her neck. *"For you, one gold piece will be just fine."*

"Deal!" Rose exclaimed. She pulled out a gold piece, laid it on the table, and picked up her purchases. Valduin and Rose emerged from the crowd as she turned around.

"You snuck away pretty quickly, there," Adelaide said with a hint of annoyance. Rose did not seem to catch her tone. She held up one of the headbands.

"This is for you!" Rose said with a warm smile. "It is made with the bones and feathers of an eagle, so it goes with your new armor."

Adelaide looked down at the halfling in stunned silence.

"Are you sure?" she asked once she had collected herself.

"Of course!" Rose replied. "I have a matching one for me, only without the feathers because they would be ridiculously long coming off my head. Kneel down and I'll put it on you. You kind of need to braid it in at the back."

Struck by this act of kindness from her new friend, Adelaide did as she was told. She sat down on her pack to the side of the halfling carts. Rose braided the headband together at the back of Adelaide's head so that the three eagle feathers hung behind her left ear. Rose then stood in front of Adelaide so she could do the same with the other headband. Adelaide stood up when she was finished, an absentminded smile on her face as she ran her fingers over the feathers in her hair.

"Very cute," Valduin snarked. "Can we go now? I would like to get back to The Tin Dragon so we can use those rooms we paid for."

Rose laughed at his impatience. "Don't worry, silly; I got you something too." She grabbed the front of Valduin's armor and pulled him down to her height. On the cloak that he wore over his armor, she attached the bone brooch with the symbol of Selaia. She released him to stand up and said, "Now the Watchful Mother can watch over you all the time."

Valduin inspected the brooch for a moment. "Thank you," he said, the attitude gone from his voice. "I hope it works."

The adventurers worked their way out of the city and back to The Tin Dragon, arriving as the sun set. Naressi greeted them from her spot behind the bar. The crowd was even more raucous than the night before, and Valduin was glad they still had rooms reserved. Retiring to their rooms, they fell asleep to the murmur of voices drifting up through the floorboards, thinking of their next foray into the Virdes Forest.

"How's your AC now with the new gear?" Logan asked Madison. "It should be much better."

"Sure is," Madison replied as she inspected her character sheet. "The only problem is I can't swing this battleaxe with two hands if I am using the shield, right? I guess I'll have to sacrifice the damage until we find some +3 mithral half-plate armor, and then I will ditch the shield," she added with a smile.

"Yeah, never gonna happen," Amelia rolled her eyes.

"The gifts were really cute, Amelia," Madison said. "Had you already thought those up?"

"I added the eagle feather thing after you got the eagle armor. And I didn't think Logan needed a headband. The holy symbol was the best I could figure for him," Amelia replied with a shrug.

"Well, I'm ready to use some of these new spells for more than pranking you two. Let's head back to the forest. We've got a quest!" Logan's eyes shone with excitement

"Oh, I forgot to get rope!" Madison cried. "Can we just say I picked up two more coils of hempen rope? I don't want to have to roleplay it; even I'm tired of shopping now."

20

The morning came, and Adelaide found herself dragging Rose out of bed again. "Come on, Rose," she implored. "Let's get going. I want to get downstairs before Naressi stops serving breakfast." She thought for a moment before adding, "Maybe she'll make us some more of those breakfast rolls we got yesterday."

"Mmmm, breakfast," Rose groaned. She rolled toward Adelaide and sat up. "Let's do it." She dragged herself out of bed and started collecting her gear. Pulling her new headband up at least got her tangled mass of hair out of her eyes, though she made no further effort to tame her unruly locks.

Adelaide swung open their door to find Valduin standing in the hallway with his back against the opposite wall, studying the book they had recovered from Galien's tomb. After she and Rose stepped out of their room, Valduin held up his hand, and to Adelaide's surprise, an identical hand, though slightly transparent, reached out from the end of Valduin's arm, between the two women, and closed the door behind them.

"Another new trick?" Rose asked. She swiped at the hand where it hung in the air in front of the door.

"Actually, no," Valduin replied as he got to his feet. "I just had not really thought about using it yet. But after watching Seer Brixim use it for pretty much everything yesterday, I thought I would give it a try."

"You get breakfast yet?" Adelaide asked, unimpressed by the display of magic.

"I went down to ask Naressi for some more of those breakfast rolls she made yesterday. She said they would be ready whenever we came down. Turns out she has sold them to a few other patrons already. They seem to be a hit," Valduin said as he smiled at Rose.

"I'm sure they are!" Rose said with a grin. "It's the only breakfast I'm ever interested in."

The party trouped down the stairs, picked up their breakfast sandwiches from the bar, and bid their hostess farewell.

"You all come back whenever you like. I'll always have rooms for the visionary chef and her friends," Naressi said as she winked at Rose.

Back on the road, the adventurers headed north. After a few hours, the forest came into view, and Rose broke the comfortable silence. "Okay, is there any way we can make this trip faster? You said we have to go all the way to where the river comes out of the mountains. We know it's almost two days of travel north from here to the river. We also know that near the river is where we got very lucky, and Venez had to save us from an army of goblinoids. Maybe we can head west first, and then northwest? At least put in one day of travel outside the forest that might get us farther along. If we reach the mountains first, we head north until we find the river. If we hit the river first, then we can follow it to the mountains. I'm just worried that too much time near such a major landmark as the river will increase the chances we run into more enemies."

"I think that's a great idea," Adelaide agreed. "Let's head west right along the edge of the forest for a day or two. The travel should be easier, and hopefully, it will be less dangerous."

Valduin winced before agreeing, "Oh, well I guess so. I was kind of excited to get to see the Valnear Viaduct. But this makes sense. Every time we are in the forest we get into trouble. We can minimize the time we spend there on this trip."

For the rest of the day's travel, the party headed west along the edge of the forest. At first, they passed through farmland that had been cultivated to the boundary of the forest, but farther from the Virdes Crossway, the land became wilder. As the sun sank behind the mountains ahead of them and darkness began to fall, Rose moved to match step with Adelaide.

"Do you get the feeling that we are being watched?" Rose murmured, trying not to change her posture or pace as they walked. "Don't look closely yet, but I'm pretty sure there has been something following us just beyond the tree line."

Adelaide did the best she could to discreetly inspect the deepening shadows within the forest but to no avail. She fell back from her friends as if taking a watch duty to justify a more thorough inspection of the forest.

After a few minutes, Adelaide returned to Rose's side. "I don't see anything," she said. "Are you sure there's something in there? Or maybe it's just getting a little too dark for my eyes."

Rose, still concerned by what she had noticed, considered their options. When she spoke up, she made sure that Valduin could hear her too. "It's getting dark. We've made a lot of progress today. Maybe it's time to make camp."

Valduin led them through the dark away from the woods until they found a small ring of trees where they could collect some firewood. As they settled down for the night within the copse, Rose kept a wary eye toward the forest. She did not see anything else suspicious over the course of the evening, so she laid out her armor on the ground and fell asleep.

"You okay with the first watch?" Adelaide asked Valduin. "I'm pretty wrecked."

"Of course. Go to sleep. I'll see you in a few hours." Valduin sat against a tree and took out his spellbook, sitting with it in his lap as he used his mage hand to add a few small branches to the campfire.

The minutes ticked by in the quiet darkness. Valduin thought about how Adelaide liked to take her watch from up in a tree. Looking at the trees around him, the lowest branch he could see was almost ten feet off the ground. He glanced at his companions to make sure they were sleeping, and then he took a run at the tree. He planted one foot on the trunk and tried to push himself up to that lowest branch. Unfortunately, the bark on the trunk of the tree crumbled under his weight, and instead of catching the branch and swinging up into the tree as he had planned, he ended up face-planting against the trunk and sliding on his stomach down to the ground.

He rolled away from the tree, holding his bleeding nose and aching forehead. He glanced over to make sure neither Rose nor Adelaide had seen him. There was no movement nor laughter from the fireside, so he guessed they were still asleep. He shuffled back to the tree he had been leaning against, and his watch ended—otherwise uneventfully—a couple of hours later.

"What happened to your face?" Rose asked in horror as Valduin woke her up for her watch.

"What are you talking about?" Valduin mumbled, trying to cover his forehead while pretending to feel for whatever Rose had noticed.

"Forget it," Rose replied with a curious half-smile. "Go to sleep. See you in the morning."

Valduin lay down and watched as Rose shuffled over and sat down against another tree near the edge of the campfire's light. He rolled over and drifted off to sleep.

Rose was convinced that she had seen something following them from the cover of the forest earlier. She had no trouble keeping a keen eye and ear out for any sign of danger from the darkness around her. With the exception of the fluttering of an occasional bat, her watch passed without incident.

As the sky was beginning to lighten in the east, Rose woke Adelaide for her watch. Once the human had gotten up, the halfling lay down next to the dwindling campfire, covered her head with her blanket, and fell back to sleep.

Adelaide took in her options, and then she leapt up to the same branch that Valduin had tried to grab hours earlier. Without any trouble, she swung herself up on top of it and climbed higher into the tree to find a comfortable spot from which to keep watch.

The ranger settled in and began cleaning her handaxes. After a while, she dropped lower in the tree to survey their surroundings. Peering into the early morning fog, she caught sight of a flicker of movement at the edge of the range of the campfire's light. Focusing on that movement, she heard light footsteps in the grass surrounding the ring of trees where they had made camp.

She dropped out of the tree as quietly as she could and grabbed Fiend's Lament from the side of her pack. She snuck to the edge of the trees and paused to locate the source of the sound. About sixty feet from where she stood, she could just make out a humanoid form alone in the darkness. She hid behind a tree and watched for a few moments, but the figure did not move. With her battleaxe in hand, she snuck out of the ring of trees and headed in a wide arc toward the figure. Closer and closer she stalked until she was within twenty feet of her target. Now, with the coming dawn behind her, she could make out the features of the silent figure.

There stood a man. He appeared to be human, with straight, brown hair that fell to the shoulder. He was not wearing armor, and he did not appear to be armed. He stood in the grass facing the forest, which was just coming into view in the early morning light.

While reassured by the apparent absence of armor and weapons, Adelaide was still suspicious. She straightened up and approached the man, keeping her weapon at the ready.

"Who are you?" she asked, and, without waiting for an answer, she continued, "Why were you sneaking up on us?"

"Oh, hello," he said. He sounded surprised. "Sneaking up on you? It would appear you were sneaking up on me." He flashed her a wide smile.

Adelaide inspected the man's face, looking for signs of deception. She found him hard to read so far, but his smile was mesmerizing. She pulled her eyes away for a moment before repeating, "Who are you?" This time the tone was less of accusation and more of curiosity.

"Adelaide, Adelaide!" the man replied. "You know me. We are just the best of friends." His smile seemed to cover his entire face, and the white of his teeth locked Adelaide's focus. She could not respond to the fact that the man knew her name when he should not have. "And as friends, I have a terribly important favor to ask of you. You will probably need Valduin and Rose's help for this."

Adelaide's mouth hung open. She stared blankly at the man. He was just so handsome. She felt herself nodding her acceptance as the man continued to talk, but Adelaide was no longer in control of her body. All she knew was that this man was her very best and most trusted friend, and she had to help him with this task.

When the man had finished giving her the instructions, he winked at her, and he headed off toward the forest. Adelaide turned and headed back to the campsite to collect her belongings and her companions to complete her new mission.

"What just happened?" Amelia asked, her voice rising in fear of the recent developments. "And what is the mission? What's on that piece of paper?"

"You don't know," Logan answered for Madison. "You and I were both asleep. We have no idea anything happened."

Madison reviewed the instructions she had received from their mystery guest. Her eyebrows went up a bit as she read, so Logan guessed there was a fair bit of danger ahead of them.

"You'll find out soon enough," she said to Amelia as she folded the paper in half and tucked it behind her character sheet.

"Well, fine," Amelia huffed. "I thought you would have a better wisdom save than that." She changed tact and said, "Okay, how about we talk about Valduin's Athletics check then? Are you going to be climbing any more trees soon? Do you want my Ring of Jumping when I go to bed?"

Logan refused to be baited. "We all roll natural ones eventually."

"I won't." Amelia stuck out her tongue. "Halflings are lucky, remember?"

"Well, either way, be glad mine came when I was rolling for something stupid and not on a super important stealth check or something."

"I still think you should have taken damage for that face-plant," Amelia teased.

Logan glared at her for a moment before he said, "Okay, Madison, I'm guessing you'll be leading the way on this side quest. Where are we headed?"

Madison sighed. "You really don't want to know. This is gonna be bad."

21

Valduin awoke to the sound of clattering metal. He sat up with a start. He spun toward the sound, and he was relieved to see it was only Adelaide pulling together her gear.

"Are you in a hurry to get somewhere?" he asked as he flopped back down.

"Oh, you know, seize the day! Right?" Adelaide said with more enthusiasm than Valduin was expecting this early in the morning. He opened one eye in time to see her reaffixing her axe to her pack. Seeing her with her weapon, he sat up again.

"Any trouble last night? Did you need that for something?"

"No, no, no," Adelaide reassured him. "Just a little cleaning. I like to take care of my tools. That way, I know they will work when I need them."

Seeing that Adelaide had finished packing, Valduin dragged himself out of his bedroll. He started collecting his own gear.

Once her pack was ready, Adelaide turned to the arduous process of waking up Rose. It took a few minutes, and a fair amount of cajoling, but she got Rose on her feet and into her armor. Before long, the group was on the move again, heading west toward the Sandgate Mountains. Not long after setting out, the scenery changed again. Close to the Virdes Crossway, there had been farmland. That had given way to untamed, rolling hills the day before. Now, there were signs of civilization again as the party started cutting across more acres of farmland planted at the edge of the forest.

"Do you know where we are?" Valduin asked Adelaide. "We must be close to a town. Do you know which one?"

"If I had to guess, I'd say Hulte. There are very few towns built right up against the Virdes like this, and Hulte is the only one I can remember," Adelaide answered. "I think this would be a good time to head into the forest. We should try to enter the mountains as close to the river as we can. If we get too far west, then we may find ourselves moving through the mountains northward and missing the river's source."

"I thought we wanted to do that?" Rose interjected. "Because the evil is in the forest. Wouldn't the mountains be better?"

"No," Adelaide said, shaking her head. "We need to start moving north now. It will only be two or three more days of travel before we reach the closest mountains. And there are plenty of things to be afraid of up there, even if they aren't evil monsters from the lower planes."

"This sounds like the right plan," Valduin reassured Rose. "Adelaide knows the mountains much better than either of us. We should follow her lead."

Rose gave in, and the party turned northward, into the forest. At first, the forest appeared to be the same as the one they had traveled through on their previous forays. However, after another hour of travel, things began to change. The leaves on the trees became drained of color, despite the summer having just begun. The wind picked up, and it brought a chill with it. Many of the trees appeared blackened, withered, diseased, or dead. Rose and Adelaide found themselves catching the sight of movement in their peripheral vision, but on turning, they would see nothing but more sickly trees.

"Does anyone else feel a little creeped out?" Rose broke the uneasy silence.

"Yes, I agree," Valduin said. "Adelaide, are you sure you want to go this way? Maybe we should keep going outside the forest for another few hours."

"Yes, I'm sure," Adelaide snapped. "I'm the ranger, remember? I am leading this expedition."

Valduin spun around to look at Adelaide, his ire piqued by her sudden attitude, but, before he could reply, the forest was rocked by an explosion. Valduin watched as a mass of dirt, sticks, and dead leaves erupted off the ground around Rose, obscuring her from his sight. As Rose screamed, a sucking sound followed the explosion, and the leaves were pulled back to the ground in the same arrangement that they had been in a moment before.

Rose's scream cut short.

Rose was gone.

Rose fell through darkness.

After the explosion of leaves around her, her head filled with cackling laughter.

She had just enough time to realize that she was falling when the darkness faded to dim light below her, approaching with terrifying speed. Despite the feeling of falling, there was no momentum to her landing. She transitioned smoothly from standing in the forest to falling through a dark tunnel to lying on a dusty, wooden floor. The laughter was gone; for the moment, her ears rang with the sound of silence. She sat up at a fluttering of wings close to her ear only to slam her forehead into the wooden ceiling of whatever structure this was.

Collecting herself, she inspected her surroundings. While she first thought she might be in a prison, as she looked around she realized that this was not a cage. There were wooden boxes built into three of the walls of this small wooden building. Poking out of half of the boxes were the heads of chickens. The chickens all appeared to be sleeping, their eyes closed. Rose, still rubbing her forehead where it had hit the ceiling, crawled out of the chicken coop. She had to roll her pack through the small doorway ahead of her so it would not get stuck; even her slight halfling form had to squeeze to get out of the coop.

Standing up outside and dusting herself off, she took in her surroundings. A handful of scrawny chickens stood around the fenced-in yard of the chicken coop. They were not pecking or scratching or even walking. They were just standing, looking at her. While this would have seemed odd to Rose, she was too distracted by the rest of the scene to pay the animals any attention.

Rose stood in a quiet clearing, surrounded by the diseased forest that she had been walking through with her friends. Standing in the center of the clearing was a large, stone hut. It was only one story high, but its thatched roof stretched to a height of nearly thirty feet. The ridge of the roof was suspended between two large, petrified trees that appeared to form the chimneys at either end of the hut; one had a thin wisp of gray smoke rising from it.

Rose was starting to climb the fence to get out of the chickens' yard when the silence of the clearing was shattered by a high-pitched scream behind her. She was so startled that she fell over the fence, landing hard on the ground outside the yard. The first scream was followed by another, deeper scream, both terrified and terrifying. Rose rolled over, frantically looking for the sources of the screams, one hand reaching for her amulet as she prepared a spell to defend herself.

Valduin rushed toward the spot from which Rose had disappeared.

"Wait!" Adelaide shouted at him as she grabbed him by his pack, holding him in place. "Just wait. Let's think for a second." She kept her grip on Valduin as she carefully scanned the surrounding forest.

Valduin stopped moving, but he jerked himself free of Adelaide's grip. "Rose is gone. She disappeared right in front of us! What's your plan? Don't you want to find her?" He was seething.

"What I *want* is to not lose you to the same trap that she just walked into," Adelaide snipped back. "Where are we? Lost in the woods. This part of the forest is clearly diseased or enchanted or cursed or something. And instead of focusing on what I need to find, now we have to look for the useless cleric. I told you she was dead weight back in Tarsam. We should have sent her home then."

Valduin narrowed his eyes at Adelaide. "What do you mean? What do you need to find? What are you looking for?"

Adelaide's aggressive stance faltered. She replied, "The same thing you are. The river. The lost city. The corruption at the center of the forest. Haven't you been paying attention?"

Valduin, his suspicion of Adelaide's motives not quite allayed, refocused on the problem of the missing halfling. "Okay, fine. Rose walked into a trap. Now she is gone. Is there anything you can do to find her?"

Adelaide, happy for the distraction from Valduin's questioning, inspected the ground around the spot Rose had been standing. Using a stick, she brushed around some of the leaves that had erupted into the air and poked at the dirt she thought would have been under Rose's feet. None of it seemed out of the ordinary to her investigation.

"I don't think I can find her. There aren't any tracks. Short of jumping in there myself, I can't tell if the magic is gone or if it reset. She could be anywhere. She could be locked up under the ground; she could have been teleported somewhere around here; she could have been sent to another plane; she could be dead! I just don't know. I say we focus on what we can control, and keep moving through the forest," Adelaide said as she got back to her feet and settled her pack on her back.

Before Valduin had a chance to protest, a high-pitched scream split the air of the forest. It was followed by another, lower-pitched scream. Valduin and Adelaide looked at each other with wide eyes, and they took off through the trees in the direction of the screaming.

Lying on her back, one hand on her amulet and the other outstretched, Rose took a moment to slow her breathing. Expecting to see at least two people behind her given the two different screams that she had heard, she was surprised to find no one. The chickens continued to mill about the fenced-in yard, either deaf to the screaming or merely oblivious. The only other movement that Rose could see was a large black bird on top of the chicken coop that was looking at her with one black eye. Rose thought that it might be a raven, but it was bigger than any raven that she had ever seen.

As Rose watched, the raven hopped a little closer to her, though staying on top of the chicken coop. It cocked its head, seemingly inspecting the halfling. It opened its beak, but instead of croaking like a normal raven, a child's scream erupted from the bird's mouth.

Rose's breath quickened once again, glancing from the raven to the hut behind her and then back to the raven. She scrambled to her feet and began to run for the tree line, glancing over her shoulder at the oversized bird as she ran. The screaming had stopped, but the raven remained, perched on top of the chicken coop, watching Rose's retreat with mute curiosity.

As Rose passed out of the clearing and back into the forest, she saw Adelaide and Valduin running right for her. "Guys! Guys! I'm here!" she shouted, turning in their direction. As Adelaide approached, Rose thought she was coming for a hug. Rose opened her arms to reciprocate. She was surprised when Adelaide instead tackled the halfling to the ground, holding a hand over her mouth and staring through the trees into the clearing from which Rose had just escaped.

"Quiet!" Adelaide shushed Rose. After Rose stopped squirming, she removed her hand from the halfling's mouth. "Were you there? Were you in the hut?"

"What? No!" Rose responded in a strained whisper. "I was in the chicken coop."

"Are you okay?" Valduin asked with genuine concern. "Who was screaming?"

Rose had freed herself from Adelaide and was getting back to her feet. "I'm fine, thanks. And it was a bird screaming. A big raven."

"That is weird," Valduin replied, looking confused. "It sounded a lot like people screaming."

"Ravens can imitate sounds they've heard," Adelaide explained over her shoulder. She was crouched behind a tree, peeking into the clearing beyond. "Now will you two be quiet? There might be someone in that house."

"House?" Valduin asked as he joined Adelaide. He looked ahead for the first time. He saw the hut between the two dead trees, with its singular window on the front of the building and the wooden door standing slightly ajar.

"We've got to check it out," Adelaide said.

"I don't know," Rose, still shaken by the experience in the chicken coop, replied. "Maybe we should just keep moving. Whoever lives out here probably prefers to be left alone."

"The door is open, and it's dark inside," Adelaide rebutted. "Maybe we find something cool. Maybe we find someone who has managed to live in the woods in spite of the demons running wild in the forest. They could have useful information for us."

"I think I am with Rose on this one," Valduin said. "We are together again. We should call this a win and move on."

"You two do what you want," Adelaide replied. "I'm at least going to take a look." She crept out into the clearing, headed for the hut.

Valduin hesitated, and then he sighed. "We should not split up," he mumbled. He stuck one hand in his component pouch and put the other hand on Rose's shoulder. "*To seek, but not to find,*" he recited in Sylvan, and she became invisible again. "Quietly," he said as he took the first few steps into the clearing.

"This is a *terrible* idea," Amelia said as she held her head in her hands. "Why are we following her?"

"Rule number one," Logan grumbled.

"Fine, we aren't splitting the party," Amelia conceded. "But why do you still want to get rid of me?" She gave her sister a glare.

"I'm sorry!" Madison said. "Right now, I have one mission, and I have to do everything in my power to complete it. Even if that means leaving one or both of you behind. And I don't want to get rid of you! As soon as Rose can prove that Adelaide really needs her in order to achieve her goals, Adelaide will stop saying those things."

"I really don't like this whole 'Adelaide' versus 'Madison' distinction you keep making, but fine," Amelia said, still looking hurt. "Next chance we get, I'll make sure Rose is super helpful to Adelaide."

22

With Adelaide in the lead, Valduin in the rear, and the invisible Rose walking in between, the party crossed the clearing to the front of the hut. As they walked, Valduin and Adelaide remained focused on the hut for signs of movement. Rose's eyes, however, drifted back to the chickens. As she looked at them, one of them put its wings up on the top rail of the fence that kept them penned and pulled itself up to look at the adventurers.

As Rose considered the strange way the chicken used its wings like arms, she finally took the time to look closer at the birds. She had not thought much about their behavior or appearance earlier, as she had been focused on getting herself out of the unusual situation of being teleported into a chicken coop. Closer to the pen now, she could get a good look at their faces. While they seemed to have all of the normal parts a chicken should have, the eyes were larger than they should have been. And they were both facing forward. The one that was peeking over the fence at them had bright green irises.

They were human eyes on a chicken's face.

Rose froze, eyes locked on those of the chicken. Not able to see her invisible companion, Valduin walked into her, knocking the halfling to the ground in a clatter of heavy armor. Adelaide spun around, glaring at Valduin.

"What happened to, 'Quietly'?" she hissed.

"I cannot see her!" Valduin hissed back as he crouched down and felt around for Rose. He grabbed what felt like an arm and helped Rose to her feet.

"Sorry," Rose mumbled, and the party covered the rest of the distance to the front of the hut in relative silence. They lined up against the wall to the side of the door, and Valduin stole a glance through the window into the darkness within the building.

What he saw reminded him vaguely of Seer Brixim's magic shop, only messier and more sinister. The rafters were hung with bundles of dried herbs and flowers, but there were also small cages hanging from chains. The walls were lined with shelves, and the shelves were crammed full of boxes, books, and jars. It was difficult for Valduin to identify most of the items from his current vantage point, but he could tell at least one jar close to him contained a large rodent floating in an amber fluid. There was a fireplace at either end of the room. In one there hung a large black cauldron over a low-burning fire. The other had two low sofas sitting in front of it, but there was no fire burning there. In between the fireplaces were a few tables of varying sizes and shapes, mostly cluttered with more jars and other items that Valduin could not identify from afar.

After he ducked back down, he relayed a bit of what he had seen, and then he added, "I do not see any people or movement, but there is a fire going, so someone was here recently. The place has a magic kind of feel to it. Rose, could you check for magical things as we go in there?"

From the space between himself and Adelaide came Rose's voice. "I mean, I can, but why are we going in there at all? This place is super creepy, those chickens are extremely weird, and there is probably some kind of magic user around. Are you planning on stealing something? Because I am not on board for that."

Adelaide cut in before Valduin could respond. "Whoever lives here is probably the one that set that trap you stepped into in the woods. They are almost definitely evil; can't you feel it? Shouldn't we at least investigate?"

Rose considered this for a moment, and then she became visible again as her eyes shone with golden light. "Okay, yes, everything here feels evil. Let's take a quick look."

Valduin crept to the door, which stood open a few inches. He swung it the rest of the way open, keeping himself as far back as he could in case some sort of trap went off. He was greeted by only the slow creak of the old door on its rusted hinges. He stepped into the single, large room with Rose and Adelaide close behind.

As Rose entered the hut, she looked around to get a sense of whether there was any magic that she could detect. Her eyes grew wide. "I'm not sure if this is good or bad," she said after a second, "but pretty much everything in here is magical. Some of these things seem stronger than others, and there are all sorts of different flavors, but all magic in some way."

"Flavors?" Adelaide asked, looking at Rose.

"The magic I can see kind of has different colors, but not like red or green. It has to do with the type of magic. Some are for causing harm, others for concealing, others for preventing harm. That kind of thing," Rose tried to explain the schools of magic to Adelaide. "But pretty much everything in this room has at least a weak aura around it." Rose took a few steps forward as she continued to take in her surroundings.

Adelaide began inspecting the shelves along the wall while Valduin looked at the various tables with their variety of strange items. He was careful not to touch anything. Rose turned in place and inspected the different magical signatures she was seeing coming off the objects in the room. After a couple of minutes of searching, she turned to Valduin and said, "I think we should get out of here. There is way too much magic here for this place to be abandoned, and I'm not going to steal something if we don't know what it does or how to use it. Whoever lives here is probably too powerful for us to confront, anyway, and they won't be happy to find us in their house."

A new voice replied to Rose's concerns calmly, causing the three adventurers to freeze. "Whatever would make you say that? I am always happy to have visitors." Valduin, Rose, and Adelaide all turned toward the source of the voice. They saw that there was now a woman standing next to the cauldron. She was elven in appearance, tall and thin, with short, brown hair. She was wearing a long, gray robe and stirring the contents of the cauldron with an iron rod.

The party was speechless. They all stood and stared at the figure. No one said a word. The woman let go of the rod, which continued to stir the contents of the cauldron on its own, and she turned to face her guests. "My name is Beulah. Most people call me Granny Beulah. Is there something I can help you with?" she asked, her voice saccharine, a warm smile on her face.

Valduin summoned the courage to speak. "When we were in the forest, our friend stepped into a trap that put her into the chicken coop out there. Was that yours?"

Beulah fixed Valduin with a stern gaze, but then her face softened. "Yes, I'm afraid it was. The, uh, chickens escape their yard sometimes. I have traps like that all around the clearing so that if they wander too far, they are brought back home. The traps only work on creatures small enough to fit in the coop, but then again, your friend is quite petite. I'm sorry if one of them caught you." Valduin accepted this answer, and he looked to Adelaide in hopes that she had some way to excuse them from this situation.

Granny Beulah looked at Adelaide as well. "Is there something I can do for *you*? Something you desire?" she asked, her words more forceful than before.

"No, I think I'm okay," Adelaide muttered. "I think we had better be going now. We have the information we need. Thank you for your time." She made a beeline for the door, grabbing Rose by the collar and half-dragging her along.

Valduin looked confused at first, but he turned to follow Adelaide when the door and the shutters on the window slammed shut.

Adelaide reached the door, but she found that she could not open it, despite there being no apparent handle, latch, or lock. She pushed against it a few times, but it did not even rattle. She spun toward Beulah and drew her battleaxe.

"Oh, my!" Beulah said in feigned shock. "What is this hostility?"

To the horror of Rose and Valduin, Adelaide rushed Beulah, raising the axe as she ran. Beulah showed no sign of fear, but instead calmly reached into a pocket of her robe, gave Adelaide a taunting smile, and vanished.

Adelaide reached the cauldron and looked around wildly, but the only movement she could see was the iron rod stirring the contents of the cauldron.

"What are you doing?" Rose shouted. "Why would you attack her? We are in way over our heads here!"

Adelaide glared at Rose while she returned her battleaxe to its spot on her pack. "She started it. She locked the door."

"Started it?" Valduin repeated. His mouth hung open as he shook his head. "You attacked her in her own house. What has gotten into you?"

Adelaide averted her eyes as she finished stowing her weapon. She made for the door again but found it still locked. As she checked the window's shutters, Beulah's voice filled the room. This time, it came from above the rafters, and it sounded raspier than it had a minute before.

"I see you wield a weapon not of this world," Beulah said. "It smells like the handiwork of Taranath. Did he send you here to taunt me and rob my home?"

At the mention of Taranath, Valduin's eyes shot upward, searching out the source of the voice. Instead of the female elf he was expecting, in the darkness above the rafters, he saw a withered creature with dark purple skin and black horns. Her golden eyes glowed as she inspected the intruders. "What do you know of Taranath?" he asked.

"I know he must be growing senile if he thinks the likes of *you* could come into my home and take my possessions without me noticing!" Beulah screeched. She let out a cackling laugh.

Rose recognized the laugh; it made the hair on her arms stand up.

Valduin replied, "I know Taranath, and that is his weapon, but he did not send us here. We happened upon your home while on a different quest."

"Interesting," Beulah considered this information for a moment, meeting Valduin's gaze with narrowed eyes. "Now, human," Beulah turned her attention to Adelaide, "you've stolen from me. I don't know what you think you're going to do with it, or why you chose that particular item, but you have taken it, nonetheless. If you are interested in leaving this place, maybe we could make a deal for the item. How does that sound?"

Valduin and Rose shared an uneasy look, and they both turned to Adelaide. Rose said to her, "You stole something? Why? Maybe you can just give it back?"

But Adelaide did not meet the eyes of her companions. "What is the deal?"

Beulah smiled as she floated down from the rafters. Rose could see the sharp claws at the tips of each of her long fingers, which seemed to have too many knuckles on them. Beulah sat down on a stool behind one of the tables and considered the three adventurers. After a few painfully quiet moments, she made her offer.

"You have two items in your pocket," she began. "One cannot be used without the other, but they are still two separate magic items. Place the items on the table." Adelaide hesitated, but she then stepped forward and placed a small, brown, clay pot with a matching lid on the table. "The cost of the lid will be information about this little quest that Taranath has given you. It has been a while since I've seen the old lizard, and I'm always interested in gossip. The cost of the pot will be a favor, to be completed now, prior to the transfer of the items. Separately, the penalty for the intrusion into my home and disruption of my work will be one favor for each of you, to be completed at a time and place as I see fit to collect on this contract. In return for the future favors, today I will not be adding you to my," she paused to select the correct word, "inventory," she concluded with grim emphasis.

Valduin spoke up before Adelaide could reply. "And what would the penalty be if we chose not to complete the favors? Or if we cannot complete them?"

"If you were to break the contract willingly by refusing to perform the tasks when I present them, then your everlasting soul would be forfeit to me, and I would place your soul in my inventory until such a time that I found the appropriate buyer for it." The hag gave a wicked smile at the shock on Valduin's face. "Now, if you were to perish during an honest attempt to complete the contract as written, certain leniency may be shown on my part. We will have to see how well you do with the first favor."

"Deal," Adelaide said.

"Lovely," replied Beulah, and she let out another loud cackle that drowned out Rose's attempt to object. Valduin, Adelaide, and Rose gasped simultaneously as they felt an icy hand reaching into their chests and pulling some part of them out, sealing the contract.

"If 'Don't make a deal with a hag' isn't on the list of rules, we need to add it," Logan moaned as he banged his forehead against the table.

"Madison, what are you doing? Why are we agreeing to do favors for the wicked witch of the weird woods?" Amelia asked woefully.

"First of all, did you just make that up? Nice alliteration. Second, I'm doing what I have to do," Madison explained, waving the paper she had received after being charmed a few hours before. "I'm still charmed! It says I need to get that clay pot and lid at any cost, using force if necessary."

"Well, that's just dandy," Amelia replied. "She's probably gonna send us to steal a baby or cut off someone's hand or something else terrible. I'm a cleric! I'm Lawful Good, remember? I'm not going to be much help when we are running errands for a hag."

"Let's just focus on right now," Logan said. "We have to give her information about Taranath and do one favor. Information is easy since we really don't have much. And how bad could one favor be?"

23

Beulah placed her elbows on the table and laced her too-long fingers together. She inspected Adelaide, and then Valduin, and then Rose. After a silence long enough to make Valduin's feet itch, she began, "So, what is Taranath up to these days? Has he declared his allegiance to one of the inner planes? An upper plane, perhaps? Or is he still adrift?"

Adelaide and Rose both looked to Valduin. He reported what he knew, "I met Taranath several years ago on the Inner Plane of Light. He helped me with something, and afterward, he gave me the ability to do magic. I had not heard from him until a few days ago when he visited me in the night."

"How mysterious," Beulah mused with a wry grin, but she let him continue.

"Well, he told me that there was a strange, evil force growing deep within the Virdes Forest. A force from another plane. He thought it was focused within the ruins of Eydon. But whatever it is, it has prevented him from entering the city or seeing into the forest. He is worried about what it might be, so he sent us to collect some items. We did that, and now he has sent us west to find Eydon and destroy the evil that is growing there,"

Valduin finished with a shrug. "That's really all we know."

Beulah considered this information for a moment, peering at Valduin through narrowed eyes all the while. She muttered, seemingly to herself, "Yes, there have been whispers. Of a power growing in the Deep In-Between." Then, louder, and directed at Valduin, she said, "Many strange things have happened in these woods. Not least of all a union of goblinoids and devils. Very well. That will do. Now, for your task. There is a rather annoying beast that has been sneaking into my yard and stealing my... chickens. I would like very much for you to find this beast and make sure it won't bother us again."

Valduin gave Rose a beseeching look. She shrugged and replied, "Killing a beast doesn't sound too bad."

"This particular creature can be quite annoying," Beulah replied. "Especially if there happens to be more than one. Now, on with your task. I have work to do, and you have an agreement to keep." She stood up and returned to the cauldron. Peering into the pot, she reached up to pull a single dried flower from a bundle hanging near the mantle. She crumbled the flower between her palms and let the fragments drift into the cauldron, which began to emit a pale, purple glow. Without looking up from the cauldron, the door swung open.

"Run along, children. Granny is busy."

Valduin, Adelaide, and Rose needed no further goading. They shuffled out of the house and into the yard.

"I guess we should start near the chicken coop, then," Rose said. "These chickens creep me out. Their eyes aren't right."

"Maybe just stop looking at them?" Valduin suggested. "Okay, Adelaide. You are up for tracking a beast. Oh, and take this." Valduin opened up his spellbook, checked something, and then said in Sylvan, *"May the old power guide you,"* as he put his hand on Adelaide's shoulder. Adelaide felt the magical warmth move through her, and her vision clarified supernaturally. Everywhere she looked, tiny details jumped out at her.

"What was that?" she asked. "Because I like it."

Valduin replied, "Just a little guidance to help you track this creature. One of my new gifts from Taranath."

Adelaide inspected the grounds of the chickens' yard, the earth around it, and the fence. As she looked, she found a couple of the pickets of the fence that had been broken off. Snagged on one of the wooden fragments were a few gray hairs. There weren't clear footprints, as the ground was hard and dry, but Adelaide could see where bits of the earth had been chipped by the claws of the beast.

"I'm getting a 'big dog' vibe from this," Adelaide said as she headed toward the tree line, bringing out the Fiend's Lament as she walked. "Hope you two aren't allergic." She crept between the trees and into the woods.

Valduin looked at Rose with wide eyes. "Is she serious? Was supposed to be a joke? Or was she trying to be ironic?" He followed the ranger, shaking his head and mumbling to himself, "This is why I should do all the talking for the group."

Rose was not listening to either Adelaide or Valduin. Trying to distract herself from the sight of the chickens, she focused on the large raven which was still perched on the chicken coop. As they had walked around the yard, the bird had watched them, adjusting its perch and moving its head to keep an eye on the adventurers. When Rose realized Valduin was leaving, she ran to keep up, not liking the feeling of turning her back on the raven or the clearing.

The group stayed close together as Adelaide tracked the beast through the forest. The farther from the clearing they went, the more the forest returned to normal. The trees were green again; the air was alive with birdsong; the sun shone brighter even as the afternoon progressed. The tracks became easier to follow on the softer ground of the living forest, and Adelaide had no trouble leading the party to a small outcropping of rocks nestled between some trees on a hillside. Within the outcropping was a dark space that looked like it could lead down into a cave or tunnel.

"I think this is it," Adelaide said as she ducked behind a tree to be out of view from the outcropping. "I don't see any movement. Do either of you?"

Rose and Valduin took turns peeking out from behind the tree, but neither could see anything that would indicate their quarry was in or around the cave.

"I don't see anything," Rose said. Valduin nodded in agreement.

"Time to be sneaky again," Valduin said as he brought out the ebony wand. After concentrating for a moment, the caps of brass shimmered with arcane energy. Valduin touched Rose on the shoulder with the wand, and the energy flowed into her, turning her invisible again. The party snuck from tree to tree toward the outcropping. They arrived at the cave entrance without any sign that their passage had been noticed.

Valduin edged up to the opening of the dark cave and peered inside. Rose and Adelaide stayed behind him by a few feet, keeping eyes on the surrounding forest.

The women heard the beast approaching before either saw it. A low, rumbling growl started behind them. They turned to see the shoulders, and then the head, of a monstrous wolf cresting over the hill above the rocky outcropping. The growling paused as the wolf let out a series of menacing barks, which were answered by a howl from somewhere deeper in the woods.

Adelaide brought out her battleaxe and shield. "You're next," she said, her voice hollow as she touched the eagle feathers in her hair and focused her magical hunter's mark on the massive beast at the top of the hill.

Rose held her amulet as she said in Halfling, "*May Selaia give you the endurance of the bear, that you may carry on through all trials.*" Becoming visible again, she touched Adelaide's forearm, and the warm, golden glow of Rose's divine magic washed over the human, enhancing her vitality.

Alerted by the barking, Valduin backed away from the cave entrance to see what was coming. His face grew pale as he took in the massive form of the wolf.

The beast charged.

It headed for the human first. Adelaide stood her ground, waiting for the beast to come within range. Valduin turned to move away from the coming melee and found himself face-to-face with another hulking wolf that was rushing through the trees toward the cave. In a panic, Valduin touched the wand to his own chest and shouted, "*One and the same,*" to summon three illusory copies of himself and try to confuse the charging wolf.

He cast the spell just in time, as the large wolf that he had nearly run into lunged at him. The attack impacted one of Valduin's duplicates, causing it to disappear as soon as it had formed. With Valduin focused on the monster charging him, he did not notice the smallest wolf in the pack leaping at him. The baby wolf managed to sink its teeth into Valduin's actual leg, drawing a scream of pain from the half-elf.

The first wolf leaped down the hill in a single bound, its massive form towering over Adelaide as it lunged to bite her. She managed to deflect the attack with her shield, knocking the wolf's head to the side. Seeing an opening, she brought the axe down on the side of the beast's neck, sinking it in deeply before tearing the blade back out with a grunt.

Rose found herself looking back and forth between the huge wolves threatening her friends and the baby wolf standing near Valduin, though the pup was still taller at the shoulder than the halfling. With a pang of guilt, she ran toward the nearest tall tree, and after activating her magic ring, she leapt up to a branch twelve feet in the air. Situating herself in a place where she felt safe from the attacking dire wolves, she grabbed her amulet and prayed, *"Selaia, grant us your aid that we may bring your light to the world."* Extending her hands to her two companions, the golden glow of divine magic bolstered both of them, healing Valduin's bleeding leg and further enhancing Adelaide's endurance.

Valduin, flanked by the two wolves, disengaged from the beasts and ran back toward Adelaide, hoping to get into a place where they could help each other. "Adelaide, I don't like this," he said, panting through the pain of the bite of the young dire wolf. "There's a baby. What are we doing?"

As Adelaide turned to reply to Valduin's question, the large wolf that had attacked Valduin rammed her in the back, its teeth tearing into her shoulder and slamming her to the ground. With a scream, Adelaide rolled over and held her shield up to protect her neck and head.

Valduin looked down at his friend, who was shaking her head as if trying to clear her mind of something. She lowered the shield and looked around as if she could not remember how she got here.

The other large wolf did not appear to notice the change in her demeanor, and its teeth sank into Adelaide's leg as she lay on the ground, drawing another howl of pain from the human.

Adelaide struggled to her feet, and she dropped her shield and axe on the ground. She touched the eagle feathers in her hair, channeling her connection with nature as she spoke to the dire wolves, "I am so sorry, please stop. We didn't mean to hurt you."

The wolves broke their aggressive stance. They appeared to glance back and forth between Adelaide and each other.

"Please, believe me," Adelaide pleaded. "Please." Her hand glowed with dark green energy, and she reached out for the shoulder of the dire wolf she had attacked. The wound on its neck closed, and its bleeding stopped.

"We don't want to hurt you," Adelaide continued to beseech the large wolves. "We were forced to come here."

The dire wolf shook its head a bit, testing the now-healed wound on its neck. Again the wolves exchanged glances. The injured wolf gave a low growl that Adelaide understood to mean, "Why were you in our home?"

"We were looking for you. You took the chickens from the old woman, didn't you? She sent us to make sure you don't take any more. She wanted us to kill you," Adelaide explained.

"The chickens are easy to catch. They are good to eat. They have more meat than they look like," the wolf growled back.

"Yes, but the woman is very evil. If you go back there she will kill you."

"She is small and old," the wolf retorted. "She cannot hurt me."

"Okay, yes, she looks small and old. But she has very strong magic. You should be afraid of her," Adelaide entreated the wolves. They looked at each other, unsure of how to respond.

"I beg you," Adelaide continued, "for my sake, for your sake, for the sake of your baby. Please promise me you won't steal any more chickens from the old lady. In fact, you should never go near that house again. There are traps in the woods. Stay out of the sick part of the forest."

For the first time, the wolf that had arrived with the baby spoke up, "We can do that. The sick forest scares me. We will find another place to hunt." The other adult bowed its head in acknowledgment.

"Thank you. And again, I am so sorry I hurt you. Does it feel better now?" Adelaide asked.

"Mostly. It still hurts a bit," the wolf shook its head again to test the injury.

Adelaide turned to Rose, who was still sitting in the tree and staring at her, eyes and mouth wide open. "Rose, can you heal this one a bit more? I already used all the healing I have."

Rose, unaware of the content of the conversation Adelaide had been having, did not approach the dire wolf that stood nearly three times taller than her. From her perch in the tree, she shouted, *Feel better!* in Halfling, sending a healing word to the wolf that completed the closure of the wound on its neck.

Fully restored, the wolf bowed to Rose and then to Adelaide. "We will leave now," it growled, and the three wolves turned and walked away, disappearing into the woods.

With a heavy sigh of relief, Adelaide crumpled to the ground, her head in her hands. Rose and Valduin approached her, and Rose patted her on the shoulder, magically healing her wounds while trying to soothe the distraught human.

"I am so sorry," Adelaide said. She took her hands away from her face. She had tears in her eyes. "I couldn't help it. It was like he was in my head, and I had to do what he wanted."

"Who was in your head?" Valduin asked, growing tense and stepping away from Adelaide again.

"The man. The man that I saw while you were sleeping. He was walking around in the dark, so I went to find him. He was probably what Rose caught following us yesterday from the forest. He was not armed, so I thought he might not be bad, but then he started talking and I couldn't stop listening. All of a sudden it felt like he was my best friend, and when he asked me to do something, I felt like that was the most important thing in the world for me to do." Adelaide hung her head, sobbing, still reeling from the battle and the realization that she had been used.

Between sobs, Adelaide continued, "And now we made a deal with a witch that I don't think we can just change our mind about. We attacked these creatures that weren't even bothering us, and I don't know what happens next. When he comes back, will I have to listen to him again? Will he still be able to control me?"

"Okay, let's focus on the positives," Rose said, sitting down next to Adelaide. "First, we didn't kill the wolves. You talked them into leaving. That was amazing. Second, we will deal with the witch. It sounded like the favors will be something she asks us for in the future, so don't even worry about that right now. Third, you are the bravest person I have ever seen. You didn't even care when that massive dire wolf was charging at you. You're a beast!" Rose finished with a wide smile.

Adelaide returned it with her own half smile. She got to her feet and said, "Thanks, Rose. Okay, let's get back to Granny Beulah so we can get on with our real mission."

"So, the dude that you talked to charmed you, and now you aren't charmed anymore, right?" Amelia asked.

"Right," Madison explained. "When I took damage, I got to roll to save again, so now the charm is gone. But we still made a deal with a hag, and we are still gonna get that little magic pot."

"Was the man planning to come back to collect the pot at some point? Did he tell you?" Logan asked, suddenly more interested.

Madison reviewed the instructions she had received after she was charmed. "Actually, yes, it says he'll find me tonight to pick it up." She grinned. "Ambush?"

"Ambush," Logan agreed with a nod.

"Are you going to tell me what you saw in the cave?" Amelia changed the subject.

"Nope," Logan replied grimly. "You had your chance to look. Please don't ask again; you really don't want to know."

24

The enchanted forest surrounding Beulah's hut was even more unsettling after dark, but with Rose's light spell shining through the trees, the party had no trouble finding their way back to the clearing. The door stood open, but this time Valduin announced their presence.

"Granny Beulah? Are you home?" he called as he knocked on the rickety wooden door.

The hag croaked from inside, "Yes, I've been waiting. And watching. Come inside."

The three adventurers stepped through the door to find Beulah seated behind the same table as earlier. She glared at the party as they entered the dark hut.

"We did it," Valduin reported. "Those wolves will not bother your chickens again."

"So, tell me. How am I to know that you completed your task? That my chickens will be safe? I see no trophy of this hunt," Beulah's gaze burned into them as Valduin, Adelaide, and Rose exchanged nervous glances.

As Valduin prepared a lie for the hag, Adelaide spoke up, "I talked to them. I explained that they were not to come around here anymore. They agreed." Adelaide laid out the facts of the encounter, assuming that the hag would see through any deception.

"Well then," Beulah replied with a grimace, "we'll just see about that. If I lose even *one* more chicken to those mangy dogs, I will consider this deal broken, and you will suffer the consequences of such a violation."

She produced the small clay pot from within her robes and placed it on the table.

"The object of your desire, pretties," she said with a wicked grin. "It has been an absolute pleasure working with you, and I look forward to our further endeavors together."

Valduin stiffened. "Are those endeavors happening now? Because we kind of already have some things to do."

"Oh, no, no," Beulah reassured him. "You can go about your little errand for Taranath. I will be looking for tasks for you. I'll come to you when I'm ready to collect on our contract. And the next time you see him, do tell him I said, 'Hello.' It has been far too long since we have talked. Now, off you go! I have work to do."

Without a word, the three adventurers filed out of the hut. After taking a moment to get their bearings in the darkness, Adelaide set their heading to the northwest. Rose lit up her amulet to help them navigate the forest as Valduin took the lead.

"We need to get out of this part of the woods. Then we can make camp," Valduin said.

Rose glanced back at the chicken yard as they left the clearing. There were no chickens to be seen, but the raven remained, perched atop the coop, its head cocked so one eye was looking at her. Making eye contact with the bird, Rose put her head down and turned to follow Valduin, picking up her pace and listening for the sound of wings behind her.

As the party moved through the twisted forest around the witch's hut, Adelaide asked Valduin, "Does it worry you at all how much she seemed to know about Taranath? She is pretty clearly evil. Why would Taranath associate with her?"

"It did cross my mind," Valduin answered. "I am not sure how I feel about it yet, though. From what I remember about the Inner Plane of Light from school, there are many powerful beings from there, and not all are necessarily good. Hags are among those evil creatures from the other inner planes. So, if she is super old and super powerful, as I suspect, it is possible that she is known among other old or powerful beings from that realm, even if she is evil."

They continued in relative silence, with only the rhythmic clinking of Rose's chainmail mixing with the nocturnal soundscape of the forest. Once they had moved beyond the reach of Beulah's corruption, Valduin picked the first large clearing he found, and they made camp.

As they sat by their small fire and prepared for sleep, Rose asked the question that had been on all of their minds during the walk. "What do we do when that guy shows up tonight?"

Adelaide answered, "I'll take the first watch. You two pretend to be asleep. When he comes to collect the pot, you can jump up, and we'll attack him."

Valduin yawned. "What could possibly go wrong?" He lay down and rolled away from her.

"No sleeping," Adelaide hissed. She threw a pinecone in his direction.

"I'm not," he shot back at her. "I can see in the dark, remember? I'm just keeping an eye over here."

Rose went through her routine of taking off her armor in preparation for bed. She lay down facing the fire and focused on listening to the forest, waiting for any sign of their guest. Adelaide moved away from the campfire and sat down against a tree. She had her battleaxe across her lap and the clay pot in her pocket. She tried her best to clear her mind, but the anger she felt about what they had done while she had been under this man's influence kept creeping back in.

After an hour or so, as midnight approached, Adelaide felt a tap on her shoulder. Turning quickly, she saw nothing close to her, but about thirty feet away there was a shape standing in the darkness. Adelaide rose and walked over to the campfire to light a torch. As she was bending over to light it, she whispered to her friends, "He's here." She stood up and headed toward the man.

"Good evening, Adelaide," the man greeted her. "Were you successful?"

Adelaide did her best to give the man a pleasant smile. "Yes, I got it," she said as she pulled out the clay pot, holding it up in one hand while her other hand squeezed the torch. It was all she could do to stop herself from rushing at him and hitting him with the flaming stick.

The man took a step toward her, hand extended. Adelaide held her ground and asked, "Why couldn't you get it yourself? Why did you need me?"

The man narrowed his eyes at Adelaide. "Give me the pot," he commanded.

Now, Adelaide's smile was real. "No," she said as she placed the pot back in her pocket and drew her axe.

The man said a short phrase in a harsh language that Adelaide did not understand. Adelaide felt something reaching into her pocket. She turned toward the feeling, swinging the axe past her side to knock away whatever had tried to pickpocket her. Despite the odd angle of the attack, Fiend's Lament did its job. A tiny, devilish entity appeared out of thin air stuck to the sharp edge of the blade. It had horns and leathery wings, and a long tail with a stinger on it. Its red skin was now covered with black blood as the axe gave off the pulse of purple energy that Adelaide recognized from the battle with the quasits.

Adelaide shook the body off her weapon, then turned back to face the man. He was glaring at her with hate in his eyes. He started to raise a hand when a spark of green energy struck him in the shoulder. Radiant yellow flames erupted in the air around him as he reeled from Valduin's attack. Rose and Valduin rushed up on either side of Adelaide, facing the man.

The man regained his footing, and, standing up straight, reconsidered his options. Looking at Rose, he gave her a dazzling smile and said, "Could you take care of these two for me? I have places to be." He then unfurled two large, leathery, blood-red wings from his back and took to the air, retreating into the darkness.

Before Adelaide could say anything, she felt a wave of pain in her hip. She looked to her side and saw Rose's hand against her. Black energy was curling through Rose's fingers and into her body. Adelaide let out a scream as she clutched her flank.

"What are you doing?" Valduin shouted when he realized that Rose had attacked Adelaide. He grabbed Adelaide, who was staggering from the attack, and tried to pull her away from the halfling. Rose drew her mace and tried to hit Adelaide again, but the small weapon bounced off the human's armor.

Adelaide regained her composure and said to Valduin, "He charmed her like he did to me. We need to hurt her. That's what cleared my head earlier." She dropped her axe, stepped forward, and kicked Rose in her unarmored chest as hard as she could. The force was enough to knock Rose onto her back, where she lay still. Adelaide and Valduin stepped toward her like they were approaching a sleeping lion, ready for anything.

"Thanks," Rose groaned from the ground after she caught her breath. "I really don't like that guy."

Adelaide let out a heavy sigh. She helped Rose to her feet. "Yeah, neither do I."

Valduin was searching the trees and sky above them. "I guess he's gone. I doubt that's the last we will see of him." He went over to inspect the body of the creature that Adelaide had killed. "What is this? Rose, do you know?"

Rose hobbled forward, holding her chest. "That is definitely an imp. That is what he was talking to. He told it to grab the pot."

"You could understand that?" Valduin asked.

"You aren't the only one that speaks other languages," Rose teased. "And yes, at the temple I learned Infernal, which is the language of devils like this imp. I'm not sure what that man is, but I can tell you he isn't human."

"Yeah, I figured that out too, thanks," Adelaide said. "Right when he flew away with those big devil wings. I guess we get to keep the pot for now. I wonder what it does. Val, can you tell?" Adelaide held out the pot for Valduin to look at.

Valduin inspected the pot for a minute as they returned to the fireside. Unable to decipher any of the glyphs carved around the edge of the pot or the lid, he returned it to Adelaide. "No idea," he replied. "Can I sleep now? Today was way more stressful than I was looking for."

The party settled in, with watches and dreams haunted by devilish forms stalking them in the night.

"Any more attitude about Wisdom saving throws?" Madison asked her younger sister.

"Ugh. No. I can't believe I failed that save. I have a decent Wisdom score, *and* I'm proficient in Wisdom saves!" Amelia lamented over her character sheet.

"Did we take the body of the imp?" Logan asked, suddenly realizing it would still be there because Madison had killed it with the magic battleaxe. "We might be able to sell it to Brixim."

"I am not dragging the body of every little thing we kill all over creation," Madison replied. "I am sure we will find some gold or gems or something somewhere on this quest."

"On another note, what was in the dire wolves' cave?" Amelia prodded Logan. "Tell me, tell me, tell me! I'm not gonna let it go."

"Nope, nope, nope," Logan replied. "Please stop asking. I don't even like thinking about it."

25

The sun was well on its way to the top of the sky by the time Valduin and Adelaide dragged themselves out of their bedrolls to eat breakfast.

"Yesterday was terrible," Adelaide groaned as she sat by the remains of their fire.

"I am sure today will be no problem at all," Rose said without a hint of sarcasm, still nestled in her blanket.

"Are you planning on staying in bed all day?" Valduin asked. He was packed and ready to start moving.

"The idea did cross my mind," replied Rose. She stuck her tongue out at Valduin.

"Come on, let's go," Adelaide said, pulling Rose to her feet. A few minutes later they were packed up and on the move. Adelaide took the lead, guiding the group northward, looking for the river that would take them to the lost city of Eydon.

The three adventurers were quiet, enjoying the warm sunlight and the noises of the living forest. After a few uneventful hours, Adelaide noticed the faint sound of rushing water.

"I think that might be the river," she said. She quickened her pace by a fraction, reassured by the presence of a landmark she had been looking for all day. Before long, they emerged from the forest into the bright sunlight of the afternoon. There was a grassy slope extending sixty feet from the tree line up to a drop-off. Adelaide approached the drop-off and found herself on the edge of a cliff, almost a hundred feet above the Virdes River. Across the river, up the other side of the canyon, the forest spread to the horizon in the north.

"Well," she said as she turned back to Valduin and Rose, "step one complete." She then looked west toward the Sandgate Mountains, which were closer than she had seen them in a long time. "Step two: to the mountains."

"Should we stay up here? Or should we go down to the riverbank?" Rose asked as she peered off the edge of the cliff.

"I think we should stay up here," Adelaide replied. "On the one hand, all sorts of bad stuff could come out of the forest. On the other hand, down there we would be trapped between the water and the cliff. I like having more room to move if we get into trouble."

"Works for me," Rose agreed with a shrug.

Valduin nodded. "You are the wilderness expert. Lead the way."

For another hour, they traveled along the ridge, listening to the rush of water from below.

Without warning, Adelaide heard another sound over the noise of the river, like a single clap of thunder. Adelaide looked up, and then around, and then at Valduin and Rose.

"Did either of you hear that?" she asked.

"It sounded like thunder," Rose replied, nodding and looking to the sky in confusion. "But there are no clouds?"

The three took a minute to survey the forest to the south, the ravine, and the rest of the forest to the north. They saw no sign of any danger, so they continued their walk.

About twenty minutes later, the noise came again, closer this time, and without a doubt from the forest to their left.

"I heard *that*," Valduin said. "Was that the same as what you two heard earlier? What do you think it was?"

"That didn't sound like thunder as much," Adelaide thought out loud, "more like an explosion."

Rose and Adelaide simultaneously took their shields off their packs. Valduin drew his wand. They stood on the edge of the cliff, peering into the forest to the south of them. One minute passed. Then five. As they were starting to relax a bit, a small form burst through the tree line and headed in their direction at a full sprint.

As the figure came closer, they could see that it was a female gnome, much younger than the last gnome that they had met. She continued running toward them, and the adventurers tensed, their weapons at the ready. The gnome, however, did not appear to have noticed them. She kept looking over her shoulder at the forest.

Adelaide followed her gaze to the trees, which were about eighty feet from the cliff edge. What she saw made her heart skip a beat. Resolving through the shadows were multiple shapes. As the shapes left the shade of the trees, Adelaide could see a dozen small goblins, with a few taller goblinoids wearing full armor behind them. None of this bothered Adelaide much, but the figure that loomed behind the taller goblins made her blood run cold. It was humanoid to the extent that it had two arms and two legs, but everything else about the monster was terrifyingly alien.

Rose recognized the fiend from her reading at the temple. At least seven feet tall with a long, thick tail, most of its greenish-brown skin was covered in four-inch-long, bony spikes. This, the leader of the approaching band, was a barbed devil.

Rose was about to relay this information to the rest of the group when the gnome reached them. "Help me! Help me!" the gnome begged as she ran to the cliff and glanced down at the river below. She appeared to consider jumping, but then she turned back to Rose, Adelaide, and Valduin. "Can you help?" she asked. Before they could reply, she drew a long, thin wand from within the short coat she was wearing.

She looked first at the wand, hesitating for a moment, and then up toward the approaching band of enemies. "I hate using the last charge," she mumbled. She pointed the wand toward the pack of goblins. A single point of red light streaked through the late-afternoon air. When it reached the center of the legion of goblinoids, there was a terrific explosion. Some of the goblins tried to jump out of the way but to no avail. At best, their limp forms were flung through the air to land with sickening thuds across the field. At worst, they were completely annihilated, large parts of their bodies reduced to ash with the remaining bits scattered on the ground.

To the horror of the adventurers, the devil seemed unfazed by the explosion. It continued its steady advance to the edge of the forest. Even more horrifying, as they watched, the devil waved its arms over its head, and there appeared a burning, swirling, red portal next to it. Through the portal stepped an identical barbed devil. They appeared to confer briefly, and then they both turned toward the party.

Considering his options, Valduin spoke an incantation in Sylvan, *"One and the same,"* and his form shifted and multiplied. To an onlooker, there were now four Valduins standing close to each other. This reminded Rose of the illusion that Venez had used to protect herself when they first met. Valduin backed up to the edge of the cliff and dropped down onto his stomach, hoping to make himself as small a target as possible.

The gnome considered the cliff again, but then she turned to face the coming monsters. She put the wand back inside her vest, and instead she brought out a short rod made of purple crystal. She pointed it at the newly-summoned devil, and three glowing, white screws emerged from the tip of the rod, appearing to grow from it. The three screws darted out of the rod, corkscrewing around each other as they flew across the field and then converging on one of the devils, leaving glowing holes across its body as it grimaced in pain.

The goblinoids that avoided the fireball, one short and one tall, raced across the field toward the adventurers, drawing bows as they ran. The short one shot an arrow that flew just over Rose's head. The tall one loosed an arrow that connected with the gnome's leg, drawing a yelp of pain.

The devils had now fully emerged from the woods. They both stretched out their hands, which burst into flames. Seeming to size up their targets, they unleashed a barrage of small balls of fire at the gnome. Two of them sailed over her head. The other two looked like they would hit her. She held up one hand to protect herself and screamed a single word while wincing with the expectation of burning pain. The two balls erupted just a foot away from her hand, the flames highlighting an invisible, arcane shield that the gnome had created around herself.

Adelaide broke into a sprint, her shield and battleaxe at the ready. She reached the goblin that had been at the vanguard of the group, and she sank her weapon deep into its chest. As she put her foot on the body to wrench the axe back out, she glared at one of the barbed devils and roared, "You're next!" Her eyes glowed with dark green light as her hunter's mark targeted the devil.

Rose, unsettled by having an arrow shot at her, surveyed the remaining enemies. After a moment, she chose the devil farther from Adelaide, held out her hand, and released a bolt of golden energy. Striking the devil in the gut, its advance faltered for a moment, and it began to glow with radiant light.

Valduin saw his chance. He and his three duplicates leapt to their feet, raised their four wands, and fired a volley of pale green eldritch blasts at the now-glowing devil. Rose could not quite tell which blast was the one that actually hit the devil, but the monster reeled from the impact. Seeing his success, the Valduins dropped back to the ground.

The gnome moved forward, standing in front of Rose now. She pointed her crystal rod at a point between the large devils and the tall goblinoid with the longbow. A deafening, ringing noise erupted from that space, and all three of them grimaced in pain. Rose also saw a tiny imp fall out of thin air next to the original barbed devil. It must have been hovering, invisible, next to it. The imp pulled itself up, looked around in a panic, and became invisible again.

The hobgoblin shook its head to clear the ringing from its ears, drew an arrow in its longbow, and, without advancing any farther, loosed another shot at the gnome. Rose watched in horror as the arrow appeared to fly true, but just before it should have sunk into the gnome's chest, she again raised a hand and screamed the single word she had used to block the balls of flame. The arrow stopped dead, less than a foot from the gnome, and dropped to the ground in front of her.

The barbed devil that Valduin had targeted with his spell glared at the half-elf. Standing near the edge of the forest, its hands burst into flames again. It hurled the two fireballs toward Valduin and his duplicates, which were all still lying near the edge of the cliff. The first one flew over their heads, disappearing toward the river below. The second one connected with one of the Valduins, who vanished in a splash of flame.

With its attention drawn to Adelaide, the other barbed devil summoned two more balls of fire and targeted the human with both attacks. Adelaide was able to deflect one with her shield, but the other hit her on the hip. Adelaide let out a roar of fury as she continued her charge toward the devil.

Before the barbed devil had even finished the act of releasing its attacks, Adelaide was on it. As her battleaxe streaked through the space around the devil, the blade collected a faint, blue energy from the air. When Adelaide connected with the devil's shoulder, the blade released the energy in a burst of blue light, crushing the barbs and spikes over the shoulder of the monster.

Rose moved in the direction of Adelaide so she could be within range to assist her friend. Walking forward, she grabbed her amulet while praying in Halfling, *"When the temptation of evil touches my mind, Selaia will give me strength."* To her surprise, there was a new warmth that emanated from the amulet. Tiny motes of golden light appeared before her, and Rose was able to send them to both the gnome and Adelaide, closing some of the wounds they had suffered.

After watching one of his duplicates destroyed by the devil's attack, Valduin got to his feet again. He took a few steps toward Adelaide, but then he decided to focus on the devil back by the tree line. He threw another spark of green energy at it and went prone again.

The gnome, invigorated by Rose's healing, surveyed her options. Her purple crystal rod came up and three more screws grew from the tip. Seeing that the hobgoblin was still on its feet, she sent two of the screws toward it. As the bright white points of light sunk into their target, it dropped to the ground. She adjusted her aim to release the third screw toward the far devil, punching another glowing hole in its chest as it hit.

The devil locked in combat with Adelaide unleashed a flurry of attacks at her. Adelaide blocked one claw attack with her shield and deflected the other with the blunt side of the axehead, but with her arms spread wide in this defensive position, the fiend's tail was able to whip around and pierce her side behind the edge of the breastplate. She grimaced, but she did not give up any of her aggressive stance toward the devil.

Pushing the claws away with both arms, she brought the axe around in a wide swing, seemingly looking to decapitate the devil. The devil, however, saw this attack coming and ducked out of the way, leaving Adelaide spinning in place with the momentum of the strike. She spun nearly all the way around before she was able to regain her footing.

As Adelaide spun to the side, Rose got a clear view of the devil, and she released another bolt of golden light at it. The beam struck the devil in the chest, and it hissed as the radiant energy burned into it. The gnome, seeing the target Rose had created, held her rod up in her left fist. While muttering in Gnomish, she used her right hand to pull back from the rod, drawing an imaginary bow. Between the rod and the fingers of her right hand appeared a glowing, green arrow, and when the gnome opened her fingers, the arrow shot across the field to the devil Adelaide was fighting. The arrow collapsed into a spray of acid as it hit the devil in the face, causing it to scream out in a deep, ragged voice.

Valduin jumped to his feet and again advanced on the action, encouraged that the party now outnumbered their enemies, which had been reduced to the two barbed devils. His two remaining mirror images moved with him, continuing to weave back and forth through his space to confound any attack. He threw an eldritch blast at the far devil again, though this one sailed over its head and disappeared into the forest. The devil returned fire with two more balls of flame, one of which destroyed another illusionary Valduin. The other attack finally struck true, and Valduin gave a yelp as the fireball burst over the front of his armor.

Adelaide's devil was still trying to wipe the acid from its face. It was looking harried, and it surveyed the field through one narrowed eye. It glanced over its shoulder and shouted something in Infernal. Before Rose could process the words, the devil turned back and laid into Adelaide, who was still off-balance from her last, overly ambitious attack.

This time, both claws raked down Adelaide's back, and she screamed out in pain. She was able to avoid the tail as it whipped toward her, and she turned the momentum from her dodge into another wild swing of her axe. This attack struck true, and another burst of blue energy crushed the barbs on the flank of the devil as it momentarily lost its footing. The devil was starting to look desperate, eyeing the forest for an escape route.

Panting, Adelaide growled, "This one doesn't leave!" She adjusted the grip on her weapon and brought up her shield, preparing for another round with the much larger devil.

In a flurry of magical attacks, Rose hit the fiend with another blast of divine energy, Valduin sent an eldritch blast that soared just over its shoulder, and the gnome released a beam of blue-white light from her rod that left a ring of frost condensed on the devil's chest. The devil, battered by the onslaught and realizing it was being overwhelmed, turned and tried to reach the tree line, but the cold of the gnome's attack made its joints stiff and its retreat slow. Adelaide, determined not to allow this monster to escape, ran it down before it could reach the forest. In another flash of blue light, she planted the blade of her axe into the devil's lower back. As the monster fell forward onto the ground, the tendrils of purple energy briefly connected to Fiend's Lament as the magic of the axe absorbed the devil's essence.

The field was quiet. The party looked to the tree line where the other devil had been standing in time to see it disappear in a flash of fire. Adelaide caught her breath as she wiped the hot, black blood of the devil from her arms. Valduin stood with his remaining duplicate, surveying the carnage left by the gnome's fireball.

Rose only now realized she was standing among the scattered remains of the pack of goblins. She turned and made her way back to the cliff's edge, trying not to think about the smell of burnt flesh. The gnome was staring into the forest, eyes darting back and forth along the tree line, looking for any sign of movement.

"Well, that was interesting," Valduin commented, walking up to the gnome as his final mirror image disappeared. "So, who are you? And what did you do to get all of them angry?"

The gnome pulled her eyes away from the forest and looked up at Valduin. "I'm Nyla. And I sort of attacked them. Thanks for all of your help, by the way." She looked at Adelaide, who was approaching them. "You were amazing! You just got in that devil's face. That was awesome!" The gnome mimicked Adelaide swinging her axe at an imaginary foe.

"Thanks," Adelaide said with a surprised smile. "Do you want to stay with us for a while? We were probably going to be making camp soon. Then we can chat?"

The gnome hesitated. "I'm supposed to be getting home." She looked up at the mountain range on the horizon; she seemed concerned. "But I don't think I'll be able to get there before tonight. I came a long way east today. Being hunted by an army of devils and goblins was not part of my plan. If it really is okay, I would love to stay the night wherever you are going. Then I can head back to Bisolone tomorrow."

"Sounds fine to me," Valduin agreed. "We should head west for another hour or two to get away from all of this, uh, evidence. Then we can make camp."

With their new companion, the adventurers pushed on toward the setting sun, keeping an eye on the forest for signs of movement. Before long, darkness had come, and they made camp on the edge of the forest for the night.

"Level four! And no one went unconscious!" Amelia cried. "I guess healing you before you hit zero hit points works better than waiting for you to go down."

"You're getting the hang of the cleric thing," Logan added with a smile.

"Why did you spend that entire battle laying on the ground, though?" Amelia asked her brother.

"Their ranged attacks are at disadvantage when I'm prone. As long as they can't get close enough to make melee attacks on me, it's better if I'm prone and just get up to shoot my eldritch blasts on my turn," he explained.

"Okay, but you look kind of silly laying down all the time," Amelia said with a giggle.

"Yeah," Madison added. She did not sound amused by Logan's tactics. "I'm in the thick of things, getting wailed on by a devil and doing all the work, and you are lounging in the grass."

"I am the caster. I am most useful at long range. You are the tank. That's how this team works." Logan sighed. "Wait, did we loot the bodies?"

"Ugh, no! I just wanted to get out of there," Madison face-palmed dramatically. "Let's just focus on getting information from the gnome, and remember to loot next time."

"And leveling up," Amelia pointed out. "Don't want to forget to do that. Oh, and why were you saying your axe was glowing blue when you hit the devil? Rose didn't get a chance to ask."

"That's my Might of the Peacekeeper ability. I get to add some damage when I attack creatures from different planes than me," Madison explained as she looked back at her character sheet. "My subclass doesn't give me anything else until level seven," she added.

"Better than nothing," Amelia replied. "I don't get to add extra damage until level eight. Just a tiny bit of extra healing before that."

26

"So, Nyla," Valduin asked the question that they had all been thinking as the party settled in around the campfire. "What in the world did you do?"

Before Nyla began her story, she thought for a moment. "Well, what do you know about gnomes?" she asked.

"I think the first time that any of us met a gnome was just a few days ago," Valduin said. Adelaide and Rose nodded in agreement. "So, not very much, I guess."

"Well, in this area, there is really only one gnome settlement, Bisolone. That's where I am from. It's in the mountains, but I'm not really supposed to say much more about the location to outsiders. Anyway, for a long time—like for generations—we have lived there. We are mostly self-sufficient, but we occasionally have some trade with the dwarves in Khal Durum and the humans in Westray. Our leaders have been friendly with the rulers of both of those cities. However, things have been strange recently. I'm not involved with those things, but from what I heard, our trade hasn't been welcome in either city for the past few months," Nyla explained. She then pointed at Adelaide's armor. "Are you a soldier of Westray?"

Adelaide ran her fingers over the emblem on the front of her armor. "No, not a soldier. I was born and raised there, though."

"You know, the halfling in the market in Tarsam said something about Westray, too," Rose recounted. "She said that there were two-headed giants guarding the official Westray coach at the front of the caravan."

Adelaide sat up at the mention of giants. "Two-headed giants? Ettins guarding the leaders of Westray? That doesn't make any sense at all; everyone in Westray hates giants. They are constantly pestering the city and the surrounding villages."

"Well, that's what the halfling said," Rose said, getting defensive. "She said that things in the caravan were a little weird this year and that there were giants with them."

"Very weird," Adelaide muttered. She withdrew into her own thoughts.

"Anyway," Nyla continued, "most of us don't know much about the goings on outside of Bisolone. There are only a few merchants that make contact with outsiders. The rest of us are just fine living and working in the city. We grow plenty of food and can mine our own materials for building and enchanting."

"Enchanting?" Valduin perked up. "Are you an enchanter? Did you make that wand you used to blow up all of those goblins?"

"All gnomes like to build things. Some have magic abilities, so they are usually enchanters. I have started to make a few of my own items, but I am not powerful enough to make a wand of fireballs yet." She pulled the thin wand out of her coat again. "This was made for me by my great-grandfather, Brixim. I'm just glad it didn't disintegrate when I used its last charge today. Brixim would have been so mad if he had to make another one."

"Brixim? Like, Seer Brixim? In Tarsam?" Rose asked, recognizing the name.

"Yes, that's him! Have you met him? He's really good at making magic items. Most of the ones I make don't end up working."

"He is the gnome that we met a few days ago," Valduin explained. "At his shop. He traded me this wand," Valduin showed Nyla the wand of recovery.

Nyla smiled. "I thought I recognized that one. He picked that up in Khal Durum last year. I'm not sure who enchanted it, but he seemed pretty excited when he bought it. You must have had something very interesting to trade for him to give that up."

Valduin and Adelaide looked at each other. "It was a good trade," Adelaide admitted.

"Okay, back to the story," Nyla refocused. "So, gnomes live in Bisolone, mostly indifferent to and unaware of the goings-on of the other cities in the Sandgate Mountains. Then comes along this guy. He looks human, and he manages to talk his way into a meeting with the city council. There are some very old gnomes there, and they aren't easy to persuade or intimidate. One of them apparently was able to see that the human appearance was a disguise, and dispelled it, revealing a fiend of some kind. Despite their attempts to capture it, it was able to escape.

"A few days later, an army of kobolds, along with some goblinoids and a bunch of fiendish creatures, attacked the city from below. For completeness's sake, I'll inform you that gnomes and kobolds hate, hate, *hate* each other. We have forever. Apparently, some kobolds tunneled into our mines, allowing access to the unguarded center of the city. They killed hundreds of gnomes.

"This is where I came in. A few other gnomes and I tracked the kobolds as they retreated, trying to find where they came from. We were able to follow them out into the open and over to the river near the old elf city. They must have been a few hundred strong, and they had a sort of camp set up in the canyon at the base of the waterfall. We attacked them in the canyon and killed many, if not most, of them. Of the ones that were left, a hundred or so chased us as we tried to get back to Bisolone. I went through my entire wand of fireballs as we ran. I'm not sure where the rest of my group is, but I'm hoping that I was enough of a distraction for them to get back to Bisolone."

As Nyla finished, she sat back and stared into the fire. There were tears in her eyes, and her hands were clenched into fists. Rose, being about the same size as Nyla, scooted over next to her and put an arm around her shoulders. Nyla did not look at Rose, but she did not resist as Rose hugged her.

"You did all you could," Rose reassured Nyla. "And I'm pretty sure we met this fiend you mentioned. We are headed to the old elf city, and we are going to destroy the evil there. For what that devil did to us, and for what he did to your people."

Nyla said nothing. She closed her eyes as the tears started to roll down her cheeks, and she rested her head on Rose's shoulder.

Trying to be as tactful as possible, Valduin asked, "Do you know what he wanted? Or why they attacked? It might help us figure out what he is doing."

Nyla sniffed, wiped the tears from her cheeks, and sat upright again. "I don't know what he said when he met with the council, but it sounds like the attackers stole a lot of stuff in addition to killing gnomes. Most of the private workshops are built deep in the city to be near the mines and the forges so they can acquire materials. From what I heard, the kobolds took all the diamonds they could find and anything that looked magical from the nearby workshops. I don't know if there were particular enchantments that they wanted, but they took a lot of items."

"Thank you, Nyla," Valduin said. "This is helpful. Did you happen to hear the name Azereth at all? That's who we heard was collecting diamonds."

Nyla thought for a second. "You know what, I think I did. After the devil met with the elder council, but before the attack, the rumors said that the meeting had something to do with someone called Azereth demanding our allegiance or assistance. Different rumors said different things about the exact demands, but that name came up a few times. The other name that I heard was Voidbringer. Do you think those are names for that devil?"

"They could be," Valduin said. "We heard about Azereth from some kobolds recently. I have never heard that other name before, though." Valduin paused for a moment, brow furrowed. "And what is with the diamonds? What we heard was Azereth did not care about any other gems. Just diamonds."

"Well, diamonds are valuable," Nyla replied with a shrug. "They can be used as currency in places where even coin isn't used. And they are useful spell components. Many of the strongest spells require diamonds."

"That devil we just fought was talking about an Azereth, too," Rose said in a matter-of-fact way that surprised Valduin.

"When were you talking to that devil?" Valduin asked. "All we did was fight it."

"Well, right before it tried to run, it shouted out in Infernal, 'Tell Azereth we couldn't stop them.' I'm guessing it was talking to the invisible imp," Rose recalled the final few moments from the battle. "I hope he doesn't put together that it was us that killed his army."

"I guess we will find out soon enough," Valduin muttered, deep in thought. "You all sleep; I will take the first watch."

The night passed uneventfully as Valduin, and then Adelaide, and then Rose took watches. In the morning, the group packed up their camp and prepared to continue on their way.

"Nyla, I had one more question," Adelaide said. "You said you killed hundreds of creatures yesterday. How did you do that?"

Nyla was quiet for a moment, and she then replied, "We were really angry. They had killed so many gnomes. I didn't think twice about retaliating in kind. Maybe one day that will weigh on me. But not today."

Rose gave Nyla another side hug at this display of insight. Then Adelaide followed up, "I can understand that. But what I meant was, what did you use? Spells? That wand of fireballs? Just in case we find ourselves in a similar situation."

"Oh, that," Nyla said. She smiled. "We used these." She produced a small, metallic object from the inside of her coat. It was oblong and just a few inches long; it fit in the palm of Nyla's small hand. There were runic engravings across its surface, and as Nyla spun it between her fingers the runes seemed to swirl and change at her touch. "This is one of the gnomes' secret weapons. They take a while to build and enchant, but they pack a

punch, especially on large groups crowded together."
She tucked the object back inside her coat and stood up,
shouldering the small pack that she had with her.

"Ah, got it," Adelaide replied, though she did not really understand what she had just seen.

"Where will you go?" Valduin asked. "You could come
with us. We plan to destroy whatever fiendish presence
we find within Eydon, whether that's Azereth, the Voidbringer, or something else. We could definitely use your
talents."

Nyla considered this for a moment before replying, "I
need to get home. I need to find my friends if they're still
alive. I need to help fortify and defend Bisolone. Good
luck to you all. I hope you are successful and safe."

"Thank you, Nyla," Rose said. "I hope your friends are
safe. I am sure we will see you again. If you talk to him,
tell Brixim we say 'Hello!'"

"I will," Nyla replied with a warm smile. She put her
hand on her chest as she cast a spell, causing the air
around her to shimmer with arcane force that created
the image of plates of armor around the gnome. She
turned toward the forest and took off at a jog, disappearing between the trees.

"She was nice!" Rose commented, at which point Valduin realized Rose was getting back into her bedroll.

"Rose, it's time to start moving!" he said as he pulled
the blanket off her. She groaned, but she got up and
started packing her gear.

Adelaide looked west, toward the Sandgate
Mountains. "We should reach the mountains today,
hopefully before dark. Then we will see what kind of
damage Nyla and her friends were able to do."

Once they had packed up and covered the remains of
their campfire, the party headed west along the ridge

that followed the river. The day was overcast. The travel was easy, though Rose kept a wary eye on the tree line as Adelaide guided them forward.

"Okay, so what do we know?" Rose asked, to neither of her companions in particular. "There is this devil guy, probably the same one that charmed Adelaide, that also showed up in the gnome city. Is he Azereth? Is he the Voidbringer? What was he trying to do? Demand their loyalty? Their help? They stole magic items and diamonds. You said you had heard about diamonds before?"

"Yes, from the kobolds," Valduin recounted. "After we left your temple, I got one of them talking. He let slip that they were mining for diamonds for Azereth. He also indicated that Azereth was not a kobold. Maybe that is the devil's name. It sounds like a devil's name. Maybe Voidbringer is what people call him. Sounds scary enough to be a nickname. I am not sure, and I do not know why they need diamonds so badly."

"Well, Nyla had some good ideas," Rose remembered. "They could be using them as money to pay for something or they could be using them as spell components. Or both. Or neither. Maybe they are planning on opening a jewelry store."

Adelaide laughed at this suggestion. "Honestly, the only thing that I am thinking about with the diamonds is that we need to find some. Even a small box of diamonds would be a nice haul on this quest. Maybe then we would be able to actually go shopping at The Lamia's Lair. Last time, it felt very much like Brixim was the one shopping, and we were just along for the ride."

"And maybe if Nyla tells him how we helped save her life, he will give us a discount!" Valduin said, suddenly realizing the connection.

"Oh great, more shopping." Rose hung her head.

The day passed quietly. As they walked, the river sunk below the cliff edge. The gorge widened into a narrow canyon as they approached the first slopes of the Sandgate Mountains. By midafternoon, the forest had receded from their left, and they had fully entered the mountains. Adelaide, who grew up in these mountains, was now navigating her favorite terrain, and she had no trouble guiding the group farther along the ridge of the canyon. The canyon had grown, and it was now about a hundred feet deep, over a hundred feet wide at the top, and nearly a hundred feet wide at the bottom.

Finally, just as dusk was approaching, they saw the waterfall. Hundreds of feet high, the waterfall filled the entire canyon with mist, and the reddish-brown stone of the canyon walls was slick with condensation. At the base of the canyon, the waterfall fell into a pool that narrowed to form the Virdes River as it stretched eastward.

Looking up, the waterfall's source was obscured. From their vantage, it appeared to emerge directly from the side of one of the mountains. This was a surprise; Adelaide would have expected it to come between the peaks. She did not take long to ponder this, though, for her attention was drawn to the floor of the canyon.

On the north side of the pool, the water spread right up to the sheer cliff wall. But on the southern side, there was a space of about sixty feet from the edge of the pool to the wall of the canyon, extending for a couple of hundred feet from the base of the waterfall. In this space were the remains of a war camp.

"I guess this is where Nyla caught up with them," Valduin said, his voice hushed in awe of the destruction below them. "She wasn't kidding. They demolished it."

Dozens of tents and small wooden buildings lay in ruins. Similar to the carnage they observed after Nyla's fireball hit the pack of goblins, they could see bodies, and body parts, strewn all across the area. There was even a section of the canyon wall that had collapsed in the attack, and a large part of the canyon floor was covered in the resulting rockslide.

"There's something moving down there," Adelaide said as they were trying to make sense of everything they were seeing. Looking where Adelaide was pointing, Rose could see three strange creatures that appeared to be picking through the destruction. "What do you think those things are? And what are they doing?"

Valduin spoke up first, "Well, I think they are either collecting things from the bodies, or possibly collecting the bodies themselves. I really don't want to think about what they might want the bodies for. But they don't look like any creature that I've ever seen or read about."

Rose inspected the closest one. She saw a creature with two arms, two legs, and a body covered in black, armored plates. It had long, oily black hair that hung from all around the top of its head, obscuring its face. It held a short, hooked blade of some kind that it was using to pull through the wreckage of one of the demolished wooden buildings, though with all of the hair in its face Rose was unsure how it could see what it was doing. Thinking through all of the books of monsters she had studied at the temple, this one was familiar.

"It's a drengarn," she said as she finally remembered the word.

"A what-yarn?" Adelaide asked.

"Drengarn. They are fiends, like devils and demons, but they come from different lower planes," Rose stopped talking and twisted her mouth in confusion.

"Everything okay?" Valduin asked, concerned.

"Yeah, I just need to think about some things," Rose finally said. "For now, I think we should make camp. It's almost night, and those things can probably see in the dark. Adelaide, can you find us a place to hide for the night up here?"

"Absolutely," Adelaide replied, surveying the mountainside above them. "This is my home turf. Come on." She led them up the slope. Before long, the party found a small, recessed area in the mountain, barely deep enough to be called a cave. They skipped the fire this night, which passed quietly except for the constant drone of the waterfall from far below them.

"Lore dump!" Logan exclaimed, studying his notes on their conversation with Nyla.

"Okay, so the diamonds and the names Azereth and Voidbringer are all important," Madison said. "I really hope we can steal some of those diamonds."

"Me too," Amelia said. "Rose needs some earrings and a necklace and maybe a couple bracelets and definitely some rings."

Madison laughed. "Why do you think they attacked the gnomes, Amelia?"

"I don't know, I kind of stopped listening at that point. Logan was taking notes."

"I can't be the only one taking notes!" Logan exclaimed. "Rule number ten: write that down. Madison, aren't you taking notes? I see you writing in your notebook."

Madison held up her notebook. "Uh, I'm mostly drawing monsters. And now I'm starting on Rose and Adelaide with lots of diamond jewelry." She smiled as Logan dropped his forehead onto the table.

27

By the next morning, the rain had started. Not heavy enough to obscure their vision, but steady enough to make the party reconsider heading out into it.

"Can we just stay here today?" Rose asked from the warmth of her bedroll. "That lost city isn't going anywhere."

"We need to keep moving," Valduin replied, his gear already packed. "After Nyla and the gnomes destroyed their army, we cannot know what they will do next. They may change their plans if they think their location has been discovered. We need to stop them here and now."

"Fine," she moaned, still not making any attempt to get up. "But do we even know who 'they' are yet?"

"No," Valduin answered. "But it's obvious they are evil and probably fiendish. Nothing good comes from the lower planes, and we have now seen creatures from several of those planes, have we not? Would you be so kind as to shine the light of Selaia into this dark place?"

Rose rolled over enough to glare at Valduin for his patronizing remark. "Fine. Let's get wet," she finally huffed and got out from under her blanket.

Adelaide stepped back into the cave from where she had been peering down toward the waterfall. "I can't see anything moving from here," she reported. "Let's try to get past the wreckage before anyone comes out from the city."

The party made their way down the slope to the edge of the cliff where they had first seen the war camp. The only thing about the scene that had changed in the night was that there was no movement visible. Adelaide studied the edge of the cliff, looking for a place to descend. After a minute or two, she found a rock to affix some rope to, and she set up to rappel down the cliff.

"I'm glad I got two lengths of rope when we went shopping," she remarked as she eyeballed the distance to the bottom of the cliff. She tied the two ropes together. "We would have had quite the jump to make from only one fifty-foot rope."

One by one, they prepared themselves for the descent. As Adelaide headed over the edge, Rose put her hand on her human friend's arm and said, "May Selaia guide you." Adelaide felt the warmth of Rose's magic and the sudden clarity of vision that Valduin had given her to track the dire wolf.

"Thanks," she said. She slipped down the side of the cliff. With the rope wrapped around one leg and pinched between her feet, she lowered herself hand-over-hand to the canyon floor.

Rose grasped the rope and prepared to drop into the canyon. Thinking for a second, she reached out and touched Valduin's arm, repeating her incantation, "May Selaia guide you." Her amulet briefly glowed with radiant energy as the spell transferred to Valduin.

"And may Taranath guide you," Valduin replied with a smile. In Sylvan, he recited his incantation, *"May the old power guide you,*" as the green light of his own magic surrounded Rose.

Rose smiled. "That's a useful spell," she commented as she let the rope slip through her gauntleted hands and walked backward down the sheer face of the cliff. A few minutes after she touched down next to Adelaide, Valduin completed the descent as well, and they surveyed the wreckage left behind by Nyla and her companions.

Just as they had surmised from the top of the canyon, this was the remains of an army camp. There were bodies of goblins, hobgoblins, bugbears, and kobolds scattered everywhere. There were puddles of black ichor that Rose assumed were the remains of various fiendish entities. Heaps of canvas from demolished tents lay scattered about, and a few small buildings had been reduced to piles of kindling.

"The entrance to the city is supposed to be behind the waterfall," Valduin recounted. "We do not want to get caught out here." He brought out his wand and touched it to Rose's shoulder. She became invisible, and Valduin concentrated on the magic of the rod to regain his spent eldritch energy. "Quietly now," he whispered as he led the way toward the waterfall.

The party crept through the remains of the camp, trying not to focus on the bodies around them. Fortunately, the heavy rain was containing the stench that had probably filled this canyon the day before. After a few minutes, they reached the place where the canyon wall had collapsed, and they were forced to go single-file between the edge of the rockslide and the edge of the water. Adelaide was in the lead with Valduin behind her. Valduin could barely hear the halfling's soft footsteps and the ever-present clinking of her armor over the roar of the waterfall.

As Adelaide made it past the narrowest point between the rockslide and the water, she froze. To her left, she saw two of the greasy-haired drengarns that they had seen the day before. One of them was up on the rockslide, digging into the mound of broken canyon wall; the other was standing behind the first, watching it work. They each held a short wooden staff with a hooked blade at the top.

"Stay quiet," Valduin whispered to Adelaide, and he disappeared in a shimmer of silvery mist, reappearing thirty feet closer to the waterfall. He scampered even farther away from the women and dove behind a crumpled tent.

Adelaide glared at him, abandoned with the invisible cleric while Valduin ran for cover. Rose and Adelaide crept forward, hoping that the fiends would remain focused on their digging.

Rose, distracted by the horrific sight of the drengarns, tripped. She stumbled forward into the back of Adelaide's legs, causing the human's knees to buckle. Adelaide yelped in surprise as she fought to keep her balance, and then she froze as both of the fiends spun to look at her.

Watching the creatures turn toward his friends, Valduin took a chance. "Abyssal or Undercommon? Abyssal or Undercommon?" he asked himself in a panic. "Let's try Abyssal." He held the end of his wand up to his mouth while pointing at the creature digging into the side of the mound. *"Leave her alone. She will destroy you. Run!"* he spoke in Abyssal into the fiend's mind.

Adelaide regained her footing, considered her options, and then decided to do what she did best. Focusing on the drengarn standing down on the ground, she grumbled, "You're next," and magically marked it as her quarry. Out came Fiend's Lament as she rushed around the edge of the rockslide and took a swing at the marked creature with the battleaxe. The fiend seemed unmoved by Adelaide's aggressive advance, and it looked down at its chest in amusement when the axe bounced off its chitinous armor.

In a flurry of movement, the drengarn retaliated, first swinging its bladed staff into Adelaide's shield and then dragging the claws on its other hand across the side of her neck. Adelaide grimaced, but she maintained her footing and her concentration in spite of the damage.

The creature up on the rockslide appeared confused. It could not place the source of the voice it had heard in its head, but Adelaide's attack reinforced the message it had received. It climbed higher on the rockslide, surveying the ground below while it tried to decide what to do.

Rose, realizing that she had blown their cover, decided to make up for it by getting in on the action early. She rushed up to the monster Adelaide was attacking, grabbing her amulet as she ran. She reached out in an attempt to magically inflict wounds on the fiend. However, in the flurry of the creature's attack on Adelaide, the back of the spear knocked Rose's invisible arm away. The spell was released and lost as Rose became visible again, standing next to the drengarn.

Watching both of his friends fail to land their attacks, Valduin stepped out from where he had been hiding and launched an eldritch blast from the wand. He aimed for the fiend Rose and Adelaide had surrounded, still hoping the other one was going to run away. The spark of energy sailed over the creature's head, leaving Valduin feeling useless and exposed.

As the fiend in front of her watched the streak of green fly past it, Adelaide landed a rising swing of the battleaxe, releasing a crushing burst of bluish, planar energy as she did.

The fiend reeled from the hit. When it regained its balance, it turned to face Adelaide, appearing to take this assault more seriously now. It swept the greasy hair back from its face, revealing sickly, sallow skin and beady, bloodshot eyes. Its mouth opened to reveal a horrid collection of jagged teeth as it let out an ear-splitting scream. As it screamed, the space around it plunged into darkness.

Taking a cue from its comrade, the other fiend looked toward Valduin. It held its arms out while it howled, and the air around Valduin grew deathly cold and filled with hailstones, pummeling the half-elf.

Rose, caught in the darkness cast by the creature she had been attacking, turned and ran in the direction of Valduin. She felt the tip of the fiend's spear catch her in the hip as she fled, but she kept running. She emerged from the darkness and could see Valduin just thirty feet ahead of her holding his hands up to deflect the torrent of hail. She held her amulet and prayed, *"Selaia, bless us that we may be your sword against evil."* She reached one hand toward Valduin and the other back to where she knew Adelaide was standing, providing Selaia's blessing for strength in battle.

Valduin stumbled through the field of hailstones toward Rose, bloodied and blue from the effects of the drengarn's spell. As he looked through the magical darkness at Adelaide, he pointed the wand at a spot between the two fiends and said, *"The deep will shatter your mind."* An explosion of thunderous sound rocked the canyon. The monster at the top of the rockslide only winced, but the one within the darkness grabbed its head and doubled over.

"It is right there!" Valduin shouted, knowing Adelaide still could not see it. "Hit it!"

"I'm trying!" Adelaide screamed back as she swung wildly into the space in front of her, hoping the drengarn had not moved. She could hear the crunching of its thick exoskeleton as the axe sunk into its torso, and in a flash, the darkness was gone. She wrenched the axe free and prepared for another swing as the creature unleashed two more attacks on her. Again, she was able to deflect the spear with her shield, but the claw coming from the right found purchase on her unarmored shoulder, spraying blood across her armor.

The fiend on the rockslide, now invested in this fight, scrambled down the pile of loose rock. After a couple of steps, it appeared to realize that the rocks were too difficult to move quickly on, and it let out another howl. This time, as it howled, it disappeared. A moment later, it reappeared in front of Rose. Rose's scream merged with the fiend's as the drengarn prepared to attack her. Rose grabbed the amulet again, and she channeled the bit of divinity granted to her by Selaia to send the small, golden points of healing light to both Adelaide and Valduin. She then raised her shield and prepared for the worst.

Valduin stood up straight as Rose's healing energy spread through him. He shouted in Sylvan, "*To the depths*," to send another spark of green energy flying from the tip of his wand at the fiend engaged with Adelaide. The spark caught the drengarn in the back of the head, causing it to lurch forward as black blood dripped from its nose and mouth. Valduin moved toward the water to keep his distance from the monsters.

Despite the critical hit Valduin had made on the fiend in front of her, Adelaide was unable to make contact as her quarry parried away her axe with its spear. The two weapons seemed to tangle briefly, and the drengarn was equally frustrated in its attacks on the human.

Rose was not so lucky. The other fiend's spear pierced her thigh, and when she dropped her shield to push the weapon away the creature's claw tore across her throat. She took a step back, her vision blurred with pain, before regaining her composure and deciding she needed to get away from this monster. Using her shield to push the fiend's claws back from her, she disengaged and headed toward the rockslide. As she ran, she activated her ring of jumping and made a terrific leap nearly to the top of the twenty-foot-high pile. She landed hard and dropped to her knees, still reeling from the last pair of attacks.

Valduin remained focused on the foe locked in combat with Adelaide. He landed another eldritch blast on it. Adelaide dealt the final blow. Fiend's Lament released Adelaide's familiar blue planar energy as it sunk into the drengarn's chest, and then the enchanted weapon soaked up the purple energy as it sealed the fiend's soul within this dying body. Without waiting for the body to hit the ground, Adelaide spun around toward the remaining drengarn. As she advanced to engage with it, she shouted, "You're next!" to move her mystical mark to it.

As soon as Adelaide reached the creature, it let out another howl, and she was plunged into darkness once more.

"I can't see *again*!" she shouted. "Val, can you do something here?"

Rose stared at the sphere of darkness on the ground below her. She wanted to help Adelaide. However, she knew she could not reach the human in time, and she would not be able to see anything even if she did. She decided to play it safe, stay put at the top of the rock-slide, and heal herself in preparation for continuing the fight.

"This is all I've got!" Valduin shouted back to Adelaide as he launched another eldritch blast at the drengarn. Adelaide could hear the creature's feet moving on the loose stones of the canyon floor as the spell made contact with it. She swung the axe wildly again, and, as before, the crunching impact with the drengarn's armored body caused the darkness to dissipate.

The creature looked back and forth between Adelaide and Valduin. Seemingly displeased with the current arrangement, it let out another scream, and it vanished.

"It's running!" Rose shouted, pointing toward the waterfall. Valduin and Adelaide spun to look down the canyon. They saw the fiend running at full speed away from them.

Valduin gave chase. When he was within range, he raised the ebony wand and loosed another thunderous explosion on the monster. The fiend stumbled in its run, but then it howled and vanished again.

Adelaide had begun to run, but after seeing the creature vanish, she stopped next to Valduin. "What now? It will tell someone we are here."

"We follow," Valduin said, disappointed that they had not been able to finish the creature off. "We need to catch it. Or at least get into the city and hide before it finds reinforcements. No time to rest; let's go."

Rose was just rejoining them as they turned to look for her. "Can you make me invisible again? And how are you both feeling?"

"Not great," Valduin replied. "And no, I am spent. We need to get into the city *now*. That thing will probably need some time to get all the way to the top of the mountain, so we have a little time, but not much. We do not want to get caught out here."

"Oh boy," Rose groaned as they started to jog toward the waterfall. "No invisibility; everyone is injured; used a bunch of spells; running into the enemy's hideout. What could possibly go wrong?"

"I cannot believe we survived that," Logan said, shaking his head. "Those were two challenge rating *five* monsters against three level four characters."

"I'm gonna say you got lucky. How many hit points did that ice storm take you down to?" Madison asked.

"I was at two! And Amelia was down to five after the critical hit on her. Awesome use of the Ring of Jumping, by the way. I thought for sure you were going down."

"Thanks! And yeah, me too," Amelia replied. "I just kept looking at my spells trying to see what could get me away from that thing after it teleported right to me. I guess the teleport was its whole action, or else it would have gotten an extra round of attacks on me there. I would have been like *dead* dead."

"We didn't loot anything! Again!" Madison realized. "If we go through this entire quest without getting any gold or gems or items, I am gonna be so mad. Adelaide's whole purpose for adventuring is to get money. She needs to *loot*!"

"Focus. Focus." Logan tried to get Madison's attention. "Get into the lost city. Try to stop that fiend from giving us away. Kill the big bad. Loot everything. We got this."

28

With Valduin in the lead, the party approached the western end of the canyon. The roar of the waterfall here was deafening. Remembering where he had seen the drengarn disappear, Valduin followed a rocky ledge into the space behind the torrent of falling water. The ledge entered a wide, shallow recess in the rock wall. The ledge was no more than five feet deep, and it extended the entire width of the waterfall until it dead-ended against the northern wall of the canyon. When Rose and Adelaide joined Valduin, he looked at them with a confused expression.

"So, where to now?" Adelaide shouted over the din of the waterfall as she surveyed the space.

Valduin shrugged. Casting his message spell so that he would not have to fight the sound of the roaring water, he said, "It was headed back here, and now it is gone. Somewhere around here is a way to get up there." Valduin pointed up and slightly into the wall. "But I do not know how. I was expecting a door or an archway or something."

Adelaide inspected the ground, looking for tracks. She followed the ledge to where it dead-ended and inspected the wall there for signs of a hidden passage. Returning to Valduin, she reported, "I got nothing. No tracks, probably from how it was teleporting. No door, no passage, no keyhole, no nothing."

"Ugh, this is the worst," Rose groaned. She sat down and let her forehead rest against her knees.

"Rose, can you help me look over here?" Adelaide shouted as she restarted her investigation at the southern end of the ledge.

"Fine. Selaia, guide her," Rose said with an exasperated sigh as she reached up and tapped Adelaide on the knee.

"Wow, thanks," Adelaide replied with a roll of her eyes. "It didn't take long for magic to get boring for you, did it?" Adelaide began inspecting every inch of the wall. As she ran her fingers over the surface, about halfway between the two ends of the ledge, her hand disappeared into the stone. She pulled her hand out and then put it through the illusion again. She stuck her head through the wall and found herself looking at a flight of stairs heading up into the mountain.

She pulled her head back out and called to the other two, "Found it!"

Valduin and Rose followed Adelaide through the illusory wall. They were now standing in a small chamber, about twenty feet deep, that ended in a fifteen-foot wide staircase. The stairs rose upward into darkness, curving to the right so that they could only see about fifteen feet ahead. There was Elvish writing in beautiful, semi-geometric patterns covering the walls, the ceiling, and the floor of the room. Looking forward, there were symbols and runes carved into the stairs themselves. Valduin could pick up words and phrases, but the meaning of the entire engraving was lost on him.

"Light," Rose said drearily, and her amulet began to glow, illuminating the room.

"I thought you usually had to *ask* Selaia for light," Valduin commented.

"I'm tired," Rose replied. "It worked. Look at all of these stairs! Are we really going to climb up an entire mountain on stairs? Where's the elevator?"

"The what?" Valduin asked.

"Uh, never mind," Rose said with a sigh. She hung her head and took the first step onto the rising staircase.

Valduin and Adelaide followed, and after a dozen steps, the room they had started in was out of sight around the curve of the staircase. As soon as they lost the view of the starting room, they saw another landing above them. The group reached the landing and looked around. This room was very similar to the one that they had started in, covered in similar symbols and runes. As Valduin drifted over to the wall to inspect the writing, Rose and Adelaide proceeded across the chamber and through the archway on the far side.

"Val," Adelaide said as she looked through the archway.

"Yeah, just a second," Valduin replied.

"No, Val, come over here," Adelaide continued.

"I just want to try to figure out what all these runes do," he said, not looking away from the ancient writing.

"Valdorkian! We know what they do!" Rose yelled at him.

"What? How?" he asked as he tore his eyes away from the carvings and walked toward his friends.

"I'm guessing they magicked us up here," Rose said. Valduin stepped up next to Rose. He was speechless. They were standing on a balcony. Through the pouring rain, he was looking down at nearly the entire length of the Virdes River, stretching through the dark green forest to the horizon. After a few moments of awestruck reverie, he looked around. To his right was an aqueduct that was flowing from behind them and pouring off the edge of the balcony, the source of the waterfall.

Turning around, he could see that they had emerged from a small building on the eastern edge of a plateau. He stepped toward the aqueduct, and as he moved out from behind the small building that held the magic staircase, the lost city of Eydon lay before him. The aqueduct that gave birth to the Virdes River ran straight as an arrow, due west through the center of the city. From where he stood, he could see dozens of bridges crossing the aqueduct, some at ground level and some suspended high in the air. On either side of the aqueduct were fifteen-foot-wide streets; lining the streets were buildings. Beautiful, elven buildings with high-pitched roofs covered with green tiles and detailed with golden crowns and gables. There were trees growing between the buildings, and ivy covering many of the rooftops that Valduin could see. In the distance were tall towers soaring over the surrounding city. Some were crumbling, with no visible roofs, but others seemed untouched by the centuries of disuse.

"Okay, where do we go?" Adelaide broke Valduin's trance.

"What do you mean? How should I know?" he asked.

"Remember the monster that we let get away?" Adelaide shook Valduin's shoulder to be sure she had his attention. "I can't tell which way he went. There are no tracks left in this downpour. It was your friend that told us how to find this place. Where do we go now?"

Valduin's turned his gaze back to the cityscape not with awe but with purpose. "We need to hide."

"As I asked before, where do you want to go?" Adelaide asked, sounding irritable and impatient.

Valduin pointed to the southwest. "We should get across the aqueduct. They will probably come straight to the top of the stairs." The party took off running west on the street that ran along the north side of the aqueduct. About a hundred feet up the street was the first bridge. As Adelaide and Valduin ran at full speed, they realized they couldn't hear Rose's clanking armor behind them. They looked back just in time to watch their armored halfling cleric stepping up onto the stone ledge that contained the aqueduct. Without even taking a running start, Rose leapt clear over the thirty-foot-wide channel. She looked back through the rain at Valduin and Adelaide and pointed at the building that she was now standing in front of. It was narrow, and taller than its neighbors, though not quite tall enough to be called a tower.

"I guess it is as good as any other building," Valduin said, shrugging at Adelaide. As they crossed the bridge, Valduin kept an eye over his shoulder, expecting to see fiends pouring up the street behind them at any moment. Adelaide was watching Rose, and just as she reached the high point at the middle of the bridge, she saw Rose jump twelve feet straight up toward a second-story window. The halfling landed on her feet on the window sill, then clawed desperately for a handhold before falling backward off the sill and into the street.

"Rose!" Adelaide shouted as she reached the southern side of the aqueduct and turned to the left, toward the building Rose was attempting to enter. Before she could take more than a couple of steps, Valduin tackled her to the ground behind the stone ledge beside of the aqueduct.

"Quiet," he hissed. "I saw something." He pointed at Rose, who was still lying on the ground, and whispered a magic message to her, saying, "If you are still alive over there, lie still. They are coming. You can reply to this message."

Moments later, he heard her voice in his head. "I'm alive. Not moving. Tell me when I can breathe again."

They lay still for what felt like hours, the rain beating down on them. Adelaide hadn't minded the rain down in the canyon, and as she lay on the ancient elven street she realized that it should be colder at the increased altitude of the plateau, but it wasn't. Somehow, the rain was comfortable. She closed her eyes, letting the water wash over her. She felt peaceful in a way that she had not felt in a very long time. Just as she let out what felt like the longest breath of her life, Valduin shook her shoulder.

"They are passed us. We need to find some cover and rest." He crawled over to where Rose was still lying on her back.

"You still with us?" he asked as he pulled the halfling to her feet.

"Ugh, yes. The door is locked. This building looked the most intact and the most interesting. Can you knock the glass out of that window up there so I can jump up and let us in?" Rose asked as she stretched her back out after her fall from the window.

"Sure," Valduin said as he glanced up and down the street to see if anyone was watching them. Seeing no one, he pointed his wand at the upper window and sent a spark of eldritch energy into it, shattering the glass.

"Okay, thanks," Rose said. She activated her magic ring again and leapt through the window. She did not even try to land on the sill this time, opting instead to dive headfirst through the opening Valduin had created. A few moments later, the front door swung open, and Valduin and Adelaide ducked inside.

"Why did I not just break open the first-floor window? Or use my mage hand to unlock the window from the inside?" Valduin asked as he pointed to the window next to the front door.

"I had to prove a point after missing the jump the first time. Lock the door. You are going to like this place." Rose turned, walked over to a long, low couch near a cold fireplace, and collapsed face down on the cushions.

Valduin took in his surroundings as Adelaide bolted the door. They were standing in someone's home. There was the hearth on the wall to the left with the couch facing it, and a cushioned chair sitting next to the couch. Across the room from the sitting area was a dining table with two chairs. On the right side of the back wall was a closed door, and on the left side was the staircase that led to the upper floors. The home was neat, if sparsely furnished.

"What was upstairs?" Valduin asked Rose. The response was muffled by the cushions of the couch that Rose had planted herself into.

"What was upstairs?" Valduin repeated, sending the message into Rose's mind. The reply was clear this time.

"A study with a lot of books," Rose replied through the spell, not lifting her head out of the pillows.

Valduin bolted up the stairs. Adelaide followed, but she did not rush. On the second floor, they found the study, as Rose had said, with two walls fully lined with bookshelves, another low couch with a table in front of it, and a desk below the broken window with the chair knocked over. Valduin guessed this was the result of Rose's flying entrance to this chamber. There was another doorway to a staircase heading up to a third floor, and Adelaide crept up while Valduin moved from one bookshelf to the next, ecstatic with this discovery.

On the third floor, Adelaide found a bedroom. The stairs entered the room from the south wall, and the other three walls of the room were covered in windows. This was a bit of a surprise to Adelaide, as she had not noticed any windows higher on the building than the one Rose had jumped through. Thinking of the illusions of the wall behind the waterfall and the entire mountaintop that they were currently beneath, she assumed this was just another enchantment.

As she stood in the center of the room, taking in the city, a shape appeared on the rooftop of the building to her right. A large shape. It was all she could do to keep from screaming as she edged backward toward the staircase, praying that the illusion that had hidden this third floor would also keep her hidden from the twelve-foot-tall ape on the adjacent rooftop. When she had made it to the staircase, she scampered down to the study where Valduin was now standing at the broken window.

He turned when he heard her enter the room. He had a finger to his lips to make sure Adelaide did not speak. He waved her over and pointed out the window.

Adelaide stepped forward and looked out. Moving along the street on the far side of the waterway was a group of bugbears, five of them, with a hobgoblin leading them. They appeared to be glancing in the windows of the buildings as they walked past.

"Do you think they are looking for us?" he whispered to Adelaide.

"I don't know. But I know what's looking for them," Adelaide replied. As if on cue, the enormous ape dropped into the field of view of the window, followed by two more apes of equal size. With a chorus of roars, they tore into the party on the street, quickly dispatching the hobgoblin and one of the bugbears. The remaining bugbears seemed unsure of what to do with their captain hanging from the mouth of one of the apes, and half of them started to run while the other two drew their weapons and laid into the beast. The bugbears did not last long, and mere seconds after they had appeared, the apes took two of the bugbear bodies and climbed up a nearby building, disappearing from sight as more roars came echoing back from multiple directions across the city.

"I know it's early," Adelaide finally broke the tense silence as she and Valduin stared in shock at the remains of the brief battle, "but we are wrecked. Let's just stay here for the rest of the day and the night. You can look through the library, we can all get a good night's sleep, and Rose and I can watch the city from the top floor. It has a good view, and I think we would be hidden there as we watch. We will be able to see if there are any other patrols or anything."

"A whole day in this library? I love this plan," Valduin replied. "You want to go check on Rose? Make sure she is still breathing?"

"Now we get a chance to loot," Logan said. "I told you our time would come."

"Wait, you want to loot this dead elf's house?" Amelia asked. "What if he was a good guy?"

"Even if he was, which we can never know, he left all this stuff behind. So, anything we find probably won't be super valuable to him. And we should make sure it gets used by us and not found by the kobolds or the goblinoids or the fiends," Logan rationalized his desire to rob the abandoned home.

"I'm in for looting," Madison said. "We haven't gotten any cool stuff recently except for that clay pot from Beulah, and we don't even know what it does."

"I'm not excited about the clay pot," Logan admitted. "You aren't supposed to trust anything a hag gives you. It will either be cursed or will be rigged to backfire."

"Adelaide doesn't know that," Madison shrugged. "And devil-man wanted it, so Adelaide thinks it must be pretty cool. She'll use it the first chance she gets. Once we identify it."

29

"Are you asleep? It's barely lunchtime," Adelaide said as she stood over the prone form of Rose.

"No," came the muffled reply. Rose raised her head out of the cushions to say, "but I am hungry. Let's see if there is any food in this place." She let her pack slide off her back onto the floor as she walked around the couch to the closed door at the back of the room. "This must be the kitchen," she said as she pushed the door open.

"The food would be like a thousand years old," Adelaide pointed out. Rose disappeared through the doorway without responding to Adelaide's comment, so Adelaide followed her.

Behind the door, they did find a kitchen, as well as another set of stairs heading down. The kitchen was small, with a counter running the length of the wall on the right and a stove against the back wall of the building. There were windows looking out the back into a sort of alleyway, but there was no back door. The shelves were stacked with plates and cups, and there were pans hanging above the stove. There was one stool in the room, but no other furniture.

"Very neat and tidy," Adelaide commented.

"Yes, it is," agreed Rose, sounding concerned. "Does it look to you like whoever lived here was planning on coming back? Everything is very neat; there are still plates and pans here. The other room is tidy, and the hearth looked like it had been cleaned since it last held a fire. And the study upstairs did not seem to have much missing from its shelves. It was still full of books."

Adelaide considered Rose's observations. "The bed was made neatly on the third floor, too," the human added. "I don't know. Maybe. Do we even know why they abandoned the city? Valduin kept saying it was a long time ago, but I'm not sure how much he knows. He's looking at the books in the library. Maybe he'll find something out. I want to see what's down there," she concluded as she stepped onto the top stair toward the basement. "Could I get some light?"

"Sure," Rose replied. She picked up a cup from the shelf below the counter and set it glowing with divine light. "Here you go." She handed the improvised torch to Adelaide. Looking around the kitchen one last time, and not seeing anything worth eating or any way to get the stove going, she headed upstairs to see what Valduin was doing.

When she entered the study, it was in a different state than the last time she had seen it. Valduin had taken dozens of books off the shelves and was sorting them into piles on the table in the center of the room. His movements were manic, and Rose watched him for a minute before getting his attention.

"Hey, you okay?" she asked.

Without looking up from the book he was flipping through, he replied, "Yes. No. Yes. Look at those." He nodded his head toward the piles of books on the table. He slapped shut the book he was holding, stuck it back on the shelf, took down the next one, and started flipping through it.

Rose looked at the piles of books and realized that Valduin had sorted them by the language they were written in. Some she recognized as Elvish, though she could not read them. Some were in other languages that she did know, including Celestial and Infernal. And some were in languages she could not identify. None appeared to be in Common.

"That's a lot of books," was all Rose could manage as she surveyed the piles.

"Here is my plan," Valduin said after inspecting and replacing three more books from the shelf in front of him. "I have looked through all of the books here. Most are in Elvish or Sylvan, and most of those I do not think are useful to us right now. Some of them are like magical textbooks, so I am guessing this person was a wizard or something. I wish I could use their magic, but I cannot. A bunch of them look like records of council proceedings here in the city. Super boring. But these," he gestured to the books in front of Rose, "might be interesting. There are some languages I do not know, so I cannot tell what is in them. But there are a few that talk about fiends, and I was hoping you could help me read through them. I want to figure out what we have gotten ourselves into."

"Sure, I can help. Maybe Selaia can too," Rose said as she touched her amulet. In Halfling she prayed, "*Selaia, guide my footsteps, and my path will ever lead to you.*" Her irises faded from their usual brown to glowing amber, her vision enhanced by the power of the magic.

"Good idea," Valduin agreed. He cast the guidance spell on himself as well.

"Wait, don't you have a spell that lets you understand any language?" Rose asked after she picked up one of the books in Infernal.

"Technically, yes. But that works *really* slowly on written text. Plus, it is more fun doing this with you," he finished, nose buried in a book, not noticing Rose's smile.

With their magically enhanced abilities, they spent the next few hours poring over the piles of books for information that might aid them in their upcoming endeavors. During this time, Adelaide finished her perusal of the basement and headed back to the top floor to keep an eye on the city. As the afternoon dragged on, the storm passed, and the sky cleared.

When Adelaide returned to the study, she said, "Alright, bookworms, please tell me you found something useful."

"This one in Infernal," Rose said to Valduin, not responding to Adelaide. The halfling held up a black leather tome with golden script on the cover. "Talks about the Astral Peace. I've seen references to it in books back at the temple. This talks about how certain archdevils tricked the demon lords into joining the Astral Peace. Without the archdevils, the Peace would have never been agreed upon. The book talks about the devils like they are heroes."

"And we saw those words in Galien's tomb," Valduin replied, excited. "At the entrance, it said, 'Here lies the Demons' Judge, Galien, Keeper of The Astral Peace.'"

"Sounds deep," Adelaide interjected, unimpressed. "Find anything useful for killing that demon that charmed me into selling my soul to a hag?"

"Well," Valduin began, setting down one book and picking up another, with a cover wrapped in golden silk and emblazoned with crimson letters, "it was probably a devil, not a demon. I am not sure what kind it was, but there are lots of different kinds, and they mostly fit into the infernal hierarchy. I did not find any description that he fits into, though. It is hard to tell since I do not think we have seen his true form. The ones we fought with Nyla, the barbed devils, are definitely part of the hierarchy, as shown here," he held the book open to a series of illustrations that included one that matched the creature they had fought. "Maybe your friend is the leader of this invasion? Maybe he's the one that calls himself Voidbringer?"

"Not my friend," Adelaide retorted. "And I'll be sure to ask him next time I see him."

"Now, the weird thing about all of this is the other things we've seen," Rose explained to Adelaide. "This is what was bothering me yesterday when we saw the first drengarns. Demons and devils hate each other, and we have encountered both. The devils we fought with Nyla, and the quasits we killed were demons. And drengarns are a whole separate kind of fiend, and they come from other lower planes. It doesn't really make sense that all of these different types of fiends would be working together, especially not working with kobolds and goblinoids too. Something is just off around here."

"There you go again with the other planes," Adelaide snarled. "I'll wipe all of them off this plane forever. Me and my axe."

"We can call that a stretch goal," Valduin said. "For now, we need to watch the city for an idea of where to find that devil. And we need to search this house for anything useful. If this really was the home of a wizard, there must be something good here. After that, I say we sleep early and head out first thing in the morning."

"Sounds good," Adelaide replied. "I've already looked in the basement and downstairs. Nothing noteworthy. Do you want to check the bedroom upstairs? And was there anything in the desk?"

"Just some nice paper and ink," Valduin replied. "I took it, although I'm not sure what I will use it for. I will take the next watch from upstairs and search the bedroom while I am up there."

Rose and Adelaide returned to the ground floor. "What was in the basement?" Rose asked as she started rooting around in her pack for food.

"Just some old furniture it looked like. A couple of chairs and a table," Adelaide replied.

"Were they wood?" Rose asked. "Could we burn them in that stove and prepare some real food?"

"Yeah, probably," Adelaide considered the suggestion. "Sure, I'll be right back." A minute later, after some loud clattering from below, Adelaide joined Rose at the stove with the remains of a chair. Before long, they were preparing the first hot meal that they had eaten since staying at the Tin Dragon.

Rapid footfalls coming down the stairs interrupted their cooking.

"I found something amazing!" Valduin shouted before he had even reached the ground floor. He burst into the kitchen holding a small wooden chest. He put the chest on the kitchen stool, flipped open the lid, and turned it to show its contents to Rose and Adelaide.

Inside the chest were two carefully tied scrolls of parchment, a small leather pouch, and a single, small, round stone engraved with glyphs. Adelaide reached for the pouch. She dumped it out into a bowl that she had taken down from one of the kitchen shelves. Inside were eight medium-sized sapphires and three large, white pearls.

"Ooh, these are nice," she muttered as she inspected the gems.

Valduin took out the two scrolls. He unrolled them on the countertop and inspected them. "These are spells," he said, his voice brimming with excitement. "This one will create a sphere of complete silence, and this one can help you identify the magical properties of an item."

"Want to use it on this?" Rose asked as she picked up the stone. "What do you think it's for? Those are magic symbols, right?"

The party took turns inspecting the stone, but none of them recognized the item or the glyphs carved into it.

"Should we use the scroll to identify Beulah's clay pot?" Adelaide asked.

"Maybe. We should sleep on it. You can only use those scrolls once, so you want to make it count," Valduin replied. "It smells amazing down here! We should eat. Then, Rose, you can take a turn on watch from upstairs. I think it will be safe to sleep here without taking watches tonight. I have not seen anyone in the street since the party that got attacked by those apes."

"Sounds fine," Rose said with a yawn. "Dinner first, then watch, then sleep. I call the bed."

Rose trudged up the stairs with her plate of food while Adelaide and Valduin sat at the dining table in the main room.

As she was eating, Valduin's voice entered Adelaide's mind, "You still thinking about ditching Rose? Whisper your reply; I wouldn't want her to hear us."

Adelaide looked across the table at Valduin as she sent a message back. "Maybe. She isn't pulling her weight."

"You say that, but you are still wearing that headband," came the next message. "She poured a lot of magic into you when we fought those dire wolves. You sure she is not growing on you?"

Adelaide reached up to touch the eagle feathers in her hair, as she had started doing whenever she was thinking of her home in Westray. "Okay, maybe a little bit. Don't analyze me," she finished with a glare.

"Will you just find out what this magic pot does?" Adelaide asked aloud as she pulled the item from her pack and placed it on the table. "The devil guy wanted it really badly. It might be super powerful."

"Yes, yes, I want to know too," Valduin acquiesced without a fight, happy to break the tension surrounding the discussion of Rose. He pulled out the scroll and unrolled it on the table next to the pot. "Here we go." He studied the scroll for a moment to figure out what to do, then he started reading the incantations and making the hand motions it prescribed. When he reached the final word, the scroll burst into flame and burned away to ash, though he felt no heat as the paper disintegrated under his fingertips.

His eyes flashed with green energy as he looked at the pot. He frowned. "It is pretty powerful, but I cannot see terribly many uses for it. I will show you." He placed the pot on the table in front of Adelaide, and then he walked to the other end of the table with the lid. He pulled a gold piece out of his pocket and placed it on the table next to the lid. He then picked the lid up and placed it over the gold piece.

"Look in the pot," he told Adelaide. She leaned over and peered inside. Within the once-empty pot lay a single gold coin.

"So, you can put on a magic show? I'm sure the little devil-kid birthday party scene is pretty competitive," she sighed and rolled her eyes. "We sold our souls for this? I really am going to kill that devil."

"Well, it's a little more powerful than this demonstration," Valduin continued. "The Inseparable Clay Pot works *everywhere*. As in, across the planes. If you want to send an object to a creature on another plane, you can give them the pot and keep the lid. Or vice versa. Then, once per day, you could send something to the other person wherever they are in the entire multiverse."

"Your big words don't make this any less of a letdown," Adelaide grumbled. "I'm going to bed before I die of disappointment." She walked across the room and flopped onto the couch. Valduin resumed eating his dinner before Adelaide called out, "You want to use that other scroll and make it silent over there so I don't have to hear you chewing?"

Valduin picked up his plate and headed for the stairs. "I'll sleep in the study. Goodnight."

"The Inseparable Clay Pot? Really? That's it?" Madison was furious.

"Hey, let's focus on the positives. The devil did not get what he wanted. Whatever he was going to use it for was probably evil," Logan tried to mollify his sister.

"I mean, it would only have been a little evil," Amelia added, not helping Logan's case. "It's a tiny pot. How big a thing could you actually send through it?"

"How about this? We learned a lot about the Astral Peace and the different fiends, right? That was useful. And we got a scroll of Silence. I can use that to prevent people from hearing Rose's armor or blocking an enemy from casting spells with verbal components," Logan continued.

"Unless you can use that scroll to enchant her armor to be silent all the time, which I doubt, I don't really see a scroll being super useful. We'll see it in your inventory at level twenty and wonder where we picked it up," Madison shut down Logan's placations.

"Fine," Logan conceded. "So, let's focus on killing your devil friend. We still need to find him. And I would like to find out what his plans are as well, if possible. Sometimes just killing the big bad doesn't actually stop the doomsday machine. We need to do both."

"Is that how you win this game?" Amelia asked innocently, and all three kids burst out laughing.

30

At first light, Valduin, Adelaide, and Rose left the safety of their hideout and started moving through the streets of Eydon. During their time watching the city from the top floor of the house, they had seen only one additional patrol. This troupe was made up of goblinoids, similar to the one that they had seen the night before, but it also had two of the black-armored drengarns accompanying it. That patrol had walked past their hideout on the opposite side of the aqueduct and turned north, moving away from them and deeper into the city.

They crept back across the bridge they had used the day before and headed in the same direction that the patrol had gone. As much as Valduin wanted to inspect every building in the ancient elven city, they stayed focused on moving quickly and stealthily. They were on a mission.

"Do we just keep going north?" Rose asked after they approached the first intersection after crossing the bridge.

"Let's stay on this street," Adelaide replied. "That way, if we don't find anything, we know how to get back to the house we stole. I'll keep an eye out for the tracks of any of those patrols."

After three more cross streets, and half an hour of sneaking from corner to corner, Adelaide found what she was looking for. She glanced around the corner of a building to look up the next cross street, and she held her hand up for her friends to stop walking. "It looks like something happened here," she whispered over her shoulder. "There are bodies in this street about fifty feet away."

"Are any of them moving?" Rose asked.

"I don't think so," she answered. After another few seconds of scanning the street, she stepped around the corner. "No movement. Let's check it out."

Adelaide stayed close to the wall. Her head moving continuously as she watched for danger up and down the street, she crept toward the bodies. Valduin and Rose followed a few feet behind the ranger. As they got closer, it became obvious these were the remnants of a battle; another battle in which the goblinoid patrol had not fared too well.

"Oh, gross," Rose said as she moved around the side of Adelaide to get a look at what they had found. Littered around the street were the bodies of goblins and bugbears. Rose moved from body to body, inspecting their wounds. They were not subtle. After just a moment, she stood up and turned to Adelaide and Valduin.

"So, remember that big ape creature from yesterday? This looks like more of the same. This one has teeth marks, and those few look like the claws got them."

Adelaide studied the scene for a moment. "It didn't get all of them," she said as she pointed to a spattering of blood heading west from the battleground. "We have a trail. Let's get out of here before any of those monsters comes back for seconds."

They quickened their pace as they followed the trail of blood west from the carnage. The trail turned a few times, winding its way north and west into the city. Adelaide did her best to remember the path they were taking, but with each turn, she became less confident that she could find their way back to their hideout.

After almost an hour of following the trail, while also trying to stay out of sight, Rose hissed for everyone to dive into an alley. Though they did not see anything amiss, Adelaide and Valduin complied. Once they were hidden, they turned to Rose for an explanation.

"What did you see?" Adelaide asked, her voice hushed.

"Movement. Something in front of a building about a hundred feet farther down this street," Rose explained.

"What kind of movement?" Valduin asked. "Something big and hairy? Or fiendish?"

"Not big, but I'm not sure what it was. I think there is someone standing in front of the building across the street. Let me look again." She crawled to the end of the alley. Peeking around the corner, she could make out two creatures in front of a large building made of black stone. Each of the creatures held a long glaive, and they stood at attention on either side of the entrance to the black building. The creatures were about six feet tall and humanoid to the extent that they had two arms and two legs, but they also had a mass of ropey tendrils hanging from their faces. Even from this distance, Rose could see the tendrils writhing as the creatures stood otherwise motionless, allowing her to identify these fiends with confidence.

Rose pulled back around the corner to confer with her companions. "So, there are definitely two bearded devils standing guard. This has to be the right place. That one book I showed you yesterday said that bearded devils are soldiers. Whoever we are trying to find must have powerful friends in the lower planes to have so many devils working for him."

"Thanks for the lesson," Adelaide snipped. "Did it say anything in those books about how to kill them other than the usual hack and slash?"

"Eh, not really," Valduin cut in. "It just said they were especially dangerous in groups. I would rather not fight them, to be honest. Maybe a distraction?"

"Can you create the image of one of those giant apes leaping down off the roof of a building and preparing to attack them? Like Venez could do?" Adelaide asked.

Valduin thought for a second. "Yeah, no. An illusion that big is outside my power. One day, maybe. Today? No."

"How about that message spell?" Rose asked. "You could try talking to them. That might freak them out."

"Do you think they speak Common, Undercommon, Elvish, Sylvan, or Abyssal?" Valduin asked.

"Well, they are devils, not demons," Rose replied. "Maybe Abyssal, but more likely Infernal. You don't speak that? I do."

"You think you could tell me what to say? And I will send it to them?" Valduin asked.

"We can try. What do we want to say? Tell him that if he doesn't run away, he will get eaten by a giant ape?" Rose considered the breadth of her Infernal vocabulary. "I'm not sure I know the word for ape. Or if they have a word for ape."

"Try insulting one of them," Adelaide suggested. "Maybe he'll think the other one said something to him."

"I like that idea," Valduin agreed. "Can you insult him in Infernal?" He asked Rose.

"Try this," Rose said with a grin, and then she uttered a string of deep, guttural syllables that surprised both Valduin and Adelaide coming from her petite form.

Valduin repeated the sounds a few times until Rose thought they sounded right. They all poked their heads around the corner. Pointing at the closer devil, Valduin did his best to repeat the Infernal insult through the message spell.

The devil whipped its head around toward its partner, though Valduin could not hear any conversation. The two devils stared each other down for a few moments, the tension silently escalating, until the first one swung its glaive into the other. Seeing it had caught its new enemy off guard, the devil followed up the glaive attack by laying into its foe with its writhing beard, which spread out to enshroud the second devil's head. As the devils pulled apart, the small spikes on the ends of the thick tendrils tore deep gashes in the devil's neck and shoulders.

Surprised by the sudden aggression, the second devil pushed the first one back with its glaive, and then it swung open the large door and ran inside the building. The first devil lost no time in giving chase. A moment later, the building was left unguarded.

"What did you say?" Adelaide asked, eyes wide at the effectiveness of the tactic.

"We said, 'We had a vote yesterday and decided you have the ugliest beard in the entire company,'" Rose said with a giggle. "Devils are very vain."

"Apparently," Valduin said with a smirk. "Okay, it is time to move."

The party rushed down the silent street, focusing more on getting inside the building than staying stealthy outside of it. As they approached the open front door, they saw that the exterior of the building was designed like a temple. Constructed completely of reflective black stone, the front of the edifice stretched almost a hundred feet high to a narrow, pointed tower roofed in dark red tiles. They had no sense of how deep the building went, but it took up almost one hundred and fifty feet wide. The doors were fifteen feet tall and made of dark wood bound together with studded, blackened iron bands. Above the doors, where they might have expected a stained-glass window, there was a pattern of overlapping discs that looked as if they had been molded directly from the obsidian surface of the temple.

The trio charged through the doors, left open by the bearded devils. They found themselves in a small vestibule that opened through an archway into a large, open chamber. They slowed their pace as they moved through the archway, taking a moment to survey the large, interior room. The cavernous space was mostly empty, with the exception of a raised area at the far end with what appeared to be an altar. The floor, walls, and ceiling were all made of the same black stone as the outside of the building. A series of lanterns embedded in the walls emitted a steady, purple glow. There was no movement, and it was not clear where the bearded devils had gone. Their attention, however, was soon consumed by the main feature in the center of the room.

The pit was a circle sixty feet in diameter. It took up most of the center of the chamber. Rose approached the edge and found herself peering down into darkness. As her eyes adjusted, she realized that there was a faint glow coming from deep within the pit, though its source was hidden. Adelaide and Valduin joined her at the edge, all of their attention focused on the deep darkness.

Valduin pointed to the far side of the pit. "There are stairs," he whispered. In front of the altar, a narrow set of stairs spiraled down the wall of the pit. "This has to be the right spot."

"Why would there be a temple like this in an elf city?" Rose asked as the group headed toward the stairs. "I'm pretty sure the symbol on the front of this building represents the lower planes."

"I do not know," Valduin admitted. "We can worry about history later. We need to figure out what is going on here right now."

"Is your plan to go down there?" Rose asked, fear creeping into her voice. "This place feels wrong. Evil. It's dark, and there could be fiends anywhere."

Adelaide chimed in, "We can't stay up here. This room is wide open; there is no place to hide. And it doesn't look like this place gets a lot of traffic. I bet all the action is down there. That's where we have to go."

Rose took a deep breath and looked around the large chamber for herself one more time. "Okay. Fine. Lead the way, Valdarun."

The party crept down the stairs. Downward they spiraled, with Valduin in the lead, his vision unimpeded by the absence of light. Afraid that light would give them away, Adelaide kept a hand on Valduin's shoulder, and Rose held Adelaide's other hand to make sure that they stayed together in the darkness. As they approached the bottom, the glow that Rose had noticed brightened. They could see several brightly lit tunnels leading out of the pit in different directions. There was a set of three tunnels on one side, and there were five tunnels entering the pit from different points around the other side. Each of the tunnels was lit with torches, and the glow from the tunnel openings was lighting the floor of the pit.

After arriving at the bottom of the stairs, Adelaide inspected the ground at the entrances to each of the tunnels, searching for an indication of which they should head through.

"I think those bearded devils went this way," she eventually indicated the left-hand tunnel of the group of three. "Do we follow them? Or do we take a different one?"

"Which one looks like it gets the most traffic? Is it the same one?" Valduin asked.

"Actually, no," Adelaide said after considering the options. "The one that slopes down in the middle of the group of three looks like it has the most movement. There is a lot of debris around those five over there. I think those are pretty new, but the pit and the three tunnels on this side are old."

"So, the bearded devils went down the one on the left, and the center one gets the most traffic," Valduin eventually said. "Let's take the one on the right. I don't want to run into those devils or anyone else while we are down here." As he said those words, Adelaide and Rose heard movement coming from one of the five tunnels behind them.

"Fine, sure, move, move," Adelaide said, pushing Valduin down the chosen tunnel. After they got through the opening, Rose glanced back to see a procession of kobolds moving across the base of the pit in the direction of the tunnel Adelaide had described as getting the most traffic. She turned to follow Valduin while holding her chainmail shirt to minimize the clinking.

The tunnel was more of a hallway, with walls constructed of stone blocks instead of being carved into the bedrock of the mountain. The party proceeded straight for a hundred feet or so, at which point there was another hallway branching to the left. Looking around the corner, the side hallway opened into a large, brightly lit room after about fifty feet.

"You both stay here," Valduin said. "I will take a look."

"Why can't we come with you?" Rose asked.

"Because you are too loud, and I do not want to use any energy to turn you invisible right now. We might be getting into a fight at any moment," Valduin replied.

"Yeah, okay," Rose conceded without argument. "Be careful."

Valduin crept down the short hallway and found himself looking at a balcony with a railing made of black metal. Peeking around the corner, he saw no one else on the balcony, so he crawled forward and peered through the bars of the railing. Below him was a chamber with an altar to his right and a large set of double doors on the wall to the left. While the walls were of the same gray stone as the hallway he had left Rose and Adelaide in, the altar looked to be made of the reflective, black stone that made up the exterior of the temple. The balcony on which Valduin lay ran the length of the chamber, and there were stairs down to the main floor at both ends.

Through the large, double doors came the line of kobolds. Dozens of the small creatures were filling a row of chests with small pouches, which Valduin assumed were full of diamonds. Two of the chests were already full, and the other two that were standing in the row would be full soon.

Standing behind the row of chests was a combination of bearded devils and bugbears. Pacing the space along the far wall of the room was a fiend that Valduin had never seen before. It looked like a seven-foot-tall vulture with long, bony arms that ended in hooked claws. Valduin matched this monster to the image of a vrock that he had seen in a book the day before.

As Valduin watched, one of the kobolds near this new monster dropped its pouch into the large chest, and there came a tinkling sound as something fell out of the pouch onto the ground. The large, winged fiend reached for what Valduin assumed were diamonds, only to have its clawed hand knocked away by the weapon of a bearded devil. The vrock retaliated against the bearded devil with its beak, and three more bearded devils took swings at it to defend their comrade. The vrock hissed at them, and then it returned to its moody pacing along the wall.

Near the altar were a handful of hobgoblins who were talking to a couple of imps. As Valduin watched, another imp flew into the room from an entrance directly across from Valduin, where there was another balcony, mirroring the one Valduin was hiding on. The imp flew down to the altar where it entered an animated discussion with the other imps.

Without warning, a silent flash of blue light lit the room from behind the altar, and there appeared the creature that Valduin had been looking for. Red-skinned, with black horns curling back from his forehead and large, leathery wings. The man that had charmed Adelaide was wearing armor now, a breastplate with glowing red runes across the front; a sword hung at his side. The imps standing on the altar turned to him and bowed their heads. They began speaking to the devil, and although Valduin could not understand what they were saying, he could tell their report was making the devil increasingly angry.

After a minute of listening, he let out a scream of rage and in a single, fluid motion the devil drew his sword and cut one of the imps in two. The chamber plunged into stunned silence. He stepped up behind the altar and addressed all of his assembled minions with forced composure as the body of the imp liquified in front of him. "The Voidbringer will open the gate tonight. We have only a few hours left to finish collecting our offering. I would not want the Voidbringer to be *disappointed*."

The devil spun on his heel and left the chamber by a door behind the altar. The rest of the creatures returned to their tasks. Everyone moved more feverishly now. Valduin crawled back through the doorway, feeling safe that the din from below would cover the sounds of his retreat.

Valduin rejoined Adelaide and Rose. "We need to find somewhere to hide for a few hours," he said. He recounted what he had seen. "Those imps could be anywhere. We need to find somewhere to lay low. Then we can come back. I think we are going to need to interrupt this 'offering' at the last second."

"Sounds fine to me, but what's the difference between that and just attacking now? Either way, we are in deep trouble. There are a lot of bad guys down there," Adelaide responded.

"If we attack now, I am certain that we do not stand a chance. I am hoping that some of the riff-raff will clear out in the meantime. Then, we can go after the diamonds and that devil," Valduin said. "In any event, we cannot stay here. Keep moving." He led the party along the passage away from the pit. A short distance beyond the large chamber, the hallway came to an end. At the end were three doors, each made of black metal untouched by rust or wear.

"Which one?" Valduin asked as Rose and Adelaide came up beside him.

Adelaide inspected the doors and the floor in front of them. "There aren't really any tracks on this stone floor. And the doors look identical." She shrugged. "Let's start straight ahead first."

Just as Adelaide reached for the handle on the door in front of her, she heard a scraping sound behind it, as if something large was being dragged across the stone floor toward the door. She stepped back and looked at Valduin. "Wrong door! Pick another one, quick!" she hissed.

Rose reached out for the door on the left, but she found it locked. Valduin grabbed the handle of the door on the right, and it swung open. They dove through and shut the door behind themselves. As their door clicked closed, the first door they had checked creaked open. The scraping sound continued past their hiding spot and down the corridor toward the altar room.

The party was standing in absolute darkness. Hesitant to reveal themselves with a light spell, Rose whispered to Valduin, "What do you see?"

What Valduin saw terrified him. They were at the end of a long chamber. A series of jail cells lined the wall on the right. The other three walls were covered with chains hanging down from the ceiling. Some of the chains had shackles on them, and one even had most of a skeleton dangling from the end of it. Bits of chain hung from the ceiling in various places around the room as well, most with sinister hooks attached to the ends.

From where Valduin stood, he could see five doors entering the jail cells on the right side of the room, and a single door at the far end of the room. After a pause, he reported back to Rose, "I think this was a prison.

Hold tight, I am going to check out the cells to see if there is anyone in them. Be ready for anything."

Valduin crept to the first cell. Lying on the floor just inside the bars was a skeleton that looked as if it had been there for centuries. Thinking about what Adelaide would say if he did not at least try to loot the body, he summoned his spectral mage hand and sent it toward the skeleton. As soon as the hand crossed the plane of the bars, however, it vanished.

Disappointed, Valduin moved on to the next cell. In this small room, he could see a pile of clothing on the floor in the back corner. Looking closer, he realized that there were patches of skin visible within the pile. He whispered into the cell, "Anyone in there?"

A moment passed, and then the pile stirred. In a moment, a humanoid creature, a bit taller than Valduin and with reddish brown skin, stood within the cell. Valduin took a step back from the bars when he realized he was looking at a female hobgoblin, a creature that he had never seen up close before. After a moment, the creature croaked out a question, "Did Azereth send you to kill me? Was Rhalzek too cowardly to do it himself? I'd wipe their whole infernal operation off this plane if he'd fight me with honor."

"Uh, I do not know who those people are," Valduin replied. "Is Azereth that devil guy?"

"The devil is Azereth, yes. Rhalzek is the traitor that sold me out and put me in here."

"Well, we do not like Azereth either. Can we get you out? Do you know where the keys are?" Valduin asked.

"The guard holds the keys," the hobgoblin said, her eyes growing wide as she pointed over Valduin's shoulder.

Not picking up on the fear in her voice, Valduin turned around and spotted a ring of keys dangling from a chain hanging from the ceiling. He sent his mage hand over to retrieve the keys, lifting the ring off the hook and floating them back to his hand. He glanced through the keys, tried a few of them, and then there was a loud creaking sound as the lock disengaged and the door swung open. When he looked up at the hobgoblin, expecting to see her happy to be free, she had instead retreated to the back of the cell, still pointing a trembling finger over Valduin's shoulder. It was then that Valduin noticed the sound of rattling chains behind him.

"Roll initiative?" Madison screamed. "What is it? What are we fighting?"

"Never trust a goblin," Amelia said dejectedly. "She is going to kill us all." She buried her face in her hands.

"It's not the hobgoblin," Logan explained to his younger sister. "It's the thing rattling the chains behind me. Probably whatever the prison guard is."

"Do you know what it is?" Madison asked. "Are there any creatures in the book that are built to be prison guards? Any chain-based monsters that you can remember?"

"Uh, there is a chain devil," Logan replied, furrowing his brow as he tried to remember the stat block. "But that's got a challenge rating of eight, I think. There's no way we would have to fight something that strong."

31

Valduin spun around to see a humanoid form wrapped in chains descending from the ceiling in the center of the chamber behind him. As the form touched down, Valduin got a good look at its face. To his horror, he found himself staring into his mother's face, half obscured by chains, with terror in her eyes. That terror washed over Valduin, and before he knew what he was doing, he was running back to the door where Adelaide and Rose were standing. As he ran, he drew his wand and shouted, *"One and the same,"* to summon his mirror images.

Knowing that Rose and Adelaide still could not see what he had seen, he blurted out, "The g-guard is in here! C-covered in chains!" He did his best to forget the form it had taken, hoping that this was just an illusion of his dead mother.

Adelaide strained her eyes trying to look deeper into the absolute darkness of the room. Accepting that she would not be able to find the enemy until Rose gave her some light, she instead put her hand against the eagle totem woven into her headband and focused on her connection to nature. Feeling that connection growing, she envisioned the fiends that she had already fought, creating a protective aura around herself. She then readied her battleaxe with a smile. "Rose, light me up," she whispered.

"You got it," came Rose's reply. Rose touched Adelaide's breastplate, setting it aglow with bright yellow light. Rose then retreated to the corner of the room as she took in the form of the chain devil. Some of its chains still linked it to the ceiling, while others snaked around its body and limbs, sliding and clanking against each other in continuous motion.

The hobgoblin left her cell at a run, staying just outside the range of the light shining from Adelaide. Her form blurred as she darted through the dark space to the wall across from her cell. She stopped and looked back and forth between the devil and the door. She appeared to be torn between the need to flee and the desire to obtain retribution against her jailer.

The devil looked from one to the next of them, and then it began to chuckle. With a few whispered words, chains all throughout the chamber came alive, writhing against the walls as hooks and blades multiplied along their lengths. The devil moved back farther into the room, though not by walking. The chains that still linked it to the ceiling lifted it a few inches above the ground and carried it along. The chains that encased its trunk and limbs moved faster and faster; some were starting to separate from its body with the momentum of their spinning movement.

The fear shaken from his mind, Valduin pointed the ebony wand toward the fiend. Under his breath he hissed in Sylvan, *"To the depths,"* and a spark of green energy appeared around his hand and spiraled down the length of the wand. The speck of light accelerated until it got to the tip of the wand, and then it streaked off into the room, bursting against the devil's chest.

Seeing her target lit up briefly, Adelaide smiled and sprinted down the room toward it. She tightened her grip on her shield and axe, as she approached the monster. The entire room was now swirling with shadows cast by the swirling mass of chains and the shining beacon that was Adelaide's armor.

Rose followed behind, putting herself in the space between Valduin and Adelaide as she reached for her amulet. "Selaia, bless us that we may bring your light into dark places," she prayed as she gave Selaia's blessing to herself and her two companions.

The hobgoblin, watching Adelaide rush toward the chain devil without hesitation, steeled herself for battle. In another blur of movement, she closed the distance to the fiend. Reaching its side, the hobgoblin let loose a flurry of punches against the chain-covered body of the devil, although the devil gave no indication as to whether she made any impact.

The devil raised its hands, the chains whirling around its body ever faster. A chain hanging on the wall behind Valduin lashed out, striking and dispelling one of his duplicates as he ducked his head away from the sudden movement. Another chain struck out at Rose and scraped against her armor, but she was able to dodge the hook on the end of it. One hit the back of the hobgoblin, wrapping around her arms and torso as she let out a grunt of pain. As a finale, the devil released two of the chains spinning around its arms toward Adelaide. Adelaide blocked the first one with her shield, but the second managed to wrap around her waist, pinning her shield arm against her and cutting into her hip with the blades along its length.

Valduin ran back toward the open jail cell, trying to get outside the reach of the bladed chain writhing against the wall behind him. Reaching the door of the cell, he released another eldritch blast into the devil, drawing a grunt from the fiend as the green energy smashed into it.

Adelaide struggled for a moment against the chain that was restraining her. After feeling the pain from the bladed chain sinking deeper into her side, she channeled her building rage into the enemy in front of her. She focused the planar energy around the fiend into the swing of her battleaxe, and in a burst of bluish light, Fiend's Lament dealt a crushing blow to the devil's shoulder. Links of chain flew apart as Adelaide laid into the monster.

Rose, unsure of the source of the attack on her, focused on the devil as she grabbed her amulet. "*Selaia, help us strike true,*" she whispered in Halfling. She felt the warmth of the divine magic spread through her hand, and she pointed at the devil to release the bolt of radiant energy. The devil hissed as the divine magic burned into it, leaving a yellow glow behind.

Apparently second-guessing her decision to engage with the chain devil, the hobgoblin slipped out of the grasp of the animated chain and tried to run for the door. Before she was able to get away, however, the devil released another chain from around its arm toward her. As the chain wrapped around her neck, the hook sunk into her shoulder, and her body went limp. Still entangled with chain, she fell to the floor, unconscious.

The animated chain hanging from the wall next to Rose lashed out at her again, and this time it found purchase on the edge of her armor. As the hook dug in, the bladed chain wrapped around her torso, and she did her best to stifle the screech that the pain drew from her. The devil's burning, red eyes met Adelaide's with equal fury, and two more chains released from the swirling mass that now shrouded it. Adelaide was able to parry the first hook with her weapon, but again the second one found its mark. She felt another set of blades tighten against her thigh.

Valduin, watching Adelaide becoming more and more entangled with the devil, took advantage of the glowing yellow target that Rose had left as he loosed another eldritch blast into the fiend. This time, the spark appeared to slip between the chains before bursting, and the devil doubled over briefly in response to the blow. Adelaide could see it was weakening. She could feel the chains wrapped around her loosening with each hit.

Adelaide raised her axe, ignoring the burning pain from the chains. She was bent on destroying this monster that did not belong in her world. With another burst of blue light, followed by the familiar purple glow of the enchantment of the Fiend's Lament, she dealt the final blow to the devil, caving in its chest. As the clanking of metal that had filled the room subsided, the limp body of the devil was left hanging by the chains that still connected it to the ceiling. The chains surrounding Adelaide, Rose, and the hobgoblin also went limp, and Rose ran to the hobgoblin, invoking Selaia to spare her life as she pulled the chains from the hobgoblin's body. The hobgoblin's breathing calmed and her bleeding stopped with the aid of Rose's healing magic.

"Rose, check the hallway. Make sure no one heard us," Valduin instructed as he ran the length of the room, looking into the other cells for any more threats. At the far end of the room, he checked the other door, which he found to be locked. Listening for a moment, he heard no sounds coming from the other side, and he breathed a sigh of relief.

Rose ran back to the door through which they had entered this chamber. First listening through the closed door, and then opening it a crack to check the hallway, she was satisfied that there were no other enemies nearby. She closed the door and headed back to the hobgoblin's side. Taking care not to do further damage, she unwound the bladed chains from the hobgoblin's neck and shoulders.

"Are you okay?" Valduin asked Adelaide as he returned to her side. He helped her extract herself from the grasp of the spiked chains. "You were amazing. Getting right up in its face like that. Not even worrying about the chains. Just clobbering it!"

"Well, I'm glad it went down since that was probably going to be my last hit on it," Adelaide replied as she leaned on Valduin. "I don't think I could have taken any more of those chains."

"Is she going to be okay?" Valduin asked Rose, nodding toward the hobgoblin. "I think she has some information about that devil that we might need."

"She'll live," Rose replied. "She's still unconscious, but she's stable. I could use some stronger magic to wake her up now if you want."

"Save your magic," Adelaide said. "Let's just take a rest here and check out the rest of this room. Maybe there will be something useful in one of these other cells. Do you still have the keys, Val?"

"Yes, I do," Valduin replied. He held up the iron ring. "Adelaide, you and the hobgoblin should rest in the open cell. You are looking pretty rough."

"Well, you don't look so great yourself," Adelaide snapped, and then she stumbled through the door of the cell and collapsed against the wall. Valduin and Rose dragged the hobgoblin into the cell and put her next to Adelaide.

Adelaide tapped on her still-shining armor. "Rose, could you turn this off so I can try to sleep?"

"Oh, yeah, sorry," Rose replied as she moved the light spell to her amulet. "Sleep. We'll loot."

"You better loot good," Adelaide mumbled as she turned over, put her head on her pack as a pillow, and closed her eyes.

Valduin and Rose moved to each of the other cells, opening them with the keys on the ring. On the skeleton in the first cell, there was nothing but the rotted remains of a robe. In two other cells they found the bodies of two kobolds, more recently deceased. In the last cell there were a few piles of clothing, presumably the belongings of the kobolds and the hobgoblin. Nothing of particular value came up as they looked through the piles, so they returned to the cell with Adelaide to stand guard and wait for the hobgoblin to awaken.

"Hit dice, let's go!" Madison encouraged her dice as she started rolling for the short rest.

"How low did you get?" Amelia asked. "I can heal you if you need. I only used a couple of spells in that battle."

"After all of my hit dice, I'm not quite full, but I'm okay for now. Save your spells. Also, Mr. Metagamer, what was that you were saying about a chain devil being too strong for us?"

"Seriously, it's got a CR of eight," Logan said, getting defensive. "But it was all three of us against one of him, and my maximum damage critical hit was clutch. Don't forget that the devil *did* almost kill the hobgoblin, and Adelaide would have gone down next round when she took the passive damage from the chains."

"I would have definitely healed you then," Amelia reassured Madison.

"Thanks, Amelia. I know," Madison said with a smile. "Are you having fun yet? I know that *I'm* glad you're playing."

"Maybe," Amelia replied with a coy smirk. "We'll see how the boss fight goes. Then I'll let you know."

"Okay, we finish the rest, get some info out of the hobgoblin, and then go hunt some more devils," Madison summarized the plan. "Also, we are not going to talk about that investigation check, you two. Neither of you remembered to use Guidance! Those dice better go to jail before this boss battle."

32

Valduin shook Adelaide awake when the hobgoblin started to groan. "Feeling a bit better?" he asked his friend. "She is waking up. We need you now."

Adelaide pulled herself back to sitting and yawned. She felt her eyes burn as Rose's glowing amulet shone in her face. "I'm up! I'm up!" she complained. She rubbed her eyes with one hand and her flank with the other. "I am definitely gonna be sore in the morning," she grumbled.

The hobgoblin opened her eyes as well. She sat up against the back wall of the cell and looked from one to the next of the adventurers that had freed her. She took a deep, meditative breath. "Thank you for your help," she began with forced composure. "I am Luvrolen. I am in your debt for freeing me from this cell and from the evil creature that held me here."

"How long have you been here?" asked Rose. She pointed at the skeleton in the cell next to them. "Did you know that guy?"

Luvrolen glanced at the skeleton. "No, that was here when I arrived. I can't say for sure how long I have been in this cell, as it is always dark in this room. But it must have been weeks since I was betrayed."

"Weeks?" Rose was incredulous. "In the dark? With that thing?" She glanced at the unmoving body wrapped in chains behind them. "How did you not go crazy?"

Luvrolen smiled, though this expression on her goblinoid face was more off-putting than reassuring to the halfling. "It would take more than darkness and pain to break my mind or my spirit."

Valduin cleared his throat to get Luvrolen's attention. "How did you end up here? Who betrayed you?" After considering other questions, he finished with, "What can you tell us about the devil?"

Luvrolen's smile turned to a grimace. "Rhalzek. That's who betrayed me, and that's how I ended up here. He was my most trusted advisor and my most competent general. I was the leader of the biggest war band in the mountains to the north. We had vision. And purpose. We were not a bunch of pillaging barbarians. We controlled everything going in or out of the Enchanted Dunes from here to the northern waters. I struck treaties with cities of elves and dwarves and humans. I knew Rhalzek missed the excitement of the old war band, but our people were thriving.

"Then came the devil. Azereth. He offered weapons and magics and legions of devils to aid us in taking control of the Sandgate Mountains and the Virdes Forest. I knew better than to make a deal with such a creature, but Rhalzek was tempted. He sold me out, handed me over to Azereth, and took control of the band. The last that I heard was that they had set themselves up near the source of the Virdes River, though I have seen nothing but this room since my betrayal."

Valduin, Adelaide, and Rose exchanged worried glances as they listened to this story. Rose spoke up first to reply, "I am sorry to be the one to tell you this, but I think most of your band is gone. We came to this place through the remains of their camp."

Luvrolen furrowed her brow. "Strange. I would not have expected Rhalzek to give up on his deal with Azereth. And I can't believe anyone else could have pulled the war band away from his control."

It was Valduin that spoke up this time. "She did not mean that they left. The camp had been destroyed. We heard that the war band helped a band of kobolds attack a gnome city. The gnomes followed them back here and loosed a terrible weapon upon them. I fear there are very few surviving members of your troupe."

Luvrolen sat in brooding silence, her gaze distant as she absorbed this information. After a few moments, she sneered and spat on the ground. "Good riddance. That treasonous filth will find themselves forever in the company of devils now. That's what they get for following Rhalzek. If I can only ensure Rhalzek shares their fate, I will be able to die happy."

"Well, maybe you'll get that chance," Valduin said, his tone grim. "We are here to kill the devil and hopefully thwart whatever he has been planning. I saw a few hobgoblins in the large chamber where the devil appeared just a couple of hours ago. I'd guess Rhalzek was among them if he is still leading the war band."

Luvrolen clenched her fists. "I can think of nothing more satisfying than ending that traitor. Especially now that the jailer has been dealt with. I will help you. When do we move?"

"There was a bunch of movement past the door just before you both awoke," Rose said. "We know that whatever Azereth has been planning is going to happen today. It could be very soon. We need to get back to the room with the altar so we can be ready for when it does happen. Whatever *it* is. Also, there was some gear in the cell at the end of the room. It seemed fairly new, compared to Mr. Bones over there. Maybe some of it is yours? Is there anything that you might need?"

Luvrolen walked down to the last cell. When she returned, she was wearing a dark blue set of leather armor with a belt that held a dozen thin daggers. "I am ready," she said with a stern nod.

Valduin cracked open the door back toward the altar room. The hall outside was quiet, and the two other doors were closed. Single file, the party crept back the way they had come, soon arriving at the side passage that led to the altar room. While the area remained quiet around them, there was a steady din coming from beyond the balcony at the end of the passage.

"Wait here," Luvrolen whispered. She crept down the hall and peeked through the bars of the railing.

A moment later, she darted back to the group. "It looks like they are ready to leave. There are several large chests lined up in the room, and each chest has two of those devils with the beards next to it. Rhalzek is there, as is Azereth. I don't know what they are waiting for, but it's happening soon. I am not letting Rhalzek get away from me."

Before Valduin could reply, there came a deafening tearing sound from within the altar room. The noise faded a fraction to a steady, roaring howl accompanied by shouting. Adelaide recognized the voice of Azereth among the shouts. She adjusted the grip on her battleaxe, roiling in the memory of him taking control of her mind. She stepped ran down the hallway and found herself standing on the balcony in the back corner of the altar room.

What she saw would have awed her had she not been so focused on the red-skinned devil standing next to the altar, accompanied by a robed and hooded hobgoblin. In front of the altar was a swirling disc of pale blue light ten feet in diameter. As Adelaide took in the room, the bearded devils were lifting the chests of diamonds and marching toward the source of the roar. One by one they carried the chests into the far side of the swirling, arcane disc and disappeared from sight. The terrifying vrock flapped its wings and swooped through the plane of light as well. Azereth shouted over the howling disc in a language that Adelaide did not understand, and for the moment, she felt confident that her arrival had gone unnoticed.

Before she could rush down the spiral staircase that stood to her right, where the balcony met the back wall of the room, she felt a hand on her shoulder. "Go be a hero," Valduin whispered, and a wave of warm, magical energy washed over her, leaving her feeling invigorated and fearless.

Rose came up behind her and said, "May Selaia protect you from these evil fiends," as she held her amulet and squeezed Adelaide's arm. The warmth of Rose's divine magic spread over her as well, and she smiled at her halfling friend.

"You could probably use a little protection, yourself," Adelaide said. She touched her eagle totem. The dark green glow of Adelaide's magic spread through her arm and into Rose's hand. Magic buffs cast, Adelaide turned back to the scene brelow them.

"Karma time," she said, not noticing Valduin cringe. The human rushed down the stairs, across the end of the raised platform that held the altar, and up behind Azereth.

Luvrolen bowed her head to Rose and Valduin. "May judgment be delivered upon the wicked," she said with a rehearsed cadence, and she vanished from the balcony in a cloud of silvery mist, reappearing in the shadows behind the altar. Without hesitation, she threw two of her long daggers at the back of the hooded hobgoblin. One of the razor-sharp blades found its mark, drawing a scream of surprised pain from Rhalzek.

Rose and Valduin moved along the balcony to get a better view of the hovering, swirling disc of light and sound. Looking at the remaining targets in the room, the last of the bearded devils disappeared through what Valduin could now see was a planar portal. Valduin pointed his wand at one of the two large barbed devils that did not look like it was heading through the portal. The pale green spark leapt down from the wand and exploded on the devil's back, drawing its attention to the balcony. Following Valduin's lead, Rose grasped her amulet and summoned her radiant, sacred flames to erupt on the same barbed devil.

Having capitalized on the element of surprise, Luvrolen stepped from the shadows and threw a second pair of daggers at Rhalzek, another one sinking into his back before he could turn to face her. When he made the turn, his eyes were wide with pain and surprise. "It isn't too nice is it, getting stabbed in the back?" Luvrolen taunted.

Valduin sent another eldritch blast at the barbed devil he had already begun targeting, finding his mark again. Surveying his position in the room, he remembered the balls of flame that the barbed devils had hurled at him last time. Without hesitation, he dropped prone on the ground. He peered through the bars of the balcony railing and hoped that he had enough cover to avoid being hit by their attacks from below.

Adelaide lifted Fiend's Lament over her head. As the blade cut through the air, it drew wisps of blue energy from the swirling portal next to her. That energy exploded outward as she landed her attack on Azereth's back. The crushing blow knocked him forward a step, and before he could do anything more, Rose summoned a shining, ethereal mace in the air above him. Righting himself, he dodged the arc of the mace as he spun to face Adelaide.

Realizing the attack had missed, Rose sent more sacred flames at the barbed devil closest to her and Valduin. This devil had gotten a lot closer as it ran up the stairs at the other end of the balcony and threw two balls of fire at her. She ducked under one, but the other burst on her shoulder, burning her neck and singeing her hair. The second barbed devil had moved from its place on the far side of the room to the middle of the chamber, and it threw its own balls of fire at Valduin. One impacted on the balcony railing, and the other hit high on the wall behind Valduin's prone form.

Azereth, meeting Adelaide's glare, kept his composure. With a smile, he said, "Hello again, Adelaide. It is so nice to see you here. Now, did you happen to bring that little item we had talked about earlier?"

For a moment, Adelaide lowered her weapon an inch, but then there was a flash of golden light in her eyes, and she smiled right back at the devil. "No more tricks," she spat at him. Giving up on the human, Azereth unfolded his leathery wings and flew up and away from Adelaide. She tried to swing at him as he retreated, but she was unable to make contact.

Rhalzek had by now composed himself after taking the hits from the pair of daggers. Turning to face Luvrolen, he shouted over the howl coming from the portal which still hovered ten feet away from him. "You got soft. I took the band where you were too scared to go!" He then chanted an incantation and pointed at the ground in front of the Luvrolen. A bead of red light shot from his fingertip toward that spot on the ground, and a massive explosion rocked the chamber as a fireball engulfed Luvrolen. The edge of the fireball also hit Adelaide where she stood just a few feet away from Rhalzek. Valduin recognized the fireball as the same spell that Nyla had cast, and he was amazed to see both Luvrolen and Adelaide still standing after the flash of light, though they did have smoke rising from various parts of their bodies.

Unfazed by the explosion, Luvrolen charged Rhalzek, letting loose a shrieking battle cry as she did. She unleashed a flurry of attacks with another dagger, drawing blood from the arm he held up to block the onslaught. He staggered from the blow, struggling to regain his footing and face Luvrolen.

Valduin, seeing that the barbed devil he had attacked had now reached the end of the balcony, got to his feet. He pointed the wand at the ceiling above Azereth's head. When he shouted his incantation this time, he did it in the grinding tongue of Abyssal. *The darkness will shatter your mind.* Even over the roar of the portal, the deafening blast of the spell echoed around the enclosed chamber, and Azereth nearly dropped from the air as he clutched at his head. Valduin moved as far from the barbed devil as he could while still staying on the balcony, and then he fell to the ground to take cover once again.

Adelaide, knowing she would not be able to reach Azereth up in the air, instead rushed to meet the incoming barbed devil. With a mighty swing of Fiend's Lament, she dealt a crushing blow to the devil's abdomen. Without hesitation, the fiend retaliated with three strikes of its own, but through a combination of successful shielding and the protection of Rose's magic, none of the attacks was able to injure Adelaide.

The other barbed devil rushed down the balcony as its hands began to glow with fire once again. Seeing Valduin prone in front of him and Rose standing just a little way beyond that, it hurled a ball of fire at each of them. Ducking his head down to the floor, Valduin was able to stay out of the way as he felt the heat of the fire pass over him. Rose was still focused on the battle below her, trying to move her spiritual weapon to get another swing at Azereth. A sudden flash of Adelaide's dark green magic next to her head signaled that Adelaide's protection spell had deflected the fire from hitting Rose.

Realizing the devil was getting close, Rose tried to summon her sacred flames on it again, but the devil was able to dodge out of the way. She ran, heading for the stairs in the back corner of the room.

Azereth, focused on Adelaide, continued his retreat until he reached the front of the room, where he hovered next to one of the large doors that stood open beside the main entrance. It was only now that Valduin noticed the imp that was perched on top of that same door. Azereth said something to it, and it flew out of the room through the large doorway. The devil turned back toward Adelaide, held up his hand, and fired his own small ball of fire at her. The attack hit her in the chest and erupted into flame, drawing a scream from the ranger that brought a smile to Azereth's face.

Rhalzek, still face-to-face with Luvrolen and harried by her repeated attacks, muttered another incantation and gave a sweeping motion with his hand as if to shoo Luvrolen away from him. As he finished the spell, the sound of another thunderous explosion filled the room, and Luvrolen flew back from Rhalzek, slamming into the back wall of the room and dropping to the floor behind the altar, unmoving. Rhalzek hobbled toward the front of the room, grinning at the finality of Luvrolen's fall.

"Is she dead? Did that kill her?" Madison asked frantically.

"I think she's just unconscious," Logan answered, though he did not sound confident in this explanation. "Amelia, will you be able to heal her?"

Amelia studied the battle map. "I think I can get to her in the next round. But do I really want to use a spell for an NPC? I don't have many left."

"That's your call," Madison said, "but we are hurting badly, we just lost one of our allies, and we haven't killed any of the enemies yet. The hobgoblin might be close, but these barbed devils had like a hundred hit points last time. We are going to need her help."

"Awesome job with the buff spells, by the way," Logan commended his sisters. "Giving them disadvantage on their attacks was a lifesaver."

"Which reminds me, are you going to stay prone for this entire battle?" Madison glared at Logan. "Because, once again, I'm in the fray getting pounded, and you are lying down."

"Ugh, fine," Logan replied, exasperated. "I'll join you next round, and you'll see why I like to stay out of the line of fire."

33

Valduin gasped as he watched Luvrolen fall. Hopping to his feet, he pushed off the wall behind him, placed one foot on the railing in front of him, and leapt off the balcony in the direction of Adelaide. As he flew through the air, silvery mist surrounded him, and he vanished. A moment later, he reappeared on the ground, just a few feet away from Adelaide. He sent an eldritch blast into the barbed devil that was engaged with the ranger as he ran up onto the platform behind the swirling portal, next to the black altar.

Adelaide used the distraction of Valduin's attack to land her own attack on the barbed devil, crushing the spikes on its shoulder with a wide swing of her axe. The devil tried again to attack Adelaide, but Rose's protective magic was too strong for it. The barbed devil on the balcony ran the rest of the way toward the back of the room, chasing after Rose. Its hands burst into flame again, and it hurled two balls of fire at her. The first just missed hitting her in the neck; it singed her hair as it flew past her and smashed into the back wall. The second shot hit her in the back, though it did not hurt her enough to break her concentration on the spell protecting Adelaide.

Rose wasted no time in her retreat. She ran from the steps to Luvrolen. She tapped the hobgoblin on the arm as she prayed aloud in Halfling, *"Selaia, we really need this one's help."* Not even looking to see the effects of the healing magic, she continued her run to the altar platform so that she could see Azereth at the front of the room. She sent her spiritual weapon across the room to him, but it was unable to cause any damage through his armor as it swung in a wide arc into his chest.

Tired of being harried by the slow-moving, floating mace, Azereth flew to the front corner of the room opposite the door he had met the imp on. He held his hand up again to release another firebolt, this time at Rose. The path of the flying ball of fire looked like it should have hit its target, but a flash of magical energy around the adventurer shielded her from the heat of the attack. Azereth looked down at Rhalzek, who was standing on the main floor below him, and hissed in Common, "What have I been paying you for? Finish them! I can barely touch them through their divine wards."

Rhalzek turned back to face the adventurers. Seeing that they had gathered close together at the side of the portal, he pointed at the ground in the middle of the group. A familiar mote of red light shot from his finger and exploded in their midst. Valduin was able to duck behind the altar and avoid most of the impact, maintaining his concentration on the heroism spell he had cast on Adelaide. Adelaide dodged most of the blast as well, but the injury brought her to the brink of unconsciousness. Rose was not so lucky, and as the smoke cleared from the explosion, Valduin and Adelaide could see their well-armored cleric lying motionless on the ground.

Rhalzek shrieked with delight. He turned to say something to Azereth, but when he opened his mouth, all that came out was blood. One of Luvrolen's daggers had sunk into his throat. She stepped out from the shadows below the balcony, her steely gaze meeting Rhalzek's wide eyes as he dropped to the floor. Satisfied with her handiwork, she turned her attention to the barbed devil that was harassing Adelaide. Determined to assist her new allies, she threw a dagger at the devil, finding her mark through the spiked hide of the fiend.

Valduin rushed to Rose's side, pulling out one of the healing potions that he had in the leather holster on his side. "Rose, it's looking bad. We need you," he whispered as he poured the potion into her mouth. Her eyes fluttered open as the magic of the potion took hold, and she grinned at the half-elf through the char marks on her face.

"Thanks, Valduin," she said, her voice tired and breathy. She rolled over and pushed herself to her knees.

Seeing that Rose was taken care of, Adelaide turned her fury back to the devil in front of her. She brought her battleaxe down on its shoulder, the blow erupting with blue energy siphoned from the massive portal that hung in the air next to them. The devil retaliated with another round of attacks, and Adelaide finally felt its claw find a gap in her armor as it tore into her shoulder. The other barbed devil reached the bottom of the stairs at the back corner of the room in its pursuit of Rose, and it threw two more balls of fire, one at Rose on the ground and one at Valduin standing over her, but both missed.

Rose got to her feet as the fire flew past her. Grabbing her amulet, she entreated her goddess, "*Selaia, we are hurting. We all could use some help.*" As she channeled her divine connection, tiny motes of golden light appeared around her and then flew into Valduin, Adelaide, and herself. All three could feel the warmth of the magical healing spread through them, soothing the burns from the last fireball.

Azereth, unfazed by the death of Rhalzek, flew the length of the balcony to get closer to Valduin. Looking him in the eye, Azereth said, "Child of the fey, it is I who could use a little help. Why don't you come over here with me?" Valduin's eyes went wide for a moment as he felt the fiend's influence pushing into his mind, but he shook it off, standing his ground. Azereth growled in frustration. "Curse you elves," he grumbled to himself. Then to the barbed devils, he shouted something in Infernal and pointed at Adelaide.

Luvrolen, seeing the barbed devils' focus on the human, moved to flank the devil Adelaide had been fighting. Daggers in both hands, she laid into the fiend's back. When the monster turned to face her, Adelaide took advantage of the distraction to land a final devastating blow to the back of its head, and it fell to the ground, tendrils of purple energy connecting its body to Fiend's Lament for a second.

After resisting Azereth's charm, Valduin ran the full length of the platform away from the flying devil, behind the altar and the howling disc of blue light. Looking over his shoulder, he could see the remaining barbed devil sprinting down the stairs below Azereth. He spun as he reached the far end of the platform, wand up, screaming in Common, "I will shatter your mind!" Another thunderous explosion detonated between the two fiends, and they both grimaced in pain.

As the final barbed devil moved toward Adelaide, who was slightly in front of the hanging portal, it came first to Rose where she had fallen at the edge of the altar platform. Rose managed to block its two claw attacks with her shield, but the tail came in low and tore into her thigh, drawing a strained screech from the halfling. As Rose tried to steady herself, she held a hand out toward the devil and her golden, sacred flames erupted across it, forcing a screech of its own.

Azereth finally joined the melee after watching the barbed devil fall to Adelaide's axe. Swooping down in front of the human, he drew the longsword from his belt. The sword burst into flames in his hand, and he swung twice at her, landing one attack that briefly stuck into her collarbone. The burning heat coming off the weapon cauterized the wound as Azereth pulled the sword back. As Adelaide howled with pain and rage, Azereth looked at the one remaining devil, shouted a command in Infernal, and then turned back to Adelaide.

Before he could say anything, though, Luvrolen appeared behind him, flanking him with Adelaide. One of her dagger attacks found a soft spot on the devil's back, drawing a grunt as the damage was starting to add up.

Valduin completed his loop around the altar and reappeared on the far side of the portal from his companions. Seeing that Azereth was hurting, he pointed at the winged devil and sent a green spark spiraling across the room, nearly crushing the arm that Azereth instinctively raised to block the attack.

With Luvrolen flanking and Azereth reeling, Adelaide summoned the planar energy she had learned to harness, the blue light leaching off the hovering portal next to her and onto the blade of Fiend's Lament. She brought the axe down on Azereth's shoulder, and the blue light exploded into him, dropping him to one knee before he regained his footing.

Adelaide and Valduin, who were focused on Azereth, heard Rose's voice cut through the commotion in the room. "It's getting away!" They glanced toward their cleric to see the barbed devil pushing her off balance and dashing through the portal. With the break in their concentration, Azereth spun around to swing his sword into Luvrolen, hitting her on the shoulder, and then he stabbed it back under his arm toward Adelaide. Unable to find purchase on the human with the attack, the devil unfurled his wings and shot into the air. He headed toward the portal behind Adelaide.

"Get down here!" Adelaide roared, and she slammed Fiend's Lament into Azereth's back as he tried to escape. The razor-sharp blade sunk deep into the devil's torso, between the wing joints. The arc of the swing caught the devil's body and brought it to the ground where he landed face-down with a sickening thud. Adelaide stood over Azereth as the head of the axe glowed purple once more, soaking up the fiend's essence and binding it to the death of this body.

For a moment, the room was still, though the ever-present howling continued unabated. Then, a roar cut through the calm. For the first time, Adelaide and Valduin looked at the front of the portal, and they both froze. Noticing their reaction, Rose walked to the front of the portal and likewise stiffened, entranced by the sight. Suspended in the air, the ten-foot diameter circle of swirling planar energy appeared to form a tunnel, only a few feet long, before opening onto an alien world.

Through the portal, they were looking out onto a narrow ridge on the edge of a volcano. The bright orange glow from below the drop-off made the entire sky appear orange. A constant wind blew across the ridge, the source of the howling that had filled the room since the gate opened so many long seconds ago.

Wisps of smoke rose from beyond the ridge before being caught up in the wind. The ridge itself was covered with chests; many more than they had seen leave this room. Adelaide could see the bearded devils that they had watched walk through the portal, but she could also see dozens, if not hundreds, of other figures moving in the background of this alien landscape. The entire horizon was made up of jagged mountain peaks, several of which had black smoke rising from them.

There was probably more to see across the plane, but Adelaide did not have much time to take it all in. Two figures much closer to her took up most of the view. Standing on the other side of the portal was a tiefling, about Adelaide's height, but ancient. He had long, stringy, silver hair that was whipping in the steady wind. He had dark red skin and black horns that curled back from the forehead and almost touched the back of his neck. He was wearing a dark red robe with black trim and holding a book open in one hand. His other hand was extended toward the portal as he chanted, staring through the gate with white, pupil-less eyes.

Over his shoulder was the creature that had let out the roar. Twenty feet tall, with maroon skin and massive cloven hooves that could have crushed her, this new fiend met Adelaide's gaze with eyes that glowed the same orange as the volcano. Adelaide stood frozen with fear as the monstrous devil lifted an enormous flail that dripped with flames as it hung in the air. The devil strode toward the portal, and Adelaide, Valduin, and Rose could hear its deep, gravelly voice penetrating their minds.

"The Voidbringer is coming. I am the chaos from which your world was born. I am the hatred that burns in your hearts. I am the temptation that draws you out of your holes in the mud. I will end the Astral Peace and unite the planes into a roiling sea of pain. The void consumes all."

The Voidbringer had now come up behind the tiefling and was staring at Adelaide where she stood over the unmoving body of Azereth. Terror washed over the adventurers as they stared up at the monstrous fiend on the other side of the gate. But before they could do anything in response to the Voidbringer's monologue, the tiefling exhaled sharply, dropped his outstretched hand, and snapped the book closed.

The portal vanished.

Silence filled the room.

"See what I mean?" Logan cried. "I come down to where you are and what happens? We get hit with a Fireball!"

"Well, if you hadn't been there to heal me, I would have been in big trouble," Amelia pointed out. "So, thank you."

"More importantly, what in the world is the Voidbringer?" Madison asked Logan. "Did that description sound like anything you can remember from the book?"

"Not really," Logan considered what he remembered from the fiends sections of the rulebooks. "Pit fiends are the biggest devils in that book, but this thing sounds more unique than that. Maybe an archdevil? I don't know those stat blocks as well," he finished with a shrug.

"Well, we know who the bad guy is for this campaign," Amelia pronounced. "We just need to find him before the whole 'sea of pain' thing starts. That sounds bad."

"Why didn't he come through and stop us from killing his helper?" Madison wondered aloud.

"I'm guessing he has lots of helpers," Logan replied. "So he probably doesn't care about one little one dying. Or maybe he expects Azereth to be reborn in his home plane like fiends usually do. That will be a nasty surprise when he realizes Adelaide killed him for good."

34

"Valduin, check the hobgoblin's body," Adelaide instructed as she bent down and started searching Azereth. He did not appear to be carrying much, but there was a heavy pouch hanging from his belt. She cut it free with the devil's longsword and took both the pouch and the sword. Valduin started walking toward Rhalzek, but Luvrolen beat him to it.

"Whatever he is carrying rightfully belongs to me," she said to Valduin. She seemed a little defensive, but Valduin did not blame her.

"Fair enough," Valduin shrugged as he looked around the room for anything else worth taking. Now that the portal was gone, along with all of the chests brimming with diamonds, the chamber was bare. There was the stone altar at the end on the raised platform. There were the four large braziers, which continued to light the room with a steady glow that led Valduin to believe they were magical. There were staircases in the four corners leading to the balconies on either side of the room. The large double doors stood open to the passage back toward the pit. Behind the altar was the door that Azereth had gone through a few hours ago, and above the door was the same symbol of overlapping discs that had been displayed on the front of the black temple.

Rose had been inspecting the altar when she spun toward the large doors. "Someone's coming!" she hissed across the room to Valduin. As soon as she said it, Valduin noticed the sound of footsteps coming down the large passageway toward the altar room.

"Where can we hide?" Adelaide asked, looking around the room frantically.

Rose had already reached the door behind the altar and pushed it open. "In here!" she called. Rose, Adelaide, Valduin, and Luvrolen dashed for the door, diving into the dark room beyond before Rose closed the door behind them.

In the darkness, Adelaide whispered to Rose, "Lock it!"

"I can't!" came the panicked reply. "There is no lock or latch. It's just a door on a hinge. Just be quiet!"

As Rose and Adelaide sat in the darkness near the door, Valduin glanced around the dark space. They were in a small chamber with a few chairs and an empty bookshelf.

"I am going look around real quick," he whispered to Adelaide, sure that she would encourage any activity that might lead to more loot. "You all stay here."

Before Adelaide could reply, she felt him leave the space next to her. "Loot good," she whispered.

Valduin inspected the chairs and then the bookshelf. As he studied the bookshelf, he noticed that the bottom shelf appeared less deep than the others. Further investigation revealed that by pushing on the back of the bottom shelf, a panel swung up. In the hidden compartment was a wooden box just a bit too small to be called a chest. Barely containing his excitement, Valduin slid the box into his pack, saving the opening for when they were out of this particular predicament.

By this time, a commotion had begun on the other side of the unlocked door. Rose and Adelaide could hear shouting in several languages.

"Do you understand anything?" Adelaide asked Rose.

"The devils found Azereth, obviously," Rose replied. "They are yelling about what to do next. There are some other voices that I don't understand, though."

"Those would be my people," Luvrolen said. "Rhalzek was not one to share power, so I doubt the remains of my band know whom to follow now."

"What are we going to do?" Adelaide asked no one in particular. "We need to get out of here. We are wrecked and tapped for magic. Is there any kind of distraction you could make, Val?"

"Not really," came his apologetic reply from deeper within the pitch-dark room.

"Is there another way out of this room?" asked Rose. "I can't see anything, and I don't want to risk making light."

"Nope, no other doors," Valduin answered. "I do not think we can wait them out, either. I watched Azereth come in here, so they all know this was his place. They will come in here looking for his stuff eventually."

"I will distract them," Luvrolen said. "You all risked your lives getting me out of that prison cell, and then you saved my life while helping me get my revenge on Rhalzek." Though only Valduin could see it, Luvrolen stood up. She muttered an incantation that he did not understand and touched the top of her head. Her appearance wavered like Valduin was seeing her through waves of heat. A moment later, she had shifted her form to look like the old tiefling they had seen through the portal. She turned to him. "Does this look right?"

Valduin tried to remember the details of the ancient tiefling's attire. "Yeah, that's really good. But, can you speak Infernal?"

"No, but neither can any of my people. I'll speak to them in Common, and I'll hope for the best. You all stay here until the coast seems clear. I'll try to get them away from this place so you can get to the surface." Luvrolen stepped up to the door. "Thank you again. I owe you my life."

Swinging the door open, Luvrolen strode forward until she was standing behind the altar. "What has become of Azereth?" she shouted in Common into the room, which fell silent as several dozen goblinoids and at least a dozen fiends of various shapes turned toward her. She pointed at the hobgoblin standing closest to Azereth's body. "You! Tell me what happened to him?"

"W-we don't know," the hobgoblin replied, eyes wide in fear as he looked at Luvrolen's tiefling form. "The imp told us there was an attack. We came as fast as we could, but all we found were the bodies."

"We must find the perpetrators of this terrible assault!" Luvrolen screeched. "The Voidbringer will require answers. Do you want to be the one to tell him Azereth has fallen?"

As Luvrolen berated the hobgoblin, Valduin, Rose, and Adelaide peered from deep within the back room, through the door that Luvrolen had left open. As they watched, they could see some of the devils narrowing their eyes and moving toward Luvrolen.

"They suspect something," Adelaide whispered to Valduin. "This isn't going to work."

"Just hold on for one more minute," Valduin entreated. He pointed at Luvrolen and whispered a message to her, "I think the devils know you are faking."

Luvrolen shifted her gaze from the hobgoblin to the fiends in the room. There were four bearded devils standing at attention, five or six greasy drengarns pacing nervously, and four barbed devils stepping toward the altar. Seeing the suspicious looks on several of their faces, Luvrolen changed tact. She started shouting in a language none of the adventurers could understand, but they guessed to be Goblin.

In another shimmer, her disguise disappeared, and Luvrolen revealed herself. She leapt up onto the altar and launched a pair of daggers into the nearest devil. A roar built up from the goblinoids in the room as they drew their weapons and rushed at the devils. Not all of the devils were taken by surprise, and they retaliated without hesitation. As the battle raged, Luvrolen looked over her shoulder toward the doorway. She shouted, "Good luck!" and descended into the fray with the remains of her war band.

Without a word, Adelaide, Valduin, and Rose took off. As they ran, Valduin loosed as many eldritch blasts as he could into the fiends he could see. Rose followed suit, raining sacred flames down on every devil in sight. Shortly, they were back in the hallway and headed to the pit that would lead them up to the temple.

As they made their way up the spiraling staircase within the pit, they could hear the sounds of many footsteps below them. Looking down at the dimly lit bottom of the pit, they saw dozens of goblinoids and devils rushing toward the commotion in the altar room, unaware that they would soon be fighting each other.

"Is it safe to make some light?" Rose asked Valduin. "Otherwise, it will be very slow going up these stairs."

"I think so," he replied. "We need to focus on moving fast right now. We should try to get back to the house we slept in last night. We know it is safe there, and we are in no state to get into another big fight."

Rose lit up her amulet as they rushed up the stairs. When they reached the top, they found the cavernous space within the black temple to be dark; night had fallen outside. They rushed out onto the street, which was quiet and still. Slowing their movement so that they could be more stealthy, they trekked back to their hideout in the ancient city, arriving without any sign that they had been seen or followed.

"What a day!" Rose exclaimed as she reclaimed her spot face-down on the sofa.

"You both were amazing," Adelaide said. She flopped into the chair next to Rose.

"That Voidbringer guy was pretty terrifying. What do you think he is? And did you see where he was? Did either of you recognize that place?" Valduin asked.

Rose rolled over to respond, "I've been thinking about that. That sort of unending mountain range seems vaguely familiar. I'm pretty sure I've seen some sort of drawing of that place in a book back at the temple, but I can't remember what it is. I know it's on a different plane, but that's it."

"Why do you think they closed the portal when they did?" Adelaide asked next. "The Voidbringer was pulling out that massive weapon like he was about to use it."

"I think he maybe just ran out of time. That portal opened before we started fighting. I think it was probably open for about a minute; I would guess that is the limit on whatever spell that was. Being able to open a portal to another plane and hold it open like that? That tiefling must be a crazy powerful wizard," Valduin replied. "Oh, Adelaide, what kind of loot did you get off Azereth?"

Adelaide perked up as she remembered the pouch. She pulled it out and dumped it on the low table in front of the couch Rose was lying on. Adelaide also pulled the longsword from its sheath and laid it down. Rose opened one eye to see their spoils, but otherwise, she lay still.

"Is this platinum?" Adelaide asked Valduin excitedly.

"I think so," he replied as he turned over one of the coins that had fallen from the pouch. "How many are there?"

"It looks like we've got thirty platinum pieces here," Adelaide said as she counted out the contents of the pouch. "And one big diamond and four smaller ones."

Valduin lifted the longsword from the table. "This is definitely magic, and we know what it does," he said, remembering the flames erupting from the sword when Azereth held it. Valduin held it out in front of himself for a moment, concentrating on the sword. When nothing happened, his stance relaxed. He said, "But I do not know how to turn it on. We will need someone to help us with that." He returned the sword to the table, unable to hide his disappointment.

Adelaide looked up from the gems to see Valduin sitting on the floor across the table from her, his back against the sofa where Rose was falling asleep. He had a weary smile on his face as he watched her appraise the gems.

"What? What's that look for?" Adelaide asked.

"We did it," Valduin answered. "We really did it. Not only are we one hundred percent, officially adventurers, but we killed that bad guy too. A really bad guy."

"Yeah, we did it." Adelaide smiled back. "You don't think that Voidbringer guy will be a problem for us again, do you? He seemed like he had a lot going on. And that monologue was a little scary."

"Why would that be our problem? I'm sure there's some super-powerful force for good out there somewhere in the multiverse that will stop him. You know, like heroes."

"I could be a hero," Adelaide said through a yawn.

"You already are." Valduin smiled again. "Well, I am ready for bed," he said as he pushed himself to his feet from beside the low table. "I will take the study again, okay? You can have the bedroom."

"Sounds fine," Adelaide replied. "Rose, you want to share the bed? It's plenty big."

Rose did not respond. Adelaide checked to make sure the halfling was still breathing. Once Adelaide was satisfied that their devout friend had only fallen asleep, she pulled Rose's pack from her back, unfolded the blanket, and tucked her in on the couch. Valduin dropped his own pack on the floor next to the sofa, made sure the front door was bolted, and staggered up the steps to the study. He collapsed on the sofa and fell asleep.

Adelaide dragged herself up to the third floor. She spent a couple of hours watching the dark city from the comfort of the bed, reliving those few seconds of seeing the Voidbringer and hearing his voice in her head. She eventually gave in to sleep, though that image of the Voidbringer followed her into her dreams.

Valduin awoke to the sound of pages being turned. From the sluggishness in his mind, he could tell he had not been asleep for long. Opening his eyes, he was not surprised to see Taranath sitting in a chair facing the sofa that Valduin was sleeping on. The tall, elf-like creature appeared to be reading from one of the books that Valduin and Rose had left stacked around the room during their research session a couple of days ago. Valduin sat up on the sofa and yawned.

"You have done quite well," Taranath said in his soft voice without looking up from the book he was reading.

"I am not so sure," Valduin replied.

"Whatever do you mean?" Taranath looked at Valduin over the top of the book. "I'm here now. When before I couldn't be. That's a success if I've ever seen one. So, what did you find?"

"The devil's name was Azereth. We killed him, but not before he was able to send a whole lot of stuff through a portal to another plane. I feel like it was important to stop him from delivering all that stuff, but we were too late."

"Well, it looks to me like you all did a splendid job." Taranath put down the book. With a wave of his hand, Valduin's spellbook appeared, hovering in the space between them. "I gave you a little something new. A couple more spells for my budding student."

The book floated over to Valduin, who took it out of the air and held it in his lap. "How exactly was Azereth preventing you from coming here? How did killing him fix that?"

"Well, I'm sure I don't know," Taranath replied, his smile faltering a fraction. "Some infernal magic or other. I try not to delve too deeply into such practices."

Valduin sat forward with a jerk when realized he had not shared the most important new information. "And we saw something else," he said. "Through the portal. There was this really old tiefling that looked like he was holding the portal open, probably a wizard or something. And the landscape was weird. They were on top of a volcano maybe, and the entire background was just mountains. And there was this creature. I think it was a devil, but nothing like the ones we have fought. It must have been fifteen or twenty feet tall, and it called itself the Voidbringer. Have you ever heard that name?"

Taranath's reply came after a half-second hesitation, "No, I've never heard that name. But I'll see what I can find out. I have friends in many places. For now, go on with your adventuring. I've got a bit of a project going on to the south of here. No rest for the weary! I'll be in touch if anything comes up that I need you to take care of. Ta ta!" With that, he disappeared.

"Insight check!" Madison screamed as Logan rolled the die.

"It's good! It's really good!" Amelia said, looking at Logan's dice tray.

"What does it say?" Madison asked frantically as Logan read the note he had been handed. "I know he's lying. He's so evil."

"He's lying," Logan said when he had finished reading, drawing groans from the girls. "But I don't know what about. It could have been anything he talked about. It might be about the thing that was blocking him from coming to Eydon or the Voidbringer or whatever he is working on."

"Yes, you do!" Madison corrected. "He definitely knows about the Voidbringer. He probably even knows where that place was that we saw through the portal!"

"Nothing we can do about that now. What next, then?" Amelia asked. "Where to?"

"You want to keep going?" Madison asked her sister.

"You still want to play?"

"Are you kidding me?" Amelia asked with a smirk. "After the whooping we just put on those devils? We definitely have to keep this party together."

"Well, then, take a long rest and level up to five," Logan replied.

"And then we are going to Westray to kill some giants!" Madison proclaimed. "Enough about Valduin. It's time for some of Adelaide's story."

Letter from the Author

Thank you so much for choosing to read *Whispers of the Voidbringer*. If you enjoyed this story of Logan, Madison, and Amelia's adventures playing as Valduin, Adelaide, and Rose, and you would like to keep up-to-date with more of their exploits, check out the website below for information:

www.VoidbringerCampaign.com

I would be very grateful if you could take a moment to rate this title, or even post a short review, wherever you found this book. These ratings and reviews will help new readers discover this book.

If you would like to get in touch, or are looking for other family-friendly content for your tabletop roleplaying games, you can find me on Facebook, Instagram, and Twitter.

Thanks again,
M. Allen Hall
@M_Allen_Hall

OPEN GAME LICENSE Version 1.0a

The following text is the property of Wizards of the Coast, Inc. and is Copyright 2000 Wizards of the Coast, Inc ("Wizards"). All Rights Reserved.

1. Definitions: (a)"Contributors" means the copyright and/or trademark owners who have contributed Open Game Content; (b)"Derivative Material" means copyrighted material including derivative works and translations (including into other computer languages), potation, modification, correction, addition, extension, upgrade, improvement, compilation, abridgment or other form in which an existing work may be recast, transformed or adapted; (c) "Distribute" means to reproduce, license, rent, lease, sell, broadcast, publicly display, transmit or otherwise distribute; (d)"Open Game Content" means the game mechanic and includes the methods, procedures, processes and routines to the extent such content does not embody the Product Identity and is an enhance- ment over the prior art and any additional content clearly identified as Open Game Content by the Contributor, and means any work covered by this License, including translations and derivative works under copyright law, but specifically excludes Product Identity. (e) "Product Identity" means product and product line names, logos and identifying marks including trade dress; artifacts; creatures characters; stories, storylines, plots, thematic elements, dialogue, incidents, language, artwork, symbols, designs, depictions, likenesses, formats, poses, concepts, themes and graphic, photographic and other visual or audio representations; names and descriptions of characters, spells, enchantments, personalities, teams, personas, likenesses and special abilities; places, locations, environments, creatures, equipment, magical or supernatural abilities or effects, logos, symbols, or graphic designs; and any other trademark or registered trademark clearly identified as Product identity by the owner of the Product Identity, and which specifically excludes the Open Game Content; (f) "Trade- mark" means the logos, names, mark, sign, motto, designs that are used by a Contributor to identify itself or its products or the associated products con- tributed to the Open Game License by the Contributor (g) "Use", "Used" or "Using" means to use, Distribute, copy, edit, format, modify, translate and otherwise create Derivative Material of Open Game Content. (h) "You" Not for resale. Permission granted to print or photocopy this document for personal use only. System Reference Document 5.1 2 or "Your" means the licensee in terms of this agreement.

2. The License: This License applies to any Open Game Content that contains a notice indicating that the Open Game Content may only be Used under and in terms of this License. You must affix such a notice to any Open Game Content that you Use. No terms may be added to or subtracted from this License except as described by the License itself. No other terms or conditions may be applied to any Open Game Content distributed using this License.

3. Offer and Acceptance: By Using the Open Game Content You indicate Your acceptance of the terms of this License.

4. Grant and Consideration: In consideration for agreeing to use this License, the Contributors grant You a perpetual, worldwide, royalty-free, nonexclusive license with the exact terms of this License to Use, the Open Game Content.

5. Representation of Authority to Contribute: If You are contributing original material as Open Game Content, You represent that Your Contributions are Your original creation and/or You have sufficient rights to grant the rights conveyed by this License.

6. Notice of License Copyright: You must update the COPYRIGHT NOTICE portion of this License to include the exact text of the COPYRIGHT NOTICE of any Open Game Content You are copying, modifying or distributing, and You must add the title, the copyright date, and the copyright holder's name to the COPYRIGHT NOTICE of any original Open Game Content you Distribute.

7. Use of Product Identity: You agree not to Use any Product Identity, including as an indication as to compatibility, except as expressly licensed in another, independent Agreement with the owner of each element of that Product Identity. You agree not to indicate compatibility or co-adaptability with any Trademark or Registered Trademark in conjunction with a work containing Open Game Content except as expressly licensed in another, independent Agreement with the owner of such Trademark or Registered Trademark. The use of any Product Identity in Open Game Content does not constitute a challenge to the ownership of that Product Identity. The owner of any Product Identity used in Open Game Content shall retain all rights, title and interest in and to that Product Identity.

8. Identification: If you distribute Open Game Content You must clearly indicate which portions of the work that you are distributing are Open Game Content.

9. Updating the License: Wizards or its designated Agents may publish updated versions of this License. You may use any authorized version of this License to copy, modify and distribute any Open Game Content originally distributed under any version of this License.

10. Copy of this License: You MUST include a copy of this License with every copy of the Open Game Content You Distribute.

11. Use of Contributor Credits: You may not market or advertise the Open Game Content using the name of any Contributor unless You have written permission from the Contributor to do so.

12. Inability to Comply: If it is impossible for You to comply with any of the terms of this License with respect to some or all of the Open Game Content due to statute, judicial order, or governmental regulation then You may not Use any Open Game Material so affected.

13. Termination: This License will terminate automatically if You fail to comply with all terms herein and fail to cure such breach within 30 days of becoming aware of the breach. All sublicenses shall survive the termination of this License.

14. Reformation: If any provision of this License is held to be unenforceable, such provision shall be reformed only to the extent necessary to make it enforceable.

Printed in Great Britain
by Amazon

44421519R00202